CATHARTA

LAUREN WESTON

NEWMAN SPRINGS PUBLISHING
320 Broad Street
Red Bank, NJ 07701

First originally published by Newman Springs Publishing 2018

ISBN 978-1-64096-044-2 (Paperback)
ISBN 978-1-64096-048-0 (Digital)

Printed in the United States of America

To Carol Linscheid, without your encouragement, your research, and your inside information, I don't know if this story would have existed. Without you as my second mother, I don't know where I would be.

PROLOGUE

*H*e woke up and found himself sprawled on a hard tile floor feeling dizzy and disoriented. He couldn't get his mind around where he was. Forcing his brain to focus, he tried to take in the things around him. The tile floor on which he lay was brick red and dirty. The ceiling above him was gray concrete and acoustic tiles. Fluorescent lights flickered somewhere in his periphery. It was familiar, but he was still having trouble placing where he was. Letting his fingertips graze the tiles, it came back to him. This was the Sixteenth Street subway station. He had worked late and was trying to catch the last train home.

Once he had that figured out, he felt moderately more at ease. Then, he set his mind to work trying to uncover why he was lying on the station platform instead of standing upright awaiting his train. Had he fallen? He assessed his body. Nothing hurt. He felt no pain, but there was a strange taste in his mouth, like old pennies, something coppery. As soon as he realized that what he tasted was blood, it vanished, nothing more than a distant memory. It was like the experience of déjà vu. As soon as you recognize the feeling for what it is, it breaks the spell and the feeling is gone.

Somewhere in the distance, he could hear a siren wailing, a fire truck or an ambulance. It was a perfectly normal sound to hear in the city, but it was odd because he was three stories underground. He shouldn't have been able to hear any street noises from down here. The sound quickly faded, and he found himself wondering if he had actually heard it at all.

Suddenly, he was struck with the sense that someone was missing. Someone had just been standing there beside him, and now, there was no one. But who was it? He couldn't remember. He pushed himself up to a sitting position and got a little bit of a head rush. Along with the dizzy feeling, reality came rushing back to him in one big, crashing wave.

He had been standing at the edge of the platform. He was waiting for the train. It was approaching. He was shoved. Someone, some stranger, was reaching for his wallet, and when he turned, the stranger pushed him. He fell. He repeated these sentences in his head a few times.

He was shoved.

A stranger pushed him.

He fell.

He didn't jump. He didn't.

But he also didn't try to stop it. He fell, and he succumbed. He let it happen. As he began to realize how he ended up lying on the subway station floor and what that meant for him now, he felt a strange sensation wash over him. He was surprised when he recognized what it was: relief.

*****

She ran through the silent streets of the city, her footsteps echoing against the tall buildings. No wind or traffic or noises of the city interrupted the sound of her feet slapping the pavement. She ran, all alone, under a slate gray sky.

In her mind, she knew it as useless. She would never get there in time. Still, she had to try. She had to do something.

She skittered to a stop at an alleyway and peered around the corner of the building. Then she saw him. He had one in his clutches. This one was just a child. Her heart sunk. The boy was so young. He had already suffered something horribly unfair to have ended up here. And now, it would get so much worse because she hadn't gotten to him in time.

"Stop!" she commanded the man in the alley, who towered over the young boy. "Let him go!" The man paid her no heed.

She could see a faint glow emanating from between the man and the boy, but it was quickly fading away. She was too late. She was always just a little too late.

The man released the boy, who stood frozen for a moment and then turned and ran down the alley, trying to get as far away from his captor as he could. Then the man turned to face her. He took a few long strides in her direction, quickly closing the gap between them. He looked down at her with something like pity. "It's better this way," he told her in a voice that was much rougher than the voice she had once known. He was no longer the man he used to be.

He stepped around her, and, with his next tread, he was gone. He practically evaporated, though she was sure he hadn't gone far.

She stepped back out of the alley and onto the street. Looking up and down the street, she saw nothing, no one. She could hear doors being pulled shut nearby. She could feel eyes all around her, hopeful for a moment, but now turning inward once more. All that faced her were empty storefronts and tightly drawn curtains. She was alone. She fell to her knees and let the tears come. She let herself cry for the little boy, for the ceaseless suffering he would now face. She let herself cry for her own failure. She let herself cry for the souls all around her, lost and helpless. But mostly, she cried for the loss of hope. She knew that she would always be just a second too late. She knew it was hopeless. She couldn't do this on her own.

CHAPTER 1

"*H*ave you ever wondered if you've already been to the place where you're going to die?" Sara Jenkins fidgeted idly with the frayed end of the drawstring on her hooded sweatshirt. She stood facing the window, looking out at the semidetached homes across the street without actually seeing them. It wasn't a question she had actually meant to ask out loud. It was just an idea that she had been preoccupied with as of late. Recently, her ideas had developed a nasty habit of spilling out of her mouth before she realized it.

The question had occurred to her when she realized how many news articles she had read recently about sudden deaths, most of them very violent. It had gotten her thinking about the various ways people met the end of their lives. Sara reasoned that a lot of people die in their homes simply because that's where they spend the most time. In those cases, the deceased had spent a lot of time in the place they would eventually die. They just hadn't known it at the time. An enormous number of people die in hospitals as a result of whatever ailment or injury brought them there in the first place. People in nursing homes probably assumed upon checking in that it would be the same place where they would permanently check out. But lately, she had seen a great many stories about people dying in places that Sara imagined they never even expected to find themselves, places that they certainly didn't expect to breathe their final breath. The previous week, there had been a story about an elderly man who was hit by a car while crossing the street at the corner of Pine and Market. Hit and run. The driver never even slowed down. The week before that, there was an article about a woman who was killed driving down highway 101. She had been caught in the crossfire of the increasingly common freeway gang shootings. When the shooter was caught, he had expressed more remorse for missing his intended target than for the life he had ended. Just yesterday, there was a story about a heavily inebriated man who had fallen onto the subway tracks right as a train was approaching. Bystanders pulled out their phones to post about what they had just seen on social media, not to call 911. How many times had those victims crossed that street or driven down that highway or boarded that train, never suspecting that one day that would be where they would meet their end?

"Christ, Sara!" Maya exclaimed. "You've got to knock it off with that morbid shit. I've got enough on my mind right now without your existential crisis." Sara turned to face her sister. The words sounded harsh, but she could tell by the look on Maya's face that she wasn't actually upset. In fact, she looked like she was barely paying attention. Maya was sprawled on the floor of the nearly empty room with her phone in her hand and a notebook and pen in her lap. Her outburst was more likely a way of changing the subject than it was about venting any sincere anger.

Sara allowed the subject to float away. "Well, you've got to knock it off with that language. You don't want the baby's first word to be 'shit,' do you?" Maya looked up from her phone. A slight smirk crossed her lips that caused her nose to wrinkle just a little. One eyebrow rose. It was her patented "I do what I want" look, which she had perfected as a child. Sara couldn't help but smile at the familiar expression.

Maya Jenkins was the younger of the two sisters. She had twenty-five years to Sara's twenty-eight. Even though she was the baby of the family, Maya had never been one to be bossed around. She tended to do whatever made her happy, which was not to say she misbehaved. They had both been pretty well-mannered kids. It just so happened that the simple things in life were what made Maya happy. Playing outside and making new friends were usually at the top of her list, and she wouldn't let anything stand in the way of those simple joys. Making new friends came easy to her. She was as outgoing and talkative as they come. Everybody loved Maya instantly.

Sara, on the other hand, was much more introverted. Socializing in general was out of her comfort zone. She relied on Maya to pull her out of her shell, lead the way, and strike up a conversation. Without the occasional shove from her little sister, Sara would have been quite content to spend her entire childhood holed up in the house with a mountain of books. Truth be told, she wouldn't mind spending her adulthood the same way.

Maya had the ability to recognize immediately what would make her happy and go for it wholeheartedly. She sometimes asked Sara, "What would make you happy?" It left Sara wondering to herself. *Am I unhappy?* She wasn't even sure how to tell anymore.

That was why Maya and Sara were so good for each other. They were perfect opposites—introvert and extrovert, type A and type B. Maya liked to live in the moment without much thought toward the future. She tended to believe that the future would take care of itself. Sara was a planner. She feared the unknown, and she felt that, with enough careful planning, the unknown could largely be avoided.

Even in appearance, they seemed rather opposite. Upon learning that they were sisters, strangers would undoubtedly comment on the fact that they looked nothing alike. Sara was tall and thin with hardly a curve to what she called her stick-figure body. She had fair skin and angular features. Her hair and her eyes were such a dark shade of brown that they were almost black. As a toddler, she had stumbled and hit her head on a coffee table, landing herself in the hospital and receiving fourteen stitches. When she was discharged, the doctors had told her parents to watch her pupils to see if they dilated, as that could be a sign of concussion. Her mom had spent the whole night fretting over that advice because Sara's eyes were so dark she could hardly make out the pupils.

Maya, in contrast, was shorter and curvier. Her skin had a natural olive tone that, every summer, bronzed nicely, while her already light hair brightened even more in the California sun. Everything about her features was round, from her button nose to her pillowy cheeks that dimpled when she smiled. Her eyes were a pale shade of blue, which had baffled both their parents. They couldn't think of a single blue-eyed person on either side of their family. The two young women seemed to be perfect inverses, but somehow still formed a matched pair. They needed one another. They balanced each other out. Despite their many opposites, they shared some of the most important values. They cared about kindness, fairness, and equality. Above all else, they valued family. Theirs was a small one, and they were fiercely protective of it. Their mother had died when Sara was in college and Maya was still a teenager. Their father had followed five years later. Cancer had taken them both. Even though both girls had already moved out on their own by the time their father passed away, Sara still thought of herself as an orphan. It doesn't matter how old you are; you never stop needing your parents. You can be an orphan at any age.

They had no other siblings, no cousins, and their grandparents also long gone. Their only remaining family was Aunt Joann, whose former home office the two young women were currently occupying. Aunt Joann had married and divorced and married and divorced, but had never had any children of her own. She doted on Sara and Maya as if they were her own daughters. Joann lived in what had been her parents' home in San Francisco's Sunset District. Joann and her big sister, Sara and Maya's mother, had grown up in the four-bedroom semidetached home in a quiet neighborhood. It was something that would be entirely unaffordable in the current market, even given Joann's successful career in marketing. Everything was much more reasonably priced back in the 1950s when Sara and Maya's grandparents had purchased the home.

Not long ago, Sara had been living in an overpriced studio apartment in the Richmond District, and Maya had been renting a room in the Mission. One evening over Sunday dinner at Aunt Joann's house, Maya had announced she was pregnant. This came as quite a shock to Sara and Joann since they hadn't even known she was dating anyone. Apparently, Maya had been having an affair with a doctor she met through her part-time job working the gift shop counter at Saint Gertrude's Memorial Hospital. Sara had admonished her little sister for getting involved with a married man. To which, Maya had replied, "But he isn't happily married." In Maya's mind, anything done in the pursuit of happiness could be considered virtuous. Sara didn't really feel that justified it, but she wasn't going to make Maya feel guilty about something that was already in the past. The doctor, Dr. Damian Carver, would not leave his wife. He had suggested Maya terminate the pregnancy. Maya had refused. He had offered her some cash to help with expenses, which she also refused. He made it clear that he wanted nothing more to do with Maya or her unborn child.

Maya was surprisingly chipper in divulging all this information, which Sara felt spoke to how resilient her baby sister's spirit truly was. Aunt Joann absorbed all this information in silence, fork suspended in midair at the dinner table. When she finally set down her utensil, she composedly stated, "I think it's time for you girls to come home." There were no protests. Deep down, Sara thought it might have been exactly what she always wanted: her family back together under one roof. She broke the lease on her studio apartment, and Maya sublet her room in the Mission. They packed up their meager belongings and moved back to the Sunset with Aunt Joann.

Now, here they stood in Joann's old office, ready to turn it into a baby's nursery. Joann had been insistent that the house was much too large for one person. She didn't need a home office anyway. She travelled so much for work that she would hardly be there to bother them. Aunt Joann understood her nieces were not girls any longer. They were women. They had their own lives. She just wanted to do what she could to enable them to live those lives as freely as possible. And that meant providing them with a safe space to shepherd in the next generation.

"Well, let's get to building this crib. I need to leave for work in an hour." Sara was a copy editor for the *San Francisco Daily News*, lovingly referred to by locals as *The Daily*. It was one of the last newspapers in the city that still did in-house printing. Sara worked the swing shift, clocking out at 10:00 p.m. right before the paper went to press. She liked to think of herself as the last guardian against typos. As a copy editor, she would occasionally suggest changes to the text of a story beyond punctuation and grammar. If she felt an article fell flat or failed to present a compelling argument, she would practically rewrite it. Of course, she would have to clear those changes with the reporter who wrote it. After all, it was their byline. The changes were rarely accepted, and Sara eventually realized all she was really accomplishing was making enemies at work. Now, she mostly stuck to fact-checking and spelling errors.

Sara had been with *The Daily* for six years. She got a job as a file clerk right out of college in 2011. In 2014, the same year her father died, she got promoted to copy editor and had been stuck there ever since. Her coworker, Tim, liked to rile her up by calling her a grammar Nazi. He did it purely to get a reaction out of her, which was the same every time. "First of all, grammar is my job. It's not something I do just to annoy people on the Internet. I'm not sitting around correcting people's use of the words 'your' and 'you're' in their Facebook rants. Secondly, I take issue with the word Nazi. Not only is it overused, but also your usage of it isn't even accurate." Then Tim would laugh and inform her that she had just proved his point, and Sara would roll her eyes. Then, they would move on to less repetitive topics of conversation. Tim would usually circle back later and remind her in a less antagonizing tone that she possessed a degree in journalism and that she ought to be writing her own articles. She hadn't gone to college and majored in proofreading with a minor in spellcheck. These types of comments usually incited Sara to defend her job as a very important part of journalism. She believed it was important, but she also suffered a deeply buried crisis of confidence. She could try to find a reporter position elsewhere. She could even push for a writing position at *The Daily*. But what if she wasn't as good at it as she thought? What if she failed? What if she walked away from stability and could never turn back?

Tim was a photographer for *The Daily*. He also worked the swing shift. His career with the paper was a couple years longer than Sara's, and he had been one of her first friends upon her arrival. In the beginning, his attentions had been interpreted by Maya as romantic interest. Sara was unconvinced. She was sure his interest was purely platonic. Besides, Sara had a rule against dating coworkers. Maya found this rule intriguing, considering this was Sara's first real job. When had this rule been invented? Maya was fairly certain that Sara couldn't see his affection for what it was because of her own self-confidence (or lack thereof). But she let it go. And in the end, Sara and Tim settled into a comfortable friendship. They had similar tastes in music. They went to concerts together. They watched football together on Sundays. These days, Tim had a serious girlfriend, and Sara often reminded Maya that she had told her so. Still, Tim was one of Sara's greatest supporters and hated to see her stay stagnant in her career. He knew she was capable of so much more, even if she didn't know it herself.

Sara had considered taking a reporter position not long ago. It happened after one of her more frustrating days at work. She had rewritten a piece about a protest against police violence that had turned violent itself. Didn't they all these days? Wasn't violence just under the surface everywhere she turned? When she had presented the rewrite to the editor in chief, he had informed her with an exasperated sigh that she was a copy editor and her job was to edit the copy, not create content. The paper ended up running the original version, which, in Sara's opinion, presented the event like a traffic report. There were a bunch of statements of fact strung together in no particular order. It said nothing about the beliefs of the protesters or what they hoped to accomplish. There was a quote attributed to a young man who "claimed to be one of the protesters." She took particular issue with the word "claimed." Was he there or wasn't he? The use of the word made it seem as though the author doubted his own source. As a journalist, if you can't trust your source, you shouldn't print it. The reporter didn't even bother to point out the irony of a violent protest against violence. Sara felt the article was soulless.

After being shut down by her boss, Sara took to the Internet for some therapeutic job hunting. She didn't intend to apply for anything. She just thought it would relieve some of her frustration to know there were other options out there for her, options where she could put her journalism degree to better use. Staying in her copy editor job felt less like settling if she knew she was making the choice to stay. It was that night, job hunting on her phone on the train ride home, that she saw a job that sounded like it was meant for her. There was an online application form. Then, there was an e-mail followed by a phone call followed by a Skype interview. Then, all of a sudden, she had been presented with a job offer—in New York City.

She told the New York editor she would have to think about it. She let the idea of relocating roll around in her mind for almost a week. Financially, it made sense. They were offering her a lot more money than she was making at *The Daily*. They were offering to pay for her move. They were offering her a position where she would be published. She would have a byline. She would have her own content read by a much more impressive subscriber count than her current paper could offer. It made sense for her career. She had nearly convinced herself that accepting the offer was the right thing to do. Then, she went to Sunday dinner at Aunt Joann's house, and Maya announced she was pregnant, and that was that. Monday morning, without breathing a word of it to her family, Sara called the editor in New York and told her that while she was very grateful to have been considered, she was going to have to decline. *Thank you, but no thank you*. Her family needed her in San Francisco.

"Where do we start with this crib?" Maya asked, looking up from her phone and notebook. She had been working on a list of potential baby names, a topic that seemed to occupy her every waking thought these days.

"We should probably start by opening the box."

Maya glanced at the box containing the crib where her baby would sleep and then back to her notebook. "What do you think about James?"

"Didn't you date a James in high school?" Sara had been the sounding board for these baby names for several weeks now and hoped she was being more helpful than discouraging, but it was hard to say.

"Oh yeah," Maya replied with a slightly disgusted look on her face. Some less than savory memory must have reared its ugly head. "What about Samantha?" she asked, hopeful again.

Sara went to work at opening the box and searching for the assembly instructions. "You know, you could save yourself about half the trouble if you just found out whether you were having a boy or a girl."

Maya looked as though Sara had slapped her. "But I want to be surprised! You're going to be there in the delivery room with me. Aren't you excited about that moment when the doctor announces 'it's a boy' or 'it's a girl'?" Maya had never been one to hide her emotions, but Sara was still a little surprised to hear a wavering in her sister's voice and see a little glint of a tear that didn't quite fall. This surprise was something she felt very strongly about.

If Sara ever had a baby, she would not be able to handle not knowing. She would want to know whether she was having a boy or girl the first second that information was available. But she shouldn't expect Maya to share this need to vanquish the unknown. "Yes," she said with a reassuring smile. "Yes, I'm definitely looking forward to that moment."

Maya wiped the tear away as Sara unloaded the pieces of the crib onto the floor. "Fucking hormones," she muttered under her breath. Sara looked at her with raised eyebrows, and Maya returned her judgmental look with a roll of her eyes. "I know… language."

Sara went back to arranging the crib parts in an orderly manner. "And what's with the sudden string of traditional names? Last week, all your ideas were Rhys and Soren and Asher. I would think Samantha would be too vanilla for you."

Maya pushed her notebook aside and finally came to join Sara in the project at hand. "You never know what name is going to be right. I want to explore all my options. I'll probably have to wait until I meet the little guy to really decide."

"Or girl," Sara added.

"Or girl," Maya seconded, clearly delighted at the prospect of another generation of women growing up in her grandparent's home. "How do you think Mom and Dad came up with our names? I don't remember ever hearing the story."

Sara felt her heart flutter as it often did when she thought of her parents. It had been three years since she lost her dad, eight since losing her mom. But it still hurt. That's the thing no one tells you about grieving: you're never done. "I don't know," she replied, trying to hide her change of mood. "I never thought to ask." It was just one more thing in a long list of questions that she had never thought to ask.

"Maybe Aunt Joann knows."

Sara smiled. Aunt Joann was their link to the past, the insight into her parents' lives that had been cut too short. "You should ask her when she gets home." Their aunt was currently out on one of her many business trips and wouldn't be returning until the following week.

The two women went to work on assembling the crib with Sara doing most of the heavy lifting and Maya insisting the instructions were unnecessary. They ended up abandoning the project, half finished with a promise to pick it back up in the morning. The time had come for Sara to catch her bus to work.

CHAPTER 2

S ara bundled herself out the glass-paneled front door of Aunt Joann's mint green house. She shivered as she fumbled for her keys in the depths of her messenger bag. Even after living in San Francisco her entire life, she had never fully adjusted to the damp chill that came with the fog. The Sunset District was nearly always socked in. She tended to swathe herself in as many layers as she could manage without looking like a Sherpa. On this mid-September afternoon, Sara was wrapped in a long sleeve T-shirt, her favorite hooded sweatshirt, and an army green jacket adorned with an excessive number of pockets, zippers, and drawstrings. As she locked the door behind her, she wrapped her scarf around her neck and pulled her knit beanie down over her ears. She made her way down the sixteen brick stairs to the cracked and uneven sidewalk, warped from years of minor earthquakes and tree root growth. As she arrived at the bus stop a few blocks away, she made a mental note to ditch the beanie before she got into the office. Otherwise, Tim would tease her about preparing for the coming blizzard.

There was an illuminated sign at the bus stop that displayed the number of minutes until the next bus arrived. At the moment. it claimed her ride would be along in five minutes, but it was nearly always wrong. Sara pondered the amount of money that had gone into equipping so many of the bus stops in the city with these useless electronic signs. Someone had been hired to design the sign itself. A crew had been formed to run power to each location. A programmer had been commissioned to write the software that would determine the whereabouts of each bus and the length of time to all its destinations. All that time, money, and energy spent on a project that never worked from day one. *That might make a good article for the paper,* Sara thought. She could conduct a study about the cost benefit of the bus stop electronic sign program. It would feel good to at least point out the idiocy of the city's spending projects. Then, Sara reminded herself that she would have to be a reporter to propose an article like that. Maybe she'd mention it in the next staff meeting anyway. She would probably have to endure the wrathful gaze of her editor in chief, Jeff. It might be worth it for the jabs she and Tim would take behind Jeff's back after the meeting. They never said anything too hurtful. It was just a way of blowing off steam.

The sign only served to irritate Sara. She stared at it for about two minutes, willing it to change, but it still displayed five minutes remaining. Sara narrowed her eyes in discontent and jabbed her headphones into her ears, turning up the volume to drown out her own annoyance. It would be so much easier to drive to and from work than to be reliant on the public transit system. But the cost of owning a vehicle in San Francisco was prohibitive, and parking was nearly impossible. Besides, if she ever really needed a ride somewhere, Tim was always willing to drive her. He had an ancient Toyota Camry station wagon, handed down to him by his parents when they moved to Daly City and had space for a nicer vehicle without worrying about the dings and dents associated parking in San Francisco. The battered vehicle was black and boxy, leading Sara to teasingly refer to it as a hearse. Tim had embraced the title, and now, they both lovingly referred to it as his hearse. Street parking was scarce near Tim's North Beach apartment, but the office had an underground garage, and management let him keep it there based on his argument that he mainly used it to drive to his shooting locations for the paper.

After eleven eternal minutes, Sara's bus finally arrived. She boarded and took a seat near the back. One of the advantages of working swing shift was that she avoided the peak commute hours. Having a nearly empty bus to herself every day meant she had peace and quiet to read, listen to music, or just get lost in thought as was her tendency lately.

A large part of Sara's recent preoccupation with violence and death stemmed from Maya's pregnancy. The baby was due within a matter of weeks, and Sara found herself wondering what kind of world this child would be inheriting. She couldn't help but feel that violence was closing in on her at all times. The world felt like a simmering pot of negativity, threatening to boil over at any moment. Somehow, San Francisco in particular seemed like it was seething with savagery. Working in the news industry didn't help matters. She was constantly exposed to some of the worst happenings in the world, but especially in her own city. She couldn't ignore it as Maya did. Maya avoided the news at all cost. She said that it was too depressing. Sara felt that, depressing or not, it was the truth and it was better to be aware of it than to live an ignorant life of bliss. Still, she questioned whether or not she dwelled on the negative too much. People see the truth they create for themselves.

She gazed out the window of the bus and saw angry people clutching their steering wheels with white-knuckled hands. She observed scowling teenagers smoking cigarettes and shooting dirty looks at passersby, daring them to make eye contact. She saw broken glass where a parked car had been vandalized. She witnessed a homeless person shouting profanity at some invisible audience. She saw anger, sadness, and injustice. What shocked her most was not the despairing negativity all around, but the sense of apathy from everyone else who observed it. Did no one else care? Had society become so numb to this way of being that it was simply accepted? Sara hoped that it wasn't as dire as she made it seem. She wished for a better world for her unborn niece or nephew. Maybe Maya was right, and she was just allowing herself too many morbid thoughts. As the bus pulled up to her stop, she made a mental note to look through the day's news with an unbiased eye. She truly wanted to see the good in the world. She just wasn't sure it was really there.

Sara disembarked the bus and walked the remaining two blocks to her office. The three-story brick and concrete building was situated on the outskirts of the financial district. It was about halfway between Fisherman's Wharf and downtown proper. Sara liked being slightly removed from the fast paced business world near Market

Street where people were constantly rushing around, buzzing with activity, oblivious to everyone but themselves.

She walked in through the double doors and gave a little wave to the guard at the front desk who returned her gesture with a grunt and an almost imperceptible nod. Sara made her way upstairs, taking care to remove her hat and scarf before she passed the door to Tim's office. She peeked in as she passed his doorway, but he wasn't there. Tim had an office and a window and a door that closed. Sara, meanwhile, lived in cubeland in the center of the office where no natural light could ever touch. Her job took place under a sky of fluorescent bulbs, surrounded by a sea of other people's paper shuffling, coffee sipping, and keyboard tapping. Sara longed for an office to call her own, although she would never admit it to Tim. She told him his office seemed stuffy, and when his door was closed most of the day, she teased him about being trapped in his cell. Of course, she was much more trapped than he was. She was stuck facing her computer monitor most of the day. He got to go out on assignments, which is probably why he wasn't in his office now.

Sara made her way to her little beige cubicle with its upholstered walls and laminate desk. She powered up her laptop and checked her e-mail for stories submitted for her edits. There was an article about a founder of a local winery who had died, a story about standardized test scores for San Francisco high schools, and a fluff piece about the thirty-year anniversary of a statue being erected. It looked like it might be a slow news day. She rifled through the papers in her inbox and uncovered her copy of *The Daily* from the day before. All staff members were supposed to read the paper in full as part of their job description, even the guard downstairs. The reasoning was that you couldn't expect subscribers to read something if the staff wouldn't. Sara decided she would take the opportunity to find something good in the world without letting her morbid thoughts cloud her vision.

There was nothing like a printed newspaper. Sara despised the trend toward Internet news, and television news was something she tried to pretend did not exist. She loved the feel of newspaper and the soft snap sound it made when she pulled it taut. It reminded her of her dad. When she was a kid, she would sit across from him at the breakfast table, eating her cereal while he read the paper. Most mornings, all she could see of her father were his two hands on either side of the publication, the black-and-white print blotting out the rest of him. She would marvel over how still he was, how attentive he seemed to everything going on in the world. She longed for the day that her arm span would be long enough to hold up a newspaper the way he did and read every last word. With these warm memories in her mind, she began searching for something positive.

She started with the local news. The first story was one she had edited the day before. It was about a fatal shooting in the Tenderloin. It was the second shooting in that neighborhood in the last two weeks. The article didn't give many details. The victim was a white male whose identity could not be released until authorities had notified his next of kin. The police didn't have much to say about it other than the fact that they believed it to be a targeted shooting. Nothing put the public in a state of panic faster than a random act of violence. If it were random, then anyone could be the next victim. As long as they believed it was a targeted attack, they could put the newspaper down and walk around in their safe little bubble with the sense that they were somehow immune to the problems of the world.

Sara moved on to the next article. They headline read "Former Deputy Pleads Guilty in Sex Scandal." It wasn't one she had edited, but she had been following the story. There was a picture of the former sheriff's deputy that looked like a mug shot. He looked miserable and unkempt. When rumors of the scandal had first begun to circulate, the articles were accompanied by photos of him from official sheriffs' events, smiling and looking well-groomed. Now that he was admitting to inappropriate conduct with an underage prostitute, the press was being very careful not to show him in any sort of flattering light. Sara reminded herself that she was the press and that maybe she shouldn't be so judgmental as she skimmed through the article and on to the next one.

It was a story about a series of muggings. They had all taken place in the early hours of the morning, and the victims had all been jogging near St. Mary's Cathedral. Police had a rough sketch of the perpetrator, but no leads yet. In most cases, the mugger hadn't gotten away with any belongings. Joggers don't usually carry much on their person. It seemed the motivation was more to terrorize the victims and less about actually acquiring anything valuable.

Sara turned the page and moved on to state and national news. Police in Los Angeles had shot an unarmed black man. Witnesses stated that during a routine traffic stop, the victim was asked to step out of the vehicle. He was shot in the back with his hands in the air while he asked what he had done wrong. The police chief gave a statement that a full investigation would be conducted. There had been so many of these stories in recent months that Sara felt the public was becoming numb to them. Violence, brutality, and injustice were becoming a way of life.

The next article was about a New Jersey man who was wanted in connection with creating YouTube videos instructing viewers how to build bombs out of common household items. The man was still at large. The videos had been removed from the website, but there was no way of knowing how many homemade bombs were already out there as a result of his instructions.

In international news, there was widespread violence and political unrest in Russia, Syria, and Pakistan. The list went on and on. There were different reasons for the wars and disturbances happening in each country around the globe. But the end result was always the same: violence, death, hatred, and more violence. Sara put the paper down and closed her eyes. She tried to tell herself that every generation before her has felt like the world was falling apart and that they needed to somehow fix it. She told herself that there was still plenty of good in the world. It just didn't make the paper. There were still more good people than bad in the world. There had to be.

She opened her eyes and saw Tim's face peeking at her over her cubicle wall. A startled yelp escaped her lips, and she nearly jumped out of her chair.

"Jesus, Tim, you scared the hell out of me!"

"Sorry," Tim said in a tone that meant he wasn't sorry at all. "I didn't want to interrupt your meditation."

Tim had a maddening way of altering his expression with microscopic movements of his face. One dark eyebrow was a millimeter higher than the other. The corners of his mouth pointed down ever so slightly, yet he still appeared to be smiling. The hint of a dimple appeared under the scruff on his face. To the untrained eye, he was merely making a factual statement. Sara knew this look meant he was making fun of her and waiting for her reaction.

"I wasn't meditating." Maybe, in a way she was, but she wasn't going to tell him that. "I was doing my homework," she said, ruffling the newspaper in his face. "It just got a little depressing, that's all."

Tim snatched the paper from her hands and flipped to the front page. "What, this? Murder? Crime? Political corruption? That's not depressing. That's our bread and butter." Sara shot him an impatient glare.

He gave in. His teasing look transformed into something more sincere. "Okay, what's got you down? Something is on your mind."

Sara bit her lower lip. She considered telling him she was worried about the state of the world, the cruelty she witnessed every day. She thought about telling him she was afraid of the chaotic life Maya's baby would have to endure. But she decided it all sounded a little too melodramatic. Instead, she asked him the same question she had posed to Maya earlier that day. "Do you think you've already been to the place where you're going to die?"

Tim's expression became thoughtful. As much as he liked to joke around with her, she knew he would take this question seriously. He wouldn't brush it off as morbid daydreaming like Maya had. He would actually think about it.

"Well"—he replied after giving it some thought—"my job takes me to a lot of crime scenes. I've been to a lot of places where other people have just died. So I'd say the chances are pretty good that, yes, I've already been to the place where I'm going to die." His eyes squinted the tiniest bit, and the set of his jaw changed a fraction of an inch. He was concerned. "Why is that on your mind?"

Sara indicated the newspaper that was still dangling from his fingertips. "All of this. People die every day. Sometimes, they're in places that seem safe. Sometimes, the places seem so random. It just makes me wonder if I could die crossing the street or waiting for the bus."

A little crease appeared between Tim's eyebrows. She had just stepped his concern up a notch. "Do you feel unsafe?"

Sara really thought about it. Was that why she couldn't get this concept out of her head? Was she afraid for her life? "No, it's not that I feel unsafe. I guess it's just hitting me that we never know when our time will be up. That, and I wish the world wasn't filled with so many heartless people."

The crease disappeared, and a trace of a smile appeared on Tim's lips. "Well then, if we could drop dead at any moment, we have to seize the day, right?"

Sara shot him a questioning look, instantly skeptical. "What did you have in mind?" She sensed he was trying to change the subject, and she found she was relieved to let him. She needed to get her mind off all this negativity.

"The Ataris are playing at Bottom of the Hill this weekend. Want to go? I'll pick you up so you don't have to die at the bus stop."

Sara's mood instantly felt lighter. Bottom of the Hill Club was one of her favorite live music venues in the city. She and Tim had seen a lot of shows there. It was small and intimate. There was no backstage area, just a hallway where bands lined up their equipment against the wall. You could mingle with the opening bands between sets. It had a casual feel that she adored. The Ataris were a band Tim and Sara both loved. Their similar tastes in music had helped to bring them together as friends. Maybe a night out would be just what she needed to lift her out of this funk.

"Sounds fun, count me in. Is Melissa going?"

Tim began fastidiously folding Sara's newspaper and dropped it back in her inbox. He was avoiding eye contact and trying to sound casual as he said, "No, we're not seeing each other anymore."

Sara's heart dropped into her stomach. Here she had been going around obsessing about the state of the world and her own mortality. All the while, her best friend had been going through a breakup. Why hadn't he mentioned it to her?

"Since when?" she asked, not even attempting to hide her shock.

Tim took a slow breath and composed his expression. He looked at her with relaxed lids over his hazel eyes and a forced small smile. "Since about a week ago."

"What happened? I thought you guys had gotten really serious." She wanted to ask him why he hadn't confided in her. Did he think she wouldn't be there for him? Had she been too preoccupied lately? Too distant? She knew he didn't like to talk much about his personal life. He was usually too busy telling Sara what she should do with her own life. He was a very private person. Still, she would think he'd share something of this caliber with her.

"She wanted me to move in with her. I said no. She wanted to know why, and I didn't really have an answer. I just knew it wasn't what I wanted." He said it as a matter of fact, like he wasn't emotionally connected to the situation at all.

"And that was it?" Tim and Melissa had been seeing each other for over a year. It seemed like it should take more than one argument to end it.

"That was it. She said she couldn't waste any more time with me if we weren't moving forward. She said it was over."

"I'm sorry." Sara had never been very close with Melissa, but the two of them had seemed like a good match. She truly was sorry for him.

Tim shrugged. "She's right. If we don't have a future together, we shouldn't waste each other's time."

Sara didn't know what to say. He clearly wanted to downplay the whole thing like it was no big deal, but she knew he must be hurting. She tried to form some words that would help ease his pain a little. Her mouth opened, but nothing came out.

"It's okay," Tim murmured, rescuing her from her speechlessness. "I'm fine with it. I'm moving on."

Sara snapped her mouth shut. It was just as well. There was nothing she could say to get him to open up about this, at least not right then, not at work. Her phone chimed on her desk, saving both of them from the awkward turn this conversation had taken. Tim looked down at it and saw it was a text from Maya.

"I'll let you get that," Tim said. "It's probably important. Saturday, Bottom of the Hill, I'll pick you up," he announced as he turned on his heels and headed back toward his office.

Sara sat there stunned for a moment and then finally called after him, "Okay." He was already well out of earshot.

She picked up her phone and checked her message from Maya. "Can u go to my old place after wrk? Roommate called. Said she found Mom's necklace." Sara set down the phone a little too hard in her irritation. She was partly annoyed by Maya's refusal to use proper grammar and spelling in text messages, but she was mostly upset by the request. She didn't mind running errands for sister, especially with her belly now bulging like a ripe watermelon. But she hated going to Maya's old apartment. The roommates never remembered her despite having met her several times. It wasn't in the greatest neighborhood either, and going after work meant being in that neighborhood well after sundown. Still, Maya had been devastated that she couldn't find their mother's necklace when she moved out. It would be worth enduring the journey to retrieve that piece of jewelry. Sara texted back, saying she would go. Then, she did her best to set aside her trepidation about the growing cruelty of the world and her worry about Tim's breakup. She settled in for an afternoon of editing.

The afternoon dragged into the evening, and finally, it was time for Sara to make her way toward the Mission District to Maya's old apartment. As expected, the roommates didn't know who she was. One of the young women peered at her through the slim crack allowed by the chain lock on the front door, interrogating her about what Maya looked like and other such things that would provide some sort of proof of her identity. When she was finally satisfied that Sara was who she claimed to be, the girl shut the door in her face to go in search of the necklace. She came back, dropped it into Sara's palm, and shut the door again without so much as a goodbye.

Sara examined the piece of jewelry. It was a small oval locket with a tiny blue gem set in the center of it. She opened the familiar trinket to reveal two pictures, one of herself and one of Maya when they were little girls. She smiled at the memory of the locket hanging

CATHARTA

from her mother's neck. It had been rare to see her without it. Sara knew how much it meant to Maya, and she was glad to be able to bring it back to her. She tucked it into the zipper pocket of her messenger bag and left the apartment for what she hoped would be the last time.

Downstairs at the bus stop, she glanced at the electronic sign stating that her bus would be arriving in five minutes. She let out an annoyed sigh. Why was it always five minutes? Looking up and down the street, she saw no sign of a bus, but she did see some teenagers. They looked like the kind of guys she didn't want to hang around with in the Mission District after dark. She glared at the electronic sign once more and decided she wasn't going to wait around for that bus. She started walking toward the subway station. The bus was convenient because it dropped her off closer to her house, but the subway had some advantages after dark. She might find some unsavory characters there too, but at least, it wasn't so exposed. Plus, you could practically set your watch by the train schedule. As she climbed the stairs down into the underground Sixteenth Street subway station, she was willing to bet that her bus still hadn't arrived.

Inside the station, it was quiet. The trains would only be running for another hour or so, and they came infrequently at this time of night. She waited at the far end of the platform near where the last train car would pull up. The platform sign indicated that her train would be along in three minutes, and she was confident that it would be exactly three minutes on the dot. She put in her headphones and peered into the dark round tunnel from which the train would emerge.

About two and a half minutes later, she began to feel a stirring. A breeze picked up in the station as the train approached, pushing a giant column of air in front of it. The train's headlights began to illuminate concentric circles of light in the dark tunnel. The wind grew, and the sound increased, overpowering the music from her headphones. A brief moment before the train appeared, it felt like the column of air slapped her in the face, whipping her hair everywhere. Just as the train was about to burst forth from the tunnel, Sara felt a sharp tug on her messenger bag. She looked down and saw a

29

grubby looking man crouched behind her. He had a wild look in his eyes, and his hands were poised to make another grab for her bag. She shouted, "Hey!" but couldn't seem to form any other words fast enough. Another man who was about halfway down the platform, turned as she yelled and began running toward Sara and her attacker. As the grubby man made another lunge toward her, she spun around a little too quickly and felt herself losing her balance. The other man from down the platform was almost upon them, hollering and trying to scare the attacker away. The grubby man scrambled to get around them both and bumped into Sara, sending her shuffling backward toward the edge of the platform. In Sara's mind, she was screaming, but no sound escaped her throat as she felt her feet go out from under her. Then the train was rushing into the station, and she was falling, and the sound and the wind were fading away. Then everything was black. Everything was silent.

CHAPTER 3

*T*he silence grew thick. It was a silence that couldn't be described as merely quiet. It was a complete absence of sound. The wind from the train was gone. The cold chill of the city fog had disappeared. Sara squeezed her eyes tightly shut, seeing nothing, feeling nothing. She waited for sensation to return to her body, but nothing came. All she could feel was her heart hammering hard inside her chest. She must be in shock. She allowed her eyes to flutter open. It was still very dark, but as her vision adjusted, she began to sense a faint fluorescent glow. Maybe she was in a hospital. Had she been hit by that train? Shouldn't she be in pain? She felt nothing. She wiggled her extremities and slowly became aware that she was lying flat on her back on a hard surface. Curiosity overcame fear, and she decided she'd try to sit up.

Propping herself up on her elbows in the dim light, she observed a long cement corridor with a red tile floor. It took a moment for recognition to dawn on her. This was no hospital. This was the Sixteenth Street subway station. She hadn't gone anywhere. But where was the train? Where was the man who had tried to help her? Where was the man who had tried to attack her? In a surge of panic, she reached down for her messenger bag. It was still there. She dragged her body up to a sitting position, crossing one leg over the other and sliding her bag into her lap. Opening the zipper pocket, she found her mother's locket was still there. She popped it open. Two smiling little girls stared back at her. She felt some small sense of relief at seeing the familiar faces. She clicked it shut again and returned it to its safe haven.

Sara glanced around at her surroundings. The station was completely empty. There wasn't a single other soul on the platform. There were no trains. There was no movement of any kind. Maybe the station had closed with her in it. That might explain the silence and her solitude. But what had happened to her? Why wouldn't someone try to help her up or at least inform her the station was closing? Even if the train hadn't hit her, she must have taken a pretty bad fall. Why did nothing hurt?

Unless she was dead.

Maybe she had fallen in front of the oncoming train, and she had died. She glanced over her shoulder at the tunnel opening. She shivered and shut her eyes. Shaking her head, she told herself she was being ridiculous. She was having morbid thoughts again. There was no way she was dead. No, the most logical explanation was that she had somehow avoided the train, fainted from fear, and then ended up accidentally locked in the subway station when it closed. That could happen, couldn't it? A thought crept in from the corners of her mind that being dead was a far more likely explanation, but she pushed the notion aside.

Slowly, carefully, she pushed herself up to a crouch. When she still felt no pain, no instability, she stood up to her full height. She wobbled a little, but found her footing. She needed to get out of the station and find help. She needed to get home. She made her way to the nearest stairs. The adjacent escalator was powered off. Sara took it as a confirmation that the station was in fact closed. There must be an emergency exit somewhere. She just had to find it. She made her way up two flights of stairs and came out at the fare gates. Her hand automatically reached for the ticket in her bag, but then she realized the gates wouldn't work if the whole station had been shut down. She exited out a side gate and found the flight of stairs that would bring her up to the street level, fully expecting that her way would be blocked by the roll-down gate that closed the station off to the public every night. But the gate was open.

Sara stood completely motionless at the bottom of the flight of stairs. She could see a little patch of sky at the top of the steps. It was a flat, pale gray, like the sky at dawn before the sun had breached the horizon. Could it be morning already? Had she been stuck in the subway station all night? She stood there, listening, for what seemed like an eternity. There should be sounds, cars, and people. She heard nothing. Gathering her courage around her, she ascended the flight of stairs and emerged near the corner of Sixteenth Street and Mission Street. This was not the Mission Street she knew. Any time, day or night, it should be littered with people, milling around on the sidewalks or sleeping in doorways. There should be cars and cabs and buses making their way through the stoplights and one-way streets. There was no one in sight. Looking up at the sky, she saw an expanse of the same flat gray she had spotted from below. It wasn't the gray of the fog she was so used to. It was the colorless clear sky that only appears in the early hours of the morning before most of the world has awoken. As she looked up, she noticed something else. The trees were nothing more than bare branches, reaching up toward the slate sky like gnarled skeletal hands. Sara hadn't paid that much attention on her way into the station, but she was certain the trees had been full of leaves. It was only the start of fall. The leaves shouldn't drop until closer to winter. She couldn't make sense of it. It was like everything was dead. She swallowed hard against that word in her throat. She wasn't dead. She couldn't allow herself to believe that. There had to be another explanation.

As she stood on the pavement, pondering her next move, she heard something like an electric crackling. It sounded like a power source somewhere was trying to come to life, sputtering and sparking. She instinctively moved toward the sound, which seemed to be coming from an alleyway up ahead. It was the first sound she'd heard since she woke up in the train station. Maybe it was a sign of life. Maybe it could help explain what had happened to her. A soft white glow was visible at the entrance to the alley, growing brighter as she approached. She slowed her pace. Then, she heard a voice. A young woman down the alley shouted, "Stop!" Sara did stop, although she was fairly certain the command wasn't directed at her. Then came a loud pop and an explosion of bright white light just before all the noise fizzled out. The alley grew dark again. The silence returned.

Sara was frozen on the spot. The fear that was coursing through her veins told her to turn and run back the way she had come from. The confusion that clouded her mind told her whoever was down that alley may have answers for her. As she stood, her body pulling her in two directions at once while her feet refused to move, the decision was made for her. The young woman who had shouted, a teenage girl from the looks of her, emerged from the alleyway. She was shielding her eyes as though trying to hold back tears. She couldn't see where she was going, and she was about to run right into Sara.

Sara caught her by the shoulders so they wouldn't have a collision. The girl was startled, but she still didn't look up. "Hey, are you okay?" As soon as she asked the question, Sara realized how preposterous it was. She, herself, was clearly not okay. How could she possibly help this girl if she were not okay? But it seemed like the natural thing to ask.

The young woman whimpered, her shoulders heaving with the sobs she was holding back. Sara reached up and swept a lock of the girl's long raven hair out of her face. "I can't stop him," the girl whispered, more to herself than to Sara.

Sara had no idea what she was talking about. Gently she asked, "You can't stop who?"

The girl sniffled, "Sorry, you must be new here." She made an effort to compose herself, standing up straight and wiping her eyes with her sleeve.

"New where? What is this place? Where am I?" Trepidation welled up inside Sara's chest like a knot. Although it looked very much like the city she knew and loved, the young woman's statement hinted at what Sara feared: this wasn't San Francisco.

"This is Catharta." Saying these words, the young woman looked up at Sara for the first time. Sara gasped and stutter stepped backward. She nearly stumbled, which brought back a gut-wrenching reminder of the train station. Panic flooded her, and she felt like she couldn't catch her breath.

The girl's eyes were like nothing she'd ever seen before. They were completely clear, like staring into a pool of water. They emitted a faint, opalescent glow. She had no irises, no pupils, just perfectly clear orbs rimmed in a forest of dark lashes, still damp with tears.

Sara managed to regain her balance, but she couldn't run. She was paralyzed with fear. Her heart was pounding so hard she felt sure it would burst out through her chest. The girl's mouth fell open in an expression of shock. She reached out one hand in Sara's direction and whispered, "Your eyes."

Sara was incredulous. She choked out, "My eyes?" She hadn't looked in a mirror since waking up in the station, but she assumed her eyes were still the same dark brown they had been her whole life. This girl's eyes, on the other hand, were something supernatural.

"Are you...," the girl hesitated, seeming to reach for a long lost word. "Are you alive?"

Her heart skipped a beat at that last word, and she feared it might have stopped altogether. Sara had reached her breaking point. This was all too much for her to take in. She dropped her face into her hands and let the tears spill out. "I don't know. I don't know if I'm alive."

The shock disappeared from the girl's face and was replaced by sympathy. She placed a hand on Sara's shoulder. "I'm sorry. I just haven't seen eyes like yours in a long time. I'm not sure, but I think it must mean you're not dead."

Sara tried to get her tears under control. "Are you?" She still couldn't bring herself to say the word out loud.

"Am I dead?"

Sara nodded, still afraid to make eye contact.

The girl gave Sara a sad smile. "My name is Ananda. What's yours?"

"Sara," she replied, stealing a brief glance at Ananda's faintly glowing eyes.

"It's nice to meet you, Sara. Why don't we go sit down somewhere and talk."

Sara was so relieved at the possibility of getting some answers. She felt like she was somehow being mothered by this stranger even though she was probably at least ten years older than Ananda. She allowed herself to be led back toward the subway station. Ananda guided her to the landing halfway down the first flight of stairs where she indicated for her to sit down. They sat across from one another, their backs against the concrete walls of the stairwell, the blank gray sky still above them, the dark cavern of the subway station below.

The silence grew uncomfortable as Ananda looked for the right words. Finally she began, "Yes, I am dead. So is everyone else in Catharta except you. I think you must be alive."

Sara was nearly convinced that she must be hallucinating. Maybe she had cracked her head open when she fell in front of the train, and this was all just a crazy, concussion-induced fever dream. "Are you a ghost?" she asked.

Ananda looked thoughtful. "I guess you could call me a ghost. But I'm not the type of ghost from campfire stories. I can't visit your plane of existence. I don't walk through walls or jump out and scare people. More accurately, what I am is a soul."

So many questions swirled through Sara's head, but she couldn't seem to form coherent thoughts. All she could manage was to vaguely repeat what Ananda had just said. "You're a soul?"

"Well," Ananda amended, "Technically, you're a soul too, Sara. But the difference is your soul still has a body. I think."

Sara pressed her palms into her eyes. She was approaching her limit of how much overwhelming information she could handle, but she needed answers. "Why do your eyes look like that?"

Ananda looked a little self-conscious, but she answered anyway. "You know how people like to say 'the eyes are the windows to the soul'? Well, I guess this is what the window looks like from the other side."

Sara nodded as if that statement had made perfect sense, but it sounded like insanity. "So if you're dead, does that mean this is heaven?" Sara had never been religious. She had vague beliefs that there was some sort of higher power out there and that something came after death. She felt organized religion was man's arrogant way of pretending to know everything about the great beyond. She believed people weren't meant to understand the greater workings of the spiritual universe. Now, Ananda was causing her to rethink her beliefs.

Ananda shook her head and gave a small mirthless laugh. "No, Catharta is not heaven. This is a place built of souls and memories. Nothing here is permanent. It's all a construction of what people recall from their lives. If someone remembers this stairwell, then here it is. Once the souls move on, the memories go with them."

"Move on to where?" Sara was growing more confused by the minute. "Is this like limbo?"

Ananda answered patiently, "You could say that. When you die, this is where your soul goes to await rebirth. Catharta is meant to give you time to reflect on the life you lived. It's where you remember everything you've ever said and done and, hopefully, learn from your mistakes for the next life."

Sara stole another glance at Ananda's eyes and found they still filled her with a sense of terror. She clung to a slight hope that this might all be some kind of bad dream. But she had never had a dream that felt so real. She had never had a dream so terrible that she couldn't wake up.

The questions were starting to spill out of her now that she had a chance to slow down and think. "So we're all recycled souls? Have I lived other lives before?"

"Undoubtedly, we all have lived many lives before. We have to be recycled, as you put it, because there are a finite number of souls in existence." For such a young woman, Ananda projected an air of wisdom. Her calm, even tone was putting Sara at ease, even if the information she was sharing seemed impossible.

"What do you mean a finite number of souls? Do you mean, like, we could run out?" The question sounded absurd even as she heard it coming off her own lips.

Ananda replied with bitter undertones that caught Sara off guard. "Oh, I'm quite sure we already have."

"So, there are people walking around earth with no soul?" Ananda gave Sara a small nod and let that knowledge sink in. Honestly, that piece of the puzzle made sense to Sara. All the cruelty, violence, and chaos in the world could be explained by people who seemed to have no conscience or no morals of any kind. Maybe they had no soul. "But why? Why are there only so many souls? Why can't new souls be created?"

"Only God can create new souls," Ananda responded evenly. With a touch of venom in her voice, she added, "And as far as I can tell, He's been out of that business for a long time." Sara stared at Ananda with awe, beginning to get used to her otherworldly eyes. "How do you know so much? You look so young, but you sound like...," she trailed off.

"An old soul?" Ananda finished for her. "I was seventeen when I died, but that seems like another lifetime ago."

"How long have you been here?"

Ananda looked up at the gray sky. "It's hard to say. Time works differently in Catharta. There are no days or nights, no seasons, no weather of any kind. But time passes very slowly here."

Sara wanted to know how much slower. "Do you remember the day you died?"

Ananda looked down at her hands in her lap and didn't respond. Sara felt she must have crossed a line. She had no reference for the etiquette for addressing a dead person, but it seemed pretty clear she wasn't supposed to come right out and ask about how they died. "I just meant the date. Maybe I could tell you how much time has passed."

Ananda nodded, but still averted her eyes. "It was November 2, 2014."

Sara replied solemnly, "That was almost three years ago."

Ananda considered that length of time thoughtfully. "It feels like a lot longer."

Both women were quiet for a moment. Sara had many more questions, but she felt she had dredged up some bad memories for Ananda, and she was afraid of saying the wrong thing. Only one question really seemed to matter anymore. "If I'm not dead, then why am I here?"

Ananda gave her a sad smile. "I wish I could tell you that. In all my time in Catharta, I've never seen a living soul before you." Sara was disheartened. If she didn't know how she got to Catharta, she didn't know how to get back home. Ananda seemed to sense her anxiety. "What were you doing when you woke up here?"

"I was waiting for the train," Sara said, peering into the station. "I fell as the train was approaching, and then everything went black."

Ananda chewed her lower lip in a thoughtful manner. "So you had a near-death experience. Maybe your soul jumped the gun."

"Could that happen?" Sara asked.

"Anything could happen."

Sara couldn't see how Ananda's theory could help her. "So how do I get back?"

Ananda looked heartbroken. "I really don't know. There are only supposed to be two kinds of gateways in Catharta. A death gateway opens to let souls in, and a rebirth gateway opens to let souls out. If you're not dead, you can't be reborn. But you didn't die, so I don't know how you got in."

Sara was becoming queasy. A sour sensation crept into her stomach, and she felt a little light-headed. "Do you mean I might be trapped here forever?"

"If it makes you feel any better, you'll be in good company." There was a sarcastic edge to Ananda's voice. As she saw Sara's face fall, she seemed to instantly realize she had said the wrong thing. "I'm sorry; I didn't mean that you're trapped here. I honestly don't know. But I do know that no soul has gotten out of Catharta in a long time."

"What do you mean? I thought you said rebirth gateways let souls out." Sara pondered, her brow furrowed in concern.

Before Ananda could answer, a man's voice bellowed from the street level above them, "Ananda!" It was a voice charged with heavy emotion. Both girls' heads whipped around in surprise. Sara sensed rage, fear, and despondency all wrapped up in the three syllables he had hollered.

Ananda leaned in close to Sara and hissed, "You need to go! Hide in the train station. He won't look there."

"But," Sara began to protest.

Ananda was already on her feet and heading up the stairs. She whispered over her shoulder, "I'll come find you. Hide!"

Dread rose in Sara's throat. She didn't know who or what was looking for her new friend, but it was obvious it wasn't good. Sara didn't know enough about the world she was in to help in any way. As she watched the young girl disappear beyond the threshold of the stairwell, she decided to do as Ananda had said. She rose to her feet and hurried down the rest of the stairs they had been sitting on. She passed through the fare gates and down the remaining two flights of stairs to the station platform. Back inside, it felt like an enormous concrete tomb. The silence combined with the stillness of the air made her feel like she was suffocating. She paced the platform from one end to the other twice, trying to clear her head. She was worried about Ananda and the man who seemed to be hunting her down. She was concerned about how she had gotten into Catharta in the first place, but more so with how she would get out. The thought kept creeping back into her mind that maybe she really was dead.

She halted her pacing when she realized she was standing in the exact spot where she had been waiting for the train before she had departed the world of the living. The hard red tiles beneath her feet felt unforgiving. The black cavern of the tunnel was ominously haunting. She couldn't remember exactly what had happened, but she was filled with an ever-growing doubt that she could have survived whatever had transpired.

Sara pressed her eyes shut. She couldn't recall ever having felt such complete and total despair. Even when she lost her parents, she didn't have such an all-encompassing feeling of loss. Losing a family member is hard, but losing yourself seemed to be even harder. She was overcome with a wave of sadness at the loss of her family, her friends, and her life. What if she could never get back there? What if she never saw Maya's face again? What if she never got to meet her new niece of nephew? The thought was more than she could bear.

A pressing impulse came over her to lie back down on the tiles, right where she had started. She didn't know where that urge came from, but she gave in to it. After all, what else did she have to do but wait? Sara eased herself onto the floor of the train platform. She lay flat on her back and let her head rest against the hard tile. She closed her eyes and wished to be home. She wanted it more than she had ever wanted anything in her entire life. She thought of Maya, Tim, and the little baby on the way. She thought of Aunt Joann and her grandparents' house and how it felt to have her tiny family reunited under one roof. She thought of her job, her daily life, and all the mundane things she took for granted. She wanted desperately to be back there again. She thought of everything she loved in the world, and a single sob escaped her lips. She was startled by the sound of her own whimper in the stifling silence, and she opened her eyes. As soon as she did, she felt a strange sensation that made her nauseous. It felt like she was moving upward very quickly, but she could see she was still lying flat on her back on the station floor. It was like being in an elevator, but the elevator was moving at breakneck speed. It began to induce a feeling of vertigo, and she was worried she was going to be sick. She tried to sit up, but found she couldn't. Some unseen force was pinning her down.

Just when she felt she couldn't take any more of this dizzying sensation, it stopped. The elevator came to a halt, but she hadn't gone anywhere. She felt her ears pop as if she had just had a major elevation change. She blinked her eyes. There was a dull pain blooming at the back of her head. She blinked again. The pain grew more intense. She noticed she no longer heard pure silence. There was a ringing in her ears. She moved her jaw ever so slightly, and her ears popped again. The ringing ceased. Then, she could hear a man's voice. It sounded like it was coming to her through an old radio with a lot of interference. She couldn't make sense of what he was saying. She blinked again.

All at once, she became aware of a person standing over her. She lurched up in shock and tried to scramble backward away from the towering figure silhouetted by fluorescent lights. She let out a yelp of fear. The man dropped to his knees and reached an abating hand in her direction. Without the backlighting, Sara could see his face, and she stopped trying to scurry away. It was the man from the train station who had tried to scare away the would-be mugger. It was a living person from the real world with eyes that had pupils and irises. They weren't clear and didn't glow. He was a kind-looking man who had a tried to help her, and here he was in the flesh, more than just a memory.

Sara became aware that he had been asking her if she was alright. She didn't know if she was. "Am I alive?" was the first thing that came to her mind.

The man gave her a look of grave concern. "Yes, you're alive. Are you hurt?"

Tears began streaming down Sara's face. "Yes, I'm hurt." She laughed out loud in spite of the pain she felt because it was nothing compared to the relief of being back in the real world, back in her body, back in her life. "What happened?"

The man was thrown off by her hysterical laughter, but answered her anyway. "A man tried to steal your purse. I scared him off, but he bumped into you. You nearly fell in front of the train. I grabbed you by your bag because that was all I could reach. You missed the train by inches, but I'm afraid you hit your head pretty hard on the floor. Are you bleeding?"

Sara pressed her palm to the back of her head. It came away clean, but she could feel a goose egg growing there. "No, I'm not bleeding." She pulled herself up to a sitting position, still too unsure of herself to stand. "How long was I out?"

"Only a minute or two." Her rescuer looked over his shoulder, down the platform. "I'm afraid the guy got away, but I can give a description of him to the police if you want. Do you want me to call the cops? Or an ambulance?"

Sara shook her head. "No police. No ambulance. I just want to go home."

The man looked deep into her eyes, probably trying to assess whether or not he should insist on the ambulance. Finally, he said, "Alright then, but you shouldn't take the train. What do you say we split a cab? That way I can make sure you get home in one piece."

Sara agreed, and the two of them made their way back out of the station as he called for a cab. On the ride home, she couldn't stop marveling at the sights and sounds of the living city. There were cars on the streets honking their horns even at this late hour. There were people on the sidewalks stumbling their way to the next bar. There were stars in the sky and leaves in the trees. There was life everywhere she looked. Her awe and amazement at such ordinary things did nothing to convince her fellow passenger that she was okay, but she assured him she was fine. It was probably just shock.

Sara learned that his name was Mitch, and he had just worked a very long day. He wouldn't normally have been in the train station at that hour. Sara shuddered to think what might have happened if he hadn't been there. But the fact of the matter was that he had been there and that she was alive and well because of it.

The driver took them to Sara's home first, even though that meant doubling back to drop Mitch off after. But he insisted he needed to know she got home safe. When the car stopped in front of Aunt Joann's front steps, Sara tried to pay the fare, but Mitch insisted it was his treat. She wanted to argue that she certainly owed him more than a cab ride, but she was too exhausted to put up much of a fight. In the end, she let him pick up the tab and go on his way. She thanked him again before he left, even though the words felt entirely inadequate. He had saved her life. There was no doubt in her mind about that.

He watched her as she climbed the sixteen steps to the front door of Aunt Joann's house, fumbled in her messenger bag for keys, and finally let herself in. She gave him a last wave of gratitude as she closed the door, and his cab pulled away from the curb.

Once inside, Sara felt fatigue set in. She wasn't sure how she was still standing. It took all the strength she could muster not to lay down on the floor and go to sleep right there. But she decided she had spent enough time lying on the floor for one night. She climbed the stairs to the second story, shedding her bag, jacket, and shoes along the way. She paused with her hand on the door to her bedroom. She couldn't bring herself to turn the knob. She couldn't stand the idea of a dark and silent room. She needed to feel life. Glancing down the hall toward Maya's room, she knew she couldn't spend the night alone. She walked the six steps to Maya's door and opened it as quietly as possible, tiptoeing across the room to her bed. Sara slid under the covers and cuddled up against her baby sister, feeling her warmth, listening to her rhythmic breaths.

They used to share a bed sometimes when they were little girls, but that was usually only when one of them had a bad dream. After their mom had died, they had bunked up again as teenagers, taking comfort in sharing their grief, clinging to the family they still had. It felt good to be close to her like this again. She promised herself she would never take these little things for granted. The closeness of loved ones was what life was all about.

Maya awoke, but in her sleepy state, she didn't find it odd that her sister was joining her for a sleepover. Instead, she scooted over to make more room. Before drifting back to sleep, she asked Sara, "Where have you been? You smell like death."

In the darkness, Sara choked back tears and laughter at the same time. "You have no idea."

CHAPTER 4

"I don't think we're supposed to have extra parts." Maya stood back and admired the baby crib they had just finished assembling, but then addressed the assorted hardware in her palm with a scowl.

Sara sat cross-legged on the floor of the nursery with the instructions spread across her lap. She stared at the page with its tiny print and incoherent diagrams, but she couldn't make the words come into focus. Even Maya's voice seemed to have a haze around the edges. She had awoken in Maya's bed alone, uncertain where she was for a moment. In the light of day, her experience the night before seemed like a bad dream. If it weren't for the pounding headache radiating from the bump on the back of her head, she might have been able to convince herself that none of it had really happened—that, and the smell that clung to her clothes. Maya had been right. She smelled like death.

She had peeled herself out of bed and taken a shower, carefully avoiding the tender lump while she washed her hair. With her wet tresses clinging to her bare shoulders, she had wiped the fog from the mirror and peered into her own eyes. She searched for her pupils in the depths of her dark irises until she felt convinced they weren't dilated. She most likely did not have a concussion. She stared for so long that she began to imagine a faint glow behind her eyes. The reminder of that image sent a shiver down her spine. Sara shook her head and cast her eyes down, forcing herself to look away from the mirror. It had to be all in her head.

After her shower, she took a couple aspirin and downed a massive amount of coffee. That had made her feel measurably better. But she was still distracted. She couldn't seem to pull herself out of the fog. It was like some part of her was still stuck in that other world, which did nothing to help her efforts to convince herself it hadn't happened. The entire experience had seemed so surreal.

She had seen plenty of people on daytime talk shows discussing their near-death experiences. They usually talked about a white light and a feeling of calm that came over them. If she was going to have a hallucination about dying, she assumed it would be something along those lines merely because the idea had been implanted in her brain. Those talk show interviews never mentioned a world built of memories that looked almost like the world of our everyday lives. They never brought up lost souls wandering around with crystal clear, glowing eyes. There was never any mention of the slate gray sky or the fact that there was no sun, no moon, no day, or night. Sara found it impossible to believe she had invented that world in her own imagination, regardless of how hard she had hit her head. She could not have conceived that place on her own, which meant it had to be real. Didn't it?

Aside from the concept, there was also the way it had felt. Sara had grabbed Ananda by the shoulders. She was solid. She felt real. Sara hadn't felt any pain while she was in Catharta, but she could feel the world around her. She had felt the stable train platform, hard and unyielding. The stairs where she sat and spoke with Ananda were undoubtedly real. Nothing about it felt like a dream. In dreams, there were no details. Everything she saw or touched in her dreams was a vague recollection of what it would have been in real life. There was no physical sensation when she touched something. In dreams, the order of events didn't necessarily make sense, and there would usually be time missing. She could be transported from one place to another instantaneously. That wasn't what she had experienced last night. In Catharta, everything seemed to obey the laws of physics, of space and time. Then, there was the memory of it all. Sara didn't often remember her dreams in much detail. Yes, she remembered every second of her time in Catharta so vividly it seemed more real than the piece of paper now spread across her lap.

Maya tossed a single bolt onto the crib assembly instructions in front of Sara, startling her and pulling her out of her reverie. "Earth to Sara," she said, playfully. She jingled her fist full of extra nuts, bolts, and washers in Sara's direction. "I said we have extra parts. Did we do something wrong?"

Sara fumbled with the paper, forcing the words to come into focus. "Um," she stalled, trying to get her brain to work. "Sorry," she said, growing frustrated with her own lapse in concentration. "No, it's okay. Those are for converting it to a toddler bed later."

She looked up and found Maya giving her a surprised look, eyebrows raised, forehead creased. "Are you feeling alright?"

Sara hesitated. She desperately wanted to talk to someone about her experience the night before. But she didn't want to worry Maya. Plus, recounting what she believed had happened out loud would probably sound absurd. Either that or it might make it sound more real. She wasn't sure which possibility scared her more.

Sara had to say something. Maya's emotional sensor had locked her in the sights, and Sara knew she wouldn't let go until she had an answer. She decided to start with the things she was sure of. "Something happened last night." Maya waited for her to go on. Sara took a deep breath. "I was in the subway station after I went to your old apartment."

Maya interrupted, "I totally forgot! Did you get Mom's necklace?" She looked giddy at the thought.

Sara was flustered by the derailment of her story. "Yeah, I got it."

"Let me see! Let me see!" Maya clapped her hands like an excited child.

Sara felt herself losing her resolve. She had to press on or she may never get the words out. "In a minute. Listen, something happened while I was waiting for the train." Maya looked concerned and took a seat in front of Sara on the floor, fully attentive. "A man tried to steal my purse."

"Oh my god, Sara! Why didn't you tell me last night? He didn't actually steal anything from you, did he? Did you get a good look at him? Did you call the police? Did you get hurt?" The flurry of questions came out in one breath, leaving no time for answers.

Sara raised her hands like a crossing guard trying to get vehicles to stop. Maya halted her barrage of questions. "No, he didn't actually take anything from me, but I did get hurt."

"Where are you hurt? Did you go to the hospital? I'll take you to Saint Gertrude's right now!"

Maya's nurturing instincts were thoughtful, but Sara shot her a warning glare anyway so that she could finish her story.

"There was another man there who scared away the mugger, but when the guy ran away, he bumped into me right as the train was coming into the station, and I fell."

Maya was silent for a beat and then managed, "Are you telling me you were hit by a train?"

Sara shook her head. "The man who helped me, Mitch, nice guy by the way." Now, it was Maya's turn to look impatient. Sara went on, "He pulled me away from the platform edge just in time, but I hit my head on the floor."

"Where?" Maya demanded.

Sara indicated the lump on the back of her head and submitted to Maya's inspection, carefully moving her still damp locks out of the way.

"That's a pretty good bump, but it doesn't look like it broke the skin or anything."

"You have an affair with one doctor and suddenly you're a medical expert," Sara teased.

Maya gave her a look that said she wasn't going to let Sara off the hook for the rest of the story now, crinkled nose, pursed lips. "So, then you called the cops and went to the hospital, right?" Her tone gave away the fact that she had already guessed Sara did neither of those things, but in Maya's opinion, she should have done both. Sara's silence served as her answer. Maya sighed in exasperation. "Okay, so what did you do next?"

Sara's eyes dropped to her hands in her lap, which were fumbling with the little bolt Maya had thrown at her. She was approaching the part of her story she wasn't sure she should share. "Well," she began slowly. "When I hit my head, I guess I blacked out."

"What?!" Maya was incredulous. "You lost consciousness, and you didn't go to the hospital? Sara, you could have a concussion. Your brain could be bleeding. Do you understand how serious that is?"

"My brain is fine," Sara insisted. Given what she was about to say to her sister, she wasn't entirely sure that was true. "Listen, I'm trying to tell you that something happened to me while I was knocked out."

Sara paused. She felt like she was teetering at the edge of a deep, icy pool, swaying back and forth. She wasn't sure she was ready to take the plunge. Silence hung between the two women for so long Maya looked like she might explode with anticipation.

Finally, Sara blurted out, "I think a part of me died." She held her sister's steady gaze and then hastily added, "Temporarily."

Maya's eyes drilled into hers with an unwavering stare for so long Sara wasn't sure she had actually heard her. Then, she reached out one hand and pressed her palm against Sara's forehead, as if checking for a fever. "Are you sure you're feeling alright? Because I'm pretty sure you've lost your mind." Sara rolled her eyes. "Seriously," Maya went on, "What do you mean you died? You're sitting right in front of me, very clearly alive."

Sara was ready to brush it off as the joke Maya seemed to think it was. But something inside her needed to get this out. She could not be the only living soul to know what she had seen. "I know it sounds crazy, but I'm being serious. When I was unconscious, I think my soul or a part of my soul traveled to this other place. It looked a lot like San Francisco, but different."

"Different?" Maya puzzled.

"Different." Sara confirmed. "More... dead," she said, unable to find a more fitting word. She waited for her little sister's reaction.

Maya shook her head in disbelief. "Hold on. You're supposed to be the skeptic. You don't believe in anything supernatural. You constantly tell me how dumb it is that I'm afraid of Friday the thirteenth. You laugh at me when I watch the Bigfoot documentaries. How can you tell me you think you came back from the dead?"

"I don't think I actually died. It was more like my soul thought I was going to die, and it jumped the gun." Sara borrowed Ananda's words. "And I mean, come on, Bigfoot?" Sara teased.

Maya ignored the jab and closed her eyes, holding up her hands as if grasping at the invisible strings of reality. "Okay, so you say it looked like the city, but more dead. What does that even mean?"

"I mean it was silent. There were no cars. There were no leaves on the trees, like they were dead. And all the people there were dead. They were ghosts."

"You met ghosts?"

"Well," Sara corrected, "I met one ghost. Her name was Ananda, and she helped me understand where I was and what was going on. She told me the place I went to was called Catharta. It's sort of like limbo. When you die, it's the place your soul goes until you're born again." She waited as Maya's mouth gaped open, but no words came out. "You don't believe me." The hurt was evident in Sara's voice.

Maya's mouth snapped shut, and she thought carefully about the next thing she would say. "It's not that I don't believe you. I believe that you believe you travelled to this ghost city or whatever. But I'm worried you might be delusional because you bruised your brain." Maya tapped her finger against Sara's forehead.

"My brain is fine," Sara began, flustered again, but then swallowed the rest of that argument. She inhaled sharply and composed herself. "I know in my heart that it was real." She hadn't been sure until those words crossed her lips, but now, she believed it with her entire being. Everything that had happened the night before, the train, Ananda, Catharta, it was all real.

Maya could see the resolve on her sister's face. They sat there across from each other for what felt like an eternity. Maya's pale blue eyes jumped back and forth, searching each of Sara's nearly black eyes in turn for some unseen truth. Finally, she said, "Okay, I believe you."

"Really?" Sara asked with skepticism. It was important to her that Maya actually did believe. If this was just lip service, it was meaningless.

Maya's face was set with determination. "Yes, really. I believe you."

Relief washed over Sara. In that moment, gaining her sister's belief and trust, she realized what she had been feeling. What had been haunting her since the night before was loneliness. In Catharta, she had awoken all alone. She had searched the empty streets and found only Ananda. And while she had been a great comfort to Sara, she had reinforced the fact that Sara didn't belong there. Upon awakening in the world of the living, she had felt isolated by the things she had seen and the knowledge she had gained about the world that comes after life. Now, she had someone to confide in. She wasn't alone in this anymore.

"So why do you think this happened to you?" Maya asked. "Do you think it was random? Or do you think you were chosen somehow?"

"What do you mean chosen?" Sara questioned.

"I mean people fall and hit their heads every day, but they're not all whisked away to the Land of Oz. Why do you think your soul went to this other realm or whatever Catharta is? And why were you allowed to return?" Now, that Maya had accepted what Sara had told her, she was anxious to explore the details and the possibilities. She had always been very into fantasy, science fiction, and anything supernatural in the slightest.

"Well," Sara thought aloud, "I'm not sure why I was chosen. I don't really understand how I got there or how I was able to get back. All I know is what I was told. The girl I told you I met, Ananda, I think she was in trouble. When I found her, she was involved in some kind of altercation. I couldn't see what happened, but it sounded bad. Afterward, she was crying. Then, right before I returned, someone was looking for her. It was a man, and he sounded angry."

Maya's eyes were wide with intrigue. "Who is this girl? Did you see the man? Do you know what he looks like? Is he a ghost too?"

"I think he must be dead. Ananda was clearly very familiar with him, and she told me she hadn't seen a living soul in ages. I think everyone there was dead, except me." She thought back and tried to remember everything Ananda had told her. Sara had been in such a state of shock and confusion; it was hard to absorb all the information the young girl had given her. She wanted to hang on to every word. A thought came back to her. "Right before he came looking for her, Ananda said something strange to me. She said that no souls had gotten out of Catharta for a long time."

"Why is that strange?" Maya was having trouble following Sara's jumbled train of thought.

"She had just finished telling me that the only way out of Catharta is through rebirth. So why would it be that no one had left recently? Unless there was some reason that they couldn't."

"So people can get stranded there like they're in purgatory?"

"It seems that way." Sara closed her eyes and tried to transport her memory back to the stairwell. She could almost see Ananda's haunting eyes. She could hear her soothing voice. She tried to put all the pieces of the puzzle back together. Her eyes flashed open in remembrance. "She said something else too. She said that there are a finite number of souls. She told me that we have already run out, that the number of people occupying this world exceeds the number of souls that exist."

Maya looked dumbfounded. She clutched her swollen belly protectively. "Are you telling me my baby could be born with no soul?"

The horror on her sister's face filled Sara with regret. The last thing she wanted to do was to give an expectant mother more to worry about. She tried to take it back. "No. I don't know. I have no idea how any of it works. All I know is what Ananda told me, and that's not much. I'm sure your baby is going to be fine."

Maya looked only slightly mollified. "Well, either way, this girl needs your help. And if you can help make sure my baby isn't born soulless, all the better." Maya reached out and grabbed Sara by the shoulders. "You have to help Ananda, Sara. And I'm going to help you do it."

"Help her?" Sara questioned. "How can I help her? I barely know anything about her, and she's on another plane of existence. I have no idea how to get back there. Even if I did, I'm not sure I could get back to the real world again."

"Sara, you were chosen." Maya was insistent. "You are the only one who can help this girl. I'm sure we can figure this out. Tell me everything you can remember." Maya began pumping her for every detail she could recall.

Sara wanted more than anything to know Ananda was okay, but she had no idea how to help her. She knew very little about her or the kind of trouble she was in. She didn't understand the rules of Catharta or why she was chosen to go there. One nagging thought kept creeping back into her mind. If she was going to do as Maya suggested and aid Ananda somehow, she would have to go back there. She would have to find a way into Catharta. It seemed impossible, and terrifying.

As if reading her mind, Maya announced, "I think you need to go see her again. I don't think we can figure out how to help her unless we know more about what's going on."

"But how? How would I even try to get back there? It's impossible." Sara wasn't sure she was mentally prepared to deal with the idea of returning to Catharta.

"Nothing is impossible. Just do everything you did to get there the first time." Maya said it so matter-of-factly, as if she often jumped into the afterlife and back.

"So, I just need to get assaulted, then crack my head open, and almost die again." Sara's voice was thick with sarcasm.

"Yeah, why not?" Maya returned her satirical tone. Then, with more sincerity, she said, "I just mean same place, same time, that sort of thing. Just do whatever you can to recreate the situation. I'll go with you if you want."

"You?" Sara asked, giving a pointed look toward Maya's rounded form. "You aren't going anywhere near that subway station after dark."

"Well, I want to help somehow."

"You can help by keeping my niece or nephew safe in there." Maya clearly didn't appreciate Sara's patronizing comment. Sara wasn't seriously entertaining the idea of trying to return to Catharta, but she wanted to appease her sister. "Listen, we'll figure it out together. But right now, I've got to get ready for work." Sara began to rise from her spot on the floor.

"Sara." Maya grabbed her hand and looked deep into her eyes. "I'm really glad you're okay."

Sara smiled. She was okay. Or at least she would be now that she had a coconspirator in all the craziness she had endured. She turned to leave the room but Maya called out to her again, stopping her in her tracks.

"What do you think of Jessica if it's a girl?"

Sara wrinkled her nose and thought it over. "Jessica Jenkins?" She let the name roll off her tongue. "She sounds like a superhero alter ego from a comic book."

Maya looked a little disgruntled. "Is that a good thing or a bad thing?"

Sara called back over her shoulder as she made her way down the hall, "That's for you to decide, Mom. I've got to get to work."

Once out the door, Sara made her way to her usual bus stop, all the while struck by the strangeness of going about her normal day. She had traveled to another world, and now here she was, waiting for the bus like she did every weekday. When she had been in Catharta, there was a part of her that felt sure none of it could be real. Now, having returned, the real world felt synthetic somehow, like some kind of illusion. How many times had she let the undependability of public transit ruin her day? Now, those types of inconveniences seemed trivial. The act of going to work itself seemed somewhat pointless. People work so hard for most of their lives, and in the end, they die, and then, it starts all over again. She had considered calling in sick, but she figured she could use the distraction. She had to get back to her normal life.

She boarded the bus when it finally arrived and took her usual seat near the back. As it wove its way out of the Sunset District, she gazed out the window. She still witnessed a lot of the negativity she had observed the day before. There were angry drivers and hoodlums who appeared to be up to no good. There was still broken glass scattered across the pavement and the occasional belligerent person screaming at no one. But she saw other things too. She saw a mom kissing her child as she dropped him off at school. She saw a woman sitting outside a coffee shop talking on the phone, smiling so intensely she was almost glowing. She saw her bus driver wave genially at the driver of a passing bus. She saw leaves on trees and heard the sounds of a vibrant bustling city. No matter what state of dismay she had felt the world was in, it was still good to be alive. She couldn't let herself lose sight of that.

Sara suddenly realized she wasn't too far from the Glen Park subway station. On a whim, with Maya's voice ringing in the back of her mind, she pulled the cord and hopped off the bus at the next stop and then walked another block to the train station. She checked the time on her phone. She could make a quick stop at the Sixteenth Street subway station and still make it to work on time. Once on the platform, she boarded the next eastbound train and traveled two stops to Sixteenth Street before off boarding.

She stepped cautiously off the train and onto the red tile floor of the platform. Her confidence immediately evaporated once she was back at that station. She wasn't even sure what she planned to do there. She supposed she was trying to collect clues as to how she had been transported to another plane of existence. But she had no idea what she thought she'd find there. She decided to make her way to the end of the platform where everything had transpired.

The station was more crowded at this time of day. There were kids heading home from school, other commuters like her trying to get to work, and a group of older ladies returning from a shopping excursion. It was hard for her to reconcile this noisy space with the pure and utter silence of the same place in Catharta. She moved past the pockets of people waiting for their train and found herself at the east end of the station exactly where she had been the night before. She stared at the floor where she had awoken in another world. Her eyes bore into the red tile, searching for a hint or a clue as to how any of it could be possible.

Ananda had mentioned gateways. Could it be that there was some sort of invisible gateway right in front of her that she simply couldn't see? And if there was, would she really want to access it? She felt convinced that it was a fluke she had made it into Catharta in the first place and nothing short of a miracle that she had made it out. Could she really entertain the idea of trying to go back there? An impulse had driven her to come back to this exact spot. That same impulse wanted her to find a way back in to Catharta, back to Ananda, back to find more answers. Sara had to decide for herself whether to follow that impulse or bury it.

The overhead speaker announced that another eastbound train would be arriving in two minutes. If she didn't get on that train, she would be late for work. The time pressure made something click in her head. She decided to follow the impulse. She needed to see Ananda again. If Maya was right and Ananda really did need her help, how could she walk away from that duty?

Maya's words echoed in Sara's head. How could she recreate the moment her soul got sucked into Catharta? She couldn't make a mugger reappear. She couldn't risk being nearly pummeled by a speeding train. But she could do something simple. She could lay down in the same spot and close her eyes. Maybe that was all she needed to do—just place herself in the invisible gateway and be whisked away to the land of the dead.

Sara looked around, feeling a little self-conscious about the number of people around. She glanced at the sign that told her the train would now be arriving in one minute and thought, *Screw it!* She took a seat on the floor, feeling very conspicuous. A teenage boy in a backpack gave her a sideways glance, but then returned his attention to his phone. Sara eased herself down onto her elbows and then all the way down to the floor until she was lying flat on her back, staring up at the fluorescent lights.

Now, she was attracting more attention. People around her were staring and murmuring to one another. She tried to block it all out. She attempted to point all her concentration toward her goal. She willed herself to tune out the sounds around her and imagine the heavy silence that filled Catharta. In her mind's eye, she pictured the deserted platform, the dead trees, and the quiet streets above. If she just wanted it badly enough, she was sure the gateway would open and swallow her up. She hoped and wished and prayed.

Nothing happened.

When she opened her eyes, one of the older women laden with shopping bags was standing over her. "Are you okay, honey?"

Sara's cheeks burned with embarrassment. In her mind, she cursed Maya for putting this stupid idea in her head. Out of the corner of her eye, she saw the teenager with the backpack take a picture of her with his phone. He'd be posting that on social media later. Look at this crazy lady I saw in the subway station.

Sara looked at the concerned old woman and propped herself back up to a sitting position. "I'm fine. I just felt dizzy for a second." The clumsy lie sounded pathetic.

"Oh," the lady uttered, fumbling in her purse for something and producing a hard candy twisted up in its plastic wrapper. "Maybe it's your blood sugar," she suggested, extending the candy toward Sara. A piece of lint clung to the end of it.

"No, thank you," Sara said as politely as she could manage. She was saved from further embarrassment by the arrival of her train. She hoisted herself up and boarded the first car. To her relief, no one else from the platform boarded with her. The doors slid shut, and she was spirited away.

She felt stupid for thinking she could get back to Catharta and even stupider for thinking she should. She was humiliated by her failure.

A few stops later, she was in downtown San Francisco. She off boarded the train and tried to forget her mortification. The walk to the office helped her shrug it off. The weather was warm for September, and the morning fog had dissipated. She didn't need her usual layers. By the time she reached the building and gave a quick nod to the guard at the front desk, she was able to nearly pretend her foolish attempt at reentering Catharta hadn't happened.

She bounded up the stairs and toward Tim's office. The light was on. She peeked around the doorway. He wasn't there. It was just as well. If he'd been there, she might have felt compelled to tell him about her experience in Catharta. Relaying the story to Maya had drained her. She wasn't sure she was ready to go through that again. Plus, she was worried he might make fun of the whole thing. Now, that she felt convinced that the ghostly realm she had visited was real, she felt oddly protective of it. She didn't want anyone making light of her encounter.

Sara made her way to her desk in the sea of cubicles. She turned on her computer and started settling in for her workday. She hadn't even finished reading her e-mails when a thought occurred to her. Ananda hadn't given her too much information to go on, but Sara knew her first name, her date of death, and her age at the time she died. That might be enough to find some information about her life. If she could find a record of Ananda in the real world, then that would be her proof that Catharta was real and that her experience there had actually happened. If she could find something to make Ananda concrete, and not just a figment of her own imagination, even she couldn't deny that it was all real.

She started with a quick Google search. She entered, "Ananda seventeen November 2, 2014," into the search bar. Over six thousand results came up. She scrolled through the first two pages, but nothing looked promising. If only she knew Ananda's last name.

Perhaps she had been from San Francisco. It made sense. Sara was from San Francisco and that's what Catharta looked like to her. Maybe meeting Ananda in the same city meant that's where she was from too. She added, "San Francisco," to her search. That brought the result count way down, but all the links pointed her toward a vegetarian restaurant she had never been to before.

Feeling defeated, Sara closed her browser. On her desktop, a particular shortcut caught her eye. It was a link to all the digital archives of *The Daily*. Maybe Ananda's death had been newsworthy. It was worth a shot. She pulled up the archives and entered some search parameters. In the date range, she entered November 2 to December 31, 2014, just to cover her bases. In the keyword field, she entered, "Ananda." Then, she had to check boxes for the types of records she wanted to pull up. She checked the boxes for news, crime, and obituaries. She clicked the search button and crossed her fingers. The result screen popped up, informing her that her query had yielded zero results for news, zero results for crime, and one result for obituaries.

She hesitated with her mouse over the link for the obituary. Her mouth felt suddenly dry. Her palms were sweaty. This was what she had been looking for. It was the proof she had been seeking. Why couldn't she bring herself to click that link? She pressed her eyes shut. Once she clicked that link, she knew that she could never unsee the results. If it were truly the obituary for the ghost she had met on the other side, she would never again be able to deny to herself that what had happened to her was real. If she learned the truth about Ananda, about who she was, Sara knew she would not be able to ignore Maya's insistence that she had an obligation to help this poor girl's lost soul.

Sara opened her eyes and, with a trembling hand, forced herself to click the button. The page seemed to take an interminable amount of time to load. When it did, Sara's breath escaped her in one fast and silent whoosh. She felt like she had been punched in the stomach. Her chest expanded, her mouth opened, but she couldn't draw in any air. When she finally did, she held the air in her lungs for as long as she could. There was a picture. In the archive, it was black and white and a little grainy. The eyes weren't clear or glowing. They were dark and very much alive. But there was no doubt about it. The beautiful young girl with the cocoa butter skin and long dark hair staring back at her was unmistakably Ananda.

CHAPTER 5

Ananda Reyes
November 1, 1997–November 2, 2014

It is with great sadness that the family of Ananda Reyes announces her sudden passing on Sunday morning. Ananda is survived by her mother, Iris, her two sisters, Jasmine and Mariel, and her step father, Greg. She will be greatly missed by her family as well as her friends at Saint Ignatius College Preparatory School where she was a senior. She was a bright star that burned out too soon. A memorial service will be held Saturday, November 15, 2014, at 1:00 p.m. at Saint Mary's Cathedral.

*T*he obituary was short. Sara read through it four times, looking for any hidden clue that might be hiding between its words. It revealed very little about who Ananda was as a person. It said nothing of her personality or the type of life she lived, information that Sara desperately craved. Perhaps the most conspicuous omission from the short text was her cause of death. It wasn't unusual to leave that out of an obituary. Oftentimes, the family of the deceased simply felt it was nobody's business. But, somehow, in this case, it felt off. How does a seventeen-year-old die suddenly on a Sunday morning? If she had been ill, they wouldn't have called it sudden. Sara also noted that Ananda had died the day after her birthday. Could that have been a coincidence? The absent cause of death reeked of something much darker than illness, something sinister.

The most important piece of information the obituary gave Sara was that Ananda was a real person. This girl wasn't a figment of her imagination. There was no way Sara could have invented this young woman with the same face and name and date of death as the real person staring back at her from her computer screen. The obituary also gave Sara another useful fact—Ananda's last name.

Sara did a couple more Internet searches, entering various combinations of the facts she had collected, Ananda's full name, the city she lived in, the school she attended, and her dates of birth and death. The results were too numerous for her to sift through. She found links to hundreds of Facebook pages and LinkedIn profiles belonging to women with the same name. There was a soccer player with the same last name and birthday in Argentina. There were a couple links leading her back to the same vegetarian restaurant she had never been to before. But there was nothing that would give more color to the seventeen years of life this girl had lived. Sara wanted to know her as a person. She wanted to know her history. She wanted to know why her life was cut so unexpectedly short and why she was now trapped in an afterlife from which she couldn't seem to escape. The desperate wanting burned hot in the pit of her stomach. Sara felt restless. She needed to do something, but she wasn't sure what.

She clicked the print icon on the obituary and sprang up from her seat. She tried to keep her pace under control as she walked the short distance to the shared printer, but her legs wanted to run. She was antsy. As she snatched the sheet of paper off the printer, she read through it again, wanting to believe she had missed something on the screen that would make her feel fulfilled and take away this disquiet. There was nothing more there, of course. She stole a glance toward the door to Tim's office and thought she might have seen a shadow move. Sara folded the printout in half and headed in that direction.

She paused just outside his door and peeked inside. He was there, seated at his desk with his back toward the doorway, staring intently at something on the screen of his laptop. His shoulders were hunched. He was motionless. It was his focused work stance. She thought of announcing her presence, maybe even trying to startle him to pay him back for his sudden appearance at her desk the day before. Then, she thought better of it. She still wasn't completely sure she should share her experience with him. Her grip tightened on the folded sheet of paper, and she felt suddenly protective of it, of Ananda. She wasn't sure she was willing to share the secret of this girl just yet. Sara moved to slip past his door as quietly as she could, but was pulled back by the sound of his voice.

"Well, hello to you too."

Sara took two steps backward and looked through his doorway. A sheepish, "Hi," was all she could manage. He still had his back to the door. Curiosity got the better of her. "How did you know I was here?"

Tim spun his chair around and addressed her with a subtly smug look on his face. "You're not as quiet as you think you are." With the tiniest shift of his eyebrows, he took on a more guarded look. "Plus, I smelled your shampoo."

Sara self-consciously ran her fingers through her hair, which was still a little damp underneath, and brought a few strands to her nose. "You look busy. I figured I shouldn't bother you." She flung her hair back over her shoulder.

"Not bugging me has never been your specialty." His chin jutted out about one millimeter. He was making fun of her.

Normally, Sara would have some sort of snarky comeback for a comment like that, but she couldn't seem to pull any normal thoughts from her brain. It was swimming with thoughts of Ananda. Instead, she uttered, "Sorry," although she wasn't sure what she was apologizing for.

Tim's eyes narrowed a fraction, his head cocked slightly to one side. He was curious. "Are you okay?"

Sara tried to pull herself together. "I'm fine. Why?"

His eyes focused on her, scrutinizing. "I don't know. You don't seem quite like yourself."

"And how should myself seem?" Sara asked, trying to play it off.

"Well, for starters," Tim said, standing up from his chair and approaching her. "Yourself would usually tell me that bugging me is your right or that nothing I'm working on could possibly be more important than whatever it was you were going to tell me." He stopped at the doorway and leaned against it. "But instead all you said was 'sorry' so, yeah, I'd say you're not quite yourself today."

Sara was annoyed with herself for being so easy to read and a little more annoyed with Tim for pointing it out. She debated just coming clean with him, telling him about the train station, about Catharta, about Ananda. She wasn't ready yet. She wasn't sure she could deal with his potential skepticism. It wasn't that Tim wouldn't believe her. He probably would. He bought into the supernatural pretty easily. He could listen to a ghost story with rapt attention, and, as Sara tried to pick it apart and prove it untrue, he would have an explanation for every piece of proof she offered. But that was the problem. That was part of the nature of their friendship. It was built on this banter that she both loved and loathed. It was fun, it was challenging, it was sometimes frustrating, but it always left them at opposite ends of the spectrum. He would likely disagree with her solely for the purpose of being contrary. If the tables were turned and Sara was suddenly the believer, he would be the skeptic just to rile her up.

After a moment's hesitation, she decided she would tell him about Catharta, but not just yet. She would try to figure out how best to approach the subject. In the meantime, she would do her best to keep her mind off it. She needed to bury the electric buzz in her brain that was telling her to find out what had happened to Ananda.

She changed the subject. "I was just going to ask you if you got tickets for the concert tomorrow." It wasn't a total lie. She would have asked him about it at some point.

A self-satisfied smile crept onto his face. "Would I ever let you down?" He moved back toward his desk and, opening a drawer, pulled out two tickets for The Ataris at The Bottom of the Hill the following night.

Sara already felt a little more at ease, talking about something besides a dead girl and making plans for the weekend. She could do this. She could still live a normal life in spite of the unearthly experience she'd had the night before.

"How much do I owe you?"

"This one's on me," Tim said, tucking the tickets back into his drawer.

"Oh, come on," Sara replied, taking refuge in their comfortable teasing of one another. "Just because you're a fancy photographer and I'm a lowly copy editor doesn't mean you have to pay my way."

"First of all," Tim shot back in mock offense, "I don't have to apologize for being fancy." Sara let out a laugh and prepared to fire back, but Tim silenced her with a raised finger. "Secondly, the only reason you're a lowly copy editor is because you're too chicken to actually write something of your own." Sara didn't have to feign offense at that comment. She opened her mouth to defend herself, but was hushed once more. Tim was on a roll. "Third, if you feel that bad about looking like a kept woman, The Ataris have a new record out. I'll let you buy me a copy at the show."

He crossed his arms over his chest. It was her turn to retaliate. "Okay, well first of all," Sara said, mimicking his tone. "I was just trying to be polite. I don't really think you're that fancy at all." Tim's mouth dropped open dramatically, his eyebrows knitted together as if that were the most offensive thing anyone had ever said to him. "Second, my job is important, and I'll write something when I damn well feel like it." He snapped his mouth shut, knowing he had touched a nerve with his comment. "And third, who calls it a record anymore. It's an album. Do you even own a record player?" As the last two words escaped her lips, a thought bloomed in her mind. She was suddenly frozen in thought, blankly staring off into the middle distance.

Tim caught the sudden loss of her attention and waved a hand in front of her eyes. "Are you okay? You look like you were just transported to another galaxy."

Sara snapped back into focus. She looked at Tim, wide-eyed, and announced, "The records office. I need to go to the county records office."

Tim was taken aback. "For what?"

Sara felt reenergized. She had a plan. She wouldn't rest until she found what she was looking for. But first, she had to get there. "I'll tell you on the way if you'll drive me."

"What, right now? Don't you have work to do?" His words sounded resistant, but his smile told her he was up for any adventure she was willing to throw at him.

But he was right; she did have work to do. She couldn't just abandon her post without permission. "I'll ask Jeff if it's okay. Will you give me a lift?"

"If the almighty Jeff allows it, who am I to disagree?" Tim said, giving a tiny, comical salute at the mention of their editor in chief. "I have an assignment at the Asian Art Museum anyway. That's not too far from the records office."

Sara grinned, feeling relieved to have someone on her side, even if he didn't really know what he was getting himself into. "Give me five minutes."

"You need to go to the county records office for what exactly?" Sara's boss, Jeff, sat behind his paper-strewn desk, rubbing his temples as if she were single-handedly responsible for his migraine.

"To fact-check a story." Sara bit her lower lip, praying he wouldn't ask for too many details. She didn't want to outright lie to him. She was trying to gather some facts, but the story she was pursuing wasn't for *The Daily*. In her six years with the paper, Sara had never once asked to leave the premises to do her job. She wasn't sure if that fact made her argument more convincing or less.

"Can't you do it online? I thought everything was online now?" Jeff returned his attention to the papers on his desk, apparently already losing interest in Sara's request. He was a heavyset man with thinning hair who always managed to look exhausted. Or maybe Sara's presence was what exhausted him.

"Not all types of records are available online. I need to be there in person," Sara answered. "Plus, Tim has an assignment in the area. He can drive me." She felt like a teenager requesting permission to stay out past curfew.

Jeff let out an exasperated sound that was something between a sigh and a growl. Sara was starting to wonder if she should have just gone without asking. Maybe no one would have even noticed if she had just left. But now she had asked, and it was too late to simply leave. If he said no, she would be stuck in the office for the rest of the day. Her heart sank at the idea of not gaining more information about Ananda. Who knew what was happening to that poor girl while Sara had been away, especially considering that time passed differently in Catharta. Ananda probably already felt like Sara had been gone a month or more. If she was going to be able to help the girl's lost soul at all, she needed to act now. It was Friday. If she missed this window, the records office wouldn't be open until Monday. Desperation was setting in. Sara searched her mind for any argument that might persuade Jeff to let her go.

A thought burst into her brain. "If you prefer, we could run the story, and if it turns out to be wrong, we'll just print a retraction next week."

Jeff was a stickler for deadlines, but he was a bigger stickler for accuracy. He kept a Post-it pinned to his bulletin board with six tally marks on it, representing the number of retractions he'd printed in all his years as editor in chief. It was a phenomenally low number of which he was very proud. He wasn't keen to add another tally to it.

His eyes darted to the bulletin board and then quickly back to his desk again. He grumbled, "Fine. As long as neither of you miss your deadlines."

"Really?" Sara asked in disbelief.

Jeff shot her a glance over the rim of his glasses that told her she should quit while she was ahead. She decided to take his silent advice.

"Thanks, Jeff. Be back soon." With that, she bolted out of his office and down the stairs toward the garage where Tim would hopefully already have the car started.

"Who are you, and what have you done with Sara?" Tim was having a hard time swallowing what she was trying to tell him.

Sara, in the passenger seat of his station wagon, closed her eyes and tried to keep calm. "I know it sounds crazy."

"You're right," Tim scoffed. "It sounds certifiable. And if I had just told you I came back from the dead, you would be the first person to check me into the psych ward. How hard did you hit your head that you suddenly believe in ghosts?"

Sara's hand automatically went to the lump on the back of her head that was still very tender. Tim stole a side-eyed glance at her while still trying to keep his attention on the road.

"I tried not to believe, I really did," Sara defended herself. "But how can I deny this?" She waved Ananda's obituary in his face.

As he brought the car to a halt at the next stop light, Tim snatched the sheet of paper out of her hand. He read through it quickly. "And you believe that this means it's all true? You travelled to another world and spoke to the soul of a dead girl, and now, you need to play Scooby-Doo and investigate her life?"

"I could not have made this up. Her name, her face, her date of death—this proves that they were all accurate. It proves that she was real." She hoped Tim could hear the insistence in her voice.

"I agree, the obituary is real, but I'm having a hard time believing you have suddenly dropped your lifelong skepticism of all things supernatural." She caught his eye just before the light turned green. None of his usual playfulness showed in his expression. It was all concern and disbelief. "You know, this obituary ran in our paper. Do you think it's possible that you remembered it somewhere in the back of your mind and that the memory surfaced while you were unconscious?"

Sara shook her head and looked out the passenger window, worried that her emotions would get the better of her. Her voice came out as little more than a whisper. "I know what I saw. I know what I felt. It was real."

They were both silent for a minute as they inched along in traffic.

Tim began again. "Say that your experience with this girl was real." Sara's instinct was to argue with him that Ananda was, in fact, real. Tim held up his hands in a show of surrender to stave off her objection. "If she was real and you wanted to help her somehow, why do you need to go to the records office?"

Sara was surprised by his question. She thought that part would be obvious. "I need to get a copy of her death certificate."

"Why?"

Sara glanced down at the obituary unfolded in her lap. "Because I need to know how she died. I'm not sure if it has something to do with the kind of trouble she's in now, but I need to know. The obituary just says she died suddenly on a Sunday morning. I'm worried something terrible happened to her, and now, she's trapped in this other world where someone equally terrible is after her."

"Lots of people die suddenly," Tim offered. "I mean, it's terrible no matter what, but it could have been something as simple as a car accident. I think you might be reading too much into it."

Sara felt depleted. She couldn't argue with him anymore. "I just need to know." Her voice cracked a little. She wasn't used to showing him this much unguarded emotion. He visibly tensed up, unsure how to react. She relieved some of the tension by pointing out a parking space. They had arrived at their destination.

Sara fumbled in her messenger bag for some change to feed the meter. "You can go to your assignment at the museum. I'll meet you back here when I'm done."

"I'll go with you," Tim said, pulling into the space.

"No, really it's fine," Sara insisted, counting her quarters.

Tim put a hand on her shoulder, and she looked up from her spare change. "No, I'm coming with you," he said firmly. His eyes looked stern, but there was the faintest hint of a smile there. He was calling a truce.

Together, they walked up the stone steps and through the glass doors of the records office. There was no one else in the lobby besides the clerk sitting behind the glass window separating the work space from the waiting area. They walked right up to her window, and she addressed them with something between boredom and contempt. "Can I help you?" she asked without looking away from her computer screen.

"Yes, I need to get a copy of a death certificate," Sara began, ready to produce the obituary with all the pertinent information.

To her surprise, the clerk got up and walked away from them without saying a word. Sara and Tim shared a look of confusion as well as mild offense. The clerk returned shortly with a carbon copy form. She slid it through the slot at the bottom of her protective window, her long acrylic nails clicking against the desk. "Fill out this form. Bring it back up here. Pens are on the table by the door." With that, they were apparently dismissed. The clerk went back to her computer screen, clicking away at the keys with the tips of her long fingernails.

Sara and Tim took a seat near the door and began to work on the form. It requested a lot of information that she didn't have, including Ananda's social security number. It also wanted to know how she was related to the deceased. She didn't think they would accept friend of the dead girl's ghost as an answer.

"What am I going to do?" Sara asked Tim. "They want me to be her mom or her lawyer or something before they're going to give me a copy."

Tim looked thoughtful. "What if we just explain it to her?"

Sara glanced up at the clerk. "You want me to tell her I temporarily died and I need to find out if my new dead friend was murdered? Somehow, I don't think she's going to go for it."

"You might be surprised," Tim said with a smirk. He was teasing, but only halfway. "Come on. Follow my lead." He stood and gestured for her to follow him to the clerk's desk.

"Hi," he said in an attempt to get her to look up from her computer monitor. "We wanted..."

She cut him off. "Form," she announced, tapping her nails on the desk near the window slot.

"You see, the thing is," Tim tried to continue.

"Form," the clerk requested again, this time finally peeling her eyes away from the computer screen. Sara shoved the half-completed form through the slot. The clerk's eyes scanned it and clearly found it unsatisfactory. With an annoyed sigh, she asked, "What is your relationship to the decedent?"

"We're not related," Sara replied, suddenly very unsure of this entire excursion.

"Sorry," the clerk said with a tone that implied she was not at all sorry. "I can't process this form."

Tim decided to get a little more forceful. He held up his press pass to the window. "Ma'am, we're from *The San Francisco Daily News*, and we need this public record to fact-check an article to be published." He sounded so official that Sara had to stifle a laugh.

The clerk looked at his badge and then leveled her gaze back on Tim, unimpressed. "Sir, I don't care if you're the press or the mayor or the damn president. If you don't have a legal relationship to the decedent, I cannot process this form." She shoved the paper back through the slot and abruptly stood and walked away again.

"Hey," barked Tim. He looked as angry as Sara had ever seen him. He was usually so calm and collected with a witty comeback for any perceived insult. Sara felt overwhelmed with gratitude that he was willing to go to such lengths to help her get the information she sought, even if he didn't fully believe in her experience.

Before Tim could yell after the clerk any further, she reappeared. She slid a different form through the slot. "Now," she said as if there had been no interruption to their conversation. "You'll have to fill out this form if you want an informational copy of the public record." She put air quotes around the last two words with her claw-like fingernails, making a mockery of Tim's demand.

Tim and Sara stared at the much simpler form she had just slid toward them, somewhat dumbfounded. As if to shoo them away the clerk added, "Pens are on the table by the door."

After filling out the form, paying a fee, and receiving an informational copy of Ananda's death certificate in a manila envelope, Sara and Tim vacated the county records office as quickly as possible. Sara was anxious to read the document she had been given, but was equally anxious to get away from the scrutinizing gaze of the surly clerk.

Leaning against the side of the station wagon, she slid the piece of paper halfway out of its envelope while Tim looked over her shoulder. She was filled with the same hesitation that she felt when she had found the obituary record. Whatever was in that envelope was something she wouldn't be able to unsee. She had started the morning insisting to Maya that there was nothing she could do to help the girl who she wasn't even sure existed. Maya's voice echoing in her mind had led to her failed attempt to try to go back to Catharta. Now, not only was she positive of Ananda's existence, but also she felt an overwhelming obligation to help her in some way. What if the cause of death was a dead end, so to speak? What if it didn't lead her any closer to the true Ananda or to Catharta? Or what if the cause of death was something so horrible and unimaginable that Sara wished she had never known it at all?

As if reading her mind, Tim said gently, "You don't have to read it." As soon as she heard his words, she decided. "I have to know."

He pursed his lips, dimpling his chin. He accepted her decision.

Sara slid the sheet of paper out of its envelope, scanning the poor-quality photocopy for the information she sought. It contained Ananda's name, date of birth, date of death, and her mother's full name. It gave her place of birth as Cebu, Philippines, and her place of death as San Francisco, California. It showed the name of the coroner who had pronounced her dead and there, next to the coroner's name was the box labeled "cause of death."

Sara's eyes wouldn't come into focus. It was as if her body didn't want to show her something her mind might not be able to handle. She blinked until she could read the words. Craniocerebral blunt-force trauma. She read the words several times over until she was sure she had understood them. She was no doctor, but she was fairly certain that this meant Ananda had died of a brain injury. More specifically, it sounded as if she had been beaten to death.

The words on the page were suddenly obscured once more. She blinked again, trying to clear her vision, only to find tears spilling down her cheeks. Her legs felt weak. She worried she was going to faint. She slid down the side of the car until she was sitting on the sidewalk. Tim sat down beside her. He took the piece of paper from her hand and slid it back into the envelope. Sara wiped her tears away with the sleeve of her sweatshirt.

"You really met her, didn't you?" Tim's voice was soft and sincere. There was no teasing undertone. Sara couldn't bring herself to look him in the eye, but if she did, she was sure she would see nothing but empathy there. She nodded. "And she really is in trouble, isn't she?" Sara nodded again. Tim put an arm around her shoulders.

"Well then, I guess you have to help her, don't you?" He sounded encouraging. Sara didn't nod in agreement. She had no idea what to do next. She wasn't sure how to go about saving Ananda from whatever fate awaited her. "And I'm going to help you help her."

Sara looked at Tim in surprise. She had assumed he would believe her eventually, but she hadn't expected him to volunteer to go with her on this fool's errand. She examined his face, the set of his jaw, the wide eyes, and the relaxed brow. He was being completely genuine. There was no teasing or challenging or friendly banter. He really meant what he said. Sara rested her head on his shoulder as a way of thanking him for being on her side, for being a good friend.

She dried her tears, and he hoisted her up. "Come on. Let's get back to work before Jeff starts to miss us."

They drove a couple blocks to the museum. Sara waited in the car while Tim completed his assignment. She clutched the manila envelope tightly all the way back to the office. Tim escorted her to her desk where she sat in a daze for the rest of the afternoon and evening. She worked through her articles. She caught some spelling errors and a punctuation problem, but was sure she had missed more than she found. She dodged Jeff the rest of the day for fear that he would ask her about her mission to the records office. Just before the end of her shift, Tim came by her desk to see if she was okay to get home by herself, and she assured him she was.

Sara made her way back to the downtown subway station in a blur. She didn't remember deciding to take the train instead of the bus. It was like she had been led there purely by muscle memory. She felt like she was dreaming. She descended the steps into the station without truly remembering her walk from the office. She couldn't recall if she had seen another living soul, if she had jaywalked, or whether the night had been foggy or clear. She decided a good night's sleep would clear her head. Maybe in the morning she would know what to do next. She boarded the first westbound train and took a seat near the door.

Four stops later, the train operator announced, "Now approaching Sixteenth Street station." Sara tried to quiet the voices inside her head. She heard echoes of Maya telling her she had to help Ananda.

She heard Tim telling her he would be there for her. Loudest of all she heard Ananda's voice telling her, "Hide in the train station. He won't look there." Who was he, and why did Sara need to hide from him?

The train came to a stop, and Sara stood without making any conscious decision to do so. She heard Ananda's voice again, calling to her. "I'll come find you. Hide!" She had hidden in the train station and, without understanding how, had then hidden in the world of the living. She wondered how long it had taken Ananda to come looking for her only to find she was gone.

The doors slid open. She felt the same urge she'd had on her way to work. It was the urge that pushed her to try to get back to Catharta. She stood in the open doorway, staring at the exact spot where she had hit her head the night before. It was just a few feet in front of her. She hesitated, her body pushing her forward, but her mind holding her back. She was awash with her memories of Catharta, of Ananda, of her failed attempt to get back there. She didn't know what to do. She stood with both feet planted firmly on the train floor, but itching to step out onto the platform.

The automated voice sounded, "The doors are closing. Please stand clear of the doors." Then, as she stood frozen in indecision, the doors slid shut, locking Sara inside, carrying her closer toward home. She took her seat again, suddenly flooded with a feeling of regret, abated only by her promise to herself that she would try again. She would find a way to get back to Catharta.

CHAPTER 6

*S*ara sat up in her bed and rubbed the sleep out of her eyes. "I thought pregnant women were supposed to be tired all the time," she grumbled to Maya who had just bounded into her room and parked herself at the foot of Sara's bed. It was just past ten in the morning. Working swing shift meant that Maya was routinely awake before her and tended to be obnoxiously perky.

"What can I say, I'm an anomaly." Maya reached over the side of her sister's bed and hoisted up her messenger bag by its long strap. "I ransacked your room while you were at work last night looking for Mom's locket. I'm assuming this is where you're hiding it." She tossed the bag in Sara's direction, hinting for her to produce the necklace.

Sara glanced around her bedroom. It did look like it had been pillaged. Drawers were partially opened. The books on her shelf were no longer lined up neat and orderly. She hadn't noticed when she'd crawled into bed the night before after an emotionally exhausting day. She hadn't slept well. Ananda's image had haunted her dreams, and she'd tossed and turned thinking of all the horrible things that could have led to the young girl's death. Bloody images flashed through her mind. Sara squeezed her eyes shut to blot them out.

"Come on, let's see it." Maya was growing impatient. She shoved the bag closer to Sara's lap.

Sara opened her messenger bag and fumbled around for the locket. She found it and held it up for her sister to see, dangling it by its chain so the pendant twirled and reflected the morning light creeping through the blinds. Maya snatched it from her and cupped it in her hands like the delicate treasure that it was. Sara watched her expression closely as she clicked the locket open and gazed at the faces of the two young girls within. A smile bloomed across her lips at the recognition of the nostalgic memento, but her eyes were sad. Sara was sure a thousand memories of their mother wearing that piece of jewelry were playing out in her mind. It doesn't matter how much time has passed. A child is never done grieving for a parent.

Sara smiled at their shared emotions, and her eyes dropped back to her bag. She noticed the corner of a folded sheet of paper sticking out. She withdrew it and unfolded it, looking again into the once lively eyes of Ananda Reyes.

Maya snapped the locket shut and looked to the paper in Sara's hands with curiosity. "What's that?" she asked.

Sara gave one last look at Ananda's lively looking portrait before handing the paper over to her sister. "That's our ghost friend."

As Maya looked over the obituary, her mouth dropped open, and she audibly gasped. "Holy shit!" she exclaimed.

"You know, the baby's ears are fully developed already," Sara reacted to Maya's profanity, but then gave her a moment to read the short blurb and take it all in.

"And this is her? You're positive?" Maya's eyes were already scanning the words for a second time.

"I'm positive that's her. She has the same name, the same age, the same date of death, and I would know that face anywhere. I can't get it out of my head." It was true, Ananda's image was tattooed on her brain. She felt she knew the girl's features better than her own at this point.

Maya looked up from the obituary with sadness woven through her expression. "She died the day after her birthday." That fact added another layer of tragedy to an already miserable tale.

Sara nodded. "My gut feeling is that it's not a coincidence." She wasn't sure she believed in coincidences at all anymore. She failed to buy into the idea that she had randomly fallen into an afterlife that she didn't know existed. She believed that it had all happened for a reason. If she could figure out what that reason was, maybe she would know what to do next.

"It doesn't say how she died though," Maya said, reviewing the page again as Sara had done the day before, hoping for new information to appear. The disappointment was evident in her voice.

"Yeah, about that," Sara replied, reaching toward her nightstand. The manila envelope containing Ananda's death certificate still rested there where Sara had dropped it the night before. "I had the same thought. So I kept digging, and this is what I found."

Sara retreated back into her blankets as Maya removed the death certificate from its sheath and carefully read over all the fields on the photocopy. Sara could tell the moment she got to the box containing the cause of death. Maya's pupils dilated as her shock registered. She met Sara's eyes. "This sounds very technical, but," she hesitated to finish her sentence.

Sara finished it for her. "But it sounds like she was beaten to death."

"Yes. Yes it does," Maya agreed solemnly. "But it doesn't give any details. It doesn't say who or how or why." She seemed as desperate for information as Sara had been the day before.

After her restless night's sleep, Sara was less desperate. She had accepted the fact that she didn't know what to do next. She didn't think she was at a dead end exactly, but she had resigned herself to the fact that she didn't know how to proceed. She held onto her promise to herself that she would find a way back to Catharta. How she would accomplish that task, she had no idea.

"It sounds like a violent crime," Sara concurred. "But death certificates don't usually give details. I did a pretty thorough search for any news items relating to the incident, but I didn't find any. Whatever happened, it apparently wasn't front-page news."

Maya gave another forlorn look at the certificate. "Well, did you check on this other record?" she asked hopefully.

Sara sat up a little straighter. "What other record?" she questioned, noting the increase in her own heart rate.

"Right here," Maya replied turning the paper around so Sara could see and indicating another box near the bottom. "It says 'related records,' and it gives a number."

Sara hastily plucked the paper from her sister's hands. Sure enough, there was a related record number there beginning with the letters PR. Sara said the letters to herself under her breath, "PR," and then to Maya she posed the question, "Do you think that could stand for police report?"

Maya gave an elusive shrug. "I don't know, but I think it's worth looking into. If this girl died a violent death, it might not have been a top headline, but there must have been a police report."

Sara's heart surged. She still didn't have a fully-fledged plan, but she at least had a next step. Then, her heart sank again. "Does this mean I have to go back to the records office? The clerk there wasn't very nice."

Maya's expression took on a look of mock seriousness. "Is somebody picking on you? Do I need to beat someone up?" Sara threw a pillow at her.

Maya laughed and then said, "I'm pretty sure you can order a copy of a police report online." She pulled her phone out of her pocket, and with just a few simple clicks, she produced a webpage with a form to order a copy of a report from the San Francisco Police Department. She turned the phone around to show Sara. "Welcome to the twenty-first century, sweetheart. All the information you could ever want. No mean clerks required."

Sara smiled at the phone and then at her sister. "I could kiss you right now."

"Save it for your hot date tonight," Maya teased.

"What date?" Sara was taken aback.

Maya shot her a look that said she was trying to get under Sara's skin. "Aren't you going to a concert with Tim tonight?"

Sara rolled her eyes. "Yes, I am. And that is definitely not a date."

Maya let it go, probably not wanting to push too many buttons. She scooped up their mother's necklace. "Why don't you wear this? Let Mom watch over you. She'll keep you safe." She leaned in and fastened the clasp at the back of Sara's neck.

Sara moved her hair out of the way and then picked up the little trinket in her hand. "You just got it back, and you're ready to give it away." She didn't admit it, but she liked the idea of her mother watching over her. She felt like she needed a little guidance and protection at the moment.

"Well, I'm just letting you borrow it. You better give it back tomorrow." Maya pointed her forefinger in Sara's face to show she was serious.

Sara smiled. "Deal." She stretched and yawned. "I'm going to go make some coffee and get to filling out this form." She pushed herself out of bed and headed toward the door. Maya followed.

As they headed down the hallway and toward the stairs, Maya asked her, "What do you think about the name Buster if it's a boy?"

Sara had to look back at her sister to see if she was joking. She wasn't. "Maya, Buster is a dog's name," she replied incredulously.

Maya looked offended. "I was thinking more like Buster Posey," she protested, referring to the San Francisco Giants' catcher and one of her many celebrity crushes.

"You want to name your baby after a catcher who was likely named after a dog?" Sara prodded her and continued down the stairs.

"You don't know for sure he was named after a dog."

Sara tried a different approach. "How would you feel if you named your son Buster and then Posey got traded to the Dodgers?"

Maya poked her in the back, and Sara nearly tumbled the rest of the way down the stairs. "Don't you dare speak that blasphemy in this house."

The girls made their way down to the kitchen, and Maya's name search continued while Sara ordered a copy of the police report.

By the time Tim came to pick her up for the show that evening, Sara was more than ready to get out of her own head for a little while. It felt good to have a plan, to know what her next step should be. But when she submitted her request for a copy of Ananda's police report, she got an automated message that it could take up to two weeks for her to receive it. Maya had told her to be patient, but she kept thinking about how much time had passed since she had seen Ananda.

When she had woken up back in the world of the living, the Good Samaritan, Mitch, had told her she'd been unconscious for a minute or two. She tried to estimate how much time she felt she had spent in Catharta. She played her experience over in her mind like a video on a loop. She had woken up, she had worked up her nerve to leave the station, she had found Ananda, they had a conversation, and then she had gone back the way she came. Her best estimate was that she had been there about twenty minutes. So that seemed to imply that time in Catharta felt roughly ten times longer than time in real life. She had been back in the real world for about forty-two hours. That meant that in Ananda's reality, Sara had left her in Catharta seventeen days ago. Once Sara had that math swirling around in her mind, it was hard to turn it off. If it really took two weeks to get the police report, by that time, five months would have passed in Catharta, although she supposed it was all relative. Ananda had died three years ago. That would be about thirty years in Catharta time. Ananda's soul had existed outside her body almost twice as long as she had actually lived.

Sara had to find a way to block out all those calculations. She needed a night out to listen to some loud music and escape from the prison of her own thoughts for a while.

Apparently, Tim wasn't going to help her with that struggle.

"You're assuming this girl is the key to accessing the gateway," he mused as they waited for the doors to open. "But you didn't know anything about her when you accessed it the first time. What if she has nothing to do with it?"

The night was cold and dry. Sara was bundled in enough layers that she would likely suffocate once they got into the warmth of the club, but for the moment, she was grateful for her armor against the chill.

"So what do you suggest?" Sara asked him with a hint of sarcasm. "Should I abandon my Ananda research and just give up?" She had informed him about the request for the police report, but she really had no other leads to go on.

"I'm not saying you should give up. I'm just saying maybe we should rethink our strategy."

She gave Tim a pointed look. "Our strategy?"

He shoved his shoulder into hers companionably. "Hey, I told you I'm in this with you. Whether you like it or not, you've got me."

Sara took a deep breath, trying to quiet the anxiety fluttering in her chest. "So what do you suggest?"

Tim looked up at the clear night sky thoughtfully. "I think we're going about this all wrong. We keep thinking more information about this girl will help get you there. But we know how Ananda got to Catharta. She died. And that is clearly not an option in your case. I think we need to focus on how you accessed the gateway the last time."

Sara looked around at the other concert goers waiting in line. She was reluctant to have this conversation surrounded by so many people, but once the show started, they wouldn't have much opportunity to talk.

"I told you, I tried that already. I went back to the subway station, I lay down in the same spot. Nothing happened."

"First of all," Tim began and Sara rolled her eyes at the oncoming lecture. "I don't think you really gave it the old college try. I think you have to recreate that night more accurately. Same place, same time, same train approaching."

Sara sighed, "Okay, and I assume there's a second of all?"

One of Tim's eyebrows peaked incrementally higher than the other. He was amused by her impatience. "Secondly," he continued, "That wasn't what I said. I'm not talking about the last time you entered Catharta. I'm talking about the last time you accessed the gateway, when you came back home."

Sara thought back to her time on the subway platform in Catharta. She shuddered a little at the memory of the despair she had felt. It had been an all-encompassing sense of despondency. She didn't enjoy the idea of revisiting that feeling.

Tim went on, "That was a much more controlled experience with the gateway. You weren't under attack, falling down, or taken off guard. It wasn't an accident. I think maybe you accessed the gateway intentionally. If you can remember everything you did to get back home, maybe you can use the gateway again." He searched her face for some glimmer of hope. "What did you do? What did you say? How did you feel?" He put a hand on her shoulder, getting her full attention. "What thoughts were in your mind?"

Sara closed her eyes to escape Tim's intense gaze and tried to recall every detail. "I felt," she hesitated. "I felt scared and desperate and," Sara opened her eyes. "Alone."

"And then what?" Tim encouraged.

Sara searched her memory. "And then I thought about my life and all the people in it and how badly I wanted to get back to them." She looked at the stars for some relief from the feeling of desperation that was creeping into her.

"And then?" Tim pushed on, giving Sara the sense she must be on the verge of some incredible breakthrough.

"And then," she thought out loud. "I cried a little." She felt embarrassed to admit that for some reason. "Then when I opened my eyes, it was like I was rocketing upward. Then, I was back here."

Tim paused for a beat and then asked, "That's it?" He looked disappointed, and Sara felt annoyed with him for it. She had been in a state of extreme distress. How could he expect her to remember every minute detail?

"That's it," she confirmed. She was saved from any further interrogation by the opening of the doors. The crowd shuffled into the venue, and Tim bought them a couple of beers.

Once Sara had a moment to relax, she felt guilty for chastising Tim, if only in her mind. After all, he was just trying to help. She vowed to herself to be more receptive to his prodding. She needed his help and support now more than ever.

There were two opening bands that Sara had never heard of, but they were both pretty good. Tim seemed to pick up on her need to escape and didn't push her anymore about Catharta between sets. By the time The Ataris took the stage, she felt glazed over, as if her entire body had been coated in a protective barrier that only music could penetrate. In a way, she felt like her old self again. She was guarded, but safe. Protected, but comfortable. Stale, but familiar. Stagnant.

She hadn't realized it until that moment, standing in the midst of a crowd and listening to one of her favorite guitarists strumming the chords of the songs she loved. Her life was going nowhere, and she had become complacent about it. Maybe that was why uncovering the mystery of Ananda gave her so much apprehension. It meant actually giving herself a purpose, working toward something. That implied a commitment to something bigger than herself and her day-to-day life. It came with the possibility of failure. It all seemed so grand and terrifying. Maybe it wasn't too late to just back out of it, give up the whole endeavor, and go back to the way things were.

She let her eyes drift toward Tim. He looked lost in the music, bobbing his head and swaying back and forth. As if sensing her eyes on him, he gave her a sidelong look. As their eyes met, the corner of his mouth turned up infinitesimally in a smile no one could possibly see but her. There was no doubt in her mind. He would never let her back out of this. He would make sure she saw it through. She needed to accept that there was no turning back. She had gotten other people involved, and it was now much too late to turn around and return to the comfortable, inert life she had led before. Maybe the first step to overcoming her fear was owning it.

The band left the stage, but the house lights remained off. They would return for an encore in a matter of minutes. In the darkness, she leaned toward Tim, very close to his ear so he could hear her over the din of the room.

"I don't have any idea what I'm doing."

Tim gave her a tiny smirk, lips curled, eyebrow cocked. "And?"

"And it's scaring the hell out of me."

Tim threw his head back and laughed. Noticing the hurt expression she wore, he explained himself. "Sara, most people are scared out of their minds most of the time. It's one of the things that makes life great. Fear lets you know you're alive."

Sara looked at the floor, not quite satisfied with his response.

Tim put an arm around her. "Hey, you're going to figure this out." She looked him in the eyes and saw sincerity there. "I believe in you."

Sara gave a small smile in response to his encouragement, and the band came back out on stage.

As they took their places, the lead singer leaned into the microphone and announced, "This song was written for a young girl who lost her way and was almost taken from us too soon. It's called My Reply, and it goes like this."

He leaned away from the mic and began plucking out the melody to one of Sara's very favorite songs. She closed her eyes and allowed herself to be absorbed by the music, this time without the guilt and fear she had felt moments before. She had to believe in herself. That was the only way she was going to get through this. It was the only way she could help Ananda.

The singer crooned, "I wish there was something I could say to erase each and every page you've been through, even though it's not my place to save you."

Sara took in the lyrics she had heard a hundred times before with fresh ears. She was trying to save Ananda from some unknown horror. She didn't know what had happened to the teenager that had ended her life so abruptly, but she was sure it was something awful. She wished she could erase that chapter of Ananda's life. The lyrics made her question her intentions again. Was it her place to save this girl whom she had only met for a matter of minutes? Yes, she decided, it was her place. It had to be. Sara had been chosen somehow. She passed through the land of the dead and back again, and that meant she was possibly the only person who could be in a position to help Ananda. It didn't matter that she barely knew the girl. It was her duty to protect Ananda now, whether she liked it or not.

The singer sang on, "These arms remain stretched out to you. Maybe someday you'll accept them. Or maybe it's too late to save a young girl's heart that's long stopped beating."

Sara was too late. She was three years too late to save Ananda from her violent end that landed her in Catharta. That was the problem. Sara had been so focused on who Ananda was in her life and what had happened to her. She hadn't realized that she was holding on to the hope that unlocking the mystery of Ananda's past would somehow help save her future. This girl's heart had long stopped beating. Sara needed to stop trying to save her from that.

The song continued, "Wake up! Wake up! You've gotta believe. Wake up! Wake up! You can't give up. Time keeps going on without us long after we're dead and gone." Sara felt more alive than she had in years. Her body pulsed with an electric zinging that she couldn't ignore. She was meant to be here tonight. She was meant to receive this message that the universe was trying to send her. All she had to do was listen, pay attention, wake up.

The last lines of the song rang out, "Just hold on to what you have. Just hold on to what you have. You will wake up tomorrow."

Sara yanked on the sleeve of Tim's shirt to get his attention. "I just had an epiphany," she said, her lips practically touching his ear so he could hear her over the final notes of the song.

"What kind of epiphany?" he asked, leaning in close.

The song ended, and the band thanked the crowd for coming out to the show as the house lights came on.

"I think I know how to get back to Catharta. Can you take me to the Sixteenth Street subway station?"

Tim's eyes opened wide with surprise. "What, right now? The subway will be closing soon. Besides, I thought you were going to wait for your police report."

Sara shook her head. "I don't think I need it. It's like you said, I'm focusing too much on her. Maybe she's not the key to getting back there. Maybe I am." He still looked hesitant. "Please, can we at least try?"

"Okay," Tim agreed. "Let's go."

He drove a little faster than Sara was comfortable with and found parking near the station at least half an hour before the last train. They made their way down to the platform, and Sara led him to the far east end of the station. The illuminated sign indicated the next San-Francisco-Airport-bound train would arrive in two minutes.

"So what's the plan? What was this epiphany you had?" Tim asked, turning to face her as she stood with her back to the tunnel's opening.

"I think it's all about what's in my head," she replied, knowing full well that wouldn't make much sense to him. "I have to believe I'm going to Catharta. I think it worked the first time because I believed I was going to die. Now, I'm hoping it's enough to believe I can go there without dying." Tim pursed his lips and gave a subtle shrug as if anything were worth a shot. Sara added, "And I think I have to accept it knowingly, with my eyes wide open. I think that's important."

He cocked his head to the side and gave her an appraising look and then said, "Alright, let's do this,"

"One more thing," Sara said cautiously.

"What?"

"I need you to not freak out over what I'm about to do." Sara examined Tim's face for acceptance.

The overhead speaker announced, "San Francisco Airport train now approaching platform one."

"Why?" He asked suspiciously. "What are you about to do?" Tim's trepidation was clearly evident on his face.

Sara flashed him her best impression of one of his barely noticeable smirks. "Just promise me. Please."

Tim noticeably flushed with anxiety or excitement, likely a little of both. "Okay. I trust you not to do anything too stupid." It was a warning, not a complete promise. Sara decided to accept it as the best she was going to get out of him.

The breeze began to stir and whip itself into a frenzy. Sara's hair billowed around her face. The sound of the oncoming train increased, and the platform rumbled under her feet. She peered over her shoulder into the tunnel that was beginning to illuminate with concentric circles of reflected light from the train's headlights. The sound was thunderous. She tried to still her heart and be patient, just another second or two. Sara subconsciously touched her mother's locket resting on her chest for good luck. She thought about Catharta, about Ananda, about how much she wanted to be there. She pushed all other thoughts out of her mind until all that remained was her pure belief that this would work.

Then, just as the train came screaming into the station, Sara suddenly pitched herself backward, throwing her body toward the platform. With her heart pounding out of her chest, she fell. She saw the panic in Tim's eyes and his barely controlled attempt to catch her. Then, the world seemed to slow down, and she was falling, eyes wide open, into a darkness that never seemed to end.

CHAPTER 7

S ara blinked. She was staring up at the concrete ceiling of the Sixteenth Street subway station. Was this the real station in the land of the living or a memory of the station in the land of the dead? She tried to pop her ears, to release the built-up pressure. They popped, but it didn't alter the pervading silence that saturated the underground space.

She sat up suddenly in disbelief and felt a little queasy as a result. Tim was gone. The train was gone. She had done it. She was back in Catharta. She touched her hand to the back of her head and found no pain there. She hadn't felt any pain the last time she had visited this other realm. Hopefully, she hadn't hurt her actual living body back in the real world. Here, in Catharta, her soul was unencumbered by the realities of throwing herself against the hard tile floor. That potential pain or injury was something she would have to face when she returned to the real world. Now, she had to do what she came here to do.

She had to find Ananda.

Sara scrambled to her feet and found her way to the same stairwell where she and Ananda had talked on her first trip to the ghost plane. She stopped briefly on the spot, halfway up, where Ananda had explained where she was and how Catharta worked, and then continued up to the street level. She was much less disoriented this time around. She knew where she was and how she had gotten there. She knew she wasn't dead. She knew she had a friend here and that armed her with a small measure of confidence.

As she emerged onto Mission Street and took in the leafless trees and slate gray sky, some of that confidence was dashed. She realized she hadn't thought much beyond this point about how to find Ananda. She had been so focused on the seemingly insurmountable obstacle of getting back to Catharta that she hadn't given much thought to where the girl would actually be. Given that Catharta looked just like the real world, she imagined it was probably just as big. Why had she assumed Ananda would be hanging around the same neighborhood?

Sara tried not to let all her hope escape. Maybe Ananda lived in this area. Lived. That wasn't the right word for it. Sara made a mental note to not use words like that if she found Ananda. When she found Ananda. She couldn't allow it to be an if.

She set off down the street and tried approaching the alley where her ghostly friend had first emerged. There was no glowing light this time. Sara rounded the corner and stood in the opening of the alleyway. It was empty, just a void framed by brick and asphalt. She felt foolish for thinking Ananda might be there. She continued down the street aimlessly. She was running out of ideas embarrassingly quickly.

Her next best idea was to call out to her absent friend. In the all-encompassing silence, her voice would probably carry to the next county. She stepped off the curb and out into the middle of Mission Street, something she would never do in the real world for fear of being run over by the constant traffic. In Catharta, there was no risk of that. Sara cupped her hands to her mouth and hollered, "Ananda!"

Her voice sounded deafening in the surrounding quiet. There was an echo. She supposed sound waves could bounce off memories of buildings. Maybe the echo itself was just a memory as well. She still didn't totally understand the physics of the ghost plane. She waited, listening for a reply or a stirring of any type of motion. She heard nothing, saw nothing. She turned around, looking down the street the other direction, toward downtown. "Ananda!" she cried out again and waited. There was no reply, but Sara suddenly felt eyes on her. She was being watched. She was sure of it. She looked up and down the street and saw no one. She glanced up at the windows of the surrounding buildings just in time to see some curtains snap shut in what was probably someone's third floor apartment. She looked at the other side of the street and saw a set of glowing eyes momentarily fixated on her before the blinds were twisted closed. All at once, she felt very exposed. There were people, souls, all around her. Catharta wasn't as desolate as it seemed. They were just in hiding; observing, but not engaging. Down the street a way was another alley, and she thought she saw someone peek their head around the corner to get a look at her. She raised a hand and waved. The head disappeared quickly into the alley.

"Hey," Sara yelled and broke into a jog toward the place where the soul had disappeared. Upon reaching the alley, she found it empty. "Hello?" she asked cautiously, wondering why these people seemed to be afraid of her. No one answered. She turned around and saw the alley on the other side of the street. Just as she turned around, a door in the side of the building bordering that alley slammed shut.

"Hello?" she called out again. She crossed Mission to the opposite alley and tried the door. It was locked. A familiar loneliness was creeping into Sara's bones. Even though she was apparently surrounded by the residents of Catharta, she felt entirely alone. She stepped back out onto the street, unsure of how to proceed. Out of the corner of her eye, she thought she saw a glowing light. She turned toward it. A few doors down from where she stood was a coffee shop with a large glass front window. Something inside the shop was illuminated. Sara advanced toward it.

As she approached the window, she cupped her hands against the glass to see in. There were people inside, two men. One man was standing with his back to the window. His body was tense, his back muscles visibly tight through his shirt, his shoulders hunched. He was holding the second man, who was facing the window, in a strange embrace, one arm wrapped around his shoulders and the other hand covering his face. The second man had his hands up in some form of surrender. His knees were buckling with fear. The glowing light Sara had seen was emanating from within the second man, from inside his chest. It was as if his heart was incandescent.

Without thinking her actions through, Sara pounded on the window. She didn't know what was happening inside the coffee shop, but it felt wrong. It felt like it needed to be stopped. As her fist rapped against the glass, the first man turned around abruptly. His face looked weary, his skin sallow, and his forehead creased high into his receding hairline. But his eyes were alert and fierce. He had the same crystal clear orbs for eyes that Ananda had. But set into this man's face, they looked worse than just supernatural and shocking. They looked evil. As his eyes locked on hers, Sara felt hate cast upon her, but there was something else in his gaze, something hard to identify. It might have been shock or curiosity. Sara recalled Ananda's own reaction at seeing her eyes, which tagged her as a living soul among the dead. Maybe that's what caught this man's attention.

As his gaze remained fixed on her, the second man's eyes fluttered open. The glowing in his chest intensified into a bright, blinding light. Sara wanted to shield her eyes, but she couldn't look away. All at once, the man was engulfed in an enormous orb of bright white light. The orb shimmered for barely a moment and then dissipated. The light faded away to nothing, and the second man was gone. The first man was left standing alone inside the coffee shop, seething with rage.

Sara took a step backward and decided she should run. Before she could move, before she could even breathe, the man was directly in front of her. The window was now nothing more than the frame of an empty shop. The door hung wide open, although Sara had never seen it open. He moved so quickly he almost left a trail. He placed his hands on her shoulders, gripping her tightly with talon-like fingers.

"What have you done?" he demanded of her.

Sara's eyes were wide with fear. She answered as honestly as she could, her voice quavering. "I have no idea what I've done."

He leaned in close. His eyes were level with hers, examining each iris in turn. "You don't belong here." It was more than a mere observation. It was an accusation. It was true. She was an intruder in this world.

Sara tried to pull away and found herself paralyzed with fear. She didn't know what to say or do. She wondered if she could will herself back to the real world. She tried to clear her mind of everything but the desire to be home, but it was useless. There was no way she could achieve that kind of focus—not with her heart racing and her pulse thundering in her ears. Besides, she was fairly sure it would only work if she were on the platform at the subway station. That's where the gateway was. She had to come up with another way to escape the clutches of this terrifying soul.

Her racing mind was interrupted by a shout from down the street. Both Sara and the man who held her captive turned as they heard a young woman shriek, "Sam!"

It was Ananda. She was running toward the pair of them at a sprint. The man, who was apparently named Sam, loosened his grip on Sara's shoulders. She didn't stop running until she was close enough to reach out and grab Sam's arm. She wrenched one of his hands away, and Sara was able to twist herself free from the grasp of his other hand. She stumbled backward a few steps, and Ananda inserted herself between the two of them.

Sara wanted to run, but she didn't know where she would go. She was also unsure if she'd be able to find Ananda again if she did run. That was a risk she couldn't take, not after coming all this way to find her. She decided the safest thing to do was to stay with the only friend she had on this plane.

"She is not one of yours!" Ananda yelled in the attacker's face. "You are not her guardian." The conviction and fury in her voice sent chills down Sara's spine. This was a girl whose wisdom exceeded her years and whose confidence exceeded her stature.

Sam snarled through bared teeth, "In Catharta, I am everyone's guardian."

Ananda shook her head. "She doesn't belong to Catharta, and she doesn't belong to you." The two of them held their eyes locked on one another, each daring the other to blink first. It was a power struggle that Sara was witnessing.

Suddenly, Sam looked up, distracted. Sara looked over her shoulder and followed his gaze to a second story window across the street. There was a bright white light seeping out from between the blinds.

Ananda noticed his shift in attention also and turned to see the light. She looked back toward Sam and said, "That is one of yours.

I believe you're needed elsewhere." She was stern, but something in Ananda's tone told Sara it pained her to say those words. She was sending him after another prey, someone else she wished she could also protect. She was making the decision to protect Sara instead.

Sam was irritated. He had lost some sort of battle that Sara couldn't fully understand. He wanted to be in two places at once, and now, he had to choose. He leaned in close to Ananda so their noses were nearly touching. Ananda didn't flinch. She held her ground. "This isn't done," he hissed. Then, in a flash, he was gone.

Ananda quickly addressed Sara. "Did he hurt you? Are you okay?"

Sara hugged her own shoulders, assessing her well-being. She could still feel where his hands had pressed into her. It didn't hurt, but it felt wrong somehow. "I'm fine. I don't think I can feel pain here."

Ananda looked her up and down and, once she seemed satisfied Sara was unharmed, asked her, "Why did you come back? When I didn't find you in the train station, I figured you found your way back into your life."

"I did," Sara confirmed. "But I was worried about you. Someone was after you. It seemed liked you needed my help. It was him, wasn't it? He was the man who was after you?"

Both women glanced up at the window where the light had appeared. It was all dark now. As they stared up at the building, it flickered, like an old television with poor reception. Its face shifted from a plain brick wall to a painted charcoal gray facade.

Sara was caught off guard. "Whoa! What was that?"

Ananda ushered her down the street. "We need to go. It's not stable here." The two girls rushed down the street in silence, and Ananda led her back into the Sixteenth Street subway station. This time, they didn't stop at the entry stairs. They went all the way down to the platform level.

They sat down on one of the concrete benches inside the station, and Sara looked around to ensure they were completely alone in their underground tomb. "What just happened up there?" she asked.

"Which part?" Ananda wanted to know. It was a fair question. Sara had just witnessed a lot of things she didn't understand.

She decided to start with the part she thought might be easiest to explain. "That building, it flickered, and then, it changed. I thought you said this place is just like the real world? That doesn't happen in the real world."

"It's not supposed to happen here either," Ananda replied morosely. "Catharta is built of memories. Souls aren't meant to spend so much time here. We're just supposed to pass through. But now, everyone has been here so long that there are people here with conflicting memories. It's making everything unstable. Are you familiar with a building called Salesforce Tower?"

Ananda was referring to the most recently constructed skyscraper in San Francisco. It was also the tallest building in the city, dominating the downtown skyline. "Yeah, I know the building. They started building it a few years ago. It's almost finished now."

"Well, not here," Ananda replied. "Sometimes it's there. Sometimes it's not. There are people here who died before the construction ever really got underway. There are other people who remember it like you do, almost finished and dwarfing the Transamerica Pyramid. Those conflicting memories make the area unstable."

Sara shuffled that answer around in her mind with the other facts she had already gathered about Catharta. It seemed to make sense. "But what happens if it becomes too unstable? What if everything here starts flickering and changing?"

Ananda shrugged. "I don't know. This has never happened before. We've never had so many souls trapped here for so long."

Sara thought she may have just put something together. "That man back there, Sam, is he the reason you're all trapped here?" Ananda nodded solemnly. "So whatever he was doing to that guy in the coffee shop, he was trying to trap his soul in Catharta?"

Ananda's interest was piqued. She lurched forward and asked, "What guy? What did you see?"

Sara tried to recall exactly what she had witnessed. "Sam was in a coffee shop with another man, and he had his hand over his face.

The guy was glowing from his chest. Then, I knocked on the window, and he let the guy go."

"Sara, tell me what you saw. What happened to the other man?" Ananda voice was urgent and insistent.

"The glowing got brighter, and then, it engulfed his whole body. Then, the light faded away, and he was gone."

Ananda's ghostly eyes were wide with astonishment. She grasped Sara's knee suddenly, causing her to jump. "Do you know what this means?"

Sara shook her head. "I have absolutely no idea what this means," she answered honestly.

"He got out!" Ananda exclaimed. Her face erupted into a grin, and Sara realized that was the first time she had seen her smile. She looked more like the young girl in her obituary photo than the weary, cynical soul that had been formed by what seemed like a lifetime in Catharta. "You saved him, Sara. You saved that man. He was reborn because of you."

Ananda leaned over and embraced her. Sara didn't know what to say, so she just hugged her back. They sat there in each other's arms until Sara finally asked, "Who is Sam?"

Ananda sat back, less jovial at the thought of the man they had just encountered. "He calls himself the Guardian. He thinks he's the keeper of souls. He used to be my friend," she answered with a sad smile.

Sara waited for more, and Ananda went on. "He died not long before I did. He was one of the first people I met when I came here. We shared the stories of our lives and our deaths. We comforted each other. We learned about what Catharta is together. We waited together to be reborn. We didn't really know what it would be like at the time, what it would look like. The light came for me first. He didn't understand what it was. We had never witnessed a rebirth before. He was scared, and he thought I was in some kind of danger. He held me tight and covered my eyes. He thought he was protecting me. My light faded out. I missed my chance to be reborn. A child somewhere was born without a soul because my soul stayed here."

"That's horrible," Sara said, her words feeling impotent. She wanted to comfort Ananda, but she knew there was nothing she could say that would help.

Ananda continued, "Once he realized what he had done, he felt awful. He didn't know how to make up for his mistake, so he just pulled away from me. We drifted apart. I don't know exactly what happened to him after that. But it seems that he realized he had the power to trap souls here in Catharta. That's what he spends his time doing now. When he senses the light coming for someone, he goes to them, and he stops it from happening. As far as I know, no one has escaped ever since."

Sara asked, "Did the light ever come for Sam?" She couldn't imagine someone trapping themselves here for all eternity willingly. It seemed unlikely he would have stopped his own rebirth, if that were even possible.

Ananda shook her head. "It's never come for him, and we don't know why. I think that's part of what turned his heart so dark. He's been here a long time, and he's never even been given a chance to get out."

Sara was relieved to find that she wasn't the only one perplexed by this guardian of souls. It sounded like he didn't really even understand himself. She still had more questions about him. "How does he move like that? He's so fast it's almost like he can teleport. Can all souls do that?"

"No," Ananda responded. "Only Sam can do that, and I don't know why. There's a lot about Sam that I don't understand." She looked thoughtful for a moment. "I can't believe you saved that man. He gets another chance at life because of you." Ananda flashed Sara another sweet smile.

Sara blushed. She hadn't meant to save the man. She hadn't even known what she was doing, but she was glad to have been of some help. "Sam isn't very happy with me about that." Sara bit her lip and then asked, "Is he going to be coming after me for revenge?"

Ananda frowned. "I don't know. But I know he won't look for you here."

That triggered a memory for Sara. "You said that last time. You told me to hide in the subway station because he wouldn't look for me here. Why is this place safe?" She looked around at the soot-stained walls and chipped tile floors. It hardly looked like a sanctuary.

"He doesn't like to come down here. This is where he died. It happened down at that end." Ananda pointed over her shoulder toward the east end of the station.

Sara glanced in that direction. "That's where I came from too." She was still pretty sure she didn't believe in coincidences anymore. There had to be some sort of connection. Maybe Sam was the key to finding out why she was able to enter and exit Catharta. "Can you tell me about how he died? Do you remember any details?"

"He was hit by a train after someone tried to mug him. There was some sort of a scuffle, and he was thrown off-balance. He fell onto the tracks right as the train was approaching."

The similarities between Sam's story and her own sent Sara's skin rippling into goose bumps, and it felt like her hair stood on end. He had to be the key; she just knew it. But she needed more to go on. She knew now that the way to help Ananda was to stop Sam from trapping souls, and to do that, she would need to learn as much as she could about him.

"What else do you remember about Sam? Do you know his full name or the date he died? Do you know where he lived or what he did for a living? Anything at all?" Sara quizzed her companion and informant.

Ananda thought for a moment. "His name is Sam Johnson. He lived in San Francisco. I think he worked in IT, but he never liked to talk about his job much. He was married, but he and his wife were estranged. And he died on…," she closed her eyes, reaching back into the depths of her memory. "September 27, 2014."

Sara repeated these facts in her mind, committing them to memory. She would need to take all these details with her back to the world of the living. She wished she had brought a pen, although she wondered if anything she wrote down here would still exist once she was transported back. That would be something she'd have to test out next time. There would be a next time. She would come back to

Catharta with a plan. But now, she had probably been here too long already. She wasn't sure how long her body could go without its soul or whatever fraction of its soul that was currently in Catharta.

"I think it's time for me to go back to my world," she said to Ananda. "But I'm going to find a way to help you, to help everyone here. I will find a way to stop Sam."

Ananda nodded, acknowledging Sara's vow but clearly holding her hope in reserve. They both stood up from their concrete bench. She followed Sara toward the east end of the station.

As they approached the spot where her invisible gateway awaited her, there was one more thing Sara wanted to ask, but she was nervous about bringing it up. She decided there was no polite way to ask, so she just spit out the question. "Ananda, how did you die?"

Ananda averted her eyes, clearly made uncomfortable by the question and the memories it stirred.

Sara quickly added, "I know you died of a brain injury. I know you were survived by your mother and your two sisters and your stepfather. I know it's really none of my business, but if you're willing to tell me, I'd like to know what happened."

Ananda closed her eyes and balled her fists. For a second, Sara thought she was going to take a swing at her, but then, she realized her friend was holding back tears.

"Shhh," Sara hushed and pulled Ananda in for a hug. "It's okay. You don't have to tell me. I shouldn't have asked. It's not my place to know something like that."

Ananda sobbed silently into Sara's chest. "I'm sorry. I'm sorry. I shouldn't have brought it up," Sara cooed.

Ananda whispered something muffled that Sara couldn't make out. She released the young girl from her embrace.

Ananda repeated, "It was my stepfather." She wiped her eyes and sniffled and then went on. "He was abusive, both verbally and physically. I used to wonder which one was worse. On my seventeenth birthday, I stayed out all night with my friends. My mom had told me I could, but I never asked him. I came home just after sun up. He was so angry. He called me a whore and accused me of drinking and doing drugs. It was honestly just an innocent night out with my friends from school, but he wouldn't listen to anything I said. Then, he hit me. He had hit me before, but not like this. This time, he didn't stop. He was unrelenting. He hit me with his bare fists until I blacked out. And then"—she hesitated and then seemed to stand up a little straighter, refusing to allow another tear to escape—"and then I died. I woke up here, and this is where I've been ever since."

Sara was dumbfounded. There were no words of consolation that seemed sufficient. "I'm so sorry. I didn't know," was all she could manage.

"How did you find out?" Ananda asked.

Sara was still trying to take in the horror Ananda had experienced, and the question caught her off guard. "What do you mean?"

"How did you know all that stuff about me, my family?"

"I knew your name and the day you died. I found your obituary and your death certificate." Sara wished the obituary were still tucked into her messenger bag so she could share it with her. Next time, she promised herself.

"Do you think you could do that again?" Ananda grasped Sara's hands, her eyes wide and hopeful.

"Do what again?" Sara puzzled.

"Could you do that same kind of research? Could you find out what happened to my stepfather?" The pleading in her voice was painful.

"What's his full name?" Sara was going to have to memorize some more information to take back with her.

"It's Greg, Gregory Hastings." She said the name as though it left a taste of bile in her mouth. She spit it out like venom.

"What do you want to know about him?" Sara didn't want to promise something she couldn't deliver.

"I want to know if he's alive. Ever since I realized what Sam was doing, I've been worried that he'll die, and then I'll be trapped here with him forever." Ananda no longer looked like the wise and hardened woman Catharta had made of her, the warrior that had stood up to Sam. She looked like the frightened teenager she was when she left the living world.

Brokenhearted, Sara promised, "I will find out what happened to him. I'll come back here and tell you everything I learn."

Ananda embraced Sara gratefully. "Thank you," she whispered.

"And remember"—Sara added—"even if he died, the only way he could come here is if he had a soul to begin with."

Ananda swallowed against the lump in her throat and seemed to take comfort in that idea.

"How will I find you?" Sara asked. "When I returned, I realized I had no idea where you were."

"I won't go far," Ananda promised. "I'll watch for you, and I'll come back here as often as I can." She indicated the subway station surrounding them.

Sara nodded in agreement. She had a plan. For the first time in a long time, she felt sure of herself. But now, she had to leave.

After giving Ananda's hand a promissory squeeze, Sara picked out her spot on the platform tiles and lay down. She closed her eyes and tried to clear her mind. She thought of the real world, of her body lying lifeless on an identical tiled floor on another plane of existence. She thought of Maya and her baby. She thought of Tim and the look of panic she had last seen on his face. She thought of Aunt Joann and the home she had provided for their family. She thought of her job and her life and the leaves on the trees. She thought of her mission to get Ananda the information she sought, to find a way to stop Sam, and to free the trapped souls of Catharta. With determination, she opened her eyes.

For a split-second, she saw Ananda's face, her mouth dropped open in awe. Then, the girl was nothing more than a blur, melting away at the edge of Sara's vision. She focused on the concrete ceiling as she felt her body being hurtled upward at an impossible speed. Her ears felt like they might cave into her head from the pressure. She felt queasy, and she wanted to close her eyes to stop the nausea. But she persisted, digging her nails into the unyielding tiles and refusing to blink.

Then, all at once, everything stopped. The concrete above her was unchanged, but she felt entirely motionless. The nausea blissfully died away. She popped her ears and looked at the place where

Ananda's face had been a moment before. She wasn't there. Instead, it was Tim standing over her looking just as petrified as when she had left him.

Sara managed a smile and croaked out the words, "Did you miss me?"

His expression changed from scared to livid. This was not one of the familiar microscopic changes of his facial features. It was possibly the most animated she had ever seen him. "Jesus fucking Christ, Sara, you could have warned me! I thought you were seriously going to throw yourself in front of that goddamn train! Then you're just lying there, unconscious. One more minute, and I was going to call you an ambulance."

Sara had never heard him swear like that before—not at her, maybe at the television after a bad call in a football game, but never at her. As if that wasn't shocking enough, Tim then scooped her half-way up off the floor and wrapped his arms around her, burying his face in her hair. He had never held her like that. If they ever hugged, it was usually a one-armed maneuver and a pat on the back. She must have really frightened him.

"I'm sorry," she said, truly meaning it. "How long was I out?"

He unwound himself from her and helped her to her feet. "I don't know, maybe three minutes? It felt like a lot longer though."

"It felt like a lot longer to me too," Sara shared.

His curiosity suddenly got the better of his anger and worry. "Did you find her? Were you able to help Ananda?"

"I found her. I found someone else too: the man who was after her before. I think I know how to help her now." Sara wasn't sure that was exactly true. She added, "At least I think I know where to start. Do you have a pen?" Sara wanted to write down all the information she had memorized before it started to fade away.

To Sara's relief, Tim gave her one of his subtle looks, one eyebrow slightly raised with lips shifted a tiny bit to one side. This was the Tim she knew. "Who uses a pen anymore?" He asked, teasing her about her apparently archaic notions of note-taking. He pulled out his phone and diligently transcribed the names, dates, and other information she conveyed to him.

He had a lot of questions. He wanted to know who these peo-ple were and why they were important. Sara couldn't deal with the interrogation at that moment. Her time spent in Catharta and the journey back had exhausted her. Tim must have noticed the fatigue in her eyes. He stopped firing questions at her.

"I'll tell you what," he said. "Let's get you home. I'm going to crash on your couch tonight, and the second you wake up in the morning, you're going to tell me and your sister absolutely every-thing that happened."

"Sir, yes sir," she replied with a lazy salute. "The second I wake up, I'll give you a full report."

As he led her out of the station, he added, "Well, maybe not the second you wake up. You can shower first. No offense, but you smell like a dumpster fire."

Sara gave herself a self-conscious sniff and corrected him, "No, I smell like death."

CHAPTER 8

"And that's when your sister pulled an Anna Karenina on me," Tim recounted, not entirely accurately, to Maya the next morning. Maya sat with rapt attention at the kitchen table, while Tim paced around the kitchen dramatically, waving his coffee mug in the air for added emphasis.

Sara, having just entered the room after her promised shower, scoffed at his retelling of their night. She was certain he had heard her approach and had added that last bit to get a rise out of her.

It worked.

"I did not throw myself under a train," she protested. "I threw myself on the platform. It was totally harmless." She had her laptop tucked under one arm and set it on the table as she took a seat across from Maya.

Tim poured her a cup of coffee. As he set it in front of her, he chastised her, "I'd hardly call it harmless considering you nearly concussed yourself earlier this week. You may want to wear a helmet next time you try to get to Catharta."

"Right," Sara replied, her voice heavy with sarcasm. "Because if I'm trying to be inconspicuous about lying unconscious on the floor of the subway station, a helmet will definitely help deflect attention."

"You have zero chance of being inconspicuous anyway, so you might as well at least attempt to prevent brain damage." Tim was giving her a deliberately serious and fatherly look, but shifted to something slightly more antagonizing when he added, "Well, any further brain damage, that is."

Sara gave him her best eye roll and was searching for a retaliatory comment when Maya snapped her fingers several times to get their attention.

"Hey, can you two stop bickering for ten seconds and tell me what happened next?" Her impatience was clearly getting the better of her.

Tim chimed in, "Yeah, that's what I'm here to find out." He took a seat at the table as well, and they both waited for Sara to share her experience in Catharta.

Sara looked back and forth between her sister and her best friend, trying to decide where to start. The previous night already seemed like a very long time ago. So much had happened while she was in Catharta. She wanted to relay it all in as much detail as she could manage. Finally, she began, "What happened next was I woke up in Catharta. I went looking for Ananda, but I couldn't find her." Maya looked instantly dismayed, so Sara added, "At least not right away. Instead, I found the man who was after her the last time I was there."

Maya's eyes widened in fear. "Is he still after her? Did he do something to her? Did he do something to you? Did he hurt you? Are you okay?"

Sara was used to Maya's inability to listen without issuing a barrage of questions. Tim, on the other hand, waited patiently for Sara to go on.

"He didn't hurt me," she replied. "It seems like nothing can physically hurt me in Catharta. He grabbed me, and he dug his fingers into me pretty hard. It was scary, but it didn't actually hurt."

"Does it hurt now?" Tim asked.

Sara raised one hand to her opposite shoulder and gave it a squeeze. It did hurt a little, like a bruise, too deep below the surface to produce any visible purple evidence. She nodded, and Tim scratched his chin thoughtfully, trying to piece together the rules of the ghost plane.

Maya was fit to burst waiting for Sara to go on. "Then what? What happened with the guy?"

Sara continued, "I interrupted him while he was trying to trap a soul in Catharta. That's what he does. He calls himself the Guardian, and he prevents people from being reborn. The man he was trying to trap got away. He gets to live another life." She smiled at the memory of Ananda's praise, even though she hadn't had any clue what she was doing in that moment. Then her expression darkened. "He was really angry with me for interfering. That's when he grabbed me. I'm not sure what he planned to do to me, but I didn't have to find out. Ananda found us. I went there thinking I was going to save her somehow, yet she ended up saving me." Saying this out loud sent self-doubt flooding through Sara's bones. She was messing around with something she couldn't possibly understand. How had she convinced herself that she could be useful to Ananda in any way?

Maya asked impatiently, "So Ananda scared this Guardian guy away?"

"She got him to leave us alone, and we went and hid in the subway station. She said he wouldn't look for us there because that's where he died. He was hit by a train." She waited for a reaction to this information and got none. "He was hit by a train in the Sixteenth Street subway station." Still nothing. "After an attempted mugging." Did she have to spell it out for them? "In the exact same spot where I was almost mugged and nearly hit by a train."

Suddenly, it sunk in. Maya almost jumped out of her chair. "That has something to do with why you were able to go to Catharta."

Sara placed one finger on her nose and pointed the other at her sister, as if she had just won a round of charades. "I think it was like an echo of the past. What happened to me was so similar to what happened to him that my soul got transported before my body realized I wasn't dead."

"So by recreating that same echo"—Tim said inquisitively—"does that mean you can come and go to Catharta as you please?"

"I think it's like you both suggested," Sara answered. "I have to recreate the situation as accurately as I can. But I think it's also important to believe. I need to believe I can go there. I have to want it. And I have to want to come back. I think that's the only way to access the gateway. When I go there, I have to accept it, eyes wide open. When I want to come back, I need to focus on everything in the real world that I want to get back to."

A look of sudden panic blossomed on Maya's face. "What would happen if someone moved your body before you came back?"

Sara felt equally panic-stricken. She hadn't considered that possibility. "I don't know." She looked to Tim who also looked wide-eyed with worry. The three of them sat in a tension filled silence for a long and heavy moment.

"Okay, new rule!" Maya declared. "You're not allowed to go to the subway station by yourself. One of us has to be with you to make sure you're not moved while you're unconscious."

Sara thought back to her failed attempt to access Catharta on her way to work when she had been surrounded by strangers. She had felt foolish at that time, but now, she fully realized how reckless she had been. She heartily agreed. "Deal, no solo trips to the ghost plane."

Tim nodded in agreement and then prodded her on. "So you and Ananda were in the station together. What happened next?"

Sara refocused on her story. "Next, Ananda answered a lot of my questions. She told me all about the Guardian. She told me that they used to be friends and that he accidentally stopped her rebirth. It was the first time he had trapped anyone in Catharta, and he didn't understand what he was doing at the time. Once he knew what he could do, he started preventing everyone's rebirth. I think his goal is to trap everyone there with him because he's bitter. He's never been given a chance to be reborn, and they don't know why."

"Maybe it's because he hasn't learned his lessons yet," Maya suggested. "Isn't that what Catharta is for? Isn't he supposed to reflect on his life and learn from it?"

"Maybe," Sara tentatively agreed.

"Or maybe"—Tim proposed—"it's just not his time yet. Maybe he's just being impatient."

"I don't know," Sara said doubtfully. "Ananda said souls were never meant to spend much time in Catharta, and I think he's way past the normal time period. In fact, the number of souls accumulating there now is making it unstable. The whole place is built out of memories. Since there are so many people there who have been trapped for so long, there are conflicting memories. I watched the face of a building change color right before my eyes. Ananda says the Salesforce Tower sometimes just disappears. She also said she doesn't know what will happen to all the souls trapped there if it becomes too unstable. She said it's unprecedented."

Maya was trying to piece together all the information into some semblance of a plan. "So, the only way to help Ananda is to stop the Guardian."

"Well"—Sara corrected—"I think that's what we have to do to help everyone in Catharta. It's also how we stop babies in the real world from being born with no soul." She gave a pointed look toward Maya's belly. "But there's something else we can do for Ananda. She had a specific request. She told me how she died, and it was as awful as we had feared."

Sara held her breath for a pregnant pause. Her audience waited, seemingly unsure if they wanted to know. "The craniocerebral blunt-force trauma that caused her death was the result of being violently beaten by her stepfather." She felt sick to her stomach just saying the words. The cause of death that had been printed on Ananda's death certificate had been rattling around in her brain for days, but allowing it to cross her lips made it feel more real. The thought of the man who had caused such trauma, savagely beating a helpless teenager, nearly made her heave.

Tim also looked a little queasy, and for once, he was at a loss for words.

Maya, on the other hand, had plenty of words. "He beat her to death?" she asked incredulously, rising from her seat and planting her palms on the surface of the table with a loud slap. "What kind of a monster so much as raises a hand to a teenage girl? And he still got a mention in her obituary? He was listed with the surviving family! Who in the hell wrote that thing? Who in their right mind would think it was okay to list a young girl's murderer in her obituary along with the people who actually loved and cared for her?" Fury was spilling out of her.

"Maybe the person who wrote it didn't know exactly what had happened, like a distant family member or something?" Sara offered, although now that Maya pointed it out, she was also disturbed by Greg's mention.

Tim chimed in, "It was probably written within the first day or two after she died. Whoever wrote it was probably in shock and wasn't thinking straight. Did she say why he attacked her?"

"Does it matter?" Maya roared. "There is no possible reason he could have had to attack her that would justify what he did. The only excuse anyone could have is self-defense and don't try to tell me he was defending himself. That girl weighed a hundred pounds soaking wet. There is no way a grown man felt threatened by her. Not to mention that she was a minor!"

Sara reached over and put her hand on top of Maya's. "Listen, I get it. It's very upsetting. And you're right, it doesn't matter why he did it. But I'm sure unbridled rage isn't good for your baby. We can't change the past, so take a deep breath and try to calm down. Just remember, this happened a long time ago, and there is still a way we can help Ananda. She had a request for me. For us."

Maya let out an indignant huff and took a seat. She closed her eyes and took a deep breath, trying to recenter herself. "Okay, so how do we help her?"

"We have to find out what happened to her stepfather," Sara replied. "She's afraid that he's going to die, and she'll be trapped in Catharta with his soul for all eternity."

"If he has one," Tim muttered under his breath, echoing Sara's exact thought the night before. His eyes were fixed blankly on a random spot on the table. He was clearly trying to control his own ferocity.

Sara was sorry to have to deliver the sad news of how Ananda had died, but she was truly touched by the reaction it evoked. Maya and Tim had never met Ananda, had never seen more than an old photograph of her. Yet they were stirred to action by the injustice she had suffered. These were two of the most important people in Sara's life, and she had never felt so much support from them, so much solidarity with them. The three of them were a team. They were going to find a way to make things right together.

Maya didn't hesitate. "So where do we start? How do we find out what happened to the evil stepfather?"

Sara placed a hand on her still closed laptop. "We start with his name, and we go from there."

Tim, realizing that was his cue, snapped out of his anger fog and pulled out his phone. Reading from the notes he had taken for Sara the night before, he asked, "Gregory Hastings? Is he the stepfather?"

Sara nodded, "Yes, the other guy is the Guardian. Tim, why don't you see if you can find out anything about the Guardian, anything that might give us a clue as to why he hasn't been reborn yet? Maya and I will see what we can find out about Greg."

Sara opened her laptop, and Maya scooted her chair around to sit alongside her, while Tim went to work searching for traces of Sam using his phone.

Sara and Maya started by Googling Greg's name. As expected, Gregory Hastings was a common enough name that they received hundreds of thousands of search results, none of which looked promising. Next, they tried searching for his name with San Francisco appended to the end. That yielded fewer results, but still no solid leads to the actual man they were hoping to track down. After clicking about a dozen links that led nowhere, Sara glanced at Tim over the top of her laptop screen. Her trained eye read his seemingly neutral expression as one of equal measures of concentration and frustration. Tiny creases formed at the corners of his mouth. His lower eyelids squinted upward, giving his eyes an entirely different shape. He was focused, but finding nothing useful.

"Here, let me drive for a second," Maya said, sliding Sara's laptop in her direction. Sara observed as her sister punched in a search for news articles containing the name Gregory Hastings, the word death, and the date of Ananda's death. She didn't need to ask Sara for a reminder of the date. The information was clearly as ingrained in Maya's mind as it was in Sara's. The details of Ananda's life and death were becoming a part of them all.

The first result was an article about a man named Gregory Hoffman who was murdered in Dallas on the same date, but in a different year. The second article was about a woman, Jessica Hastings, whose dog had been killed by a neighbor as the result of an argument over a shared parking space. It was looking like another dead end.

Sara glanced at Tim again. His brow was furrowed in disappointment. He gave a small shake of his head, not finding what he was looking for. She hoped he would find something useful for Ananda's sake and for the souls trapped in Catharta, but mostly, she just felt appreciation that he wanted this so badly. He wanted to get to the bottom of this as much as she did.

Sara was distracted from her silent observation of her friend by Maya's sudden declaration of success. "Oh my god, I think this is him!"

Sara turned her attention back to the screen, and Tim jumped up from his chair, coming to stand behind them and see what Maya had found. It was a report from a local news broadcasting station's website. It was dated November 4, 2014, two days after Ananda had died. The video was accompanied by the caption "Tenderloin Teen Killed, Domestic Abuse Suspected."

"Television news?" Sara asked with distaste.

Tim gave her a little poke in the back. "Don't be such a media snob. There is a whole world of journalism outside the printed newspaper."

Sara shrugged him away, stubbornly holding on to her bias against this particular medium. The three of them fell into a concentrated hush as Maya clicked play on the video.

It opened with a shot of two newscasters, a man and a woman, seated behind the news desk looking groomed and polished. The female newscaster began the story.

"Police were called to an apartment building on the two-hundred block of Turk Street in the Tenderloin district early Sunday morning to investigate the death of a seventeen-year-old girl. The teen had allegedly been beaten to death."

The practiced look on the woman's face depicted the sorrow and gravity the viewers expected with this type of story. A box appeared in the upper right corner of the screen depicting an unflattering picture of a man who was presumably Ananda's stepfather. It appeared to be a mug shot. His graying hair was shaggy and hung across his forehead at awkward angles. His blotchy skin and bulbous red nose hinted at alcoholism. But what struck Sara most were his eyes. They were a strange shade of gray with no depth, not even a hint of color. They gave him a villainous look. But mostly they just looked empty, hollow, dead. If the eyes truly were the windows to the soul, Sara felt convinced this man's window was vacant.

The newscaster went on, "The victim's stepfather, Gregory Hastings, is a person of interest in the investigation. Emergency dispatchers received a call just before 7:00 a.m. from the victim's mother requesting medical attention for her daughter. When first responders arrived, they pronounced the teenager dead at the scene. Our field reporter Deborah Lewis is at the scene with more. Deborah?"

Greg's mug shot disappeared, and the scene shifted to a split screen between the newscaster at the station and the field reporter standing in front of an apartment building. It was after-dark, but the harsh lights from the camera illuminated Deborah and the gray stone face of the building behind her. There was an awkward pause while the field reporter waited to hear her cue in her earpiece, one of Sara's biggest annoyances with televised news. Then she began, and the split screen disappeared, focusing solely on the reporter in front of the apartment.

"Well, Catherine, I'm here at the Turk Street apartment where the young victim was found dead just two days ago. As you can see, there are still remnants of crime scene tape behind me." She stepped aside momentarily to allow the cameraman to get a shot of a fragment of yellow and black tape clinging stubbornly to the hinge of the building's front door. "The building has been reopened to residents, but the apartment where the incident occurred has been vacant since the police pronounced it a crime scene Sunday morning. The victim's mother, who is staying with friends while the investigation continues, has no plans to return to the apartment even after it is cleared. That grieving mother was understandably too distraught to speak with us, but I was able to speak with the victim's sister regarding the incident."

The scene cut to a prerecorded interview in a small, cozy-looking room, which was probably no more than a stage set. If the cameras were to pan out, the shot would likely reveal dusty concrete floors and high ceilings with exposed duct work just outside of the framework of comfortable arm chairs and a tastefully chosen houseplant in the background. The field reporter was seated in the right-hand chair. The young woman, who was apparently Ananda's sister, was on the left.

The sisters didn't look much alike. Where Ananda's face was long and oval, punctuated by sharp cheekbones and a delicately tapered chin, her sister's was round, without a point in sight. There was no hint of Ananda's almond-shaped eyes in her sister's gaze, although, to be fair, it was clear her sister had been crying, probably for the previous two days. Her eyes were red and puffy. This video segment was not likely to be a good representation of what she normally looked like. Her clothes were rumpled; her hair was unkempt. She had barely pulled herself together enough to make it to this interview.

The girl's name appeared on the screen below her face: Mariel Reyes. The interview began with Mariel speaking. Whatever question the field reporter had asked went unheard.

Mariel was clearly holding back tears as she said, "My mom called me before she even called the police. She was so scared. She didn't know what to do. At first, I couldn't tell what was wrong because she was so hysterical. When I realized it was something about my baby sister, I told her to hang up and call the police. I rushed over there, but the whole place was already on lockdown when I arrived." She produced a tissue from somewhere and wiped her eyes.

The field reporter, Deborah, asked her, "You don't live at the apartment with your mother?"

Mariel shook her head. "I moved out two years ago, as soon as I finished high school. I knew then that it wasn't safe."

"But your sister, she was still in school?" Deborah prodded.

Mariel sniffled, "She had one more year. I knew it would be a hard year for her, but I never thought…," her voice trailed off as she tried in vain to stifle her tears.

Deborah gave her a respectful amount of time to compose herself and then asked, "Would you mind sharing with our audience why you agreed to speak with us?"

Mariel turned to look directly into the lens of the camera. "Because I want people to learn from my mistake. If you don't feel safe in your own home, do something about it. Get out and take everyone you love with you. Call the police. Seek help. Do something. Whatever you do, don't be complacent about it. Don't assume it will get better with time. Don't wait for the problem to fix itself. No one has the right to hurt you. Get out while you can. Don't let what happened to my sister happen to you or to anyone you care about." Her voice was breaking, but the fierceness of her gaze held strong.

The prerecorded version of Deborah thanked Mariel for her time and then the scene cut back to Deborah standing on the sidewalk in front of Ananda's building. "As you can see, that was a very emotional moment for the sister of the young victim. The girl's stepfather is the only suspect at this time, and Mr. Hastings is currently in police custody. Back to you, Catherine and Bill."

The video cut back to the two newscasters in the studio. Bill thanked her for her report and then seemed about to move onto the next segment when the video ended, leaving him stranded in an awkward freeze-frame, mouth agape, one eye half-closed.

Sara, Maya, and Tim were equally frozen for a moment, trying to absorb all they had just seen and pointlessly hoping for more information from the concluded news story.

Sara spoke first, "They never even mentioned her name." She stood and backed away from the table, wanting to somehow distance herself from everything she had just witnessed. She felt heartbroken for Ananda on a whole new level. Her death had made the news, but they never named her. They didn't show her face. The world never got to know who she was.

Tim consoled her, "A lot of times, they don't give the identity when the victim is a minor."

Sara agreed, "That's true. And it explains why she didn't come up in any of my news searches before. I was searching for her by name. What I needed was the name of her murderer."

"Speaking of which," Maya interjected. "We still don't know what happened to him. All this tells us is that he was in police custody three years ago. How are we going to find out where he ended up or if he's still alive now?"

Sara thought for a moment. "Well, we know the cops took him in. I'm sure they pressed charges. There must have been a trial."

"The Superior Court of San Francisco has a website," Tim offered, following Sara's train of thought. "They show the verdicts of all the cases they hear."

"I'm on it!" announced Maya, focusing back on Sara's computer.

Sara turned to Tim. "Did you find anything on our Guardian?"

Tim's brow furrowed slightly, and he shook his head. "Nothing useful. I found eleven Facebook profiles that have the same name, but most of them don't have profile pictures, and they're all private anyway. He didn't come up in any news searches either."

Sara was disappointed, but unsurprised. "I feel like I need a better idea of who he was in life if I'm going to be able to stop him in death."

"There might be more information on his death certificate," Tim offered. "Maybe his next of kin?"

Sara looked at him with anxiety in her eyes. "So I guess I'm going back to the records office tomorrow." She did not relish the idea of facing that surly clerk again. At least, this time she would know what to ask for.

Tim's mouth curled up in a one-sided smile, revealing a hint of a dimple. "We are going back to the records office tomorrow."

Sara's heart warmed a little at his offer to accompany her. Again, she was reminded that she truly was not in this alone. "Okay," she agreed. "But let's go before work so we're not subject to Jeff's decree of whether or not we can leave."

"Yes," Tim seconded. "Benevolent ruler Jeff can giveth, and he can taketh away."

"To be fair"—Sara conceded—"he had every right to question why a little peon like me would need to go on an excursion like that."

"Sara, you know you could graduate from peon any time you wanted if you would just write something and submit it to him. You're wasting your potential fixing other people's run-on sentences." His tone was teasing and pleading at the same time.

Sara was in no mood for one of his lectures. "Yeah, thanks Dad. I'll get right on that." She was aiming for sarcasm, but her voice betrayed the real pain she felt at his apparent disappointment in her.

Maya interrupted what could have turned into an argument by announcing, "The People versus Gregory J. Hastings."

Sara and Tim turned their attention back to Maya and her findings. What she had found was the verdict from the trial.

Sara displayed some of her sister's usual impatience as she waited for her to read what the verdict had been. "Well, what does it say? Was he convicted?"

Maya's eyes scanned the small print on the document before her. As she found what she was looking for she began to read aloud. "The Supreme Court of California finds the defendant Gregory J. Hastings guilty of murder in the first degree with two additional aggravating factors: a history of domestic violence and the victim being a minor."

Maya turned to face Tim and Sara. For a moment, the three of them stared at one another in silence.

Then, Tim spoke, "So he was convicted. Where is he now?"

"In prison, I would assume," Maya replied, turning back toward the screen and scanning for any additional information. "This document is from the date of the verdict. Doesn't sentencing usually happen later?"

"I think there's usually a separate date for a sentencing hearing," Sara said, surprising herself with how little she knew about the justice system. She supposed it's not something the average person spends much time worrying about since they never plan on committing such a heinous crime.

"Here," Maya declared, finding a link near the bottom of the page. "Sentencing Hearing for Gregory J. Hastings. It's dated about a month after the verdict."

Tim and Sara leaned in closer, trying to read over her shoulder. The document was filled with a whole lot of legalese that was little more than gibberish to Sara. Why was everything related to government agencies so painfully slow and complicated?

Before either of the two onlookers could spot anything useful among the legal drivel, Maya found what she was searching for. She turned once more to face her audience, eyes wide, face frozen.

"He was sentenced to death."

Silence hung in the air once more as they all tried to take in what this might mean. In Sara's mind, she pictured Greg on an executioner's table with a needle in his arm, about to receive a lethal injection. She pictured the man materializing in Catharta and hunting down Ananda, wanting to punish her for the consequences he had suffered. She pictured Ananda, having to face her attacker, knowing she would be trapped with the most sinister man she had ever known for the rest of eternity. Sara's stomach turned over, and she felt her knees begin to buckle.

As she took a seat to keep from falling over, Tim asked, "But that doesn't mean he's dead, right? I mean, California hasn't actually executed a prisoner in years, right?"

Both girls stared back at him with blank looks. Maya gave a hopeless shrug and shook her head. At least, Sara wasn't alone in her ignorance of the workings of the justice system.

Tim punched some information into his phone and, with a mild look of relief, confirmed, "The last prisoner put to death in California was in 2006, almost a decade before this guy was convicted."

"So he's alive," Maya stated, wanting it to be a fact.

"Do we know that?" Sara asked. "I mean, people die in prison all the time. How do we know he's still on death row?" Tension filled the room as Sara was swarmed by feelings of failure. She knew she hadn't actually done anything yet, hadn't actually proven or disproven anything. Yet somehow, she felt she had let Ananda down. There was only one thing that girl needed protection from, and Sara suddenly believed she had failed to provide her with that protection. She could feel herself spiraling down into a dark well of self-doubt.

Maya pulled her out of her downward spiral when, with a decisive look on her face, she stated, "I know one way we could find out. Who is up for a field trip?" Sara and Tim exchanged a confused look.

"A field trip to where exactly?" Tim asked.

Maya rose to her feet and smiled, brimming with all the self-confidence that had fully escaped Sara. Then, she announced, "We're going to San Quentin."

CHAPTER 9

"What do you think of the name Quentin?" Maya asked from the backseat of Tim's station wagon as they barreled down the highway toward the prison that had inspired this thought.

"You cannot be serious," Sara responded without turning around from her spot in the passenger seat. "Maya, do you really want to name your son after a state prison?"

"Hey," Tim interjected on Maya's behalf. "It could be a cute girl's name too."

Sara shot him a side-eyed glance and said, "Not helping."

"I wouldn't necessarily be naming my baby after the prison. I was thinking more like Quentin Tarantino," Maya said thoughtfully.

"What a great role model for a young child," Sara quipped with heavy sarcasm. "Baby's first movie can be Reservoir Dogs."

Without turning around, Sara could tell her sister had crossed her arms in a defensive pose and was pouting. "You hate all my baby name ideas."

"You're free to name your kid whatever you want," Sara replied. "But you asked for my opinion, so I gave it to you."

Maya leaned forward to place her face nearly on Sara's shoulder, less pouty now. "Why don't you suggest a name then? If this were your baby, what would you name it?"

Sara threw her hands up in surrender. "Oh no, I'm not playing that game. I'll suggest a name, and you'll latch onto it, and when the kid is a couple years old, you'll decide you don't like it, and you'll blame me for all eternity. No suggestions from me." Then she thought for a moment, "Although I would suggest not Greg," she added, contemplating the murderer they were hoping to visit when they arrived at their destination.

The occupants of the car fell into silence as they all reflected on the purpose of their journey. They weren't just out for a Sunday drive. They were essentially doing a welfare check on a death row inmate. Sara wanted desperately to be able to return to Ananda and tell her that her murderer was alive and locked away where he couldn't hurt anyone else. She wanted to tell her friend that she need not worry about his soul joining hers in the afterlife in which she was trapped. But the fact of the matter was, no matter what they found when they reached their destination, Greg wouldn't stay alive forever. Even if they arrived at the prison today and found him alive and well, that didn't mean he would live indefinitely. He could be killed in a prison riot or die of some undetected illness. He could commit suicide or die of a drug overdose, which Sara understood was a bigger problem than you might think within the prison system. The state could start actually putting prisoners to death again. His life could be taken at any time. As long as Ananda remained trapped in Catharta, she would have valid reason to fear seeing her killer again, that is, provided he actually had a soul.

If they were to arrive at the prison and find Greg to be still among the living, all that meant was that they needed to focus on stopping the Guardian, Sam. Sam needed to be stopped so that Ananda could be reborn. That was the only way she would ever be truly free of her fear. That task, however, seemed impossible at the moment. Tim had been unable to find anything on Sam Johnson that might help them figure out who he was or how he could be stopped. Sara would need to check the records office the next day, and if that didn't help, she may need to return to Ananda to see if she had any other information on him.

She decided to focus on the more achievable goal of tracking down Greg Hastings, which in itself didn't seem entirely likely.

"Remind me why we believe this guy is at San Quentin?" Sara asked, looking for reassurance that they were on the right path.

"Because that's where California's death row is," Maya said, reciting from the Wikipedia page she had found on the subject.

"With the exception of thirty-two inmates who are in special medical facilities, the other seven-hundred-something male inmates with death sentences are at San Quentin. The odds are in our favor that he'll be there."

"And then what?" asked Tim. Both girls looked at him for further explanation. "What do we do if we find out he's there?"

Maya answered matter-of-factly, "We ask to talk to him. Today is Sunday. It's a visitation day."

Sara felt her stomach turn over. "Do we have to? If he's there and he's alive, isn't that enough? I can go back and tell Ananda that he's alive, and she doesn't have to worry about running into him in Catharta." Even as she said the words, she knew the reason she couldn't do that. If she was doing a welfare check on this man, she had to make sure he was more than just alive. She had to gain some sort of assurance she could expect him to remain in the world of the living for the foreseeable future. There would always be uncertainty in life and death, but she had to at least see the state this man was in.

"This is what Ananda asked of you," Maya reminded her. "The least you can do is talk to him."

Sara knew her sister was right. "If you're practicing your mom guilt, it's working." Still apprehensive about the task at hand, she asked, "How do we get in to see him? I mean, do they let total strangers visit an inmate? Are we supposed to know him somehow? Do we need a valid reason to see him? Couldn't he refuse to see us?"

Tim had a suggestion. "What if you tell them we're from *The Daily*, and we want to do a piece on his story? If he's the sociopath we think he is, he probably couldn't resist that kind of attention."

Maya shook her head. "No, I think we should just be honest. We'll tell them we're friends of the family. We don't have to tell them the family member we're friends with is the stepdaughter he killed."

Sara felt more comfortable with Maya's honest approach, but she was still nervous. "What will we say to him if we do get to see him? Where do we even begin?"

Maya, always prepared with an answer for everything, replied, "Why not be honest with him too? Tell him about Ananda's soul. Tell him about Catharta. Who cares if he thinks we're crazy. We're not here to impress this guy."

Sara bit her bottom lip. She was uncomfortable with the idea of talking about Catharta outside of the confines of her little brain trust. She certainly didn't feel Greg was owed any kind of information about Ananda. But Maya had a point. It really didn't matter what this prisoner thought of them. If all went well, they would meet with him briefly and then never have to see him again.

Tim, sensing her apprehension, said, "Why don't we take it one thing at a time. Let's see if he's there first and if we can get in to see him. We'll worry about what to say to him when the time comes."

The car slowed to a stop as they approached the gates of San Quentin. Located about twenty miles north of the city and situated at the tip of a point overlooking the San Francisco Bay, the prison sat on a sprawling piece of land that would have been worth millions if not billions to a real estate developer. Residents would have paid top dollar to have an apartment with the view afforded by this property. Yet the actual occupants, the inmates, would probably rather be absolutely anywhere else. Sara felt confident that the beauty of the view was lost on them. With the uneasiness she was currently feeling, it was lost on her as well.

The gates were open with no guard out front. The sign indicated the direction to turn for visitor parking. Tim hesitated to make the turn. His grip on the steering wheel tightened.

"Are we sure we're ready for this?" he asked his passengers.

"Yes!" Maya exclaimed, always excited, rarely patient. "What else did we come out here for?"

Despite Maya's eagerness, Tim's foot held fast on the brake pedal. He looked at Sara. "Are you ready?"

Sara stared at the open gate while fiddling nervously with the drawstring of her sweatshirt. She was asking herself the same question. Was she ready to face the convicted murderer of one of her friends? Could she look this incarcerated man in the face, knowing full well he had taken the life of an innocent teenager? The thought made her feel ill, but then she thought of Ananda. She thought of the kind eyes and innocent face in her obituary photo. She thought of the fierceness with which Ananda had protected her against the Guardian, the soul of the man who had trapped her in purgatory. She thought of the fear in Ananda's trembling voice when she had told Sara how afraid she was of meeting her stepfather again in Catharta. She thought of the lost soul of her friend, and she made up her mind.

"I'm ready. Let's do this." Her voice was barely above a whisper, but there was resolve behind it. She was ready to meet this man.

Tim pulled through the gates and found a parking spot easily. Considering the number of prisoners housed here and the fact that today was a visitation day, there were surprisingly few cars in the visitor lot. Sara wondered how many inmates got visits on a regular basis. She thought family members of the imprisoned ought to feel some sort of obligation to come visit their incarcerated kin. These people had no other contact with the outside world. The lives of those they loved went on without them. It seemed the least they could do was come for a visit. Then Sara realized she was relating this experience to that of visiting a sick family member in the hospital or a beloved grandparent in a nursing home. Those were people who were stuck in isolation through no fault of their own. The residents of San Quentin had earned their imprisonment through heinous deeds. Their loneliness and solitude were well deserved. Also, since this site served as the only death row for the entire state, it probably wasn't geographically convenient for many visitors. It had only taken the three of them about forty minutes to drive here, but for family members outside of the Bay Area, even as far south as San Diego, it could mean an overnight trip. Sara was reminded of her own trips to visit her mother at a hospital in Los Angeles when the local doctors had been unable to stop her cancer from consuming her. She wished she could have been there every day, but the distance and the fact that she was still in school made it impossible. She had to settle for visiting one weekend per month and frequent phone calls. But, again, her mother's isolation occurred through no fault of her own. If Gregory Hastings were a relative of hers and she knew exactly what he had done to land himself in his current situation, would she feel any obligation to visit him? Probably not.

The trio stepped out of the station wagon in silence and followed the signs that directed them toward the visitor entrance. There, they were met with a metal detector and a pair of very efficient guards who searched them to make sure none of them were carrying any contraband. They were then ushered to a row of lockers where they were instructed to deposit everything they had on them with the exception of their identification. They would not be allowed to bring any personal items into the visitation room.

Once they had been stripped of their belongings, they approached the check-in counter where a friendly, but bored correctional officer was waiting for them. She had her hair pulled back in a tight bun and was sitting at her station with her back as straight as a soldier.

She perked up a little at the sight of them, probably grateful to have something to do on what was apparently a pretty uneventful day. With a vague smile and sleepy eyes she asked, "What's the name of the inmate you wish to visit?"

Sara, who had been wrapped up in the strangeness of the place and the procedures, was caught off guard. She hadn't realized how confining it would feel being inside a prison, if only a few steps inside the front doors. She hesitated before stuttering, "Greg. Gregory. Gregory J. Hastings." Tim and Maya, hanging back slightly, seemed equally uncomfortable with the sudden shift in their surroundings. They were brought back to attention by Sara's quavering voice.

"Inmate number?" the officer asked.

Sara's heart sunk. She didn't know his inmate number. Was she supposed to have that information? Would she be barred from seeing him without it? She opened her mouth, but no sound came out.

Tim volunteered, "We don't have his inmate number. Is there some other way to look him up?"

"No problem," the guard said, turning her attention to the ancient-looking computer in front of her. While she clicked away at her keyboard, Sara exchanged a worried glance with Tim and Maya. Somehow, it felt like they were doing something criminal, like they were trying to get away with something.

"Okay," the guard said, bringing their attention back to her. "What is the name of the visitor?"

The phrasing of the question struck Sara as strange. "Do you mean my name?"

The officer glanced at the three of them in turn. "I need the names of anyone who wishes to visit the inmate."

Maya was probably the least intimidated by this unfamiliar process. She interjected with a question. "Are we all allowed to visit?"

The guard was patient, but, realizing this group of visitors had no idea what they were doing, spoke to them like they were children. "Yes, as long as you're all on the visitor list, you can all see him, but only one person at a time can visit."

Sara felt the blood drain out of her face. She must have looked like a ghost. There was a visitor list. Of course, there was a visitor list. This was a fruitless trip. They wouldn't be able to see Greg. They probably wouldn't even be able to confirm if this was where he was being held or if he was still alive. She would have to return to Catharta and tell Ananda she had failed in the one task she had been given. She felt her heart sink into the pit of her stomach.

"Great!" Maya exclaimed as Sara was losing all hope. "So how do we get on the visitor list?" It was such a simple question, and Sara wasn't sure why she hadn't thought of it herself. The officer pulled some forms from somewhere beneath her desk. Handing them to Maya, she explained, "You fill out this form, and I scan your ID. Once I get you entered in the system, you can see the inmate."

"Thank you so much," Maya said, accepting the forms and flashing the guard a dimpled smile. She grabbed Sara and spun her around, escorting her to some chairs against the opposite wall.

Taking a seat, Sara felt nauseated. A moment before, she was sure she had failed in her mission. Now, it seemed like everything may work out thanks to a very simple question from her sister. Sara didn't know why she was so quick to doubt herself. Why did she give up so easily? In the back of her mind, she realized a small part of her had been relieved to think she had been unsuccessful because it meant she wouldn't have to face the murderer she had come to see. Maybe she was so quick to accept failure because it meant she could stop trying. It was easier to give up. The more effort she put into something, the worse it would feel when she didn't succeed. Why couldn't she recognize the fact that failure wasn't the only option? She had to be more confident in herself. She had to keep pushing forward instead of crumbling at the first sign of an obstacle, no matter how daunting that obstacle may be. She recognized that some of her current queasiness was due to the idea of looking Greg in the eye.

"Alright, we really only need to fill out the form for you," Maya said to Sara.

"Yeah," Tim agreed. "I don't see any reason we need to talk to him too." He indicated himself and Maya.

Sara's brain wasn't working quickly enough to comprehend what they both seemed to have grasped immediately. All she knew was it sounded like they wanted her to go on alone. "What? What do you mean?"

Maya met Sara's panicked eyes in surprise. "Well, she said we can only visit him one at a time. If you're able to visit him, then there's not really any reason for Tim and I to talk to him too."

Tim added, "Plus, we don't even know if he'll agree to see you. I'd say it's even less likely he'd agree to meet with a parade of strangers. Our best bet is for you to talk to him."

"But why me?" Sara asked. Her fuzzy mind was catching up. She knew why it had to be her, but the question had already escaped her mouth.

"Because"—Maya responded, patiently, but slightly patronizingly—"Ananda asked you to do this. You know her. You have to report back to her. It has to be you."

Sara nodded her silent agreement while swallowing the lump in her throat. Maya took a seat next to her sister and went to work filling in the form on her behalf. Tim, sensing Sara's anxiety, took a seat on the other side of her and put an arm around her shoulders.

"Listen, Champ," he began in his best pep talk voice. He was staring at her down his nose, and his jaw jutted out ever so slightly, giving him a look something like a drill sergeant. He was trying to hide his sincere words of encouragement behind humor to make her more comfortable. She wasn't in a joking mood, but the attempt was thoughtful. "You're going to go in there and face this guy. You're going to stand up to him, call him names, ask him questions, whatever you feel is right. You're going to remember that he's incarcerated and you are free. You're in charge here. You're going to remember that no matter what kind of awful things he's done, he is just a man. You are better than him. You are stronger than him. You are in control. Understood?"

He sounded like a football coach giving a halftime speech in the locker room. It actually did make her smile a tiny bit, and she felt marginally more relaxed, although her confidence still seemed to be lacking. His mouth puckered a little in a half smirk. He was clearly satisfied with himself.

"Understood," Sara replied.

"Okay, I think that's it," Maya announced, looking over the form.

The three of them approached the security desk again and handed over the form and Sara's ID. The corrections officer typed all the information into her archaic computer and then finally said, "Okay, Miss Jenkins, you're on the inmate's visitor list. Please have a seat, and you'll be called when he's ready to see you." With that, they were left to wait.

The three of them sat in awkward silence. Sara wanted to ask her cohorts what would come next. She didn't know what to say to Greg when she saw him. But given that they were the only people in the waiting area, the guard would be unable to help overhearing them. There was no easy way to discuss Catharta without coming off sounding like a lunatic. Sara was already surprised that her sister and her best friend believed her and hadn't shipped her off to the loony bin. She didn't want to come off sounding like a crazy person in front of a stranger and risk getting locked up herself. Plus, anything she might ask about Greg would make it sound like she had no legitimate reason to see him. She didn't want to draw any more attention to the fact that this man was a complete stranger to her. So, she sat in silence, stewing over what she might say to her friend's killer and taking a little guilt-inducing solace in the fact that he may still refuse to see her.

Just as the thought crossed her mind, a large, intimidating corrections officer with a deep and booming voice burst forth from a door down the hall a few paces. "Sara Jenkins, you're inmate is ready for you," he bellowed with the practiced tone and rhythm of a man who made this statement several times a day.

Sara stood abruptly, and Maya and Tim did as well. She turned and gave them a tentative glance. The anxiety must have been written all over her face.

"It will be fine," Maya reassured her. "Just do what we came here to do, and then we can all go home."

Tim's nearly blank stare held the faintest hint of a smile, and there was something hard to define in his eyes. Playfulness? Or maybe confidence? Sara could use a little of that right about now. "You got this," he told her calmly.

Sara nodded and tried to appear stronger than she felt. She faced the awaiting officer and followed him back through the doorway through which he had come. As she heard the door click shut behind her, she felt more alone than she ever could have imagined.

She was led through a series of locked doors until they finally arrived in a cramped room, the sight of which sent all the oxygen rushing out of her lungs. She wasn't sure what she had expected. Maybe she had been picturing an interrogation room like in one of the police dramas on TV with a table in the center where she would sit across from the prisoner with a wall of two-way mirrors behind her. Or maybe she had pictured something more like in prison movies with a row of desks running down a long narrow room with impenetrable glass separating the inmates from the visitors. The only method of communication is a phone receiver you needed to use to make contact. But that was not what awaited her.

The room she entered was filled with cages. There was no other way to describe them. They were boxes of steel bars only slightly larger than a phone booth with a small metal bench within each one. There were ten of them lined up against the far wall and a small standing-height desk next to the door they had just passed through. To the left was a red sign with black lettering that read in all caps, DO THE NEXT RIGHT THING. Sara guessed that was San Quentin's version of a motivational poster. She swallowed hard as she glanced around the room, trying to take it all in and adjust to her surroundings. All the cages were empty except for one, and there was a metal folding chair propped up facing it. Within the bars of that tiny cell was the man she recognized as Gregory J. Hastings. Ananda's killer sat before her, his empty gray eyes boring into her soul. Cold sweat prickled the palms of her hands and her mouth went dry.

He looked considerably older than he had in the mug shot photo she had seen on the news report. Three years had passed since that time, but even so, it was evident that prison had aged him rapidly. His once unkempt hair was shaved down to a short buzz cut, but she could tell it was much grayer than it had been. His skin looked sallow and waxy. His eyes were sunken into his skull and were framed in a spider web of age lines. She couldn't see much of his body under his prison jumpsuit, but the sagging skin around his jowls and neck indicated a loss in weight. He looked like he was wasting away.

He sat motionless, waiting for Sara to make the first move. The guard, who had taken his place behind the standing desk, clearly positioned to enable him to oversee this meeting, cleared his throat. "Miss," he muttered, causing Sara to nearly jump out of her skin. "You can have a seat if you like." He gestured toward the folding chair.

Sara tried to regain a normal heart rate and nodded, slowly approaching her seat. As she lowered herself onto the chair, Greg never took his eyes off of her. She couldn't imagine what he must be thinking, who he guessed she was or what she might be doing here. She took some small satisfaction in knowing she had disrupted his day, thrown him off-balance. A part of her wanted to explain nothing about herself, to leave him wondering for the rest of his life what this visit had been about. But she knew she would likely have to reveal something to get the information she needed.

They sat across from one another, caught up in a staring contest, each testing the other to see who would blink first, neither wanting to break the silence. The tension built, and Greg revealed nothing to her. She thought he would ask her name or why she'd come to see him. The curiosity must be getting to him, but his poker face was too good.

Finally, feeling she was wasting time, Sara spoke first. "You're Greg Hastings?" She immediately regretted the words. It felt like she had given up some control by speaking first. She had shifted the power to him.

At last he moved. A menacing grin rose on his lips. "You already know the answer to that question, don't you, sweetheart? The question is who are you?" His voice seemed too high pitched for the size of him. It didn't fit, and she found it unsettling. His tone was like acid, and the way he said the word "sweetheart" made her want to go home and take a shower.

Sara took a steadying breath before responding, determined not to let him have all the power. "I'm Ananda's friend," she replied and waited for a reaction. He gave her nothing, not even a hint of recognition. She added, "You know, the innocent girl you murdered in cold blood." She felt proud of the calmness with which she'd gotten the words out. If she was going to play his game, she was going to play it well.

He stared at her blankly for a few seconds and then let out a harsh laugh. It was one loud, "Ha!" followed by silence and more staring.

Sara refused to ask him what was so funny, but eventually, Greg volunteered, "Sorry, I thought I heard you say that little whore was innocent."

Sara felt her blood boil. She was sure her cheeks had turned bright red in anger, but she wasn't going to give him any other indication he'd gotten a rise out of her. She reminded herself of Maya's advice to be honest and of Tim's pep talk. She had to stay focused to get the information she sought. She needed to steer the conversation back to him, to his well-being.

"So you feel justified in your actions? You feel you should be a free man?" If he had some delusion he might get out of prison someday, that at least meant he wasn't a likely suicide risk.

Greg sat back against the bars behind him, clearly enjoying this exchange. "She had it coming if that's what you mean." He must have suspected she was after some sort of information, and he was determined not to give it to her. He was on guard, but he wanted to toy with her. He glanced up thoughtfully and continued, "In fact, I'm sure I would be a free man right now if the judge had been a man. But she was a woman, a mother. She was soft. She bought into that same innocent girl sob story you seem to have swallowed too." His eyes narrowed, and he leaned toward her. "If that judge had been a man, if he'd been a father like me, I would have walked. He would have related. That little skank deserved what she got."

"You were not her father." Sara was having trouble pretending to be calm and rational.

"I was the closest she had. Her daddy was dead. I kept a roof over her head and clothes on her back. I kept her family from getting deported. And how did she repay me? That ungrateful bitch went whoring herself around behind my back. Any father with half a brain in his head would have done what I did. She got what she deserved." He was studying Sara closely, looking for a reaction.

Sara was losing her patience. She reminded herself of her goals. She needed to know if there was any risk of him dying imminently and whether or not he had a soul. It was hard to say how much of what he said was how he truly felt and how much was lies he spit out to try to upset her. But either way, it seemed clear he had zero remorse for killing Ananda. She felt certain that the body of the man before her contained no soul. She decided a sudden change of topic might throw him off his feet.

"As far as I can see, the only one who got what they deserved is you." She indicated the steel cage surrounding him. "How is your health, Mr. Hastings?"

Her nonsequitur seemed to have the desired effect. His brow furrowed, and he seemed unsure of how to react. "My health?" he asked, stalling. "What's it to you?"

"It seems to me that illness could take hold quickly in such close quarters. I'm just curious if this fine facility is looking after you." He probably assumed Sara wished ill health upon him, although that couldn't be further from the truth.

"This fine facility"—he said, adding a mocking emphasis when he repeated her words—"is looking after me just fine. Don't you worry, sweetheart. They want to keep me alive right up until the day they kill me."

He seemed satisfied he had given her the answer she didn't want. She gave him no reaction either way. "What about family history? Are there any hereditary diseases in your bloodline?"

He gave her a quizzical look. He had been in control of the game they were playing, but now, he wasn't sure of the rules anymore. He couldn't figure out her angle. It was agitating him. He tried to regain the balance of power.

"How is it you said you knew that little bitch?"

"Ananda is my friend," Sara answered in a calm, even tone.

A sneer appeared on Greg's face. "I think you mean she was your friend. Past tense. In case you forgot, the girl is dead."

Sara gave him the sweetest smile she could manage. "No, I mean I am her friend. Present tense. She has moved on to a better place, and she's doing just fine there," Sara replied confidently, only slightly bending the truth of Ananda's current circumstances. "And that better place is somewhere I'm sure you will never go once they finally send that lethal injection coursing through your veins." She was sure she must sound a little nutty to him. Maybe he thought she was crazy or fancied herself a psychic medium. But she reminded herself of Maya's words. It didn't matter what this man thought of her. She went on, "The reason you will never go there and you will never see her again is because the place Ananda went is for people with souls. And you, Mr. Hastings, don't have one."

Sara rose suddenly to her feet. She was ready to storm out and as far away from Greg as she could get, but she realized the door she'd come through would likely be locked. She turned and walked toward the officer so he could escort her out. She prayed Greg wouldn't say anything. She felt she deserved the last word in this exchange. The officer pulled a set of keys from his belt and approached the door. Only when Sara heard the key click and the lock disengage, did she chance one last look at the prisoner in his cage.

Greg was left looking confused and a little angry. As the guard swung the door open, Sara decided to give him some parting words. "Have a nice life, Mr. Hastings. I'll be sure to let Ananda know you're doing just fine."

His mouth dropped open to shoot back with some reply, but he wasn't quick enough. The door clicked shut behind Sara, and she smiled to herself as she followed the officer back the way they had come.

In the waiting area, Tim and Maya sprang to their feet as soon as Sara came into view.

Maya rushed toward her, questions flowing out of her like a faucet. "Was it him? Did you talk to him? What did he say? Is his health good? Does Ananda have anything to worry about?"

Conscious of the prison employees within earshot, Sara kept her voice low and tried to reign in Maya's anxiety. "I got the information she asked me to get. Let's just go home." They had a long drive ahead of them. She would be able to fill them in on the way.

Sara was anxious to put as much distance between herself and Ananda's murderer as possible. She felt she had learned all she needed to know about him, enough to satisfy Ananda's request. He wasn't sick or dying, and even if he did die while Ananda remained stuck in Catharta, she felt confident that he didn't have a soul anyway. She would count that obtained knowledge as a small win. Now, she was faced with the more daunting task of figuring out how to stop the Guardian. That would take all of her focus. As the three of them turned to collect their belongings and head back out of the building, Tim gave her a tiny, affectionate punch in the arm. The smile on his face was more than just a hint for once, and the look in his eye was most definitely pride.

"I told you that you could do this," he said.

A little self-confidence bloomed inside of Sara. She had done it. With the help of her sister and her best friend, she had done it.

CHAPTER 10

"Oh god, it's her again." Sara had stopped short just a few steps inside the records office and found herself faced with the same surly employee who had been there the week before. All the confidence she had gathered the day before seemed to vanish.

On the ride home from San Quentin, she had filled in Tim and Maya on her conversation with Greg Hastings. It had left a sick feeling in the pit of her stomach to relive her brief time with the convicted murderer. But it had also reminded her that she accomplished something that had seemed wholly unlikely when she started out. She had faced the challenge set before her head on, and she had accomplished what she meant to do. She could return to Ananda with the information she had asked for. With that task behind them, they had returned home, and Tim and Sara tried to find out more information on the Guardian, but had turned up nothing. Maya had opted to rest. She got tired very easily this late in her pregnancy, and the trip to the prison seemed to have taken a lot out of her. That fruitless search for Sam Johnson with Tim the day before was what had led Sara to the records office on this Monday morning.

Tim, who was standing barely a pace behind her, said encouragingly, "She won't bite." He placed a hand gently against the small of Sara's back and urged her forward.

Sara approached the front counter, and the clerk failed to acknowledge her presence yet again. She cleared her throat to get the woman's attention.

"How can I help you?" the clerk asked without looking away from her computer monitor, her talon-like nails clicking away.

Sara was at least armed with the right request this time. "I need a form to get an informational copy of a death certificate."

The clerk stopped typing and looked at Sara and Tim for the first time. She showed no sign of recognition. Either she didn't remember them or she just didn't care that they were repeat visitors. Given the empty state they had found the office in on both visits, Sara presumed it was the latter. The woman then stood reluctantly and disappeared into the mysterious back of the office where all the elusive forms seemed to be kept. She returned with a familiar-looking sheet of paper and instructed them, "Fill this out. Pens are on the table by the door." With that, she went back to whatever was so interesting on her computer monitor.

Having filled one of these forms out just a few days earlier, Sara was able to plug in the limited information it requested quickly and return it to the clerk's desk. The woman took the form from her and went to work typing and clicking away. After a minute or so, the clerk slid the paper back toward Sara and stated plainly, "No such record. Is there anything else I can help you with?" The tone of her voice implied she sincerely hoped there was nothing else she could help them with.

"What do you mean no such record?" Sara asked in disbelief. This was her last lead on tracking down Sam's history in the world of the living, and it was evaporating before her eyes.

"I mean"—the clerk said with a heavy sigh—"That there is no death certificate on record for this man."

"But how can that be? That doesn't make any sense." Sara was trying to piece together how this could be possible. Maybe she had spelled his name incorrectly. Maybe the clerk had keyed something in wrong. This had to be a mistake.

The clerk raised her eyebrows at Sara, clearly annoyed that this girl would question her authority. Then, in the most patronizing voice she could muster, the woman asked, "Are you sure this man is dead?"

It was Sara's turn to be annoyed. "Yes, I'm positive he's dead," she said, stopping just shy of adding that she had personally met his ghost. She tried her best to keep the snotty edge out of her voice, but it was impossible.

The clerk countered back with another question. "Are you sure he died in the county of San Francisco?"

"Yes, I'm sure." Sara was indignant.

Tim had his doubts. "Are you?"

Sara turned to face him, wounded by his lack of faith. "Yes, he died in the Sixteenth Street subway station. That's well within San Francisco city limits."

"That's where we think he died. That's according to what he told Ananda. Couldn't she have gotten it wrong? Or isn't it possible that he lied about it?" Tim gave a sideways glance toward the clerk who had sat back in her chair and crossed her arms. She was examining the pair of them as though they were clinically insane. Sara couldn't exactly blame her. Tim was talking about Sam posthumously explaining his own death.

"Why would he lie to her? They were friends at the time." Sara couldn't believe Tim wasn't backing her up on this. Here she had been ready to stand up to the intimidating records office employee, and then her teammate wasn't even supporting her.

Tim threw up his hands in a gesture of surrender. "I'm just saying, maybe we need more information."

Sara glared at him through squinted eyes, wavering between anger and sadness. Finally, she turned to the clerk and said, "Thank you for your help."

In an overly sugarcoated tone, the clerk replied, "My pleasure to be of service." She then returned to her computer screen as Sara headed for the door.

Tim raced after her, but didn't catch her until they were both outside. "Hey!" he called to get her to stop. "I'm just trying to help."

"Are you?" she questioned him. "Are you trying to help, or are you trying to poke holes in the tiny bit of information I've actually been able to put together? Are you trying to point out the impossibility of this job I've been tasked with? I never asked for this, you know." She felt betrayed. Tim had promised to help her, to support her through this journey she was on. He had to know how hard it was for her to find the confidence within herself to go through with this whole scheme. Why would he try to make her doubt herself? How could he feel that was helpful?

"I know you didn't." Tim was using a calm voice to try to soothe her, but it only made her more irritated with him. "Listen, let's just go to work. We'll figure out another lead on this guy. He's dead, not nonexistent. There has to be a record of him somewhere."

Sara pressed her eyes shut. She knew he was right, as annoying as that was to her at the moment. She would just have to keep digging. The stubborn side of her wanted to tell him she would make her own way to the office, but she realized that was really pointless since they were going to the exact same place, and his car was sitting just a few steps away. "Fine," she said. "Let's go to work."

They didn't speak the whole way to the office. Upon arriving, Sara bolted straight to her desk, not wanting to give Tim a chance to spend any more time telling her she was wrong. She got her work done in record time, meeting all her deadlines with room to spare. Her anger at Tim's lack of support and her determination to avoid thinking about Sam Johnson for the moment gave her the focus she had been lacking at work ever since stumbling upon Catharta.

Once all her work was done, however, she had no more distractions, and her mind turned back to the Guardian. She still had about an hour left in her shift. She might as well make good use of her time. She decided to search *The Daily* digital archives again using the new information she had about Sam: his name, his date of death, and his place of death, which she was still convinced was the Sixteenth Street subway station. She would not let Tim work his doubts into her head. It had taken a lot of time and effort to build up this much confidence, and she was hurt that he would attempt to take that away from her.

She checked obituaries. She even extended her search out a couple months after the day he died. Sometimes, it takes the grieving family a while to get something like that together. She found nothing. She searched the news, the crime reports, and even transit reports since it was an occurrence in the subway system. Nothing came up. This man was mugged, hit by a train, and then died. How had that not been reported in the news? Sara thought of her own experience the night she first visited Catharta. The same series of events had nearly happened to her. If she had been hit by the train that night, if that Good Samaritan hadn't been there to pull her out of harm's way, would her death have gone unnoticed? She wouldn't necessarily expect a front-page headline, but some mention would be nice. She felt a chill at the thought of all the deaths that go unreported every day. Countless souls slipped into the abyss, and the world went on without so much as a flinch. The thought was even more unsettling with the knowledge that these souls would stay stuck in purgatory forever unless she could do something to stop Sam and his mission to trap everyone in Catharta.

She physically shuddered at the thought just as Tim sidled up to her desk and asked, "Are you cold?"

She looked up and met his eyes. She couldn't read his expression. He must have known Sara was still irritated with him. He was trying to keep his face neutral until he figured out just how upset she actually was.

She thought about telling him her chill was from thoughts of Sam and the burden she carried of stopping him, but she figured he might take that openness as forgiveness and she wasn't quite ready to give him that yet. She thought about giving him some snarky retort, but he might see any sign of joking as permission to bury their earlier argument and she wasn't ready for that either. In the end, she just replied with a plain, flat, "No."

He looked down, conscious of the coldness of her response. To avoid looking her in the eye, he tried to get a look at her computer monitor. He recognized the archive search page. "Were you looking for the Guardian?" Sara nodded blankly.

"So was I. I tried different spellings of his name too. I tried Samuel in case that's what Sam is short for. I tried Jonson without the H. Nothing came up."

Sara glanced back at her own search results that had yielded nothing useful. "Same here," she agreed.

"It's weird," Tim said, more conversational now. "It's like this guy just silently disappeared. I don't see how something like that could happen, and he doesn't even get a mention."

Sara had, of course, had the same thought, but she didn't feel much like agreeing with him. Instead, she volunteered some of her own search techniques. "I even checked the transit reports since he died in the subway system." She knew she was baiting him, daring him to disagree with her again, but she couldn't stop herself.

Tim hesitated, clearly wondering about the dangers of pursuing this line of conversation. Eventually, he said, "I think we need to be more open-minded about that. There is no death certificate for Sam in the county records office. I think it's probably true that he was hit by a train at Sixteenth Street, but we have to at least consider the possibility that he actually died somewhere else."

The calmness of his voice felt like an itch too far beneath the skin's surface to scratch. She wished he would have just left her alone for the rest of the evening. But now that he was here, she couldn't ignore him.

"Don't you think a person knows where they died?" The question was absurd. How could either of them pretend to know the rules of death and afterlife? Yet Sara felt she had a little authority on the subject having actually been to the afterlife. "If he believes he died in the subway station, it's because that's where he woke up in Catharta. And he wouldn't have lied to Ananda. He wasn't evil back then. They were each other's only friends."

Tim's face hardened at her bristly tone. He couldn't hold back anymore. "If only you had so much blind confidence in your writing skills, you'd be one of the lead reporters at this paper."

That was a low blow. He knew she didn't like it when he pried into her career like that. He was purposely trying to rile her up. It reminded her of her meeting with Greg the day before. That man had wanted nothing more than to toy with Sara, to make her emotions bubble over. She tried to harness some of the control she had exercised with the inmate.

"There is nothing wrong with being a copy editor." She kept her voice as even as she could manage, but it still wavered noticeably.

Tim's eyes narrowed fractionally, and his jaw set just a bit to the left. He was trying to stop himself from needling her further, but he couldn't take it anymore. With bitterness in his voice he said, "You're right. There's nothing wrong with it, but you're better than this. You could be so much more, but you'll never try because you're too scared. You're scared to death of living. You're so afraid of failure that you simply never try. You owe it to yourself to try."

That was it. Any semblance of control Sara had been holding onto evaporated. She shot to her feet to better look him in the eye. "You know what, Tim? I don't need blind confidence to know that I could be a writer. Do you know how I know?" She didn't pause for him to answer. "I know I could be a writer because I had a job offer. It was a reporter position at a way bigger paper than this one, and I didn't take it because it was in New York. I thought about it, and I turned it down because I decided that my life here was more important than my career. I decided staying near my family was more important. I decided that being here for my sister and her baby was more important. I decided that working with my best friend was more important. But maybe I should have rethought that last part since apparently my life choices aren't good enough for you. What kind of friend does that make you, Tim?"

Tim's eyes were wide, and his jaw went slack after her outburst. He had to have known his comments were going to upset her, but he clearly hadn't been prepared for her response. "I didn't know," was all he could manage in reply.

"No, you didn't," Sara said, not ready to let go of her rage just yet. "Because I never told anyone. I never said a word because it's my life and my choice. Maybe I would have mentioned it if you weren't always so busy telling me what I should and shouldn't be."

Conscious of the fact that they had attracted the attention of the few people left in the office and unable to look Tim in the eye any longer, Sara stormed off. She wasn't sure where she was going. Her shift wasn't over, so she couldn't leave, but she couldn't go back to her desk either. She headed for the stairs for lack of any other direction. When she reached the security desk on the first floor, she looked out the front doors longingly, wishing she could go home and crawl into bed and forget this day had happened. But, on an impulse, she turned and headed down the stairs to the basement instead. At the bottom of the stairs, she paused next to the door to the underground parking garage where Tim's hearse-like vehicle was parked. Then, she turned to face the storage area that occupied the other half of the basement.

For a moment, she just stood in the dimly lit space, taking deep breaths of the stale air and trying to calm the restless energy that was coursing through her. When she felt measurably calmer, she took a look around. This storage space was filled with old newspapers. There was a print copy of every paper *The Daily* had ever published since its inception. The smell of old newsprint was actually soothing to her, and she approached some of the filing drawers, inspecting the labels. She didn't come down here often, but she knew the archives were all filed by date. She decided that so long as she was down here hiding from Tim, she may as well make herself useful. She looked for the drawer labeled "Fall 2014." Pulling the cabinet open, she located the paper from the date of Sam's death. She skimmed through the entire thing. It had been published not long after Sara had been promoted to copy editor from file clerk. She could still pick out the articles she had edited. She thought about the strangeness of the way memories worked. It seemed that the older a memory was, the more concrete it was. She could remember changing a comma to a semicolon in an article she edited three years ago, but she couldn't tell you what clothes she had worn last week.

The paper didn't even hint at anything that might have to do with Sam. She moved on to the issue from the following day, scanning headlines, looking for anything remotely connected to an incident in the subway system. It was like stepping back in time. She turned page after page, learning a great deal about what was going on in San Francisco three years earlier, but nothing that helped her find out what had become of the Guardian.

She was about ready to move on to the next day when something on one of the last pages caught her attention. A couple of times a week, the paper ran a column called The Police Blotter. It was just a collection of blurbs they received from the police department giving brief summaries of interesting things they had encountered. Mostly, it consisted of briefings on emergency dispatch calls received and investigations that were resolved in less than one day. Essentially, it was crime news that didn't warrant a full article for each incident. A few sentences were all each occurrence received, and it usually included no names and very few details. Because of the nature of the column, it wasn't included in the digital archives. It was too hard to index since the column covered a multitude of incidents with very few specifics. It wouldn't have come up in her search of the database. Near the end of this particular column was a two-sentence blurb that seemed to stop Sara's heart for just a moment.

Paramedics were dispatched to the Sixteenth Street subway station after a man was reportedly struck by a train. The victim was transported to Saint Gertrude Memorial Hospital where he remains in critical care.

She read those two sentences over and over until they were burned into her brain. This had to be about Sam. It just had to be, which meant that Tim had been right, Sam hadn't died in the train station. She glanced up at the ceiling thinking of Tim sitting in his office two floors above. She felt a pang of guilt for the way she had blown up at him. Then, she reminded herself she was mad at him for not supporting her and for telling her how to live her life, not just for doubting her. Either way, she would tell him he had been right about Sam, eventually.

She returned her attention to the paper. It didn't make sense. Her understanding had been that when people died, their souls woke up in the same physical location in Catharta. When she fell and bumped her head in the subway station and was transported there herself, she came to in the exact same spot on the platform. If Sam had woken up in Saint Gertrude's, why would he think he had died at Sixteenth Street? She shook off the thought. She couldn't pretend to understand all the rules of the ghost plane. Besides, the rules didn't seem to apply to Sam. The way he moved and the fact that he couldn't be reborn, everything about him pointed to the fact that he was different. He was an exception to the rules.

Sara remembered her trip to the records office that morning that had yielded no results. If there was no death certificate on file, maybe he had been transferred to another hospital in a different county. If she could find out where he had actually died and could get a copy of that death certificate, maybe she could find out more about him and figure out why his soul was different. She needed to know what happened to him after he was taken to Saint Gertrude.

Pulling her phone out of her sweatshirt pocket, she called Maya. Only after it rang three times did Sara realize the lateness of the hour and that Maya was probably sleeping. She almost hung up, but then the call connected, and she heard her sister's groggy voice.

"Sara? Are you okay? What time is it?"

Even in a half-sleep state, Maya was full of questions.

"Hey," Sara greeted her in return. "I'm fine. Sorry to call so late. I just need you to send me Dr. Carver's number."

Maya sounded suddenly more alert and a little suspicious as she asked, "Why?" Maya knew Sara had nothing nice to say about the illegitimate father of her baby. She was reluctant to give her sister a direct line to speak to the man himself.

"Don't worry," Sara reassured her. "It's nothing about you or the baby. I just need some information from him. I think I'm onto something."

Maya was now not only alert but also excited. "Is this about the Guardian? What did you find out? Did you get his death certificate? Do you know what happened to him?"

"I don't know anything yet. I just have a lead. Send me the good doctor's number, and I'll explain everything in the morning."

Maya let out a huff of impatience, but Sara could hear some shuffling around as her sister searched her contacts. Sara's phone buzzed against her ear.

"Okay, I just sent it to you."

"Thanks. Now, go back to sleep," Sara instructed.

"Fat chance of that," Maya replied. "But I'll try. Get home safe."

Sara hung up and checked the text message from Maya. She saved Damian Carver's number to her contacts and intended to call him right then and there. Her thumb hesitated over the call button. It was late. There was a good chance he was in bed, asleep, next to his wife who knew nothing of the impending birth of her husband's love child. It was too late to call; she knew that. But she didn't care too much about sparing his beauty sleep, and she really wanted answers now. She compromised with herself. She sent him a text message. It seemed a little less invasive. She composed the message: "This is Sara Jenkins, Maya's sister. I need a favor." She thought about putting the nature of the favor in the message but decided against it. She needed a reply from him. She needed to know he would agree. If she sent the whole message in one shot, she may not get any confirmation from him. By leaving it open-ended, she hoped to pique his curiosity. She tapped the send button.

Sara stared at her phone and held her breath. Maybe she should have called. If he picked up, at least she would know he was hearing her. What if he didn't see this text until the morning? How long should she wait? She startled and nearly dropped the phone when it buzzed in her hand. He had replied.

"it's your sisters choice to keep that baby i told her i want nothing to do with it"

Sara rolled her eyes at his lack of capital letters and punctuation. At least, he had replied.

She texted back, "It has nothing to do with Maya or the baby. I need medical records for a patient that was taken to your hospital three years ago."

He texted back right away. "that violates HIPPA regulations"

She had expected that response. She sent another message in return. "What regulations did you violate when you impregnated a member of the hospital staff? By the way, how did your wife take the news of your infidelity?"

Sara had no intention of actually contacting the doctor's wife. Maya would never forgive her for it. Hopefully, Damian wouldn't call her bluff.

There was a long pause before her phone buzzed again. She imagined him glancing over at his sleeping wife, wondering if he dare ignore Sara's request. A devious smile spread across her lips as she read his response. "whats the patients name and date of admission"

Sara sent him the information he requested about Sam and then noticed the time. Her shift had ended ten minutes ago. She took a quick photo of the blurb in the newspaper about Sam's incident and then tucked the paper back in its spot in the archive drawer. Then, she raced back upstairs to gather her things and get out the door. She noted Tim's light was off before she passed by his office. He must have already gone home, much to her relief.

Once Sara was out on the street, she felt clear minded again. Her fight with Tim was pushed on the back burner. She had finally found some proof of what happened to the Guardian, and she had a good lead on getting more information on him. She had accomplished something today, even when she had nearly chalked it up as a lost cause, and she felt good about it. She breathed in the damp night air, and she felt proud of herself. She walked through the dark city, among the shadows of skyscrapers. Before she realized it, she was standing at the steps that lead down into the Embarcadero subway station. Apparently, her subconscious had decided she would not be taking the bus home tonight. She would be taking the train instead.

She made her way down to the platform level and boarded the next train into the city. As usual, at this time of night, the train was largely deserted. There was a young couple who had fallen asleep on each other's shoulders and a middle-aged man reading a newspaper at one end of the car. At the other end of the car was a man in an ill-fitting suit who appeared to be in need of a shower. He was standing in the middle of the aisle and seemed to be having a conversation with himself or with some invisible companion. Sara took a seat near the young couple. As the train moved along its route, she caught bits and pieces of what the man standing at the other end of the train car was saying, but not enough to make sense of it. It sounded like he was reciting news headlines.

The doors opened at Civic Center, and there was a crazy-looking woman on the platform, stomping her feet and flailing her arms, shouting misquotations from the Bible. "Judge or be judged! As I walk through the valley of death! Fear no evil!" A transit policeman approached her from the stairwell, and she fled in the opposite direction, screaming, "You are not god!"

The doors shut, and Sara could hear the man at the other end of the train car again. She strained to make out his words. He was saying, "A nineteen-year-old Caucasian female committed suicide in the Mission District. She was found with a note on her body. It read 'It feels so good to be invisible. Thank you for not acknowledging me.'"

The train came to a stop, and the doors slid open. Sara found herself once again confronted with the platform at the Sixteenth Street subway station. Before she could reason with herself, before she could overthink it, before she could convince herself not to, Sara sprang to her feet. She stepped off the train onto the platform and only had a second to contemplate the wisdom of this move before the train doors slid shut behind her and her decision was cemented. The train rumbled out of the station, and everything was quiet.

Another train wouldn't be along for several minutes, which gave Sara time to process what her impulses wanted her to do. She had promised Tim and Maya that she wouldn't go to Catharta alone. But she knew Maya would forgive her. She would understand. Tim would be pissed, but to hell with him. She was pissed at him too. She paced the length of the platform and found it completely empty. She listened at each stairway and escalator for any sign that someone might be approaching, but she heard nothing. She appeared to have the station all to herself tonight. She paced the platform a while longer.

She could go to Catharta. She would only stay ten minutes. That would only be about one minute in the real world. What could possibly go wrong in one minute when there was no one in sight? She glanced at the sign overhead. Another train would be along in two minutes. She made her way to the east end of the platform and gazed into the dark tunnel. A breeze began to stir. She made a bargain with herself. She would go to Catharta. She promised herself that if she didn't find Ananda immediately, she would come right back.

The wind grew more intense, blowing her hair in all directions. She could feel the platform beneath her feet begin to tremble as the train made its way in her direction. The headlights, still not fully visible around the bend in the tunnel, began to illuminate concentric circles of light within the dark, soot-stained tunnel. Sara took her place on the platform. As the train burst forth into the station, she pitched herself backward, sweeping her own feet out from under herself. As she fell backward, eyes wide open, she caught sight of an errant spark from the electric third rail. It was the last spot of brightness she saw. Then, she was falling, forever, into a bottomless pit. The lights, the sound of the train, and the wind all faded into nothingness until everything was dark and silent.

CHAPTER 11

*S*ara inhaled sharply and blinked rapidly, willing her body into motion or whatever constituted a body in Catharta. Maybe it was just a memory of her body. Either way, she needed to move. Time was of the essence. She sat up, fighting off the dizziness that was fogging her brain, and looked around. It was hard to say, because the station had been empty to begin with, but there was no train at the platform. She was pretty sure she was in Catharta. A satisfied feeling came over her that she had truly figured out this whole gateway thing. She could come and go as she pleased. She was in control. That feeling of satisfaction was quickly replaced by a feeling of urgency. She didn't have much time. She didn't fully understand the consequences of leaving her soulless body unattended in the world of the living. She had to find Ananda quickly before she was faced with finding out what those consequences might be.

She forced herself to her feet, ignoring the fuzzy feeling in her brain, and took off at a run down the platform toward the stairwell at the opposite end of the station, noting as she ran that there was still no sign of life. As she approached the stairwell, she saw light pouring in from above, light from a slate gray sky. She was definitely in Catharta; otherwise, it would still be dark outside. She took the stairs two at a time, thinking she should be out of breath. Maybe breathlessness from physical exertion was something that went along with having a physical body, and hers had been left behind. It made her feel invincible. She wondered if her body back in the real world was panting or if her heart rate had increased. Sara had to remind herself that she was no superhero. She could be physically hurt from things that happened to her in Catharta. She just wouldn't feel the pain until later, like when the Guardian had dug his hands into her shoulders. She also reminded herself that her physical body was lying unattended on the subway station floor back in the world of the living. She had to hurry.

At the top of the stairs, she blindly turned to head toward Mission Street without a real plan, wondering which way she should go to find her friend, and nearly ran right into Ananda. Both girls let out a little startled yelp, and then, they embraced one another.

"You're here," Sara said, glowing with relief.

"I told you I wouldn't go far." Ananda's voice was reassuring, almost motherly. It gave Sara a warm feeling in the pit of her stomach.

Sara pulled back and looked her friend in her supernatural eyes, which she grew more accustomed to all time. She couldn't believe her luck at finding her friend so quickly, just when time was the most important. Those haunting, glowing orbs gazed back at her with apprehension.

"I don't have much time," Sara told her in a rush, the words tumbling out of her. "I'm not really supposed to be here right now. But I wanted you to know I met your stepfather."

Ananda's eyes widened. "He's alive?" She reached out and grabbed Sara's hands, seemingly needing to steady herself.

Sara nodded in confirmation. "He's alive, and I met him. He's awful," she said, making a disgusted face as she tasted the memory of him. Sara physically shuddered at the recollection of her encounter with the murderer. She shook it off and went on. "He was convicted of your murder. He's at San Quentin." She hesitated, not wanting to alarm Ananda, but wanting to give her the full details of all she had learned. "He was sentenced to death."

Ananda looked as though she had been punched in the stomach. She backed up a few steps and doubled over. Sara put a hand on Ananda's shoulder and leaned down, trying to catch her eye.

"They're going to kill him," Ananda whispered. She was envisioning her worst fear coming true, meeting the most wicked man she had ever met once again in the afterlife and being tormented by him for all eternity.

"They're not going to kill him anytime soon," Sara tried to sound reassuring, channeling Maya's casual confidence. "California hasn't put an inmate to death in over a decade, and there are more than seven-hundred people on death row right now. Even if they started executing prisoners again today, I'm sure there are a lot of people ahead of him."

Ananda stood up a little straighter and took a deep breath, trying to calm herself. Her hands were still balled up in little fists of anxiety. "So he's alive, and he will be for a while." She took a deep breath and processed that information. Her ghostly eyes looked sad but thoughtful. "That should make me feel better." She locked eyes with Sara. "Why doesn't that make me feel better?"

Sara couldn't imagine what it must be like to finally get news from the other side like this. Ananda had been on the ghost plane for what felt like thirty years, longer than Sara had been alive, and she had been haunted by this fear the entire time. She had existed in a state of not knowing for several decades, and now, she finally learned something new about her killer. It had to be a lot to take in.

Sara tried to think through the psychology of learning something like this. "It probably doesn't make you feel better because you know no one lives forever, and right now, you feel like you're trapped here forever. You're worried that he's still going to end up here someday." Sara tried to mimic the motherly tone Ananda had used moments before. It didn't seem to have the same effect. "But honestly, Ananda, I don't think you ever have to worry about seeing him again. That man is soulless. I spoke to him about what he did to you. He didn't show even the slightest sign of remorse. Even with all this time to think about what he's done, he feels that his crime was justified. He's been in solitary confinement for years, and he doesn't feel even a little bit guilty about what he did. Undoubtedly, he will die someday, but when he does, he won't be coming here. He has no soul. When he dies, he will just be gone. Erased." She tried to infuse this statement with as much confidence as she could manage. Of course, there was no test to prove that Greg Hastings was soulless. Still, Sara felt that she was as sure as she could possibly be. She had looked into the man's eyes. They were dead. They were supposed to be a window to the soul, but in that man, they were a window into nothingness.

Ananda searched Sara's eyes, looking for a sign that there was truth behind her words. Seeming satisfied, she nodded. But she still seemed forlorn. "If only I could get out of here, then I would never have to find out if you're right or not."

"Well, I'm working on that too." Sara wanted nothing more than to reassure this girl that there would be an end to her struggle, that she would be reborn again someday, and that all of Catharta would be set free. But she still had so many unknowns. The best she could do was to reassure Ananda that she would keep trying. She would not give up.

Ananda gave her a skeptical look. "What do you mean you're working on it?"

"I mean I'm trying to find more information on the Guardian. If I can find out more about his life, maybe I can figure out how to stop him." Sara was conscious of the time that had already ticked by, but if there was anything else Ananda could tell her about the Guardian, she needed to take that opportunity.

Ananda shook her head and looked at Sara with something like pity. She clearly thought this mission was a waste of time. "Sara, there's no way. Sam is…"

A man's voice close to Sara's ear cut Ananda off. "Sam is what?"

Both girls jumped and turned to find themselves faced with none other than the Guardian himself. Sara instinctively grabbed Ananda's hand, unsure if she was trying to play the protector or the protected. Sam's tall and imposing form seemed to tower over the two of them. He had the ability to appear much larger than he really was. His broad shoulders gave him the look of some sort of winged demon, ready to take flight at any moment. Sara felt frozen where she stood. Her muscles itched to flee, to get as far away from him as she could, but fear pinned her to the spot. It was better that way anyhow. She needed to confront him. What better source of information could there be than Sam himself? She was overcome with the compelling urge to punch this man in the face, as if that would solve anything. She stood her ground and tried to think of what to say to him. How could she get information from this man who clearly despised her?

He repeated his question more slowly. "Sam is what?"

The question was directed at Ananda, but he never took his eyes off Sara. His frightening eyes bore into her, daring her to speak, to move, to breathe.

Ananda answered, "Sam is a coward." Those were clearly not the words she had intended to say to Sara, but there was no doubt she meant them when she said them.

"How so?" he asked, still not unlocking his crystal clear orbs from Sara's eyes, so full of life.

"You're afraid of letting people go," Ananda fired back. "You collect souls like they're tchotchkes even though these people mean nothing to you. You only do it because you're so desperately afraid of being alone." The venom in her accusation even made Sara flinch.

Sam shot Ananda a disdainful look, but didn't respond. He returned his attention to Sara. "Why do you keep coming back here? You're alive. Why don't you go live?" He made a motion with his hand as if he were shooing her away like a pesky insect.

"Because I want to help you," Sara replied, swallowing her fear, and trying to hold her voice steady. "I want to help everyone here. Everyone deserves a second chance at life. Even you. You have to see that what you're doing is wrong. You're denying everyone their second chance just because yours hasn't come yet."

Sam laughed a slow maniacal chuckle. "You are so naive," he accused. "This is the most righteous thing I've ever done. Are you blind? Can't you see that?"

Sara furrowed her brow, trying to understand how he could have convinced himself that what he was doing was right. Ananda rolled her eyes, probably having heard this argument before.

Sam explained, "Your world is a sad and desolate place, filled with pain and loneliness. Life is pain. This place"—he said, looking around to take in their surroundings—"is a gift. There is no pain here. There is no death. The more people we collect here, the less loneliness there is. The souls I guard are far better off here than on the other side. I keep them safe here. I am their guardian."

149

"That's not true!" Sara protested. "You are not their guardian. You are their jail keeper." He shook his head as though she just couldn't understand his righteousness. Sara pressed on. "Look, I'm sorry about whatever happened to you in your life that made you so bitter, but my world is not the desolate place you make it out to be. Most of these people lived long and happy lives, and they deserve a chance to have that again. You deserve a chance to experience that too. You can't keep trapping everyone here. Everyone deserves a second chance."

"Obviously not everyone," he spat out bitterly, eyes narrowed. He had been in Catharta longer than anyone else. Of course, he would be bitter about that.

"I'm going to find out why you haven't been reborn," Sara promised him. "I'm going to help you, whether you want my help or not. But you can't keep trapping souls here. You're making my world a soulless place. This must stop!"

"You're toying with things you could not begin to understand, Sara," he snarled at her. She took a step back, startled that he had remembered her name. It made her feel marked, like she was on his hit list. "You're nothing more than a tourist here. Go back to the hell you crawled out of." He turned to leave, at a normal pace, rather than the breakneck speed she'd seen him demonstrate before.

Sara wasn't sure why, but she felt she couldn't let him go. She needed something more from him. She needed him to want to change. When he was nearly half a block away, she blurted out, "You didn't die in the subway station!"

Sam stopped walking, but didn't turn around.

Sara repeated, "You didn't die in the subway station. You say there are things here that I don't understand, but there's a lot you don't know yourself. I know that you were mugged and shoved over the edge of the platform. I know you were hit by a train. I know that when the paramedics arrived at the Sixteenth Street station that night, you were still breathing. Your heart was still beating. There was still warm blood coursing through your veins. They took you to the hospital. You did not die on that train platform."

In less than a breath, he had turned and was nearly on top of her, one clawlike hand gripping her throat. "You're wrong!" he roared in her face. "You weren't there. You don't know what happened. You could not begin to understand."

Sara felt paralyzed by fear, and Ananda had jumped in and was trying to pry his hand off of her, shouting protests that Sara couldn't quite bring into focus. She managed to choke out, "I do know, and I'm going to prove it. I'm going to help you, whether you want my help or not."

Sam released his grip, shoulders heaving with each breath, overcome by rage. He let out a primal yell, and then, he was gone. In a flash, he simply disappeared. There was a slight trail indicating that he had taken off down Mission Street somewhere. Sara felt an immense relief to be free of his presence. When he was standing right in front of her, he became all-encompassing, like the rest of the world, the rest of Catharta, faded into the background. He was powerful. That much was undeniable. She reminded herself that he was still just the soul of a man who was lost and scared. He was different from the rest of the souls here for reasons she couldn't yet explain. But he was still just a man.

She turned to Ananda, suddenly realizing once again that she had stayed much longer than she had intended. "I need to go."

Ananda stopped her. "What do you mean he didn't die in the subway station? How do you know that?" Her expression was wide-eyed and wild. After spending so much time in Catharta where every moment was the same as the last, she had just taken in a lot of new information in a short period of time. It seemed to be overwhelming her.

Anxious, but not wanting to abandon Ananda without the answers she wanted, Sara imparted, "I found something in the newspaper that said he was taken to Saint Gertrude after he was hit by the train. I tried to get a copy of his death certificate, and it didn't exist, which means he probably didn't even die in San Francisco. He must have been transferred somewhere else. I have a doctor at Saint Gertrude working on getting me his medical records from his time there. It should tell me where he went when they discharged him."

Ananda took in this new information, grinding her teeth a little as she mulled it over. "But that doesn't make any sense. He entered Catharta through the gateway in the train station, the same gateway you've been using. That has to be where he died."

Sara felt validated. She'd had the same thought, which is why she had been so convinced that Tim was wrong to doubt her. She may not fully understand the rules of the spirit plane, but Ananda was an expert, and she thought the same thing. Sam had to have died on that train platform.

Still, records don't lie. There must be some other explanation. She fumbled for a suggestion. "I know it seems that way, but I'm going to get to the bottom of it. I'm going to find out what really happened to him. I don't doubt that he came through that gateway, but we know he's different. He moves so fast, and he can't be reborn. Maybe this is part of the reason why he's different. If I can find out why he breaks all the rules of Catharta, maybe I can figure out how to stop him."

A whisper of doubt crossed Ananda's face, but her words were encouraging anyhow. "I believe in you. You can do this. Maybe this is the reason you came here to begin with. Maybe you were meant to save us all."

"I hope so," Sara replied, allowing that trace of doubt wash over her even though she knew she should try to ignore it. It was seeping into her pores before she even realized it. Maybe hope was all she had. Maybe hope wasn't enough. "I have to go. I've been here too long."

"Go. I'll be nearby when you come back." Sara turned to head back down the stairs into the subway station, but Ananda called after her, halting her steps. "And Sara, thank you. Thank you for going to see my stepfather. I'm sure that wasn't"—she hesitated, pursing her lips and looking for the right word, finally settling on—"pleasant."

Sara was inclined to tell her it was nothing, but she knew it wasn't nothing. It had been a difficult, stomach-churning task. But she would do it all again just to see the grateful look on Ananda's face. Instead of downplaying her efforts as she was inclined to do, she responded, "You're welcome."

"Thank you for everything you've done for me, for all of us. Thank you for everything you're going to do." Ananda smiled. Sara wasn't sure she had ever seen such a true and genuine smile on Ananda's face. It was a smile untainted by sadness. She looked like a seventeen-year-old girl again, rather than the wizened woman she had become in Catharta. She was beautiful. Sara simply smiled back and then turned to head down the stairs. She had been in Catharta far too long. She tried not to think about her body that she had carelessly abandoned back in the world of the living. Hopefully, the platform was still empty, and her body was still unmoved. She rushed through the station and found her place at the east end of the platform. Lying down on her back, she pressed her eyes closed and took a deep breath. She tried to let go of her conversation with Sam. She tried to ignore the strange sensation that his fingers were still wrapped around her throat, digging into her skin. She tried to mentally let go of Ananda and Catharta and everything she needed to leave behind once again. She had to set it all aside for now. She'd be back soon enough. She focused instead on the present in her real life. She thought of Maya who had hopefully managed to get back to sleep. She thought of the tiny baby curled up in her sister's belly, unaware of the chaos going on in the world outside. She thought of Aunt Joann and the home she had provided for all of them. She thought of her job and her daily life and all the little things she usually took for granted about the real world, like sunsets and the city fog and the sound of busy people bustling around. In the end, she let herself think of Tim too. She was still upset with him, but she knew she'd get over it eventually. After all, he was her best friend. She thought of all of this and then let her eyes snap open.

Staring up at the concrete ceiling, she felt that familiar, sickening sensation. She was rocketing upward, out of control. Her vision told her she was stationary, but the queasy feeling in her guts told her she was riding an elevator to another dimension. The pressure on her head swelled. Her stomach threatened to empty itself. She wanted to close her eyes, but she stayed strong. Just as she thought she couldn't take it anymore, it all stopped. She came to rest in the same spot on the floor of the Sixteenth Street subway station, staring up at the same concrete ceiling with flickering fluorescent lights in her peripheral vision.

Sara held her breath. She didn't hear anyone. She didn't detect any motion nearby. She breathed a sigh of relief as she popped her ears. She had done it. She had gone to Catharta by herself. She had done what she needed to do, and she had returned her soul to her body, unmolested, unmoved. She knew it didn't justify the risk she had taken. Maya would still be mad, but at least, she would be relieved that Sara was safe.

She rolled her head slightly to the right. There was no train at the platform. She had been gone long enough for it to have departed already. That was fine, there would be another train along shortly that would get her home. She wiggled her toes, trying to bring the blood flow back to her extremities and trying to reduce the head rush she knew she'd feel when she finally sat up. She wiggled her fingers, and her left hand brushed against something, startling her. She recoiled, balling her fingers into a tight fist. Sara found herself unable to move anything more than her fingers, not breathing, not blinking. Had she imagined it? No, she had definitely felt something there. Maybe it was one of her own possessions, flung onto the platform when she had thrown herself into another world. She gathered her courage, and her fist loosened. Her fingers reached slowly back to the left, cautiously searching out whatever unexpected object was there. Then she felt it, and her heart stopped. Short nails. Thick fingers. A warm hand. There was a person lying next to her. Another living soul. And Sara couldn't move.

CHAPTER 12

S ara held her breath. An endless stream of thoughts cascaded through her mind. Her first impulse was that the person lying next to her was Sam. She didn't know what made her think that. Sam was dead. The dead couldn't travel back to the world of the living. Or could they? She was alive, and she could travel to the land of the dead. But Sam had just run away from her in Catharta. Why would he want to follow her here when he was trying to distance himself from her there? Even if he could travel back to the real world, why would he want to? He had just professed his hatred of it. Sara's next thought was that her soul hadn't actually landed in her body when she returned to real life. She was having an out of body experience, her soul lying next to her lifeless body. But that didn't make sense either. She knew what her own hand felt like. The hand she had brushed her fingers against was too masculine, too rough, too unfamiliar. She noted the pain she felt around her neck where Sam had grabbed her. No, she was firmly back in her own body. Otherwise, she wouldn't be able to feel that pain. This was someone else lying next to her. It could be a complete stranger. Her mind flashed back to the man who had tried to steal her messenger bag in this very spot just a few nights ago, his wild eyes, his animal-like stance. The thought of someone like that lying next to her helpless body filled her with terror. All these thoughts whipped through her mind in only a matter of seconds.

Then, he spoke.

"I knew you would come here."

Sara finally exhaled having heard the familiar timbre of Tim's voice. She was able to move again, turn her head, and look at the person beside her. He was lying flat on his back alongside her, staring up at the ceiling.

"You scared the hell out of me!" she accused.

He tipped his head in her direction and raised his eyebrow a fraction of an inch, giving her a stony, side-eyed glare. "Really?" he asked, his voice leaden with sarcasm and judgment.

Of course, she had scared him too. It was his turn to be mad. She had broken a promise to him. She had gone to Catharta alone. She had put herself at risk, mostly because she was angry with him. She tried to summon that anger, but it seemed distant, too far away to reach. They both looked back up at the ceiling.

"Your stubbornness knows no bounds," he uttered. Sara couldn't exactly argue with him without sounding even more stubborn. Besides, she knew he was right.

Instead, she asked, "How are you here right now? I searched the whole platform. I was alone when the train arrived, and I couldn't have been gone more than a couple minutes."

Tim disagreed. "You were gone at least four minutes. And I got here the same way you did: on a train."

Sara looked to her right, toward the edge of the platform where the train would have been. "You were on the train that I...," she began.

"That you threw yourself in front of? Yeah, I was," Tim finished for her. "So was a very nice lady who was really concerned about you. She wanted to call you an ambulance. It took some serious convincing to get her to stay on that train."

Sara felt foolish. She had convinced herself that she was all alone. How had she not considered the fact that every train entering the station would be carrying passengers? Passengers who might mean to do her harm or take advantage of her vulnerable state. Or even well-meaning people like the lady Tim met who could unintentionally do her harm just because they didn't understand that she had traveled to another plane of existence. The risk that she'd taken had been bigger than she had realized. Tim had every right to be upset with her.

"I'm sorry," she told him, still looking straight up, unable to look him in the eye.

Tim let the silence build long enough that Sara became unsure if he had heard her. Then he said, "I'm sorry too."

Sara thought she heard his dark hair rustle against the platform as he turned his head in her direction. She couldn't look at him.

He went on, "I have no right to tell you what to do with your career or with your life, and I never meant to imply that what you do for a living isn't good enough. If it makes you happy, then it's plenty good enough. All this time I thought I was encouraging you, just giving you the extra little push you might need. But it's not my place to push you in any direction you don't want to go. I honestly had no idea about that job offer. I'm glad you considered it, but if you decided it's not for you, then I have no business telling you what you should or shouldn't do." He paused, sounding unfinished. Sara waited. Then, he continued. "I just want to know one thing, but you don't have to tell me if you don't want to." He sounded uncharacteristically nervous. "I just want to know how big a part of that decision I played."

Sara shifted a little, suddenly unexplainably nervous as well. "I told you, I didn't want to leave Maya, and I didn't want to leave my home here. I didn't want to leave my life in this city, and you're a part of that too."

"How big a part?" He was insistent, looking for some sort of reassurance she couldn't quite understand.

She reached over and intertwined her long, slender fingers with his thick, rough ones. "A big part, Tim. You're important to me."

Hand in hand, they stared at the ceiling in silence for a while longer. The silence was broken by the overhead speaker announcing that the next train would be arriving in two minutes.

"Come on," Tim said, pushing himself up off the brick red tiles. "That's your ride out of here. Let's get you home."

He offered her a hand and hoisted her up to a standing position. Once on her feet, she moved to pull her hand away. He held onto it. She looked at their interlocked fingers and then at his eyes, framed with concern and something like sadness.

"Just so you know"—he told her—"you're important to me too."

Sara smiled at him, and he smiled back, releasing her hand. The rumble of the train could be heard in the distance. The air stirred around them. The sound of metal wheels racing along metal rails filled the cavernous space. Then, the train roared into the station. Sara felt a slight pain at the back of her head from falling in front of the previous train, coupled with the pain around her neck from Sam's grip. She was relieved to be taking this train back home to her family instead of taking it to Catharta.

The train slid to a stop, and the doors opened. Tim and Sara stepped onboard. Sara flung her hair over her shoulder, and Tim poked at her neck. Putting on an exaggerated voice like an overexcited teenager he asked, "Oh my god, is that a hickey?"

Sara instinctively touched the spot he had poked and tried to examine her reflection in the darkened windows of the train. She twisted her head from side to side, and Tim noticed the pattern of the marks on her neck. He dropped his teasing tone and asked seriously, "Are those bruises?"

Sara nodded.

"What happened there?" he asked. "What happened in Catharta?"

The doors slid shut, and they trundled on toward home. "Can we talk about it tomorrow?"

Tim glanced between her exhausted eyes and her purple-dotted neck. Then, he gave in. "Yeah, we can talk about it tomorrow. Let's just get you home."

In the morning, Sara was the first one up. Maya was stirring by the time Sara got out of the shower, but the elder sister was still the first one downstairs. There, she found Tim, still asleep on the couch. She watched him for a bit, noting that he looked like a little boy while he slept. Underneath all of that scruff, he had a baby face. She considered letting him sleep, but she really needed coffee, and the sound of the grinder was going to rouse him anyway. She gave him a gentle nudge on the shoulder to wake him.

Tim sat up with a start and took a second to remember where he was. Then, he buried his head in his hands and let out an inarticulate grumble. He wasn't really a morning person.

Sara teased him, "You better not make this business of crashing on the couch into a habit. Aunt Joann will be back from her business trip on Wednesday, and she's not big on strays."

He rubbed the sleep from his eyes. "Well, maybe if I could be assured you would actually go home after work, I wouldn't have to escort you." There was a bite to his voice reminiscent of their fight the day before, but Sara let it slide, given that he had literally only woken up a few seconds earlier.

"Okay, princess"—Sara mocked—"one extra strong cup of coffee coming right up."

As Sara went to work making some coffee, she didn't hear Maya approach her from behind over the sound of the grinder running. As soon as it stopped, Maya asked, "So what was that all about?"

Sara jumped a mile and nearly spilled the grounds she had just made. "What the hell, Maya?" she exclaimed, trying to calm her racing heart.

"Jeez, you're a little jumpy. You sure you need that caffeine?" Maya backed off a bit, but could not contain her questions. "So what's the deal? Why did you need Damian's number last night? Did you call him? And what's he doing here?" she asked, indicating toward Tim who was finally making his way off the couch. "Did something happen? Did you go back to Catharta?"

Sara set the coffee to brew, and she and Tim shared a knowing look. She was about to get yelled at by her little sister. She decided to get it over with and answer the last question first. "Yes, I went back to Catharta."

"Alone," Tim interjected.

"What?!" Maya exclaimed. "You didn't! Tell me you didn't."

Sara glared at Tim, but she knew she deserved it. She had broken her promise. She needed to accept the consequences. Still, he should have let her confess.

"Thanks tattletale. I was going to work up to that part." She looked back at Maya. "Yes, I went back to Catharta alone. It was stupid, and I know I shouldn't have done it. I promise you it will never happen again."

Maya was wearing her best motherly scowl and was making no attempt to hide her disappointment. "You don't even know the risk of what you're doing. How could you take that sort of chance?"

"I know! I know!" Sara felt terrible, but she let the guilt wash over her. After all, she deserved it. She had to own her mistake. "It was reckless. I know that now." Maya was still standing with her arms crossed, waiting for something more. "I'm sorry," Sara added, and she truly meant it. She had broken a promise and put herself at personal risk because she had been angry with Tim and frustrated that she hadn't been able to find out more information about the Guardian.

Sara's apology seemed to soften Maya some, but she still looked concerned. "Are you okay? Obviously you survived the return trip."

"I'm fine. It turned out I wasn't as alone as I thought." Sara gave Tim a look that she hoped expressed the fact that she was thankful he had been there for her. "But I saw Ananda again."

Sensing they were about to get the full story, Maya and Tim took a seat at the table. Sara told them what had happened. "I went to Catharta, and I found Ananda almost right away. I think she's been waiting for me. I told her about meeting her stepfather and that he's alive and we expect he'll stay that way for quite a while. It wasn't much consolation to her, but I think she was relieved to finally know."

"See," Maya said, "you helped her, just like I knew you would. Just like you were meant to do."

"I'm starting to believe I'm meant to do more than that." She looked back and forth between her sister and her best friend as they waited anxiously for her to continue. "I saw the Guardian again too."

"Your neck." Tim was piecing it together. Or maybe he had figured it out the night before and was just looking for confirmation. Sara's hand instinctively went to her throat and grazed the bruises she knew were still there. Four on the left, one on the right, one for each digit Sam had gripped her with. "He did that to you, didn't he?"

Maya jumped up to investigate, examining the marks that the Guardian had left her with. "He did this to you?" She was disgusted. Fury burned in her eyes.

"Yes, he did this to me. But what I was trying to say is that I think I'm meant to do something else in Catharta. I think I'm meant to stop him." Maya sat back down, looking helpless, knowing she was unable to protect her sister. "And I think the only way to stop him is to help him."

"Help him?" Maya was in disbelief. "Why should you do anything to help that evil man? He's trapping souls there with him, and he's making our world soulless. And look what he did to you! Why should you lift a finger to help him?"

"Because I think that's the only way to save all those souls," Sara defended her plan. "I tried talking to him. I tried reasoning with him that what he was doing was wrong. He won't hear it. He thinks our world is a wasteland and that the souls of the dead are better off there with him. He makes Catharta out to be some sort of pain-free paradise. He honestly believes he's doing the right thing."

"He's delusional," Tim declared.

Sara agreed, "Probably. But the point is he's not going to stop on his own. I prevented him from trapping a soul one time, but I just got lucky. I had the element of surprise working to my advantage. The only way to stop him is to get him out of Catharta."

Maya's eyes widened. "You mean bring him back here? But he's dead. He'd be a zombie."

"Not really," Tim said thoughtfully. "Zombies are reanimated dead bodies. The Guardian doesn't have a body. He's just a soul. I think he'd be more like a ghost."

The coffeemaker beeped, indicating it was finished, and Tim and Maya both jumped a little. Sara closed her eyes and shook her head. They weren't following, and they were getting way off track. She poured the coffee as she went on. "Listen, he won't be a zombie or a ghost. I'm not talking about bringing his soul back here with me. I'm talking about helping him to be reborn."

Maya waited for Sara to say something more and, when she didn't, asked, "How exactly do you plan to do that? Even he and Ananda don't know why he can't be reborn."

"I know, but I intend to find out. That was why I needed your doctor's number last night." Sara pulled her phone out of her back pocket and pulled up the photo she had taken of the blurb in the archived newspaper. She laid it on the table and waited for her audience to absorb the words written there.

Maya was the first to say something. "He didn't die in the train station."

Tim looked at Sara, clearly remembering his words in the records office the previous day that had sent them on a downward spiral. He was treading on dangerous ground and didn't want to say the wrong thing.

Sara took the guesswork out of it for him. "No, he didn't. I guess I should have been more open-minded about that." Tim gave her a small smile and thankfully refrained from saying "I told you so." Sara smiled back.

"The thing is," Sara continued, "he really believes he died on that platform. That's exactly where his soul woke up in Catharta and that's where the gateway still is, the gateway that I'm using. Something doesn't add up, and I think if I can figure out what happened to his body that night, I might be able to figure out how to help his soul be reborn."

"That's why you needed to talk to Damian," Maya finally understood.

"He's getting me the medical records," Sara said triumphantly. "Hopefully, that will be the last piece of the puzzle we need to figure this thing out."

After coffee and breakfast and a lot more questions from Maya, Sara finally convinced everyone that they needed to simply wait for the medical records and that speculation was going to get them nowhere. Reluctantly, Maya agreed, and as their shift approached, Tim and Sara made their way to the office.

They decided to take the bus instead of the train. Passing through Sixteenth Street again at this point would only reignite all the what-ifs in their minds. What if Sam's soulless body had been transported so far from the gateway that he couldn't get back into it? But then why did his spirit possess those ghostly eyes? When Sara travelled to Catharta, her eyes looked just as they did in life because she was still alive. Her heart was still beating. Her body was still taking in oxygen. Sam's body was still alive when he was taken from the train station. At what point did his eyes change? Maybe when his body had been removed from the spot where his soul had left it? Maybe when his soul had been out of his body for too long? Would that happen to Sara if she lingered in Catharta too long? Would she change? Would she be unable to return to her life? With a shudder, she shook off the idea. It was pointless to speculate. She just had to wait for the medical records and deal with whatever information they contained.

She stole a glance at Tim in the seat next to her. He hadn't said a word since they had boarded the bus. He looked as tangled up in his own thoughts as she was. She stared out the window instead. She tried to see what Sam saw in the world. She passed figures on the streets who looked sad, angry, desperate, and alone. She saw homelessness and crime, dirt, and callousness. She saw exhaustion written on people's faces. She saw a city full of people just trying to protect themselves as best they could and get by. But she also saw life, happiness, togetherness, and vibrancy. The world was what you made of it. You would see whatever you were looking for. Something happened to Sam in his life that made him look for the negative. Sara just wished she knew what that was.

She shook off thoughts of the Guardian as they came to their stop and off boarded. They walked the short distance to the office in silence and entered the building equally quietly. The guard gave them a surreptitious look, probably realizing this was the second day in a row that they had arrived at work together. He quickly lost interest and went back to reading his paper.

Tim and Sara climbed the stairs together and stopped outside Tim's office.

"So," Tim hesitated, looking for discrete words as their coworkers walked around them. "Let me know if you hear anything."

He was talking about the medical records of course. "I will," she reassured him, and then, they went their separate ways with some unnamed awkwardness still hanging between them.

At her desk, Sara found it was a slow news day. She didn't have much work to keep her occupied, and the fluff pieces they had her editing weren't providing much of a distraction. About halfway through her shift, Sara's phone buzzed, providing the distraction she needed. She picked it up, expecting a text message from Maya with more questions. It was Dr. Carver. She quickly opened the message, her heart beating a little faster. She read the text, which said, "uploaded records to secure dropbox," followed by a link. Another text came through almost immediately. It read, "download what u need and save offline. Delete this msg. I'm deleting dropbox acct at end of day today."

Clearly, the doctor was trying to cover his tracks. With her pulse racing, Sara clicked the link and opened the document she found there. She forwarded it to her e-mail so she could read it on the computer instead of her phone. She recognized that she was just adding one more electronic trail to this document that was supposed to be strictly confidential, but she didn't care. To hell with Damian Carver's professional integrity. The file took a surprisingly long time to send.

She downloaded it from her e-mail and saved it to her hard drive. Opening the file, she felt her mouth go dry and her throat constrict. She became hyperconscious of the sore spots dotted around her throat. She forced her eyes and brain to focus on the document in front of her. Why did she long for so much information, but when it was presented to her, her brain tried to shut it out?

The first page seemed to be all Sam's personal information. The first thing that caught her eye was his date of birth: August 5, 1976. The year was different, but the day was the same. That was Sara's birthday. He was born exactly thirteen years earlier than her. It listed his full name as well, Sam Eli Johnson. A chill went down her spine as she recited her own name in her head: Sara Elizabeth Jenkins. They had the same initials too. She was sure none of this was a coincidence, but she put a pin in that for the time being. She needed to keep reading. She needed to find out what had happened to him.

Sara scrolled through a page or two of medical records, full of abbreviations, some of which she recognized. It started with the night he was admitted, September 27, 2014. They had taken his vitals, blood pressure, temperature, and oxygen level. She was no doctor, but none of the results looked good. It appeared he'd had surgery to relieve the pressure on his brain. She told herself she would look up the details of the procedure later, but it sounded like they had removed a portion of his skull to make room for the swelling. The thought of it made her stomach turn over, but she pressed on. She scrolled and scrolled through pages of vital readings and medication administrations, searching for the part where he had been transferred to another facility. He had to have been transferred out of San Francisco. That was the only explanation as to why his death certificate wasn't in the records office. She kept scrolling through more medications, more vitals, and another surgery to put a plate in his head and more records with date and time stamps that were beginning to stretch into days and weeks. This wasn't making any sense. She decided to jump to the end of the record. On the last page was another record of his blood pressure and his oxygen level. It was dated September 25, 2017.

That was yesterday.

This couldn't be right. There had to have been some kind of mistake. The date must be a typo. She scrolled up and down through the document, noting there were vital readings for every single day. They went on and on, stretching out over the course of nearly three years. This couldn't be right. Dr. Carver must have given her the wrong record. This couldn't be the same guy. Sam was dead. There was no way his heart was pumping at seventy beats per minute yesterday.

She closed the file, unable to look at it anymore. She grabbed her phone and got up from her desk, summoning all her self-control to keep herself from running through the office. At Tim's door, she paused. He wasn't there, but his light was on. He was out on assignment. He'd be back. For lack of a better place to go, she raced up to the roof. At least up there, she could make a phone call in privacy. She walked out onto the rooftop and found her way to the railing at the side of the building that overlooked the San Francisco Bay.

165

As impatient as she felt, she paused and forced herself to catch her breath before unlocking her phone.

She scrolled through her contacts, thinking at first of calling Tim. He was on assignment, and he would have his cell phone on him, but he would be busy. He may not be able to pick up. Then she considered calling Maya, but the inevitable barrage of questions she would receive made her realize who she needed to call. She needed answers, not more questions. She called Dr. Carver. The phone rang three times, and she was ready to yell an obscenity to release some of her impatience, when he picked up.

He didn't greet her with any sort of pleasantry. Instead, he simply asked, "Did you delete the text message?"

The question caught Sara off guard. "What? No, but I will. Listen, this can't be right. I don't think this is the same guy. The guy I was looking for came in after being hit by a subway train. He should have died shortly thereafter."

Damian huffed with impatience. "It's the guy. I asked about him. He was mugged and hit by a train, and they brought him here. He's been in a coma ever since."

Sara felt like a planet knocked off of its axis, spinning off into the infinite darkness of space. None of this fit with any of the conjectures or possible explanations she'd come up with. This made no sense. She had met Sam's ghost. How could he still be alive?

She couldn't tell the doctor any of that. She had to try to keep calm. "What do you know about his condition? Is there a chance he could wake up from this coma? Would he be able to lead a normal life again?" She was already trying to formulate a plan in her head to get Sam's soul back into his body. If this truly was the correct patient record and Sam's body had a little bit of life left in it, maybe it wasn't too late to fix what had been broken. It seemed far-fetched, but at least, it was a plan.

"No," the doctor asserted plainly. "There's no way this guy is ever waking up. Even if he could, he would be so brain damaged he wouldn't be able to function." So much for bedside manner. "He breathes on his own. He doesn't need a vent. But we've got him on a feeding tube. If he was awake, he would be in pretty much the same condition, except the poor sap would know what was going on. That's no kind of life."

Another thought occurred to Sara. "Isn't Saint Gertrude an emergency hospital? Why is he still there? Shouldn't he have been transferred somewhere else by now?"

"Yeah, he should have been transferred to a long-term care facility or a nursing home by now." Damian sounded as though Sam's continued residence in the hospital was some sort of personal affront to him. "The thing is, we need his next of kin to sign the release papers for his transfer. No one returns our calls. No one comes to visit."

That sounded strange to Sara too. "But isn't he married? Shouldn't his wife be coming to visit him?"

"She came once, the day after he was admitted. She hasn't been back since. Nobody has."

The thought of Sam's solitude broke her heart. He had been in a coma for three years, and nobody had even come to check on him. His own wife didn't care enough to even return a phone call. No wonder he had become so bitter. When she tried to imagine what his life must have been like, Sara could begin to understand why Sam thought the world of the living was such a lonely, desolate place.

"Sara." The sound of Damian's voice brought her back to the present. She didn't like the sound of her own name coming out of this man's mouth. "I have to go. Delete that text message."

"I will," Sara reassured him, although she didn't feel like doing him any favors. "Hey, one more thing." The doctor was silent. She had to check the screen of her phone to make sure the call was still connected. It was. "What's his room number?"

Sara assumed he would need to look it up or get back to her, but to her surprise, he had the answer ready. "MedSurg unit, room one-twenty." He must have been able to tell she was taken aback by the readiness of the information. He added, "I went to see him this morning. The guy looks like a ghost."

Sara pressed her eyes shut. Damian had no idea how right he was. Without much true gratefulness in her voice she said, "Thank you, Dr. Carver." There was a pause, and then, the call disconnected without so much as a goodbye.

Sara gazed out over the bay. A container ship passing through blocked her view of Oakland and Emeryville across the water. She breathed the damp foggy air and tried to make sense of it all.

Sam was alive. He had been alive all this time, and his soul didn't know it. She thought about the life he must have had. Not a single family member or friend had come to visit him in his three-year stay at the hospital. No one had come to speak to the doctors or find out about his condition. Not even his own wife. How disconnected had he been from all his loved ones before his accident that they didn't care to see him afterward? It would have been so easy to paint him as a monster if she didn't know these little details of his life. But isn't that true of everyone? We can make a person out to be whomever we want as long as we don't know the real person they are on the inside. Knowing who a person is in their soul makes them human. No human with a soul can be a monster.

Sara wanted to form a plan. She wanted to figure out how to save Sam. But she couldn't focus. She couldn't think beyond the sadness of the life he had lived and the loneliness he now existed in. That was all he was doing: existing. He wasn't living anymore. Staring out over the rippling water reflecting the late afternoon sun, Sara placed her hand around her own throat, exactly where Sam's hand had been. She placed her fingers on his purple imprints, and she let herself shed one tear for the man she knew as the Guardian.

CHAPTER 13

S ara stood on the rooftop long enough for the container ship to pass by and continue on under the Bay Bridge. She felt anchored to the spot, as if she were a tree that had tangled its roots deep into the earth beneath her. She could not will herself to move. She had to wait for the earth to move her. This changed everything. Sam was alive. Before gaining this knowledge, she felt like she was helping a creature, a supernatural being, from some science fiction movie. He didn't seem entirely real, and that distance from reality made the whole thing a little easier for her to face. It all seemed somewhat fake. Now, she was talking about a living, breathing person, a person still in her own world. Sam was no longer some historical figure who may or may not have died in a subway station three years ago. He was a human being. She wasn't just messing around with Catharta. She was messing around with her own reality too.

The ringing of her phone startled Sara out of her frozen state. She looked at the screen. It was Tim. She connected the call.

"Hey," she greeted him. "Where are you?"

"Where am I?" he asked in surprise. "I'm at your desk with a cup of coffee for you, and it's getting colder by the minute. Where are you?"

She hesitated, but then answered, "I'm on the roof." For some reason, she felt ridiculous admitting this fact, like a child hiding under her bed from invisible monsters.

There was a long pause followed by Tim saying, "I'll be right there."

The call disconnected, and Sara forced her feet to move. She had probably only been standing in that spot for ten minutes, but she felt like a statue, cold and stony. She was colder than she had any right to be on this mild September afternoon, fading into evening. In a way, she wished she were a statue. Statues had no responsibilities. They didn't have to make decisions or try to do the right thing or even think. They just existed, and that was enough for everyone. No one expected anything more from them.

Tim emerged onto the rooftop with a cup of Blue Bottle coffee in each hand. His assignment must have been near the ferry building. They were both coffee snobs and couldn't stomach the brown sludge that was available in the office, so Tim tended to bring her the good stuff whenever his job allowed it.

"Thank you," she said as she took the cup from him gratefully and tapped the rim of her cup against his. They both turned to face the water. They sipped in silence for a moment before Tim asked, "So what happened? You don't normally make a habit of hanging out on the roof."

Sara fussed with the cardboard liner around her coffee cup, unsure where to begin. Saying it out loud was going to make it feel more real. She didn't feel prepared. She had discussed Sam with Damian, but he didn't even know half of the story. Tim knew everything. He was going to force her to face the implications of the Guardian's living state.

"Sara," Tim prodded her.

He'd probably said her name a thousand times over the course of their friendship, but somehow, the sound of it shocked her. It was the opposite of how she had felt when the Guardian had said her name—singled out, marked. Coming out of Tim's mouth, it sounded safe and sheltered, protected.

She told him, "The doctor sent me the medical records."

Tim straightened a little, looking anxious. "And?" he pushed her onward.

Sara looked into Tim's eyes. "He's alive. The Guardian, Sam, he's still alive. That's why there's no death certificate for him. He never died."

Tim went pale, but he had no words. His only response was a slack-jawed, wide-eyed stare. Sara felt validated that at least she wasn't the only one to be so rocked by this information. She went on. "He was still alive when the paramedics got there. They took him to Saint Gertrude. He's still there today, in a coma. He's been there almost three years, and he's only had one visitor in all that time. His soulless body just stays there, all alone. That's why he can't be reborn. He's not dead." The words were tumbling out of her now, seemingly in no particular order. She didn't want to hold anything back. She wanted someone to share the burden of this knowledge with her. She needed to get it out of her.

"Are you sure it's not some kind of mistake?" Tim was in the same state of denial that Sara had been in upon first learning Sam was alive. "We don't know a whole lot about this guy. What if the coma patient isn't the same person?"

Tim's initial reaction was so similar to her own that she almost laughed. "I talked to Dr. Carver. There are too many similarities. I think it has to be our Guardian."

Tim was once again speechless, so Sara added one more thing, a fear she hadn't put into words yet, not even inside her own head. "Tim, I think that's what would happen to me if someone moved my body while I was in Catharta. When I went there by myself, I could have ended up trapped there forever, just like Sam."

Hearing the quaver in her voice, Tim put one arm around her shoulders. "That's all the more reason for you not to go to Catharta by yourself." He looked lost in thought for a moment, like he had drifted away across the bay. Then, he suggested, "What if I went for you?"

Sara was taken aback, "To Catharta?"

"Why not? I told you I'd help you, that I'd be here to support you. Why not at least let me try? It could take some of the burden off you."

She knew he was trying to be helpful, so she didn't want to simply shut him down, but she didn't think it would even be possible for him to go to Catharta. "What would you do when you got there?

You don't know Ananda or the Guardian. Plus, we don't even have a plan yet. I don't know what the next move should be."

He looked disappointed. He really just wanted to help. She tried to assuage his feelings. "I don't really think you have a choice anyway. I think it has to be me. The medical records gave his full name and his date of birth. We have the same initials and the same birthday. Between those connections and the similar events that brought me there in the first place…"

"It's like Catharta thinks you're him," Tim finished the thought for her.

Sara nodded. "I think the ghost plane is trying to finish what it started."

They stared out at the bay again, both their brains cranking at full speed. Then Tim said, "Well I think I know what your next move should be." Sara looked at him questioningly.

"You need to make sure this is the same guy. There's no point speculating if there's a chance it might be a different person lying in that hospital bed. You need to go see him."

This felt reminiscent of being told she needed to go visit Greg Hastings in prison. The responsibility resting on her shoulders felt like it might crush her.

Noting her reluctance, Tim added. "You're the only person who knows what he looks like. Besides, at least you won't have to talk to him."

She knew he was right. That should be the next step. She was still nervous about cementing him in this world as a real person. She reminded herself that the person lying in that hospital bed was a real person whether she went to see him or not. Avoiding it didn't make it any less true. "What do I do if it's him? What does that prove and where do I go from there?"

"You do what you've been doing all along," Tim coached her. "You cross that bridge when you come to it. Look how far you've come and how much you've learned in just a few days. You've gone from not knowing what Catharta was, to understanding how it works, to knowing Sam's plan and now possibly having tracked down his body. You're doing just fine so far." He had managed to say all this with sincerity. There was no teasing tone or cocked eyebrow that she was so accustomed to. He wasn't trying to sound like her father or her football coach. He was just supporting her and encouraging her as a friend, just like he had promised her he would.

"You're right," she admitted. "I guess I don't have to have all the answers right now. It sure would make everything a lot easier though." She took another sip of coffee. She wasn't sure if it was the hot beverage or the confidence Tim was trying to instill in her, but she felt warmer, less stiff. She tried to form concrete steps to the tiny beginning of a plan she was holding onto. "Well, I can't go now. Jeff would never grant me another excursion. I'm not sure what visiting hours are, but I'm pretty sure they won't let me in after work tonight. I guess I'll have to go tomorrow." She felt like she was losing something more than just time, just another day. She needed to resolve something soon. She needed to figure this out, and she didn't want to have to wait another day to get to that next step.

"If only you knew someone who could get you in after hours." Tim gave her a goading look, eyes slightly narrowed, lips pursed to one side. She wasn't catching on. "Someone who, maybe, used to work there. Someone who seems to become best friends with practically everyone she ever meets. Someone who probably has friends working at the hospital tonight."

His suggestion suddenly seemed obvious. "Maya," Sara concluded. "Why didn't I think of that? She knows half the hospital."

She pulled out her phone and called her sister. Maya picked up on the first ring. "Tell me you found something interesting."

Sara smiled at her sister's lack of patience even for simple things like saying hello when she answered the phone. "I did find something interesting, and now, I need your help."

Maya squealed in excitement, and Sara went on with her request. "Can you meet me at Saint Gertrude when I get off work? If you're not too tired, that is. Baby comes first."

Sounding a little suspicious, Maya asked, "Does this have anything to do with Damian? I told you before, I've made peace with him. I have no need to confront him about anything. And he hasn't seen me since I've been so obviously pregnant. I don't want to upset him by letting him see me like this."

Maya was always so concerned about other people's feelings, even the deadbeat dad of her unborn child. She reassured her little sister this had nothing to do with Dr. Carver. "He won't even be there. This is about the Guardian. But I need your help getting me into the MedSurg unit. Could you make some calls and see if you know anyone who's working tonight?"

"I'm on it!" she declared. Then, she hung up without saying goodbye.

Sara turned to Tim. "Well, it looks like I might have a way in tonight." She tried to sound happy and accomplished, but she was sure the trepidation came through her voice.

"I wish I could come with you," Tim said. Sara hadn't realized that she was assuming he'd be along for this caper. Now that she knew he wouldn't be there, she felt a little abandoned. She wasn't sure why. Maya would be there. All she was doing was looking at a coma patient to see if his image matched the soul that she knew.

The disappointment must have shown on her face, because Tim quickly offered an explanation. "Melissa is coming over tonight. She has some of my stuff. I have some of her stuff. I guess she feels it's been enough time that we should do the breakup exchange."

Sara was flush with embarrassment. She had initially been so hurt that Tim had been reluctant to share the news of his breakup with Melissa. But since finding out last week, she had barely thought about it. In truth, she had completely forgotten about Melissa. She felt horribly selfish now for occupying all his time and obsessing over her own problems when he must be hurting still. He really hadn't talked much about how he felt about the relationship ending, but from the little he'd told her, it sounded like she had initiated the breakup. As guarded as he could be with his emotions, Sara knew Tim must be at least a little heartbroken.

She also felt a pang of jealousy. It surprised her to find that emotion within herself. Tim had spent a lot of time with her lately, but she couldn't very well expect him to spend every waking minute by her side until she figured out how to fix the problems of Catharta. He had a life outside of her current dilemma. She couldn't allow herself to feel jealous of his needing to attend to that life. She buried that jealousy as deeply as she could.

She wanted to get him to open up about his split from Melissa a little, although she knew that might be a wasted effort. "Is this the first time you've seen her since the breakup?" she asked.

Tim nodded, still staring out over the water.

"Are you going to be okay seeing her again? Are you ready?" Again, Tim nodded.

Sara searched her mind for something other than a yes or no question, but anything else felt too invasive. She thought of how helpful Tim had been to her lately, talking her through her self-doubt and accompanying her to all sorts of unusual places at odd hours. She offered, "Would it make it easier if I came with you?" Sara didn't want to abandon her plans to go to the hospital that night, but she would do it if it meant being there for her best friend in his time of need.

To her surprise, Tim laughed. With his eyes still locked on the bay, he replied, "No, that would actually make it exponentially worse."

Sara was a little hurt that he had denied her offer so quickly, but she swallowed it. If her company wasn't what he needed, she wouldn't force it on him.

"Listen," he said, finally turning to face her. He was smiling, but there were some other unreadable emotions behind his expression. "I'm going to be fine. I'm a big boy. I can handle my own breakup. She'll probably only be there a few minutes. You have something more important you need to take care of."

Sara nodded. He was right. She needed to focus on her next step. She drained the rest of her coffee. "If you change your mind," Sara began, but Tim didn't let her finish.

He placed an arm around her shoulders and gave her a little squeeze. "Thanks."

They stared at the water a few moments longer and then decided they had been missing in action long enough. They made their way back down to their respective desks to finish out the workday.

Sara moved through the rest of her day like a sleepwalker, fairly sure she was accomplishing something, but unsure of what. She was pretty confident she had edited all her stories and met all her deadlines, but she couldn't tell you what a single article was about. As soon as she noticed some other members of swing shift heading for the exit, she packed up her things and got ready to go.

Stopping by Tim's office on her way out, she found he was still there, hunched over his computer with his back to the door.

"You heading out soon?" she asked, startling him a little. She got a little thrill out of seeing him jump. He was always so in tune to his surroundings. Or maybe he was just in tune with her whereabouts. Either way, she felt a small satisfaction out of having snuck up on him. Then she felt guilty, seeing how discomposed he looked. "Are you going to be alright?"

Tim raked his fingers through his hair and put his face back together into one of his calm and collected looks. "I'll be fine." Then, looking her up and down, he asked, "Will you be alright?"

Sara was still anxious about seeing Sam, but she kept telling herself she was just going to the hospital with Maya. She wasn't allowing herself to think much beyond that. Just like Tim had suggested, she was taking it one step at a time. She forced a smile. "I'm going to be fine too."

They remained in awkward silence for a moment, both thinking of the unsavory tasks ahead of them, before Sara said, "I'll see you tomorrow, Tim."

When he didn't reply, she turned and left. She needed to catch her bus. She didn't want to leave Maya hanging out in the Mission District by herself at night.

Sara found her sister milling around the gift shop where she used to work, just inside the main lobby at Saint Gertrude.

"There you are," she said as Sara approached. Before Sara could greet her in return, Maya announced, "So I got you a way in. I know the charge nurse working the MedSurg unit tonight. She's going to let us in. She wanted to know why, and I told her I had no idea, that I was just doing a favor for my sister, which is true. So are you going to tell me why we're here?"

Sara glanced around the lobby and saw no one but a security guard at the far end. She decided this was as good a place as any to fill Maya in on what she had learned earlier in the day.

"We're here to see the Guardian," she whispered.

"The Guardian?" Maya asked a little too loudly for Sara's comfort. Hearing the echo of her own voice, she lowered it and asked, "Then shouldn't we be going to the morgue, not the medical surgical unit?"

Sara just slowly shook her head.

Maya gave a little puppy head tilt of confusion. "But then what's in the MedSurg unit?" Sara stared at her, willing her to figure it out.

It clicked in Maya's head. She clapped her hand to her mouth to cover her sudden gasp. Then, she whispered, "He's alive?" Sara nodded her head in confirmation, and Maya asked, "But how? Since when? How did you find out?"

Sara answered, "He's been here since the night of the incident. The doc got me his medical records. He's alive, but he's in a coma with basically zero chance of ever recovering."

Maya's eyes were wide with shock and disbelief. "And you're sure it's him?"

"That's exactly what we're here to find out." She looped her arm through Maya's and turned her sister toward the elevator. The security guard never looked up from his desk. Maya took them to the correct floor and then led Sara down long, identical looking hallways. She could never understand how people found their way around these places. There were no windows, and every direction you turned looked exactly like the way you had come.

They turned one last corner, and the hallway opened up to a nurses' station. A redheaded woman in scrubs sat behind the counter and looked up, startled, as they approached. Upon seeing Maya, she softened. "Maya!" she greeted Sara's sister.

"Rachel!" Maya greeted in return.

Rachel stood and came around from behind her station. She opened her arms wide as if to give Maya a hug, but instead placed one hand on either side of the pregnant woman's beach ball of a belly. "You've gotten so big! You must be about to pop any day."

Sara felt uncomfortable watching what seemed to be a very intimate moment between her sister and a stranger. Maya must have sensed her discomfort, so she made introductions. "Rachel, this is my sister, Sara. Sara, this is Rachel. She's the charge nurse in this unit."

The two women shook hands. "Nice to meet you," Sara said. "Sorry to barge in on you like this."

"It's no bother," Rachel insisted. "It's a slow night anyway. But Maya didn't really tell me what you need. I'm not sure how I can help you."

"Well," Sara began sheepishly. "I know it's after visiting hours, but I was hoping I could go in and visit the patient in room one-twenty."

Rachel raised her eyebrows in surprise. "One-twenty? Do you know that guy? He doesn't get visitors."

Sara didn't want to give any more information than she absolutely had to. "I don't really know him. I'd just really like to see him if I could."

Rachel went back to her station. "He's not due for vitals until tomorrow. No one will be going in or out of there. Just"—Rachel fidgeted nervously—"try not to let yourself be seen, okay?"

"I'll be quick," Sara promised. Rachel pointed Sara in the right direction, and Maya hung back to talk to her old friend. Sara left the two women, Rachel filling Maya in on the latest hospital gossip, and went in search of room one-twenty.

She found the room, looked both ways down the hallway, and then quietly slipped inside. The room was dim. The overhead lights were off. There was a curtain pulled shut, blocking the view of the only bed in the room. The only light emanated from behind that curtain. Sara instinctively felt drawn to it, but she wasn't ready to move in that direction just yet. In her mind, she was still trying to come up with some possible explanation of how this might not be the same Sam. There could be another man with the same name. It was obviously a very common name. There could even be another man with the same name who also had an accident in the Sixteenth Street subway station. It was possible. But on the same date? A little less possible. She realized she was stalling, bargaining with herself or with some unseen power. A part of her wanted to pull back that curtain and see someone else lying there in that hospital bed. She wanted Sam to be dead, a ghost, a resident of Catharta. She wasn't sure how to deal with him being a living, breathing human being. But if it wasn't him lying in that hospital bed, that would be even worse, wouldn't it? Then she would be no closer to solving the mystery of Sam than she was on the day she met him. She wouldn't know what to do next. She might even be forced to give up.

This was ridiculous. She had come all this way. She just needed to walk another ten feet and find out one way or the other. Forcefully, she took one slow, deliberate step forward and then another and another, until she was standing within arm's reach of the curtain. She hesitated again. She wished Tim or Maya were here with her. They wouldn't let her chicken out. They would force her hand, make her do what she came here to do. She tried to channel some of their confidence or manifest one of Tim's pep talks. There was no one else here to push her. She had to find the strength within herself.

She pulled back the curtain.

All the air escaped her lungs. Her blood pulsed through her ears, deafening her in the silence of the hospital room. Her skin crawled as if she didn't fit inside it any longer. She pressed her eyes shut, silently wishing she had a time machine that could take her back in time just ten seconds so she could unsee this.

What she saw looked like a corpse. There was a husk of a man lying in the hospital bed, looking scrawny and pale. Monitors were attached to his chest and arms, letting Rachel at the nurses' station know that he was still alive, if only just barely. An IV snaked its way into his arm, giving him the fluids and nutrients that were keeping him clinging to this life. His eyes were closed, and they were sunk deep into his head, just below his high forehead. His hair was sparser and more matted. The pallor of his skin made him appear gray, almost translucent. But there was no doubt that this was Sam Johnson. This was the body of the man she knew as the Guardian.

Sara had been at the side of many hospital beds. She had seen both her parents wasting away like this, tubes keeping them alive. She was all too familiar with the sterile smell of the room, the dryness of the air, and the beeping and humming of the machines. But this was different. With her parents, she knew she was in the process of saying goodbye. Now, she was saying hello for the first time to the physical form of Sam, knowing full well what he had become since he died, or nearly died. She still didn't fully understand how his soul could be wreaking such havoc on the other side, while his body remained breathing in this world.

She felt like she might faint, and she looked around the room for a place to sit down. The usual visitor chairs had been removed, probably put to better use in other rooms once everyone realized no one would be coming to visit this man. To avoid collapsing, she was forced to step forward and place her hands on the bed, bringing her even closer to the ghost of a man.

Sara closed her eyes and took a few deep breaths to steady herself. She had done what she came here to do. She had confirmed that the Guardian was still alive, that he was here, that his body was exactly where his medical record said it would be. She could turn and leave if she wanted to. Somehow that freedom emboldened her. She had accomplished what she came here for, but now, there was one more thing she wanted to do.

Slowly, cautiously, she edged toward the head of the bed. As she stood alongside the man's shoulder, she leaned in closer to get a better look at his face. It was heavily creased, not with the normal smile lines and crow's feet that come with age. Every inch of his skin was a canvas of very fine, crisscross lines, like the floor of a dry riverbed, marked by the flow of the water and then left to dry up into a rough crust.

To work up her nerve, she placed her palm on top of his hand. She pulled back at first after feeling how cold he was. He wasn't as cold as a dead person would be, but much colder than any living person ought to be. She forced herself to put her hand back on top of his. She let some of her warmth flow into him. When she felt brave enough, she turned so she could place both hands on either side of his face. It felt far too intimate, but she reminded herself that she knew this man's soul. Nothing could be more intimate than that.

Gently, she placed a thumb on each of his eyelids. With the delicacy she might use to handle butterfly wings, she lifted his lids. A part of her expected to see the familiar glowing orbs she knew from Catharta staring back at her with the same intensity and wildness she was used to. What she saw were blue eyes with pinhole pupils, so pale they looked almost clear. The light color was like a small nod to the crystal clear eyes his soul now possessed. She wondered if his eyes were always such a light blue or if they had become dim and ashen in his invalid state.

She stared into eyes that didn't look back at her, that looked at nothingness. She stared at them and thought of the dead gray eyes of Gregory Hastings. She thought of looking into that murderer's eyes and knowing within the depths of herself that he had no soul. Now, she looked into the eyes of Sam Johnson, and with the same conviction, she knew that he did have a soul. It was more than just knowing that his soul existed in the ghost plane. She was looking at his soul now. Some fractured piece of him still resided in this body, and suddenly, it all made sense.

Sam wasn't tethered by the rules of Catharta because his soul there was incomplete. Part of it was still in the world of the living. That's why he could move the way he did, disobeying the laws of physics all the other souls were bound by. That was why he couldn't be reborn. It wasn't just that his body was still alive, but Catharta was refusing to birth an incomplete soul. That must be why the gateway was still open. The ghost plane was desperately trying to finish what it started. That's why it had left an open door, like a magnet, trying to draw in the rest of this man. It was trying to collect what it was owed.

Sara carefully lowered his eyelids. She wondered if there could be another gateway here, waiting for the day his body finally gave up, and the remainder of his broken soul escaped. She tried to sense the gateway, but then realized it was a wasted effort. She couldn't sense the gateway at the Sixteenth Street subway station. She only knew it was there because she had accidentally fallen into it. If Sam did die here, would this tiny fragment of his soul be strong enough to travel to Catharta? Would he be able to find his way back to the Guardian?

Could his soul be made whole again? She didn't know, but she had an idea who might.

Just as Tim had said, she had taken this next step of coming to see Sam, and now, she knew where to go next. She had to go back to Catharta.

She leaned in and whispered, "I'm going to find a way to fix this. I promise." She gave Sam's hand one final, tiny pat, and then she backed away from the hospital bed. She drew the curtain back into place and silently slipped out of the room.

She reunited with Maya back at the nurses' station where she was still chatting with Rachel. As Sara approached, Maya asked awkwardly, "Did you, um, get what you needed?" Sara nodded, "Yeah, but we have to go."

Maya and Rachel said a quick goodbye with a promise to stay in touch, and then, Maya and Sara were rushing down the hallway toward the elevator and out of the hospital. Once they were out the front doors, Maya asked, "So, was it him?"

"It was him," Sara confirmed.

Maya grabbed Sara's arm and squeezed in a show of shock or excitement and attempted to pull her in the direction of the bus stop, which was probably how she had arrived at the hospital earlier that evening.

"No," Sara insisted, pulling her in the other direction. "We need to take the subway home."

Maya gave her a knowing look and followed along toward the station entrance. Once they made their way to the platform, the overhead voice indicated the next train would be arriving in four minutes. Sara decided to take the opportunity to warn Maya about what she was about to witness since she had yet to accompany her on one of these journeys.

"So, I know Tim has put some ideas in your head about me throwing myself in front of the train. I promise you it's not that dramatic. But I am going to fall down backward, and you can't try to catch me. Got it?"

Maya was ecstatic about being included in this part of Sara's mission. She enthusiastically agreed, "Got it!"

"And once I'm down"—Sara continued—"you can't let anyone move me. I'm pretty sure that's how the Guardian got trapped between two worlds."

"Don't worry, I won't let anyone come near you," Maya said, glancing around the quiet platform to ensure no one needed to be immediately fended off.

The overhead speaker announced that a San Francisco airport train was now approaching the platform. That was Sara's ride.

"Here we go. Are you ready?"

Maya answered with one curt nod, all business now.

Sara took her place on the platform. She touched one finger to her mother's locket that still hung around her neck. She had gotten into this tangled mess because she had gone to retrieve the necklace for Maya, yet she was the one who had been wearing it ever since. It felt like much more than a memory or a family heirloom. It was a talisman now.

The air around the two women began to swirl. Sara's dark, wavy hair billowed around her shoulders as did Maya's lighter, straighter locks. The platform began to rumble as the train approached. The sound of the wind preceded the sound of the train barreling through the tunnel toward the Sixteenth Street subway station. Sara looked over her shoulder and saw the beginning of concentric circles of light illuminating the tunnel from the train's headlights. As it rounded the bend in the tunnel, the reflected light shot down the length of the steel rails, first one then the other, like the tails of two parallel shooting stars. Then, in a wail of thunderous noise, the train burst forth from the mouth of the tunnel. That was Sara's cue. She pitched herself back, letting her feet be swept out from beneath her. She did a trust fall, feeling secure in the knowledge that Catharta would catch her. Eyes wide open, she fell back, hearing a small yelp escape her sister, but true to her duty, Maya did nothing to try to stop her. And then she was falling into a deep, dark nothingness, like sinking into a black sea. She fell until there was no light and no sound. There was nothing left of the world, and all that was left of her was her soul.

CHAPTER 14

*W*aking up in Catharta was like escaping into a dream. Back in the real world, Sara was wiped out. She'd had a long, emotionally exhausting day, and her body was begging her to go home and crawl into bed. Here in Catharta, she couldn't feel any of the physical symptoms of exhaustion. She couldn't feel the pain she knew should be forming at the back of her head from throwing herself onto the unforgiving tile of the train platform yet again. She couldn't feel much of anything. In a way, it was a relief.

Then, she remembered her sense of urgency. There was always a sense of urgency when she was in Catharta. She didn't know how long she could stay here without risking becoming trapped. Even with Maya guarding her body, she couldn't be sure no harm would come to her back in the world of the living. There was too much uncertainty. She couldn't risk wasting time.

Sara pushed herself up to a sitting position and looked around. Maya had vanished, as had the train at the platform. She wondered on that for a second. The train station was here because she remembered it, because most of the residents of Catharta remembered it. She remembered the train too. Why was it never here? She shook it off. She had to accept that she would never fully understand the rules of the ghost plane.

Standing up, she rushed toward the opposite end of the station and ascended the stairs. As she stepped out onto the pavement of Mission Street, she blinked away the brightness of the slate gray sky. It wasn't so blinding as a sunny day in San Francisco should be, but much brighter than the cavernous depths of the subway station.

She glanced around. No one was in sight. She needed to find Ananda quickly. She decided to call out to her. While in Catharta, she often felt a need to maintain the quiet of her surroundings and speak in hushed tones, like whispering in a library. But she couldn't see Ananda anywhere, and she trusted she was nearby somewhere just as she had promised she would be. Sara stepped out into the center of Mission and cupped her hands around her mouth, calling out Ananda's name. She stood perfectly still and listened, but heard nothing. Sara turned to face the other way and called out to her friend again. She waited, but heard nothing, which is why she nearly jumped out of her skin when she felt a hand placed upon her shoulder. Whipping around, she found herself face to face with the Guardian.

Of course, she hadn't heard his approach. He moved soundlessly, instantaneously. It was almost as if he could astral project himself anywhere he wanted to be. Sara took a couple long strides back from him, not anxious to be within reach of his talon-like hands again. She knew that the news she brought with her was likely to set off his hair-trigger temper.

"Back again I see," he growled. "You just can't seem to stay away."

Sara gathered her courage. This was the first time she'd been alone with him since the moment they had met. She tried to block out his intimidating form and picture him more like the withered carcass she had just encountered at the hospital. It helped him seem less frightening.

"I'm back because my business here isn't finished." She felt a surprising strength behind her own voice, but the anger and hatred of this man was gone. That wasn't what fueled her courage any longer. She could no longer envision him as the villain she had made him out to be. His life was too sad. His mere existence, living in suspension, was too pathetic. She couldn't hate him anymore. Instead, she felt sorry for him.

"Your kind has no business being here. If you really want to stay in Catharta, I'd invite you to drop dead." The sarcasm and venom in his tone hurt a little, but Sara knew he was just lashing out. The last time she had seen him she'd told him that everything he believed about his own death was a lie. His attempts to discredit and dismiss her were his way of protecting the story he had built about himself and the persona he tried to present. How could she begin to tell him that he wasn't actually dead at all? That what he considered "her kind" was, in fact, his kind too. He was one of the living.

They were both distracted by footsteps approaching. Ananda emerged from between two tall buildings and rushed toward them, commanding, "Don't you dare touch her!"

"Oh good!" Sam said with an exaggerated flourish. "Ananda has come to collect her pet. You really ought to keep her on a leash if you're going to let her keep coming back here."

Ananda reached the point where they were standing and came to a halt. "I don't let her do anything. She's free to come and go as she pleases, unlike the rest of your prisoners."

Sam threw up his hands in defense. "No one here is a prisoner. They're here because it's safer for them. I'm keeping them free from pain. I'm keeping them happy."

"Look around!" Ananda shouted, spinning in a circle in the empty street. "Do you see one happy person? Do you see anyone at all? No, you don't. They're all in hiding because they're terrified of you!"

"I'm not," Sara interjected. It wasn't entirely true. A big part of her was still petrified by this sinister man. But she tried again to think not of the towering soul with glowing eyes before her, but of the weak and scrawny man in the hospital bed whose eyes still held a whisper of a soul. That man was someone she was not afraid of. "I'm not afraid of you because I know what you are."

The Guardian folded his arms across his chest smugly. "Is that right? And what exactly am I?"

"You're alive," Sara uttered. The three of them stood motionless while she waited for this information to sink in.

Sam just eyed her suspiciously as Ananda said, "That's not possible. Sara, look at your eyes and look at his. You're alive. He's not."

"He is," Sara insisted. "I've just come from visiting his body. I watched him breathe. He's alive."

Sam's posture drooped and then quickly returned to something more aggressive. "Lies," he spat, glaring down at her with contempt.

Sara shook her head calmly. "It's true, and I think I can prove it. But I need you to come with me."

"I'm dead! I'm a ghost! You come here with your wild stories, trying to upset the peace of this place. You're trying to drag the misery of your world into mine. I won't allow it!" He was crumbling inside, and it broke Sara's heart.

"You're not dead," she told him gently, but insistently. "That's why you haven't been reborn yet. Your life isn't over." She looked into his clear, faintly glowing eyes, less viscous now, more broken. He wanted to believe.

He turned away from her and shouted into the empty street, "It's not true!"

Sara feared he was about to bolt. She couldn't lose him now. If he left, he would find a way to convince himself she was lying, and she might miss her only chance to help him. In an attempt to keep him from running, she began reciting everything she knew about him.

"Sam Eli Johnson, born August 5, 1976. Married with no children. You were struck by a train on September 27, 2014. You were taken to Saint Gertrude Memorial Hospital. You had two separate operations, and your living body still resides in room one-twenty of the MedSurg unit. That's where I want to take you. Will you come with me?"

Sara held her breath, waiting for a response. In the corner of her eye, she thought she saw a building flicker. There were too many competing memories here. She was worried about the stability of the place where they were standing, but she held her gaze, staring at the back of the Guardian's head.

Slowly, he turned around. His face was a web of conflict. Part of him truly wanted to believe her. She could see that. But a big part of him was controlled by the character he had invented for himself to cope with being trapped in Catharta. The Guardian was not who Sam really was. The terrorizing image and threatening tone he had taken on were just defense mechanisms against his own fears and uncertainties. The real Sam was still somewhere inside this figure. But he had been buried by what felt to him like thirty years trapped in Catharta.

Sara wanted to scream at him that she saw right through him. He should drop the act already and just go with her. She knew it was what he wanted deep down. He wanted hope. He wanted to know there was something more than the stasis that imprisoned him. But she didn't. She waited, silently, but shouting in her mind for him to let her help him.

"And do what?" he finally responded. "You want me to go with you to what end?"

Sara hadn't really thought about why she needed Sam to go with her to the hospital so badly. Like Tim had suggested, she was taking everything one step at a time. She had seen Sam's body and known that she needed to go to Catharta. She had gone to Catharta and seen Sam's spirit and known that she needed to take him to the spot where his body lay. Now, he wanted to know what she intended if she got him there. She wasn't prepared to think that far ahead yet.

Unable to think of a solid plan for once she got him there and guessing he may be more responsive to a challenge than a plea, she asked, "Do you have somewhere more important to be? If I'm wrong, you have the rest of eternity to be anywhere else but at that hospital. So you might as well come with me this one time. Unless, of course, you're afraid."

"There is no fear in Catharta. There is no pain." His response was firm, but something had softened inside him. She was sure she nearly had him convinced.

Ananda jumped in. "Prove it. Go to the hospital. Prove you're not afraid."

That was enough. He and Ananda had too much history together. He could not back down from her challenge. Sam glared at Ananda and then back to Sara. "I'll see you there."

In a flash, he was gone, nothing more than a faint trail of a man leading off in the direction of Saint Gertrude. Sara and Ananda looked at one another in amazement. Neither could believe they had gotten the Guardian to bend to their will. They headed off in the direction of the hospital at a run.

"How can Sam still be alive? How can his body go on living without his soul?" Ananda asked, still somewhat disbelieving. It sounded rhetorical, but Sara answered anyway.

"I think a part of his soul is still in his body. I think the soul of Sam that you know is fractured. He's missing a piece. I think that's why the gateway is still open, waiting for the rest of him to pass through. That tiny piece of his soul is keeping his body clinging to life, and the fact that it's missing in this world is keeping him from being reborn."

They were approaching the hospital. Ananda slowed and asked, "Can this be fixed? Is there any hope for him?"

"I don't know," Sara answered honestly. In truth, she felt Ananda was much more qualified to answer that question than she was. Ananda knew the way Catharta worked. But they were walking down an unfamiliar path. It was all guesswork for both of them. "But I have to at least try."

The two women entered the lobby of the hospital, and Sara led her friend up a set of stairs to the level of the MedSurg unit. Apparently, elevators didn't work in Catharta any more than escalators or subway trains. They wound their way through the identical hallways, having to double back once, and finally found the nurses' station where Sara had met Nurse Rachel earlier that evening. She peered cautiously around the corner that led to room one-twenty. Sam was standing motionless outside the closed door. Had he waited for them? Or was he paralyzed with fear and trepidation as Sara had been when faced with the same hospital room? She took Ananda's hand and led her in the direction of the Guardian.

They approached him cautiously, not wanting to startle him although he undoubtedly knew they were there. As they stood along-side him, Sara found herself unsure of what to say. She wanted to urge him forward, but she recognized that this was a delicate situation. In the end, she didn't have to say anything. Sam broke the silence.

"I'm dead. I went to the place where I was meant to die. I died there. People don't come back from that." His voice was calm and even. His words indicated his denial, but his tone showed no sign of distress.

Sara shivered as an eerie feeling crept over her. His words, although they sounded less grim in light of her experiences over the past five days, reminded her of her own thoughts and musings, thoughts for which her sister had accused her of being morbid. She wondered if she had more in common with Sam than their initials and a birthday. His thoughts were familiar to her, as if they could have been her own.

"You did die, Sam. The you that is here right now is dead. But you're not whole. Part of you has gone on living all this time. That part of you is in another world, but just on the other side of this door." Sara reached out and put one hand on the doorknob. When Sam didn't stop her, she turned it, and swung the door open.

Within the room was the same pale blue curtain Sara remembered, drawn shut around the bed, a faint light shining from somewhere within its folds. Sara waited for the Guardian to take the first step.

When he finally moved forward into the room, it was like he was gliding, propelled forward by instinct, not deliberate intention. Sara followed with Ananda close behind. Once they were all inside the room, Sara stepped around Sam and approached the curtain. She gripped the fabric in one hand and turned to see if Sam was prepared. He remained motionless and flinty. Sara decided that was the best indication she was going to get that he was ready.

She pulled the curtain back and revealed an empty hospital bed, a heart monitor, and an IV bag on a pole, both hooked up to nothing. The monitor didn't beep and showed no readings.

The IV bag didn't drip, but sat in the corner filled with fluids that went to no use.

Sara shut her eyes and shook her head in disappointment, and Ananda put a hand on her shoulder. "I thought," Sara began, but her voice trailed off. She didn't know what she had thought. Or rather, it hadn't dawned on her what she had expected to find until she realized it wasn't there. Ridiculous as she felt for her mistake, she admitted, "I thought he'd be here. I thought that this place was made out of memories. I remember him, vividly, lying in this bed. If I remember him, why can't he be here?"

"It doesn't work that way," Sam muttered sourly.

Ananda agreed, "It doesn't matter how clearly you remember. If someone or something is alive, it doesn't exist in Catharta. If he were here, that would mean he'd have died." Sensing Sara's disappointment, she added, "This proves your point though. He's still alive."

Sara let it all sink in. That all made sense, and she saw now that she should have known Sam's living body wouldn't be here anymore than her own body was in the subway station when she transported to the ghost plane. She thought maybe they'd be able to see a glimmer of his soul. But there was nothing visible at all.

Then, a thought occurred to her. The gateway on the platform at Sixteenth Street wasn't visible either. Maybe there was a gateway here that they couldn't see. Maybe there was a portal that could take Sam's soul back to his body. It may be true that he couldn't be reborn, but perhaps he could still finish the life he was meant to live. Maybe if the pieces of his soul were reunited in the world of the living, everything would be set right. He could go on living as Sam Johnson. The souls of Catharta could move on to their next lives. Their imprisonment would be over, and Sara's world wouldn't be filled with soulless people. Maya's baby wouldn't be born without a soul. It seemed like too much to hope for, but she had to try. She had come this far. The least she could do was try.

She turned to face Sam squarely. Gently, but firmly, she commanded him, "You need to lie down on the bed."

He turned to look at her, and she saw a hint of the Guardian she knew, powerful and defiant. "Why?" he demanded to know.

"Your body is still alive in this very spot back in my world. A piece of your soul goes on living there. You need to reunite your soul. You need to go back to the world of the living."

She knew he despised her world or had at least convinced himself that he did. She suspected this would be a hard sell. He let his eyes drift back to the empty bed, looking detached.

Noticing his hesitation, Sara took him by the shoulders, garnering his full attention. "Look, I know that you think my world is full of pain and suffering." She thought of his lack of visitors and his wife who couldn't be bothered to answer a phone call. "I know you think it's a lonely place. But I think you were dealt a bad hand. Something happened to you in your life as Sam Johnson, and you were unhappy. But I promise you it doesn't have to be that way. If you go back to this life, you can make something else of it."

He looked doubtful, so she added, "Even if you can't be happy in that life, you at least give yourself a chance at another one. As long as you stay here with your soul broken into two pieces, you can't be reborn, forced to remember every detail of the life that left you so sad. But if you put yourself back together, you will get another chance. You'll live again, with a clean slate, with none of the hurt or loneliness that haunted you in this life." She bit her lip and held her breath, hoping her words would be enough. "But the first step is lying down on this bed."

Sam stood perfectly still, looking back at her eyes, but looking right through her. His face was awash with the turmoil of his emotions. He stood in silence for so long she thought she had lost him.

Finally, he asked, "How does it work?" He broke free of her hold and faced the bed again. "What do I have to do?"

"Lie down on the bed and close your eyes." Sara and Ananda waited as he hoisted himself onto the bed. Once on his back, staring up at the ceiling, he reluctantly closed his eyes. His lids fluttered.

Sara stepped closer to his shoulder. She was tempted to place her hand on top of his as she had done with his comatose body, but she decided against it. "Now," she instructed, "you have to think of everything you miss from the other world. Think of your family, your wife," she suggested. A deep scowl creased his forehead. "Think of your job and your home and your day-to-day life. Hold whatever you miss at the front of your mind. Think of how badly you want to get back to it and then"—she paused, hoping to give him time to come up with something he truly missed—"open your eyes."

Sam's eyes snapped open, and he looked directly up at the acoustic tiled ceiling again. Sara could almost feel the familiar sensation she would get of it were her returning to the real world, the sickening speed, the impression of rocketing upward although no motion could be observed. The jarring stop and the feeling of pressure in her head building almost to its breaking point.

Sam turned to look at her and whispered the word, "Nothing."

"Nothing happened," Sara agreed with disappointment.

Sam shook his head. "No, I mean there's nothing I want to go back to."

Sara felt momentarily ashamed of her happy life. There was virtually no limit to the things in her life she would miss if she were trapped in Catharta. Yet here this man couldn't come up with one. It was unfair. Surely, there must be something.

"What about little things?" Sara asked. "Like sleeping in on Sundays or watching sports or hobbies. You must have had a hobby."

Sam looked blankly back toward the ceiling.

"I miss the rain," Ananda said forlornly from behind Sara.

"How about the sun and the moon and the leaves on the trees, the city fog, anything?" Sara was grasping at straws now. She wasn't sure missing the weather would be enough to get him back.

Sam pushed himself up to a sitting position and spun so his legs dangled off the bed and hung his head. "You're wasting your time. I told you, there's nothing in that world that I want. There's nothing but pain there. It's better here."

He pushed himself off the bed and slowly made his way out of the room. Sara moved to follow him, trying to form more arguments in her head as to why he shouldn't give up. Ananda held her back.

"Let him go. He won't hear you now anyway. His mind isn't here anymore."

Sara was crestfallen, but she obeyed. "What do you mean his mind isn't here?"

Ananda carefully drew the curtain back around the bed. "He tries to never think of his life before. He doesn't like to talk about it. Whatever his life was like, he was very unhappy. We just forced him to confront that life, and now, he's back there, living that unhappiness." She thought for a minute and added, "I think his one consolation of being stuck in Catharta was knowing that his life was behind him. Now, he knows it's not. A part of him is still living it. I think to him that's worse than dying. He wanted that closure."

Sara felt awful for awakening this sadness in the Guardian, but she had to tell him the truth. She had to bring him here. She had to try. What did it mean that Sam couldn't access the gateway? Did it mean the gateway wasn't there at all? Or was it simply that he didn't have the tools to get back there because there was nothing in his life he wanted to return to? Maybe that was just the way the gateway worked for Sara. Maybe Sam needed to find his own trigger. She was back to the unknown. Not knowing what to do next made her feel like she was falling, not plummeting like a stone, but floating downward, slowly and aimlessly, like a feather set adrift in the wind.

"I need to be getting back," she said to avoid being overcome with a sense of failure. Ananda put an arm around her and led her out of the room. They made their way through the winding hallways toward the stairwell.

Ananda must have sensed Sara's defeat. She offered her some encouragement. "I know you're going to figure this out, Sara."

The words bounced off of her. She couldn't absorb them right now. She felt too deflated and lost. She thought about returning to her body in the real world, of facing Maya and telling her she had accomplished nothing. She was no closer to solving this problem than she was before she had dragged her sister out on this late night excursion.

As if reading her mind, Ananda said, "You are getting closer. It might not feel like it right now, but you are. You found out why Sam can't be reborn. That's more information than we've had in all our time in Catharta. Now, you just have to find out what to do with that information. This is uncharted territory. You can't expect to figure it out on the first try."

Sara knew in her heart Ananda was right. She was grateful to be surrounded by such supportive friends, both in life and in death. As they descended the stairs toward the lobby, Sara tried to imagine some alternate reality in which she and Ananda might have met in real life and been friends. She knew it was unlikely, given their age difference, that Ananda probably would have been going off to college soon, that their lives probably would have pushed them further apart, not closer together. But still, she liked the idea that their souls could have met in the world of the living. The thought was both comforting and tragic, knowing that Ananda's life had been cut so short.

As they made their way through the hospital lobby, Sara told her companion, "Thank you for believing in me. I'm not sure why it's so hard for me to believe in myself." Ananda gave Sara a sad smile and a little pat on the shoulder, and they made their way toward the doors. They were stopped short by a voice calling out from behind them, "Sara?"

The voice was familiar and warm, yet at the same time foreign and strange. She had heard that voice say her name thousands of times, and it usually made her feel safe and loved. But now, it felt wrong. It felt impossible. She must be mistaken. It couldn't be him.

She turned around slowly, cautiously, and let her eyes sweep through the lobby. There at the far end, near the corridor that led to the stairway they had just come down, was the man that had called her name. He was barefoot. He still wore the same hospital gown she had last seen him in. Sara felt her knees buckle beneath her, and now, she really was falling. Ananda reached out to steady her, but still Sara crumpled to the floor. With what felt like the last bit of breath in her lungs, she managed to whisper, "Dad."

CHAPTER 15

*H*e was running toward her now, his bare feet padding softly against the laminated tile floor. The rhythm of his strides seemed to match the beat of Sara's racing heart. She was calcified, unable to stand, unable to move. He was running toward her, but never seeming to get any closer. Then all at once, he was upon her, crouched down with his arms wrapped around her like the wings of a great bird, enveloping and cocooning her. She wanted to stay wrapped in his embrace for eternity.

It was her father. She hadn't seen him in nearly three years, not since she had held his hand at his bedside in this very hospital as he breathed his last breath. He hadn't been himself, even then. He wasn't quite a whole person anymore. His body had been trying to let go of the physical world even though his soul had clung tightly to it. For the last days of his life, he had existed in a dreamlike state. He had a few lucid moments, but mostly, he responded to any questions like a person talking in their sleep, disconnected and irrational, but calm. He had seemed so calm. Maybe that was just the drugs they had him on. Somehow, it had made everything seem worse to Sara. She knew it was best that he wasn't in pain, but it seemed unfair that every part of him should be so numb at the time when he should be saying goodbye. It was his last chance to feel anything. But then he had slipped away, and she was left to feel everything.

Now, he was here with her again. For a moment, she forgot all about the Guardian and Ananda and the whole of Catharta. All that existed was her dad. In that moment, she believed this was why she had come here. This was why Catharta kept calling to her. This is who she had been brought here to see.

No, that was selfish. All of this could not simply be for the purpose of reuniting her with her father. He was trapped here just like everyone else. She couldn't make this all about her and her longing to have her father back in her life. She was sent here not only to help him but also to help everyone.

How had she not done the math before? She should have known he'd likely still be here. Sam had died in September 2014. Her father had died in November of the same year. She didn't know exactly when Sam had discovered he couldn't be reborn or when he learned he could condemn other souls to his same fate, but two months in the real world was something like two years in Catharta. The Guardian was probably incarcerating souls in the ghost plane long before her dad showed up.

Her racing mind slowed down just long enough to realize her dad was speaking to her through his sobs. "What happened Sara? What happened to you?"

Her brain couldn't grasp the question. Her synapses fired but made no connection. What had happened to her? When? What did he mean? And then the crushing realization hit her.

"I'm not dead, Dad. Nothing happened to me. I'm still alive."

He pulled away from her, gripping her shoulders tightly and examining her face in confusion. Seeing his ghostly clear eyes sweeping over her face sent a shiver through her whole body. She had grown accustomed to those faintly luminescent eyes set into Ananda's face and even the more sinister-looking glow emanating from the Guardian, but not her own father. It was wrong. Everything about it was wrong.

"You're alive?" he asked, desperately wanting to believe, but finding it impossible. As much as Sara had longed to see him again, her dad had hoped to never see his daughters here in Catharta because that would mean their lives were over.

"Look at my eyes," Sara directed him. He did, examining each one in turn. "I'm alive, Dad. I promise you."

He hugged her tightly to himself once more, this time in relief. When he pulled away again, he asked, "How are you here?" Confusion was etched on his face.

"Well," Sara said, unsure where to begin that story. She looked over her shoulder for Ananda, but found that her friend had made herself scarce to give the father and daughter some privacy. "I found a gateway. It was an accident at first, but now, I seem to be able to come and go any time."

Her father looked worried. "That sounds dangerous. This place is nothing to play around with."

"I know," Sara agreed. "But I'm here for a purpose."

His brow furrowed in concern as he asked, "You aren't here looking for me, are you?"

"No," Sara confessed. She felt an odd sense of guilt, as if maybe she should have been searching for her dad all this time. But he looked relieved. He didn't want to be the reason for Sara putting herself in harm's way. "I'm here because of the Guardian."

His eyes widened. Now, he truly was worried. "Sara, do you know what he his? Do you know what he does? You shouldn't get involved with him. It's not safe."

"I know exactly what he is," she replied in the most reassuring voice she could muster. "That's why I'm here. I know that he can't be reborn and that he's stopping everyone else from being reborn too. He's trapping you and everyone else here with him. He's making the world of the living a soulless place. I have to stop him."

Her father considered that, but looked unsettled. "Why you? Why do you have to stop him?"

Sara had been asking herself that same question since her first journey to Catharta. She still didn't have a really solid answer, so she simply told him, "I was chosen. I was sent here, and I'm pretty sure stopping him is what I'm meant to do. I have to do it for everyone who's stuck here, and I have to do it to make sure Maya's baby isn't born without a soul."

His jaw dropped open, and his eyes searched her questioningly. "Maya?" was all he managed to utter.

Nodding, Sara confirmed, "Maya's pregnant. The baby could be here any day now." After an extended pause, he asked her, "Is she...," but then trailed off.

"She's not married," Sara said, filling in the blank for him. "She's not even seeing the father anymore."

Her dad shook his head, "I was going to ask if she's happy."

Sara was surprised that with the shocking revelation she had just dropped on him that his only question was about Maya's happiness. She supposed spending so much time in Catharta made you focus on what was really important.

"Yes," she assured him. "She's very happy. And she's going to make a great mom. She has the support she needs. We both moved in with Aunt Joann. She's already taken leave from all her various jobs. She's just waiting for the baby to arrive now. Her only fear is that it will be born without a soul. That's why it's so important for me to keep coming back here. I need to stop the Guardian."

Looking into the face of the man who had loved and protected her for her entire life suddenly made the confidence she'd been trying to hold onto evaporate. Her eyes fell to the floor as she admitted, "But I'm not sure how. I have no idea what I'm doing, and my last attempt to fix things just failed miserably. I feel like Catharta chose me for this purpose, but I'm not the right person for the job."

Tears began to well up in Sara's eyes, and she had to choke back a sob. Her father shifted his position so that he sat next to her where she remained in a heap on the floor. He placed an arm around her shoulder and squeezed her tightly to himself.

"Sara, do you remember when you were about ten years old and you told me you were sick the day of soccer tryouts and you couldn't go?" Sara nodded. "But you weren't sick, were you?" She shook her head. "You were afraid you weren't going to be good enough for the team, so you just wanted to stay home and never try. I didn't force you, but sometimes, I wish I had. Maybe you just needed that little push so that you could see how much potential you had."

That stung a little bit. She understood he was trying to give her the confidence she needed to solve the problem of the Guardian. He wanted her to believe that if she just had a little push, she would see she was the right person for the job. Since her fight with Tim, she had spent a lot of time questioning whether or not she was living up to her full potential.

Her father went on. "When it came time to apply for colleges, you only applied to one. It was the closest to our home, and it was one of the least competitive to get into. Most kids your age were shooting for the stars, and you applied to a safety school." He seemed to sense his message wasn't quite having the effect he had hoped. "What I'm trying to say is that your choices were always fine with me. I just wanted you to be happy. But I want you to know that your only limitations are the ones you put on yourself. If you believe in yourself, Sara, you can do anything."

"I always wanted to make you proud, Dad." This line of conversation wasn't helping her build her confidence or giving her any clues as to what to do about Sam, but it felt important. "I just didn't want to mess anything up. It was easier to play it safe, take the path of least resistance. That way, I wouldn't fail, and you would still be proud of me."

Her father looked discouraged. He was trying to explain something deeper to her, and she wasn't getting it. She was still focused on childish dreams of parental approval.

Finally, he asked her, "How do you measure your potential?"

"How should I know?" Sara asked sourly. "Everyone seems to think I'm not living up to mine."

He squeezed her a little tighter. "It doesn't matter what anyone else thinks—not your friends, not your colleagues, not your parents. You measure it by happiness. If you're happy, then you've lived up to your potential. If you're unhappy, it's time to make a change."

He put one finger under her chin, guiding her eyes toward his. "Are you happy?"

She wanted to tell him yes, that she was happy, that he didn't have to worry about her, and that she was living her life to her full potential. But she wasn't sure. She didn't think she was unhappy exactly, but lately, there had been an undefined gnawing feeling at the edges of her consciousness. Something in her life was incomplete or unfulfilled. She just couldn't quite name it.

As she searched for an honest answer within herself, a look of sudden panic swept across her father's face. "What?" she asked, all at once frozen in fear.

"Your eyes," he whispered. "They just flickered."

"Flickered?" Sara asked, thinking of the unexpectedly changing buildings she'd seen in the less stable parts of Catharta.

"Flickered," he confirmed. "Like they were glowing, just for a second."

"Oh no!" Sara exclaimed, scrambling to her feet. "I think I've been here too long. I have to go." She turned toward the front doors of the hospital lobby, but stopped. She had just reunited with her father after spending the last three years believing she would never see him again. It felt impossible to just walk away from him now. "I'm sorry, Dad. I'll come back again. I'm sorry, but I have to go."

He hugged her and said, "It feels so good to be reunited with you, if only for a moment. I'm so glad you came here. My soul feels whole again."

Sara soaked up his embrace, but something sparked in her mind. "Dad, you're a genius!" she declared.

He smiled at her, a little bemused, but didn't ask for an explanation. She kissed him on the cheek and then fled, her brain in a whirl of thoughts and emotions. The most prominent emotion was fear. She needed to get back to the gateway before she ended up trapped in Catharta just like Sam. She found Ananda just outside the front doors and told her urgently, "I have to go."

The two women sprinted through the streets of San Francisco, past abandoned apartment buildings, markets, and coffee shops. They ran down the center of streets, no traffic to bar their path. The sound of their shoes against the pavement was the only noise to be heard, echoing off the surrounding brick and concrete. They skidded toward the stairs leading down into the Sixteenth Street subway station, making a quick descent and finding their way to the east end of the platform.

As she lay herself down on the grimy red tiles, Sara told Ananda, "I might know what to do. I might have an idea of how to help Sam. I'm coming back tomorrow night, so stay close."

"Okay," Ananda said, clearly wanting more information, but understanding that time was short.

Sara closed her eyes, but then had one last thought. She looked up at Ananda, towering over her now that Sara was on the floor. "I know it won't be easy, but if you could be here in the station when I get back, that would help." Ananda nodded her understanding. "And if there's any way you can convince Sam to be here too," she added.

Doubt spread across Ananda's expression.

"I know it's a big request," Sara admitted.

"I'll do what I can," Ananda promised. "You need to go!"

Sara closed her eyes. Clearing her mind, she thought of her life back at home. She thought of Maya and Aunt Joann and their little house in the inner Sunset. She thought of Maya's baby and of herself becoming an aunt. She thought of Tim and the newspaper and her daily life. She thought of good coffee and foggy days, and she did her best not to think about her father because the desire to stay here with him was far too strong. When she felt ready, she opened her eyes.

Then, she was rocketing upward once more. Her view of the concrete and acoustic tiled ceiling was unchanged, but the edges of her vision blurred. The pressure in her head built up, clogging up her ears. Nausea overwhelmed her until she could think of little else. She stayed strong, racing toward the real world, racing toward her living body and her sister and the life she had left behind. Then, it all came to a sudden stop. She had arrived.

CHAPTER 16

Staring up at the concrete ceiling, Sara bit the inside of her cheek so hard it bled a little. She could taste the tiny drops of coppery, salty blood on her tongue. Her teeth connected with the nerve endings beneath her flesh, sending signals firing to the pain receptors in her brain, begging her to stop. It hurt. She needed it to hurt. She needed to know that she was back in her body in the world of the living where pain was real, not just a distant memory. Catharta had not trapped her. Her body had not rejected its escaped soul. She was alive. The soul she had so carelessly flung into another dimension had returned to its rightful place in one piece, unfractured. She released the hold on her inner cheek with relief and began to wiggle her fingers and toes, slowly bringing life back into her body.

She shifted her jaw ever so slightly in an automatic and almost involuntary motion and felt a distinctive pop in her ears. The relief of the pressure on her head felt heavenly. Her hearing, which had been muffled and distorted, became suddenly clearer. Everything sounded deep and echoey by comparison for a second. Then, it returned to normal, more or less. It was like waking up from a heavy sleep. It didn't happen all at once, but in stages. Only when her ears cleared did she hear her sister speaking rapidly to someone. Maya's voice was an unnaturally high-pitched squawk, alerting Sara that her little sister was in a state of panic. Something was wrong. She sat up quickly and all at once wished she hadn't. The blood drained from her brain with the sudden change in position, and she almost fell back onto the platform. She allowed herself to lean back onto her elbows, but refused to lie down completely. She needed to be alert.

Pressing her eyes shut, squeezing her hands into tight fists, and taking a few deep breaths, she brought herself back to reality. She had to focus. She recognized Maya's voice clearly, but her brain refused to make sense of the words. Sara had no idea what her sister was saying, but she knew something upsetting was happening. Maya, who was usually so calm and chipper, sounded angry and frenetic. When she opened her eyes again, Sara could see Maya's back, her arms flailing wildly. She was talking to someone, almost yelling at them, but Sara couldn't see who. From her spot on the floor, Maya's form blocked out the other person. She had to stand up to find out what was going on. Sara gathered her feet under herself and forced her way up slowly, making sure she didn't lose her balance. This must have been the most time she'd spent in Catharta all at once. The extra time outside of her body made the return trip that much more disorienting, but she had to keep it together. She had to find out what had Maya so worked up. Once she was finally standing, she could see the other person on the platform in front of her sister.

Maya was yelling at a cop.

"You can't lay a finger on her without her permission! I know my rights!" Maya exclaimed frantically, her forefinger pointed dangerously close to the policeman's nose.

"Ma'am, I'm going to need you to calm down," the officer replied impatiently.

Sara approached and placed a hand on her sister's shoulder, both to steady herself and to alert Maya to her presence back in the world of the living.

Maya jumped and spun around. She embraced her sister tightly and hissed, "Oh, thank God!" This situation had apparently been getting out of hand for a while now, and Maya was relieved to see she now had some backup. Then, she turned to address the cop again, ready to assail him with another barrage of demands and threats.

Finding her voice, Sara intervened before Maya could get started. "Is there a problem officer?"

Having apparently only then noticed that Sara was no longer lying on the station platform, the policeman dropped his agitation with Maya and showed some genuine concern. "Are you okay, miss?

You appeared to be unconscious, and I wanted to get you some medical attention, but...," he managed to say before Maya cut him off.

"But I told him you were fine. You just needed to lie down for a minute." She looked at the officer defiantly and added, "Isn't that right?"

"That's right," Sara backed her sister up. "I'm just really tired. I needed to lie down for a minute."

The officer clearly didn't quite believe this story. Sara couldn't blame him. She imagined that her body, devoid of its soul, lying on the floor of the station, appeared to be either dead or dying. He looked back and forth between the two women probably trying to assess whether or not they were on drugs. "This is hardly the place for a nap."

Sara looked back at the tiled floor she had just been lying on. Under normal circumstances, she would avoid touching the filthy subway station platform at all costs. She thought of the thousands of feet that tread these brick red tiles every day, feet that had been dragged along the sidewalks and the streets and the gutters of San Francisco.

"No," she agreed. "No place for a nap."

She could hear a train approaching, the stale air in the station beginning to stir once more. She checked the overhead sign and noted that this train would get them home.

Glancing down at the name badge on his uniform, Sara told the cop, "If it's okay with you, Officer Bailey, we're just going to board this next train and go home."

"Are you refusing medical attention?" he asked, his impatience returning.

"Yes, I am refusing medical attention," Sara confirmed.

Officer Bailey stared at the two women as the train rumbled into the station. "Okay," he finally said. "You two ladies get home safe." He looked worn-out and defeated, like he just wanted to be done with whatever mischief these two women were up to.

Sara smiled in thanks, but he didn't move, just stared at them uncomfortably until the train pulled to a stop and the doors opened. Maya continued to stare back at him with a sense of challenge in her eyes. With the train doors standing open behind them, Sara grabbed her by the elbow and pulled her onto the train. Even as the doors shut and they pulled away from the platform, the policeman watched them go, wanting to make sure these two strange ladies left the station and became someone else's problem.

Once they had pulled into the darkness of the tunnel, far away from the cop's gaze, Maya finally relaxed, her job of guarding her sister's temporarily soulless body finally complete. She turned to Sara with a dreamy look in her eyes and asked, "Hey, what do you think of the name Bailey?"

Sara shook her head in disbelief. Of all the questions she thought must be on the tip of Maya's tongue, this was one she hadn't expected.

"You are impossible," she told her sister with an exhausted laugh. "Let's just go home."

The next morning, Sara was up well before Maya despite having overslept a bit herself. As she poured her second cup of coffee, she was struck with a pang of guilt at having kept her very pregnant sister out so late. She also felt grateful that she had a sibling who was willing to do anything for her, even drag her exhausted body out into the city in the middle of the night and stand up to a cop.

She hadn't told Maya anything that had transpired in Catharta the night before, claiming she was too tired. In truth, she worried if she told her sister she had seen their dead father, Maya wouldn't get any sleep at all. She needed her rest and so did the baby. As it was, Sara had a restless night's sleep, replaying her conversation with her dad over and over.

Still, she felt guilty about this omission, and she waited impatiently for Maya to wake up, her gaze repeatedly drifting toward the stairway. She wanted to own up to this small betrayal.

Everything she did while waiting for Maya to awaken felt absurd. She had showered and dressed. She had ground and brewed coffee and checked her e-mail. It felt ridiculous to be going about the mundanities of her everyday life after having just spoken to her father's soul. She felt physical pain at the thought of knowing where he was and knowing she could go speak to him anytime she wanted.

A wound had been reopened. It reminded her of a blinding headache that you thought you had cured, but that returned with a vengeance the moment the drugs wore off. The experience of being close to him and speaking to him followed by the sudden loss of his presence once more made things like getting out of bed and getting dressed seem trivial and worthless.

It made her question her life. Every day, she got up and went to work. She hung out with her family and her friends, but she didn't really do anything. All the little things that had made her feel accomplished in her past now seemed pointless. Her life was stagnant, like a pond, sitting perfectly still and growing a thick layer of algae. Maybe Tim was right, and her father too. Maybe she was just afraid of trying for something bigger, something more important and fulfilling. No, she decided, she wasn't afraid of trying. She was afraid of failing, and that fear prevented her from trying altogether.

Just as she felt herself spiraling into this thought pattern that would likely lead to self-pity, but no real change in her fears or in the way she lived her life, Maya came bounding down the stairs, bringing her back to reality.

She still wore her pajamas and hadn't brushed her hair yet. On her feet were a pair of Sara's slippers. Since they had both moved back in with Aunt Joann, Sara had noticed the return of this old habit of Maya, borrowing her things without asking permission. In the beginning, she had pretended to be annoyed by it as she had been when they were teenagers living together in their parents' house. But in truth, she sort of liked it. She liked feeling that reminder of a happier time when their family was still whole and they were sheltered and protected. The whole world was filled with possibilities at that time. She hadn't felt stuck. She had felt full of potential rather than constantly feeling she wasn't living up to her potential. She was reminded again of her father telling her the only limitations she faced were the ones she placed upon herself. She shook off the thought. She didn't have time for a pity parade today.

"Well"—Maya said in lieu of a morning greeting—"what happened last night? Tell me everything."

Sara thought of her trip to Catharta. She knew Maya would be upset with her for withholding the information about their dad. She should probably blurt out that part first, but she just couldn't do it. She had to work up to that part of the story. Besides, if she told Maya she had spoken to their dad, she knew her sister would be incapable of listening to the rest of the story. Reminding herself that she had a plan now and that she needed Maya's help, she decided to save Dad for last.

"I went to the hospital," she began.

Maya cocked a curious eyebrow at her sister like she might be losing her mind. "Um, I know. I was with you, remember?"

Sara was confused for a second and then realized what Maya was talking about. "No, I know you and I went to the hospital together. I mean in Catharta. I found Ananda and the Guardian, and I convinced them to come with me to the hospital. I took them to the same room where I saw his body when I went to the hospital with you in the real world. I took him to the same hospital bed."

Maya looked dumbfounded. "You convinced him to come with you? Did he hurt you? You shouldn't be palling around with this guy when you know what he's capable of."

"I don't think he's really like that," Sara said, shaking her head. She felt she had really gotten to know Sam as a person, having seen a different side of him. She also knew she hadn't done a very good job of conveying that to either Maya or Tim. "I think it's an act he puts on. He's playing a character because that's the only way he knows to cope."

"Really?" Maya replied sarcastically, eyebrows arched high. "So those bruises I still see on your neck are just a coping mechanism?"

Sara's hand went self-consciously to her throat, and she flipped her hair over her shoulders to make the marks left by Sam's fingers less noticeable.

"I'm not saying he hasn't done bad things. All I mean is that he's not bad at heart. He's just broken."

"Obviously," Maya agreed with an eye roll.

This recounting of her night wasn't going the way Sara had expected. She tried to get it back on track.

"So we went to the hospital." Maya dropped the attitude and was once again paying attention. "I got him to lie down on the bed in the same spot where his body was lying in the real world."

It took a second, but then Maya figured out exactly what her sister had been trying to accomplish with this move. "You thought he could go back to his body? You want him to be alive again? Did it work? Is he alive? Should we go back to the hospital?" The questions spilled out in a single breath.

Sara gave her a disappointed look in response, the failure washing over her again.

"It didn't work," Maya deduced.

"It didn't work," Sara confirmed. "I thought it might work the same way it works with me, you know? I just lie down in the same spot where my body is and think about wanting to come back to my life."

"Maybe it only works that way because your body is still at the gateway," Maya suggested.

"Maybe," Sara said hesitantly. "I thought there might be a second gateway around his body's living soul. I think it has more to do with the fact that he doesn't want to come back to his life. I don't know what happened in his life to make him so miserable. It seems like his marriage wasn't a happy one. I'm sure there's more to it than that though. Whatever it is that made him so miserable in life also made it so there's nothing he wants to go back to. He couldn't think of a single thing he missed from the world of the living."

"But it's not like he has much going for him in Catharta either," Maya protested. "What's the difference?"

"He won't admit it, but I think deep down, he's still hoping he'll be reborn somehow, that he'll get a second chance at a better life. But the longer he waits, the more bitter he becomes. So he pretends it doesn't bother him that he's stuck there, and he collects souls along the way. Misery loves company."

Maya looked satisfied with this explanation, but disappointed in the outcome of her sister's attempt to stop the Guardian. "So if you can't get him back into his comatose body, what can you do? How can you stop him?"

"Well," Sara said, still chewing on the guilt of her omission about their father. "I have a plan that I think will work. I'm going to need your help. I'll have to get Tim on board too. I still think the only way to stop the Guardian is to help him, and I think I finally know how to do that."

"I'll do anything!" Maya exclaimed. "Just tell me what you need me to do."

She couldn't hold it back any longer. "Before we talk about the plan, there's something important I need to tell you."

Maya waited expectantly.

Sara decided to just blurt it out. "I saw Dad."

Maya stared at her, unblinking. Sara gave her a moment to let the weight of this news sink in. The moment stretched on. Sara became more and more uncomfortable, unable to read the frozen expression on her sister's face.

Finally, Maya spoke with a slow gravity that sounded alien to her normally perky, bubbly personality. "Tell me what you mean. Exactly."

"I mean," Sara said, feeling somehow guiltier now that this news was out in the air. "I saw Dad's soul. He's in Catharta. He's trapped there by the Guardian, just like everybody else."

Sara still couldn't read her sister's emotions, but when she spoke again, her voice was shaking. "You saw him? Or you talked to him?"

Sara swallowed nervously. "I talked to him."

Finally, Maya exploded. "Sara, how the fuck could you keep something like that from me? Those should have been the first words out of your mouth when you woke up in the train station last night. You saw our father? You saw our dead father, and you didn't think that was important to mention?" Tears were welling up in her eyes. Sara felt awful.

Sara wanted to say something about Maya's foul language to lighten the mood, but sensed it wouldn't help. "I knew if I told you this last night you wouldn't have slept, and I had already kept you out so late. You need your rest, for the baby."

"Don't you pull the baby card on me," Maya shot back, but the bite was gone from her voice. She was in shock. That was all. She had a point, Sara should have told her, but she understood. Now, Maya's brain was working on the implications of her dad's soul still being there. With renewed softness in her tone, she began her slew of questions. "What did you talk to him about? What did he say? How did he look?"

Sara started with the easiest question. She conjured up her father's image in her mind. "He looked the same. He was still at the hospital, still wearing one of those pale blue gowns that ties in the back. He didn't have all the tubes and monitors attached to him anymore. He didn't look sick anymore, or at least not as sick. His eyes didn't look so vacant."

She thought of his clear glowing eyes and shivered a little. But it was true that at the end of his life, the thing that made him look truly sick—the thing that made it undeniable that he was dying—was the absent look in his eyes, like his soul was already retreating. At least in Catharta, that was gone.

Sara had been replaying their conversation over and over in her head for most of the night. One of the most painful parts was the moment he first saw her. "He thought I was dead." She choked a little on the words. "He thought I had died and that's why I was in Catharta. It took him a minute to understand what I was actually doing there."

Sara thought about how strange it seemed to be grieved by a loved one while you were still alive to see it. Watching her father sob over what he believed was the tragic death of his eldest daughter seemed impossible. In truth, it was bizarre to think of a dead person experiencing grief at all. She tended to think of people in a purely biological way. Those types of emotions were tied to particular receptors in the brain. Outside factors like losing a loved one put the body in a state of stress that caused a flux in serotonin and cortisol and other hormones that triggered emotional reactions from the brain. Those reactions presented in different ways in different people, but no matter what, she had always thought of it as a physical reaction, something that stemmed from nerves and brain matter and flesh. Only now did she realize that the physical and biological aspect was only a small part of it. Your body is the thing you walk around in all day. Your soul is who you are. That's what you feel with. Your soul is your emotional core. You don't need a body to grieve the dead.

Maya wanted more. She urged Sara on. "So once he realized you're still alive, then what?"

"I told him what I was doing there, that I needed to stop the Guardian so everyone could be free. He didn't like the idea of it. I think Dad is scared of him or at least scared of me interacting with him." Sara reflected on that too. Even in death, a parent never stops feeling protective of their child.

"But you explained to him why this is important, right? You've been chosen. You have a duty now. You have to see this through." Maya was clearly worried that their father had somehow managed to talk her out of saving the souls of Catharta.

Again, Sara felt that pain of knowing exactly where her father was and not staying there to be with him. It was tempting to abandon her entire mission, to leave him there, frozen in a time capsule, where she could visit him anytime she wanted, talk to him and get advice, hug him, and tell him she loved him. But that wasn't right. If she did that, she was no different than Sam. If she didn't follow through with her duty to save the Guardian and thereby free all the souls of Catharta, she was no better than the monster that had trapped them there in the first place. She couldn't be selfish. She needed to see this through.

Sara nodded to put her sister's mind at ease. She would not back down. Their dad understood why it was important that she not give up.

"I told him you're pregnant." Maya's face lit up in a flurry of emotions. She seemed surprised, like she hadn't foreseen herself being included in this posthumous exchange between father and daughter. Then, she seemed worried or embarrassed. She was pregnant out of wedlock, something she had never had to confess to her parents. She had probably never considered how it might have made her feel to disclose that information to her dad. Then, curiosity bloomed again.

"What did he say about it? About me being pregnant?" She waited anxiously for an answer, clutching her belly protectively, one arm draped over the top, the other cradling it underneath.

Sara smiled at the motherly pose. "He just wanted to know if you were happy." Maya's eyes were wide with an unasked question. "I told him you were." She looked relieved, so Sara went on. "I told him we had moved in with Aunt Joann and that we would make sure you have all the help and support you need. He seemed to like that idea, us living together again."

"Did you tell him about the father? About my," she hesitated, "situation?"

This was the first time Sara believed she had ever seen her sister show any sort of embarrassment over what had happened between her and Dr. Carver. Maya was the type to live life moment to moment, heedless of consequences and entirely without regrets. It wasn't that she didn't have a conscience. She had a clear sense of morals. She just didn't saddle herself with all the guilt that Sara was so prone to. She accepted her actions and their consequences and moved on.

"I told him you weren't married to the father and that he wasn't involved. Dad truly didn't care. He really only cared that you're happy." Maya finally looked content.

Sara considered telling her sister the next part of the conversation. The part where her dad had tried to give her the confidence to do what she needed to do next to help Sam and thereby help everyone trapped in Catharta, including her own father. Then, she thought about disclosing how his words had really made her feel, like she wasn't good enough, like she should have done more with her life by now, like she would never amount to anything because she was always standing in her own way.

As she tried to form the words to share this part of her experience, she realized how pathetic it all sounded. If she tried to explain her self-doubt to her sister who always seemed to have boundless confidence, she would just get another lecture on how she was good enough. She'd had enough of those lectures to realize they had no effect on her. She didn't know what she had to do to make herself feel better about her life, her choices, but she knew it had to come from within herself somehow. Other people's words were useless in trying to bring about change in herself. So she swallowed that part of the story, vowing not to feel guilty about that small omission because that part was private.

The part that came after that, however, was going to make Maya nervous. "I probably would have stayed there with him all night," she began.

"Well, it's a good thing you didn't," Maya interjected. "That cop was likely to arrest me just to get me out of the way so he could call you an ambulance. Then, we'd both be screwed."

"I was saying," Sara said pointedly, playfully ignoring Maya's interruption. "I probably would have stayed there all night, but something happened. Dad said my eyes flickered."

"Flickered?" Maya queried. "What do you mean flickered?"

"I mean one minute they looked like they do now, and the next minute, they looked dead, like the eyes of a ghost, like Ananda's and the Guardian's and everyone else in Catharta." Maya was still working out the implications of what that meant. Sara went on, "He said it was just for a second, but I think I know what it meant."

She waited for Maya to put it together herself, but when her sister stared back blankly, Sara delivered the punch line. "I think it means I could get trapped there just like the Guardian."

"But if no one moved your body," Maya began.

"I still believe that would cause a problem too, but I think the simple act of being there too long might be enough to get me stuck between life and death. If I stayed there too long, I might not be able to get back. A living soul isn't meant to be outside of its body for that long."

Maya was whipping herself into a panic now. "How long is too long? How would I know if you were at risk? Can I wake you up? If you've been out for too long, could I just slap your or something? Bring you back to reality? You should take a watch with you next time."

Sara thought about that. "I don't think a watch would work in the ghost plane. Nothing mechanical there seems to function—the trains, the cars, and the escalators. I have a feeling a watch would be the same story. Besides, time passes differently there. I don't really know how long is too long." Maya looked disgruntled. Sara addressed some of her other questions. "And I don't think there's anything you can do on this side to get me back. If my soul isn't at the gateway, it wouldn't work."

"Well then, you can't go back." Maya stomped the linoleum floor as if wanting to indicate she was putting her foot down both literally and figuratively.

"Weren't you just telling me how I had a responsibility to see this through?" There was a teasing undertone in Sara's voice that Maya clearly did not appreciate.

Sara dropped the sass and arranged her face in a more serious expression. "Look, I get why you're worried, but the thing is I only need to go back there one more time." Maya looked skeptical, so she added, "And I promise I'll be really quick. I'll be careful."

Maya huffed out a little sigh of defeat. "Okay, why do you only need to go back one time?"

"Right before I left, Dad said something, and now, I think I know how to end all this. I know how to help the Guardian, and once that's done, everyone in Catharta should be safe too, Dad included. But like I said, I'm going to need your help. I hope you don't have any plans tonight."

Maya listened raptly as Sara explained the details of her plan that she hoped would save Sam and save all the lost souls in the ghost plane, ensure Maya's baby was born with a soul, and bring an end to this journey she had unwittingly embarked upon only a week ago.

While Maya had a lot of questions, she was pretty much immediately on board and once again enthusiastic about Sara's return to Catharta. She seemed to let go of her anxiety about the risk Sara was taking, like a child absentmindedly letting go of a balloon. Her fervency was contagious and allowed Sara to buy into her own plan a little bit more. She still wasn't entirely sure this would work, but she had to try something, and she worried she was running out of time. Now, she just needed to get Tim on board.

It was way too early for her to go to the office, but she grabbed her messenger bag and headed out the glass-paneled front door of the mint green house anyway, calling out a reminder to Maya that Aunt Joann would be home from her business trip that evening. She made her way on down the sixteen brick steps and headed out to catch her bus. There was a special stop she wanted to make on her way to work.

CHAPTER 17

S ara rose up from her usual seat at the back of the bus and stepped off when it reached the Presidio. This little corner of San Francisco always seemed like another world to her. Compared to the rest of the city, it looked absurdly flat. In reality, it wasn't all that flat. It had some small hills, but nothing like the other neighborhoods of her hometown. Walking up Broadway could feel like climbing a mountain. Tourists flocked to the windy path that zigzagged up the steep slope of Lombard Street as well as to see the wild parrots on the challenging climb up Telegraph Hill to Coit Tower. Those types of hills characterized the city Sara knew and loved. They were part of what made it feel like home. By comparison, the Presidio was the flat lands of the city. The financial district didn't have many hills either, but that fact was more or less lost in the tall buildings. Here in the Presidio, the relative flatness was undeniable, and it made for breathtaking views. The sprawling former military fort that sat just south of the Golden Gate Bridge was filled with a smattering of one- and two-story buildings, all with some sort of historic military significance that Sara had never bothered to learn. Everything about the area looked old, like it had been frozen in time. The Presidio had no signs of modernization, unlike the flashy skyscrapers downtown and the trendy apartment buildings south of Market. It had all been left largely as it was in the early 1800s. It made Sara feel like an alien, encroaching upon a civilization that knew nothing of her kind.

Large stone pillars and iron gates standing open framed the entrance to San Francisco National Cemetery. It was one of only two places in the city where you could still bury your loved ones in the ground, the other being located at Mission Dolores Church. There were also a handful of places where you could have ashes interred, but as far as a traditional burial, the options were slim. In the early 1900s, the city of San Francisco had closed all the other cemeteries and graveyards and forced the exhumation and relocation of hundreds of graves to the city of Colma. For that reason, Sara had always thought of Colma as a city of ghosts. Having been to Catharta, she would probably change that opinion. She had been to the true city of ghosts, and it was unlike anything she could have imagined.

Sara made her way up the paved path toward the lush green grass and gleaming white headstones sprawling out before her. It was a tranquil place, always very quiet, never many visitors, especially on a weekday. She walked the path she knew all too well, up to where the trail crested and you could get a view of the bay. She veered toward the back of the grounds near a copse of trees over which peaked the towers of the Golden Gate Bridge. There was a smattering of sailboats out on the water today. The morning fog was starting to burn off. It would be a beautiful afternoon on the water, she thought, as she made her way along the row, taking care not to tread on any graves.

When she reached the location she sought, she sat down in the grass, directly between the final resting places of her mother and father, facing their headstones. She placed a hand on the grass to either side of her, wanting to connect herself to the earth that entombed her parents, wanting to feel closer to them in any way she could.

This was a ritual she had designed for herself and taken part in ever since shortly after her mom had died eight years earlier. She used to studiously ignore the spot where her father's grave would someday be while he was still alive, not wanting to think about losing another parent. Now, she paid equal homage to both plots.

This is where Sara came on her parents' birthdays, on Mother's Day and Father's Day, on their wedding anniversary, and any day she felt she needed their guidance. This is where she came when she felt adrift, like the boats out on the water that day. Feeling close to her parents gave her back her sail and her rudder. It gave her a way to stop drifting and guide herself back home.

She rarely thought about what she wanted to say to them before arriving. She simply showed up with a need aching in her chest and then talked her way through it after she arrived. As she sat with her fingers entwined with grass, gathering her thoughts, she realized she had always assumed her parents were together somewhere, reunited in the afterlife. The religious beliefs she was raised with fell somewhere on the spectrum between vague and nonexistent. She had never thought specifically about heaven or hell. She had never fully formed an image of what she thought life after death would look like. But she certainly always believed something came after this life, and she had decided for herself long ago that her parents were together in whatever that something might be.

A sour feeling seeped into her guts now knowing that it wasn't true. They weren't together. There was no eternal haven for the dead. There was something that came after this life, but it wasn't anything like what she had expected. It was meant to be a short stay in a place where you could reflect on the life you had lived followed by another life altogether. Her mother had already moved onto that stage. Her soul had passed through Catharta and was off living another life somewhere. Sara tried to imagine what her mother's new life might be like. She was probably about eight years old. Sara tried to summon a picture in her mind of her mother as a little girl again, but a different little girl, or maybe she was a little boy in this life. Maybe she was a different nationality or living in a different country. Sara tried to picture it, and she failed. She decided matters of the soul may be too much for mere mortals to comprehend.

Then her thoughts drifted to her father, still trapped in the ghost plane, unable to move on to his next life and unable to gain another chance at happiness. It seemed horribly unfair. She had to accept that her parents weren't living out eternity together in some imaginary afterlife like she had always pictured in her head, but it made her sick to her stomach to think that they weren't even on the same plane of existence. Her mom had moved on to a new life with no memory of the past. Or maybe there were some faint memories that carried over, like an imprint or a shadow, something you never really noticed but always carried with you. Either way, she had moved on, and her dad was trapped, damned to haunt a place where he remembered everything but could change nothing. He couldn't do anything to free himself.

But Sara could.

She balled her hands into fists and felt little blades of grass break free of their roots with a satisfying snap, becoming stuck between her fingers. She suddenly realized what she had come here to say. She touched her fingertips to her mother's locket, still hanging around her neck.

That connection to her mom gave her the strength to find her voice.

"Hi, Mom. Hi, Dad. I miss you." It was how she always began. This time, however, missing them felt like a lead weight in her heart. The recent embrace from her dad made the loss of her parents feel that much more fresh and raw. She sighed and blinked back some tears. Then, she launched into what she was truly feeling. "I'm involved in things I don't fully understand," she said to her parents' headstones. "I'm trying to understand. I really am, but it's all so new and frightening and unfathomable. There is no set of instructions for what I'm trying to do. There's no road map I can reference. I'm pretty much making things up as I go along, and you know me, that's not what I do. I plan. I wait. I don't take risks." She closed her eyes and drew in a deep breath; then, she opened her eyes and went on. "But I'm going to take a risk. It's a big one. I may not fully understand the task I've been given, but I know enough about what I'm doing to know I can't give up. If I give up, I'm failing hundreds if not thousands of souls who need my help. I would be condemning you to an eternity of misery," she said, stroking the grass covering her father's grave. "I can't do that."

She looked out over the water again, gathering her thoughts once more. "I have a plan, and I'm going to go through with it tonight. I don't know if it will work, but if it's ever going to work, it has to be tonight. But the thing is, this is going to make everything real. This goes beyond messing with the fates of a bunch of dead people in a place no one knows exists. What I'm planning to do will affect real people, people who are still alive."

Sara contemplated the lives that would be affected by her plan. She thought of Maya, who had so readily agreed to help her, probably without thinking through the consequences. She thought of Tim whose help she still needed to ask for. He might be harder to convince. She didn't allow herself to think of the other lives that might be impacted by her decisions. If she did, she was afraid she would chicken out. She needed to stay strong.

"I wish you were here to tell me I'm doing the right thing," she said, although in her heart, she wasn't sure she could take it if they told her what she was doing was wrong. She wanted their reassurance, but knew she couldn't take their rejection. "I would feel so much better about all of it if I knew I had your blessing." She considered the fact that her father's soul still existed in a place that she could access it—that she could go tell him her plan, ask what he thought of it, and get his permission. But no. The next time she went to Catharta would be tonight. If this plan was ever going to work, it had to be tonight. Besides, what if he advised against it? She was out of ideas and out of options. She wouldn't know what to do if he told her no. She had to do this. She had to take the plunge, even if it terrified her.

"If I fail, I could face some pretty serious consequences." The thought of failure at this point, after she had tried so hard, after she had come this far, turned her stomach. It made her want to lie down in this very spot and give up on life.

Then, a thought occurred to her. "Even if I succeed, I could face some serious consequences." It was true. She was planning on taking real-world actions that would have real-world implications. Success or failure didn't get her out of that mess. She found the thought oddly comforting. She shouldn't have. If anything, the thought of facing some sort of punishment for her actions either way should have frightened her more. But the idea that the consequences she might end up facing didn't depend on her success made it seem less scary to try, to put out the effort, to take the risk.

She felt better for a split-second, but that relief dredged up other emotions she'd been battling with lately. The feelings formed into a question that she blurted out before she even fully processed the thought. "Why am I so afraid to fail? Everyone fails. It's normal. No one likes it. But I'm afraid of it to the point of paralysis. That fear drives me to simply never try. My whole life, I've never really pushed myself out of my comfort zone. Why did you guys let me get away with that?" she asked the silent grave markers. It wasn't fair to blame her parents for her own fears and hang-ups. She felt instantly guilty for even saying it out loud.

The words made sense to her logically. People faced failure every day, and they survived. Why did she think she should be any different? Why should she be so afraid to take a little risk and go for something she wanted? But the logic didn't matter. Her fear wasn't logical; she knew that. It was irrational, and the only way to fight that was with irrationality. Maybe that was the key. Maybe she had to do something totally reckless and irrational to snap herself out of her paralysis. It was an idea. She'd have to spend some more time thinking about what that might be.

She also realized she had insulated herself from her fear by convincing herself she didn't want any more out of life. If there was nothing she wanted, nothing she knew she should strive to achieve, then she couldn't be accused of not taking the risks to get it. But she had been doing that her whole life. She had buried her deepest desires even from herself to the point that she had no clue what she wanted out of life. She had no barometer anymore for whether or not she was happy.

"What do I want?" she asked, not just of her parents, but of herself and the cemetery at large. "I think something is missing from my life, and I don't know what it is. Even if I could find the courage to try and risk failing, what would I try for? What would make me happy? What would make me feel fulfilled?"

She could feel her mind shrink away from her own question. Accepting mediocrity had become a way of life for her. She couldn't force herself to dream, to hope, to wish. She didn't know where to begin.

Frustrated with herself and with what had dissolved into a very rambling, one-way conversation with her dead parents, she glanced out at the water again, searching for something to ground her, something to bring her scattered thoughts back together.

As she stared out at the bobbing sailboats, a memory suddenly came crashing down on her like a tidal wave, washing away reality, the cemetery, the grass, and the headstones. Everything around her disintegrated and retreated into her peripheral vision. All she could see was the memory. It was all that was real.

It was a dream she'd had when she was perhaps ten years old. She was in a body of water. She was sure it wasn't the ocean or the bay, but it wasn't a lake or river either. The water was gray. Not a dirty, murky gray, but the unique colorless shade of deep, crystal clear water reflecting a slate gray sky. There were no waves. The water was still save for tiny little ripples on the surface, breaking up the glassiness of it all. She was cold and naked and alone, and she couldn't see shore in any direction. She didn't know how she had gotten there, but she knew she had to find a way out. She picked a direction at random and tried to swim, hoping to find dry land. But the more she moved and kicked and flailed, the more the water churned. It started as tiny, lapping waves like you might see at the edge of a lake on a calm day; but it escalated into crashing, tumbling sheets of water with a rip current so strong it threatened to suck her under. The panic rising in her chest made her kick harder, which only caused the water to become more turbulent. She kicked and swam and gulped for air until she had no energy left in her bones, until she could move no more. Breathless and terrified, she stopped moving. She gave in. The water began to settle once more. She allowed herself to sink lower in the water as it calmed. She found there was something like a sandbar below her. If she stood on her tiptoes and craned her neck back, she could just barely keep her head above the surface. She knew in her gut that the shore was close, if she could just figure out which direction to swim. But she was equally sure that if she stepped off of her tiny sandbar she would drown. So she stayed out in the middle, cold and afraid, never reaching for the edge. She resigned herself to standing perfectly still in the icy, motionless water, forever, if she had to.

A chill ran down Sara's spine, shaking her back to reality. She felt cold all over despite the sunshine peeking through the dissipating fog. She had come to this place to make herself feel better, to feel reassured, to find her way. Instead, she felt worse than when she had arrived. Sitting in this spot, talking to the graves of a woman who was off living another life somewhere and a man who was trapped in a different dimension wasn't going to do her any good, not today, anyway, maybe not ever again.

She stood up and brushed the grass from her hands and her jeans. Normally, she said a standard goodbye to her parents when she left, letting them know she loved them, that she missed them, and that she would be back again soon. But not this time. It felt pointless. The carcasses beneath the earth couldn't hear her. Those bodies didn't belong to her mom and dad any more than the dirt or the grass or the headstones did. Their souls weren't here, weren't listening, weren't watching over her. Sara made her way back toward the paved path feeling very alone.

On a random impulse, before reaching the pavement, she veered off her usual path, winding her way through the graves, not toward the exit, but toward the copse of trees, toward the water, toward nothing in particular. She walked with no direction, hoping each step would take her closer to some sort of understanding, some semblance of reassurance that she wasn't about to do something she would regret for the rest of her life. She tried to stop thinking about the upsetting thoughts and memories swirling in her brain and instead focus on her plan, on convincing Tim to help her through the night she had ahead of her. She walked until she reached the last row of graves, and then she fell to her knees, never breaking her gaze from the sailboats bobbing along in the bay. She wanted to let her fears and her anxiety and all her responsibilities flow like a river spilling out into that bay. She wanted to walk away from all of it. Knowing she couldn't leave it all behind made her feel claustrophobic, trapped. Then she thought of all the people trapped in Catharta, her father included. She thought of the tiny baby in Maya's belly, waiting to be born and receive a soul that may never come. She thought of all the evils of the world, all the wars and violence and crime. She thought of all the people walking around the planet, empty vessels devoid of a soul. The thought of these things along with her own unescapable sense of responsibility and guilt piled on top of all the other emotions she was feeling.

Disgusted with herself, she broke her staring contest with the water. She looked at the last row of headstones sitting immediately in front of her, initially without actually seeing them. She was looking through them. Then something caught her eye. It all began to come into focus. The grave marker to her left sparked something in her subconscious and took a moment to register with her conscious mind. She read it, unable to believe what she was seeing. She read it again, to be sure. The words carved into the gleaming white stone seemed impossible, yet here they were, plain as day.

ANANDA REYES
NOVEMBER 1, 1997 ~ NOVEMBER 2, 2014
BELOVED DAUGHTER AND SISTER
REST WITH THE ANGELS

Something had brought Sara here to this spot, some force she couldn't understand. Her parents might not be here; they might not be listening to her rambling reverie or offering her advice. But something, some force, had guided her here. Of that much, she could be sure.

Sara crawled on her hands and knees across the damp grass toward the headstone, no longer cautious about disturbing graves. She ran her fingers along the chiseled letters, needing to touch them, needing some reassurance that what she was seeing was real. When she felt the cold, unyielding stone beneath her fingertips and the sharp corners of the carved letters, she knew she couldn't deny it. This was Ananda's grave. This was her final resting place. She had been here all along, mere steps away from Sara's parents.

Something inside of Sara broke just then, glass shattering beneath a crushing weight, and she collapsed onto Ananda's burial plot, hugging the earth. She allowed herself to cry, huge gulping sobs. She cried for the loss of Ananda's young life. She cried for the lack of empty plots beside this one, knowing Ananda's remains would never be joined by those of her family. She would be alone here for the rest of eternity. Sara cried for the loss of her parents. She cried for the journey she was on that she had never wanted to take. She cried because she pitied herself and the somehow incomplete life she was living. But mostly, she cried because it was all just too much. The world had dealt her a hand, and it was more than she felt she could bear. The weight of a thousand souls rested upon her shoulders. She cried for those souls, and she cried for herself. She cried until no more tears would come. Even then, she continued to lie prone on the grass covering the body of a girl she'd never met in life, but who she felt she owed everything to in death. She felt like she could lie there for the rest of her existence, unmoving. But of course, she couldn't. She had to keep moving forward.

Hiccupping with her eyes red and puffy, she attempted to pull herself together. She had to get to the office soon. She had a long day ahead of her and an even longer night. She had work to do.

CHAPTER 18

The bus pulled up to carry Sara away from the Presidio and off to work. She felt distinctly dissatisfied. She hadn't gotten what she came here for. She hadn't gained any clarity or peace of mind. She didn't feel any more confident or tranquil than when she had arrived. In fact, she felt significantly worse off. She probably shouldn't have come here at all, not today, anyway.

She had a moment to examine her reflection in the glass doors before they folded open to allow her to board the bus. Her clothes were damp and rumpled from the grass and the fog. Her eyes were red, and her whole face looked puffy from all the crying she had done. Her hair was a mess. But there was something else she couldn't quite place, something about her own reflection she didn't recognize. She looked older, tired, more rundown. It was probably the result of the stress she had been under lately coupled with too many late nights. Yet she couldn't help but wonder if somehow spending so much time in the land of the dead was sucking some of the life out of her. Every time she went to Catharta, did she leave a little bit of her life on that platform? Did she leave a tiny piece of her soul behind? The thought gave her just one more thing to fret over. At least, she could take comfort in the fact that she would only be going to the ghost plane one more time. Tonight would be her last trip, that is, if her plan worked. It had to work. She couldn't consider the alternative, or she would lose her nerve.

Sara suddenly realized the bus was standing with its doors open, and the driver was looking at her expectantly, wondering if she was going to board or if she was just standing at an otherwise empty bus stop simply to vex him. She hastily boarded the bus, paid her fare, and took a seat all the way at the back.

The bus took her past Crissy Field, through the Marina District, around Russian Hill, and finally landed her in the financial district. Along the way, she saw broken shop windows, graffiti depicting violent images and hate speech, and plenty of hurried men and women walking through the city with scowls on their faces. She saw anger and violence and hatred everywhere she looked. She even saw a homeless woman shove a pedestrian off the curb into oncoming traffic. Luckily, the oncoming car stopped short, and no one was hurt, but Sara was struck by the senselessness of it all. Could all the negativity she saw in the world be chalked up to an ever-growing number of soulless bodies walking around, wreaking havoc? Surely, that couldn't be the only cause. Sam had only been trapping souls for three years. The people born without a soul as a direct result of the Guardian's actions would only be toddlers at this point. But as Ananda had pointed out, there is a finite number of souls. Maybe we really did run out a long time ago. Maybe it was just more obvious in the most densely populated areas like San Francisco, where souls were in greatest need.

It made Sara's goal of stopping Sam and freeing the souls of Catharta seem meaningless. What good would it do for the world at large? There were still more people than souls in the world. So what was the point?

Her mind returned again to her father. That was the point. Sara couldn't fix all the problems of the world of the living, but she could at least help her dad. She could at least help the souls that wanted to move on but couldn't. She might not make a dent in the violence and anger and hatred she saw all around her, but she could make a difference for those lost souls. Maybe they would be reborn into doers of good. Maybe some of them would be able to make a difference in the balance of good and evil. Maybe whatever little bit of positivity Sara could bring into the world by stopping the Guardian would multiply and grow into something much bigger. She needed to hold onto that small and distant hope if she was going to succeed.

She would allow herself to believe in that possibility, at least, to get her through tonight.

Sara off boarded the bus a couple blocks from the office, holding on tightly to her messenger bag and the fragile shell of confidence she was trying to build up around herself. She made her way through the doors, past the disinterested security guard, up the stairs, and paused outside Tim's office. She wasn't prepared yet to divulge her plan to him and try to get him to agree to help her, but she was surprised to find his light off and his workstation seemingly untouched.

She checked the time. She was about ten minutes late. She hoped nobody had noticed her tardiness. But what concerned her more was that Tim was never late. They worked the same shift, but he nearly always made it to the office before her. He could have been sent out on assignment, she reasoned, but it seemed unlikely. The fact that his light hadn't been turned on made it seem more likely that he hadn't made it to work yet.

Sara made her way to her desk, and as soon as she sat down, she sent a text to Tim asking where he was. Within a few seconds, a little thought bubble appeared on her screen indicating he was writing a response. She waited. The thought bubble disappeared, but no response came. Then, a new thought bubble appeared. He had written something, deleted it, and started over again. This time, the response arrived saying he'd be there in ten minutes.

There was a sense of relief knowing he wasn't dead in a ditch somewhere, but Sara was still concerned. Being late was very out of character for him. She hoped he wasn't having a bad day. She really needed his help tonight, but as his friend, she didn't want to pile her problems on him if he was already having troubles of his own.

Rather than let the night ahead distract and dismay her, Sara delved into her work, paying more attention to it than she had at any point in the past week. Her mind had been occupied with Catharta and Sam and Ananda and with the role she had to play in trying to fix everything. She hadn't been able to focus in the office. But now, work was a welcome distraction. She proofed everything twice, found plenty of typos, spotted several incorrect uses of "there" and "their," and stopped just shy of suggesting a full rewrite of a piece on declining ridership and increased sanitation complaints in the subway system.

She got so caught up in her work that she forgot to go check and see if Tim ever made it to the office until it was time for her lunch break. She finished up the article she was working on and made her way back to his office.

Tiptoeing up to the door, she paused and peeked in. He was there. His light was on as was his computer, but he wasn't looking at it. He had his elbows propped up on the desk and was cradling his head in his hands. He looked like he was sleeping sitting up or maybe nursing a headache. Sara wasn't sure how to approach without startling him, but apparently, he already knew she was there.

"Come on in," he announced with a hint of reluctance in his voice, his forehead still resting on his palms, his back still facing the door.

Sara took a step into his office and leaned back against the doorframe. "How do you always do that?" she asked.

He tilted his head up slowly and let his hands fall to the surface of the desk with a thunk. He spun around then to face her. Something was off about him. It was subtle, but he didn't quite look like himself. His hair looked like he'd been raking his fingers through it all day. His skin had an unfamiliar pallor to it, like there was somehow less life to it. The main thing, though, was his eyes. They looked tired. They looked beyond tired. They were weary, like he hadn't slept in a week. It wasn't that they were red or puffy or that the lids were droopy. It was something else, something harder to pinpoint. It was like they had lost their shine. What used to be hazel was now just plain gray. Maybe she was imagining it.

He hadn't answered her, so she repeated her question. "How do you always know when I'm standing here?"

She expected a sarcastic remark, perhaps like an insinuation that he just said "come on in" every ten minutes just in case. Or maybe something more factual, like the often pointed out fact that she's not as quiet as she thinks she is.

Apparently, he couldn't come up with anything. Instead, he leaned forward and rubbed his eyes, mumbling, "I don't know."

"Are you okay? You don't look so hot?" He looked like he had been up all night or like he was hungover or maybe both.

He rubbed his eyes with his fists and then dragged his palms down the length of his face. He inhaled deeply, the sound amplified by his hands in front of his nose. Then, he looked at her again. He looked more like himself then, but not in an authentic way. It was more like he was trying to pull himself together for her benefit.

"I'm fine."

He was decidedly not fine.

"Have you eaten? Do you want to go grab some food with me?" Maybe if Sara got him out of the office, he'd snap out of it. She needed a little time to assess what was going on with him before she dropped her bombshell of a plan on him.

He looked at her and then looked at his computer, probably realizing he had work he ought to have been doing. Then, he decided to abandon it, at least temporarily. "Yeah, I could eat."

They went to a little cafe around the corner. The thing about working swing shift was that it really limited your lunch options. They ended up eating lunch at dinner time when a lot of the financial district had already shut down for the night. But this little cafe stayed open. It was always a quiet place to grab a bite to eat, and the staff knew them well. A lot of times, they would just get something to go and walk back to the office, but Sara wanted a little more privacy to confess what she had planned for the evening. She also thought Tim could use a little time away from his desk to deal with whatever he was going through.

Sara let him get a few sips of coffee in before trying to engage him in conversation.

"So what's going on with you?" she asked once it looked like the caffeine was starting to hit him.

"Nothing's going on with me," Tim replied unconvincingly.

"Tim," Sara said pointedly. If she wore glasses, she would have glared at him over the rims to drive home the point that she wasn't buying it.

"What?" he asked, feigning innocence.

She continued to stare relentlessly until he squirmed beneath her gaze.

"Fine," he gave in. "It's not nothing. It's just all this crap with Melissa. But I don't want to talk about it right now. Okay?"

Melissa. Sara had forgotten all about Melissa. Tim's ex-girlfriend was the whole reason he couldn't come with her to the hospital the previous night. They were getting together to do the post-break up exchange of possessions. Sara felt like a horrible friend for having forgotten, especially considering that, from the looks of Tim, it hadn't gone well.

Tim took her continued staring as a sign she was going to keep pressing him for information. Apparently, he couldn't see the guilt that was filling her up and threatening to spill out. To try to throw off her scrutiny, he put on his armor of sarcasm.

"Why don't you tell me about your wild and exciting night instead? What was it you were doing? Going out dancing with the girls? Drinking all night? Getting arrested?"

Sara set aside her guilt and decided to temporarily let him off the hook for disclosing whatever had gone so terribly wrong the night before. "Well," she began, matching his sarcasm. "There was no dancing or drinking, but the night did end with Maya having an altercation with a cop."

Tim almost choked on his coffee. Clearly, he was intrigued. "Go on."

"So we went to the hospital, and you were right, Maya had a friend who was able to get me into the MedSurg unit."

Tim looked quite self-satisfied at being told he was right about something. He was also impatient to hear what happened. "So was he there? Did you see him? Did you see Sam?"

Sara paused for dramatic effect. Regardless of the rough night he'd had, it felt more natural to antagonize him a little bit. This was their thing. It was how they interacted. When she felt she had made him wait long enough, she said, "It was him. Sam is alive. He's been in a coma at Saint Gertrude's all this time."

Tim let the gravity of the information hit him. Then, he asked, "So what did you do?"

"I went to see Sam. The real Sam." Sara paused. She suddenly wasn't sure what she meant by real. Sam's body was there in the hospital in what she called the real world. A piece of his soul was there too. But the Sam she could talk to and interact with was in Catharta, a place she still sort of thought of as make-believe. "I went to see Ghost Sam in Catharta," she clarified.

"And you didn't go alone, right?" Tim gave her a very serious, almost scolding look, eyebrows knit together, jaw set, teeth clenched.

"Of course not, Maya was with me." Sara had learned her lesson. She would keep her promise. She would not go to Catharta and leave her body unattended in the subway station.

Tim dropped the stern look, and his head hung a little lower. "I should have been there," he mumbled at his dinner plate. Some of that weariness she had noticed at the office returned to his face. He was thinking about the previous night, and all the places he would have rather been than at his apartment with Melissa.

"Hey," Sara said, trying to break through his foul mood. She reached across the table and put her hand on top of his. That got his attention. "It was fine. Like I said, Maya was there. And you didn't even let me get to the part about the cop yet." Sara gave him a mischievous smile, and Tim seemed to snap back out of his funk.

Once he looked more composed, she went on. "So I went to Catharta, and I found Ananda and the Guardian, and I convinced them both to go with me to the hospital. I took Sam to the room where his body is in the real world."

Tim's mind was already jumping ahead of the story. "You wanted to get him back into his body." Sara nodded. "How did you convince him to go with you?" he asked. His eyes subconsciously went to her throat, remembering the time the Guardian had attacked her.

Sara felt a little hurt that he seemed so surprised she was able to talk him into going with her. "Hey," she said, defensively. "I can be persuasive." She sat back in her chair and folded her arms in mock defiance. She wasn't actually that offended, but didn't want to let him off the hook so easily.

"I forgot," Tim said, raising his hands in defeat. "You are a master of charisma and have the ability to bend others to your will."

"Damn straight," Sara replied with the ghost of a smile on her lips.

"So?" Tim asked, expectantly.

"So what?" Sara asked in return. She was getting caught up in the comfort of their usual banter and had lost the thread of her own story.

"So did it work?" Tim blurted out. "Did you get him back in his body? Is he alive? Like, all the way alive?"

The failure of the previous night came back to Sara like a punch in the gut. "No," she answered, defeated. "It didn't work. He's still in Catharta and, as far as I know, still trapping souls there with him at this very moment."

It stung all over again having to repeat this failure out loud. It also left her with an exhausted feeling. If she had succeeded the night before, if she had been able to get Sam back in his living, breathing body, she would be done. She wouldn't have to go back to Catharta again. She wouldn't have to get up the nerve to go through with this plan tonight. The souls of the ghost plane would be free and so would she.

If Tim felt any disappointment, he didn't let it show. His face didn't change at all, not even one of his subtle, barely perceptible changes that drove her to madness sometimes. He didn't respond, so she went on.

"The night wasn't a total loss though. I got to see my dad." She said it casually, as if she dropped by to see him every day.

Tim's mouth fell open. He set down his coffee cup and gripped the edge of the table like he needed to hold onto something to keep himself in reality.

"Your dad?" he asked in disbelief. "You saw your dad?"

Sara nodded and shrugged, still trying to pretend it was no big deal. She didn't trust herself to speak. She couldn't risk dissolving into a sobbing pile of sadness like she had at the cemetery earlier that day. But Tim wasn't fooled. He could see the sting of tears in her eyes.

After a long pause, Tim breathed out the words, "Oh, Sara." There were no other words. What could he say? He understood how close she had been to her father. He had even met her father on several occasions. Knowing her dad was still there, trapped in the land of souls, probably made all of this much more real for Tim.

Sara blinked back the tears before they fell. Hearing her name come off Tim's lips made it a little easier to hold back her emotions. It made her feel safe. When she felt she could speak again, she said, "I know."

She did know. She knew what Tim was feeling. He was putting together that her dad's soul had been stuck in limbo all this time. He was realizing what that meant for Sara's mission to stop the Guardian, how much more important it had just become. He realized the mix of emotions it must have brought up for Sara to see him again. He probably realized that regardless of how disastrous his evening with his ex may have been, it was nothing compared to the roller coaster ride Sara had been on.

"I'm sorry," he said, just above a whisper.

"I know," Sara choked out again. She cleared her throat and tried to regain her train of thought. "But something good came out of it. He said something to me, something that sparked an idea in my mind. I think I know why Sam can't be reborn, and I'm pretty sure I know how to fix it. I think I know how to help everyone in Catharta, my dad included."

Tim's lips pursed and twitched to one side. His eyebrows rose. He was intrigued. She let him hang in suspense a little longer until he finally had to ask, "So why can't he be reborn? How are you going to fix it?"

Sara's eyes widened hopefully. "Well, I have a plan, but I'm going to need your help."

She went on to explain to Tim what she had planned for their evening, Maya's role in her plan, and his own involvement in the whole scheme. He listened attentively and she was surprised he only interrupted a few times with questions or to point out what a huge risk she was talking about taking. She had expected he would have a lot more questions, a lot more fatherly warnings, but he seemed to be on board with the whole thing. She was relieved. She could have handled it if he said he didn't want to be involved. She would have been able to deal with it if he didn't approve. But she didn't think she could take it if he tried to talk her out of it. She had been too close to talking herself out of this whole caper throughout the day. If he told her she shouldn't go through with it, she might just have to agree with him. But that would be quitting. That would be taking the comfortable path and the easy way out just like she had been doing her whole life. For once, she had to take a risk. She had to see this through.

When she was done, she told him, "That's it. That's the whole plan, and I'm just praying it works."

He didn't react. This time it was his turn to leave her hanging in suspense. Finally, she had to ask, "So, what do you think? Will you help me?"

He leaned back in his chair and looked up at the ceiling with his hands folded behind his head, as if he were giving the question his deep consideration.

She waited. Finally, when this posture had gone on a comically long time, she had to ask, "Are you done?" Impatience edged its way into her voice, and she couldn't contain her eye roll.

He leaned forward and gave her an earnest look, like his eyes were boring into hers.

"I'm in." She allowed herself a small sigh of relief. "You know I'm in."

Sara's phone chimed, interrupting their staring contest. She checked it and saw a text message from her sister.

"Well, needless to say, Maya is in too. And it sounds like she's already made her phone calls and gathered the stuff I need. She says she'll meet us at the hospital at eleven."

Tim checked the time. "We should get back to the office. I've got a lot of work to do before then."

"I'll get us a couple more coffees to go," Sara offered.

They made the short walk back to the office in silence. Sara wanted to press him further about what had happened with Melissa the night before, but he had said he wasn't ready to talk about it. Plus, he seemed to be in a much better mood, and she didn't want to spoil that. In the end, they parted ways when they got to the door to his office without discussing anything more.

Sara went back to work, but all the focus she felt she had regained in the first half of her shift was gone. As the clock ticked closer to quitting time, she grew more and more anxious about the tasks ahead of her. There were so many ways it could go wrong. Even if everything went exactly according to plan, it may still not work. Then, she would be back to square one. She tried her best to push that possibility out of her mind, but it stayed stubbornly lodged at the forefront.

By the time her shift was up, she wasn't even sure she had completed all her articles. If she'd missed any major typos, she would have to deal with the wrath of Jeff the following day. But that was tomorrow's problem. Besides, she was fully aware her mind was not going to let her get any more work done anyway. It was time to go.

As if reading her mind, Tim materialized outside her cubicle. He held up his station wagon keys and jingled them in the air. "I've got the keys to the hearse. Let's go."

The car ride to the hospital seemed interminable. Sara watched the buildings go by from the passenger seat of Tim's car without really seeing them. Everything was going by in a blur, yet she felt they weren't making any progress through downtown. There was little to no traffic at this hour. The stop lights didn't take that long. Yet somehow, she felt she was never going to arrive at her destination. The thought simultaneously filled her with complacency and dread. She didn't really want to do this. There was no part of her that thought this was a good idea. The logical part of her mind told her she should chalk this past week up to some sort of hallucination or mental breakdown and simply abandon the whole idea. But in her heart and in her guts, she knew she had to do this. She had to get there and get it over with. That was the part of her that felt like she was never going to arrive at the hospital. She would be stuck in Tim's passenger seat for the rest of eternity.

She needed to get her mind off it before she overthought everything and screwed it up or, worse, chickened out altogether. Tim had the radio on, but it wasn't helping. She needed to talk. She needed to think about something else.

Before she thought it through all the way, she asked Tim, "So do you want to tell me what happened with Melissa last night?" She immediately bit her lip. She hadn't meant to bring that up again. She knew he said that he wasn't ready to talk about it, but it was the first thing that came to mind. She just needed to talk about something besides ghosts.

Tim sucked in a sharp breath and held it for a second. She had made him uncomfortable, which in turn was making her uncomfortable. But on the plus side, she was feeling less anxious about their imminent arrival at the hospital.

The silence gathered around them as if the car had filled with water. Sara couldn't hear anything except her own heart pounding in her ears.

Finally, Tim spoke. "Yeah. Well. Melissa came over last night to get her things. She didn't have much stuff at my apartment. Just some clothes, a phone charger, a toothbrush." He paused there and Sara wondered for a moment if that was all she was going to get out of him, an inventory of items his ex-girlfriend had left at his place. But then, he added, "She said she wanted to try again."

Sara hesitated for a moment. She couldn't tell how he felt about that. She wasn't even sure if that meant they were together now or not. Unsure of what to say, she finally settled on, "So that's good news, right?" He gripped the steering wheel tighter and didn't respond.

"I mean," Sara continued. "You said she was the one who broke up with you, right? If she wants to try again, isn't that a good thing?"

"I guess," Tim replied unconvincingly. "Here's the thing." He bristled as he searched for his next words. He looked like a dog with its hackles raised. He took each hand off the wheel in turn and wiped it on his jeans. He was sweating, which was making Sara's palms sweat in return.

"She broke up with me because I didn't want us to move in together."

"Right," Sara responded. "You told me that part already. So did she change her mind?"

"Not really," Tim said. "She just said she wants to try again. She wants to start over. She's fine with us not living together, but she said

237

she needs a bigger commitment from me. She wanted me to make her some promises. I'm just not ready to make those promises. I don't know that I ever will be."

There was more to this story, and Sara wasn't sure yet if he expected her to put it together herself or if he was still working up to it. She wasn't getting it, so she prompted him. "What kind of promises?"

He closed his eyes for a moment, and Sara's gaze immediately shot to the road in front of them, as if she could guide the car for him. He opened his eyes again.

"I didn't want to do this right now," he said, more to himself than to her.

Sara was frozen. Her mouth was dry. Her pulse was racing. She had no idea what was going on, but she had never in her life seen Tim so riled. He was her best friend. She thought she knew him, but she had never seen this side of him. She didn't even understand what this side of him was.

"Okay," he finally said, trying to relax his shoulders a bit. "Melissa did break up with me because I couldn't commit to her, but there's more to it than that. She wanted me to move in with her. I said no. She said she couldn't waste any more time with me if we didn't have a future together." Sara knew all this already. She still didn't get what had him so agitated.

"Last night, when she came over, she said she was willing to try again, that she wouldn't push me to move in with her. But first, she wanted me to promise that the reason I couldn't commit wasn't you."

"Wasn't me?" It came out a whisper. Sara couldn't make any sense of what she was hearing. What did she have to do with any of this?

"She accused me of trying to keep myself available for you. She thinks I'm waiting around for you to decide you have feelings for me. And she's not wrong."

The words were rushing out of him now, like water from a burst pipe. Sara wanted to plug the leak long enough to absorb what he was saying, but she couldn't stop him. She couldn't speak. She couldn't even move.

"She's not wrong, and I told her so, and she said it was over. She couldn't be with me if she knew she was my second choice, if she knew I'd rather be with you. Not that I can blame her for that. No one should settle for being someone's fallback plan. Do you want the honest-to-god truth, Sara?"

He turned and looked at her then, looking away from the road for just a moment. His eyes were wide and wild. He looked like he was going to be sick. She felt like a deer in the headlights. She couldn't respond to his question. She couldn't look away from his gaze.

He didn't wait for her to respond. "The truth is I'm in love with you. I've been in love with you for a long time. I've been waiting around hoping that one day, you'll wake up and decide you love me too. But maybe I'm the one who's dreaming. Maybe I'm the one who needs to wake up."

Sara didn't have any time to react. Suddenly, the car was stopped. Tim put it in park, the engine still idling. The passenger door was whipped open, and Sara turned to find herself staring at Maya, standing in the darkness of the parking lot, framed by the hospital entrance doors.

Her sister quickly shoved a bag into her lap and stated matter-of-factly, "Here are the scrubs. Shift change is in ten minutes. The orders will go through in fifteen. Are you ready?" Sara had to ask herself the same question. Was she ready?

CHAPTER 19

S ara stared into the mirror in the lobby restroom of the hospital, trying to recognize her own reflection. She didn't look like herself. She had stripped off her layers until she wore just jeans and a t-shirt; then she had pulled on the cornflower blue scrubs Maya had obtained for her over her clothes. She had clipped Maya's hospital badge to her waistband where it would be less noticeable than on the breast pocket of her shirt. She also made sure it hung the wrong way, showing only the barcode on the back. She didn't look enough like her sister for anyone to believe the smiling dimpled face pictured on the front belonged to Sara. Plus, she didn't want anyone noticing the words "Gift Shop" displayed prominently next to Maya's photo. She had pulled her long, dark hair back into an uncharacteristic ponytail. There was very little about herself that she recognized except her mother's locket hanging around her neck. She tucked it inside her shirt.

Maya pounded on the bathroom door. "Are you almost ready?" She asked. "You're running out of time."

Sara unlocked the bathroom door. She handed the pile of her own discarded clothes to her sister, and in return, Maya handed her a paper face mask and a pair of purple latex gloves.

Maya began to rattle off instructions. "I'm going to take these to the car," she said, holding up Sara's bundle of clothes. "Then I'm going to head for the south side exit. I'll probably be there in like ten minutes." She let out a small groan and pressed her hand to her lower back. Sara momentarily forgot the stress of the task ahead of her and turned all her concern toward her sister.

"Are you okay? Is the baby okay?"

Maya waved her off. "I'm fine. My back is killing me today, but it's no big deal. It comes in waves. I'll be fine in a minute."

Sara looked her up and down appraisingly. "Are you sure?"

"I'm positive. Just focus on what you need to do. After this is all over, you can worry about me all you want. But for right now, you have a more important job."

Considering this was Sara's plan, Maya sure was taking charge. Sara didn't mind though. She could barely bring herself to think, much less speak. It was good to feel like someone else was running the show. She nodded to acknowledge her sister's instructions. "Okay, well you've got about two minutes until shift change. You better go." Sara nodded again and turned toward the elevators.

"Hey," Maya said, catching her by the arm. Sara thought she was going to give her a last-minute pep talk or some words of encouragement, but all she did was tug at the paper mask in Sara's hand. "Put it on."

She looked down at the mask like it wasn't real. None of this seemed real. She couldn't really be going through with this idiotic plan. Maybe if she pretended none of this was really happening, she wouldn't have to think about it until it was all over. In her mind, she told herself this was all happening in her imagination. It was all a dream. The thought did nothing to drown out the rush of blood in her eardrums or the anxiety rising in her chest. People talk about getting butterflies in their stomach when they're nervous. Sara didn't have that sensation exactly. It felt more like a swarm of bees in her lungs.

Sara pulled the mask to her face under the guise of germ control when really it was a tactic to hide her face. She looped the elastic straps behind her ears and headed off through the lobby. She left her sister behind her, refusing to look back for fear of losing her nerve. As she approached the stairwell, she pulled on the gloves as well. Her palms immediately began to sweat, making the latex cling to her skin uncomfortably.

As she climbed the stairs, the mask close to her face made her already heightened breathing escalate to the border of hyperventilation. It would have been easier if she could have taken the elevator, but Maya had warned her she should avoid as many security cameras as possible, and the stairwell didn't have any.

When she got up to the floor where the MedSurg unit was, she paused and looked around. This maze of hallways was one thing she was worried about. She didn't have much time to double back if she took a wrong turn, and she certainly couldn't ask anyone which way to go since she was supposed to be a hospital employee. She also had to find a spare gurney before she made it to the unit. She closed her eyes and tried to catch her breath. She reminded herself that she had walked these halls twice the night before, once in the real world and once in Catharta. She should be able to find her way. She headed out in what she was pretty sure was the right direction.

She ended up only taking one wrong turn, but it was a fortunate one. She turned down a hallway and found herself approaching Diagnostic Imaging and noticed an abandoned gurney up against the wall between two x-ray rooms. Making sure she wasn't visible from the check-in desk, she dragged the rolling bed back the way from which she had come. Checking the signs overhead, she realized where she had gone wrong and got back on track on her way to the MedSurg unit.

The hallways were thankfully empty, but as she approached the unit where Sam resided, she could hear a bustling of activity around the next corner that would bring her to the nurses' station. She checked the time. It was shift change. That meant there were twice as many nurses on the floor. She hoped the commotion of passing off patient information and the extra bodies on the floor would make it easier for her to blend in. It was true—she looked just like every other nurse in the hospital, but the gurney drew attention. She wasn't sure she would be able to get past the nurses' station to Sam's room without being questioned.

She hesitated at the T-junction of the hallways, waiting for the best time to make a right turn and head toward the nurses, trying to figure out how she should approach. Should she be quick and quiet and keep her head down? Should she try to move slowly and leisurely and maybe give a friendly wave? Neither option seemed like a good one.

She peeked around the corner to her left. The hallway stretched out with patient rooms along the right side and wall art on the left. It was the kind of art you only seem to find in hospitals, abstract shapes in muted colors that complement the bland beige of the walls. At the end of the corridor, it looked like it turned right. Sara wondered if it looped around. If it did, maybe she wouldn't have to walk by the nurses' station at all.

Taking a chance, she pushed the gurney down the left hallway and followed it to its end, taking slow, measured steps without ever glancing back at the nurses. When she turned the corner, the sounds of shift change faded away and another long hallway stretched out in front of her. Again, there were patient rooms along the right-hand side, and again, it seemed to take a right turn at the end of the hall. She quickened her pace now, knowing that she was well out of view of the nurses' station, but she didn't want to run in case there was someone in one of the rooms with a door standing open. As she passed each open room, she tried not to look in, but just scan it with her peripheral vision. She detected no movement, and most of the lights were down low. The patients inside were resting, their machines hissing and beeping away.

At the end of the hallway, she took another right and felt more confident rushing down the corridor. All the doors in this hallway were shut. She was essentially opposite the nurses' station in this loop of the unit. She reasoned they probably tried to fill up the closest rooms first to better keep an eye on the patients. She wondered why Sam hadn't been exiled to this distant stretch of rooms long ago to make room for higher-priority patients.

One more right turn and she was able to confirm that this was, in fact, a loop. She could see the final turn she needed up ahead. As she rushed toward the last turn, she was stopped short as a man in cornflower blue scrubs emerged from one of the patient rooms. Sara was frozen in her tracks. In her mind, she tried to tell herself to keep going, to act casual, to pretend she belonged there. But her feet wouldn't go. The nurse doubled back into the room from which he had just come without looking in Sara's direction. Maybe he forgot something. Maybe he had been called back by the patient. Would he step out into the hallway again in a matter of seconds or a matter of minutes? Sara had no way of knowing. If she resumed her trek down the hall now, she might risk being right alongside the room when he came out again and then there would be no avoiding him. But this might be her only chance to get past him unnoticed. As she stood, paralyzed with indecision, the door to the patient's room clicked closed. She wasn't sure if he had shut it on purpose or if it had just accidentally swung closed behind him, but it didn't matter. She seized the moment.

Breaking into a full on run, she sprinted down the hallway, pushing the gurney in front of her as quietly as she could manage. She made it past the room the nurse had entered and down to the final turn in the hallway, where she skidded to a halt. She peeked around the corner and noted several other nurses still milling around their station. None of them were looking in her direction. Sam's door stood halfway between her and them. It was closed. She glanced back over her shoulder as she heard a door swing open behind her. The nurse she had passed would be coming out of the patient's room in a matter of seconds and would probably be heading straight for the nurses' station. She had to move now.

Shoving the gurney ahead of her, she rounded the corner as quickly as she could manage to get out of the line of site of the nurse approaching from behind and then tried to slow to a more reasonable pace so as not to attract the attention of any of the nurses at the station. She kept her head down, but her eyes on the nurses' station. There was a lot of movement, but so far, no one coming Sara's way. She focused on steadying her breathing, counting her steps, anything she could think of to keep from panicking. She needed to keep it together. Just a few more steps and she would be at Sam's door.

Breathe in. Breathe out. Slow, even steps.

Her hand was on the doorknob. She swung the gurney wide so that she could back into the room, pulling the bed behind her.

Breathe in. Breathe out.

She could hear the shoes of the male nurse from the other hallway, squeaking against the linoleum. He'd be rounding that corner any second.

Breathe in. Breathe out.

She pulled the gurney into the room and moved out of the way so that the door could swing shut behind her. It had one of those controlled hinges to keep it from slamming. It hissed closed at a maddeningly slow pace. Sara resisted the urge to push it closed faster, knowing that would only draw more attention. The nurse's shoes squeaked down the hallway.

Breathe in. Breathe out.

The door clicked shut, and she was enveloped in darkness. She held her breath and waited motionlessly as she heard the nurse's shoes squeak by and on toward the station down the hall without so much as a heartbeat's hesitation. Sara pulled off the paper face mask and allowed her breathing to follow its own frenetic rhythm rather than try to force it. She had done it. She was in the room.

She waited until her heart had slowed to a steady thump rather than a panicked pounding; then, she turned around. She was faced again with the pale blue curtain surrounding Sam's hospital bed. She approached it cautiously and stretched out one hand to pull it open. A thought burst into her mind unexpectedly. What if she pulled back the fabric and found Sam sitting up, wide awake, healthy, and alive. That was absurd. The man had been in a coma for three years; he wouldn't wake up tonight. Then she pictured the bed empty, Sam gone, as if he had never been there at all. Maybe she had imagined him the whole time. Maybe Sam never existed at all. She didn't know why she thought of that. Sam was definitely real. Dr. Carver had seen him. Charge Nurse Rachel had seen him. Sara had touched him with her own hands and had looked into his eyes with hers. He was real. The thought of him being awake or being nonexistent wasn't a funny idea to her at all, but for some reason a laugh bubbled up in her throat. She let it escape her mouth, and it sounded foreign to her. It sounded like the laugh of someone gripped by hysteria. She was losing it. She had to try to keep it together. She took another deep breath and pulled back the curtain.

Sam was there, just as he had been the night before. His skin was pale and papery. His eyes were set deep under his prominent brow bones. His mouth was agape and his eyes were open just a sliver.

She felt like someone reached a hand into her chest and gripped her heart, squeezing it to get it to stop beating. She ached to help this man. She felt somehow personally responsible for the unhappy life he had lived and for the fact that his suffering wasn't yet over. She hadn't caused this pain, but she could fix it. She just had to find the courage to follow through.

It would be so easy to just stay in this room forever, to put a hold on her plan, on life, and just stay here, never moving forward. But she couldn't do that. Maya and Tim were waiting for her. This had to happen tonight. She had to keep going.

She approached Sam's bedside. She placed one hand on his chest and another on his forehead. Leaning in close she whispered, "I'm going to help you. I promise I won't give up."

Sara turned her attention to the machine Sam was hooked up to. Maya had warned her she had to shut the machine down, rather than just pull off the wires and electrodes running under Sam's hospital gown. Otherwise, she risked setting off a series of alarms at the nurses' station and bringing a whole lot of unwanted attention to this room. She shut the machine down and then, for good measure, unplugged it from the wall just in case. Then she began unhooking all the little wires that had been monitoring his heartbeat and his blood oxygen level for the past three years.

It was strange to stand so close to Sam's body, to touch his skin, to listen to his shallow breathing. She couldn't connect this shell of a human to the Guardian that was awaiting her return in Catharta. The Sam of the ghost plane seemed gargantuan. He was all broad shoulders and long arms and piercing eyes. The Sam before her now was just a wisp of a man. This was the real ghost.

Sara turned off his IV drip and laid the bag across his chest. She wasn't going to try to remove the line from his arm. Maya had given her some instructions on how to shut down the machine, but neither of them was a nurse. She didn't trust herself to mess with something that was connected to Sam's vein. She was just lucky he wasn't on a ventilator.

Once he was fully disconnected, Sara wheeled the gurney alongside his hospital bed. She lowered the bedside rail so that the two mattresses were even with one another with no obstructions in the way. This was one part of the plan she was nervous about. She had witnessed this maneuver many times when her mother was in the hospital. Usually, two musclebound nurses would be called in. They would lift her mom by the sheets beneath her and slide her over to the other bed. Her mom didn't weigh a ton, and the staff that did the moving always looked so strong. Sara was uncertain if she would be able to pull off the same move by herself. But she had no choice. Tim and Maya each had their own role to play in this caper, and neither one of them was able to be with her here in this room. She had to do this on her own.

She gathered her strength and gripped the sheets, both underneath and on top of him. She pressed her hip against the gurney so it wouldn't slide around, and then, she heaved. She nearly tumbled backward from her overcompensation as Sam glided easily onto the gurney. He was featherlight. There was practically nothing left of him. His muscle mass had disappeared from being immobile for so long. He had been kept alive by liquid nutrients in an IV bag for three years. He was little more than a skeleton and a dilapidated collection of organs.

Again, Sara thought about his lack of visitors. This man had a wife. He was in here disappearing day by day, and his spouse was out there somewhere living her life. She knew there were two sides to every story, and there was probably a reason Sam's wife didn't want to see him, but in the moment, Sara couldn't excuse it. She couldn't look at this husk of a human being and fathom any reasonable explanation as to why his wife wouldn't at least come to see him or return a phone call from the hospital. He shouldn't be here. He should be in some sort of long-term care facility with people who are experts in his condition, who know how to make sure he's comfortable.

Rage was bubbling up inside her, and she pushed it back down. She had to stay focused. She could stew over Sam's miserable life later. Right now, she had to get him out of here. She tore her eyes off of him and looked over her shoulder at the door. She had to go back out there.

Shift change had surely settled down by now. The nurses might be making their rounds, checking in with their patients, crawling all over the hallways. Or they might still be hanging around the nurses' station getting settled in. Sara had no way of knowing because whatever was happening out there was happening on the other side of that closed door. She felt blind.

She pulled the paper mask back onto her face, breathing in her own hot, damp breath. She crept toward the door and edged it open just a crack. Looking down the hallway, she could see at least two nurses seated at the station, their heads down, maybe focused on paperwork. She pressed her ear to the opening in the door. Footsteps could be heard squeaking around in the distance, but she couldn't tell which direction they came from.

A decision had to be made. Straight past the nurses' station was the quickest way out of the unit and the nurses seemed distracted, but she would definitely encounter them. She could loop back around the way she had come, but who knew how many hospital employees might be walking those halls now.

She wished someone else were here to tell her what to do. To buy herself a little time, she moved the gurney into position, ready to make her exit. She pulled the sheet up under Sam's chin and gently closed his eyes. Still feeling indecisive, she asked Sam's comatose body, "Which way do you think we should go?"

As if the world were trying to send her a signal, Sam's head fell ever so slightly to his right, toward the nurses' station. Sara accepted it as his choice.

"Okay, we'll take the shortest route. Wish me luck." With that, Sara quietly swung the door open and pushed the gurney out into the hall.

The gurney was no harder to push with Sam's weight on it. If anything, it turned a little easier. Sara swung it so he was pointed down the hallway, feet first. She waited until the door clicked shut behind her before she began her slow and steady trek down the hall. Her plan was to keep her head down and push on past the nurses' station and hopefully not be noticed. She didn't see any other nurses walking this stretch of hallway, just the tops of two heads behind the counter at the station, still focused on something on the desk in front of them. One was a brunette and one was a redhead. Sara prayed the redhead wasn't Maya's friend Rachel who she had met the night before. The mask covered her face from her nose to her chin, but she was still worried she might be recognized.

The panic was rising in her chest again. The swarm of bees were humming. She wanted to run. She wanted to get out of this unit and off of the floor as quickly as possible, but she knew she couldn't do that. She hoped she was walking at a normal pace, not so quick as to draw attention but not so slow as to appear as if she had nowhere to be. She felt like she was crawling.

She was almost alongside the nurses' station now. A few more steps, and she'd be right in front of them. Another ten feet after that, she could turn the corner and be gone. She just had to keep putting one foot in front of the other.

Eyes forward. Steady breathing. Left foot. Right foot.

She was right in front of them now, close enough to the station desk that they wouldn't see the gurney unless they looked up over the counter in front of them. Maybe she just looked like a lone nurse pacing the halls. Maybe they wouldn't even realize she had a patient with her.

Eyes ahead. Don't hesitate. Don't break your pace. Left foot. Right foot.

She had reached the end of the station. Another ten paces, and she could turn the corner, get out of sight.

Left foot. Right foot.

One of the nurses spoke. "Who do you got there?"

Sara took two more steps. Maybe she could pretend she hadn't heard the question. Maybe the question wasn't even directed at her. Should she just keep going?

"Hey there," the voice called after her. The tone was friendly but insistent. This nurse would not be ignored.

Sara stopped and looked back over her shoulder, trying to look loose and casual in spite of the fact that her entire body had gone rigid. It was the redhead. To Sara's relief, it wasn't Rachel. At least, this woman wouldn't recognize her.

"I said who do you got there?" the nurse repeated.

Sara's mind raced. How should she respond? How did nurses refer to their patients? Should she give a first name? A last name? Both?

The brunette seated at the desk took note of the interaction going on in front of her and peeked over the counter.

"Is that one-twenty?" she asked, the surprise evident in her voice. She had referred to Sam by his room number. Was that how nurses referred to their patients? Sara never would have come up with that.

"Yeah," she agreed. "This is one-twenty."

"Is he finally getting transferred?" the brunette asked. She seemed to be more familiar with Sam than her red-headed counterpart.

Sara's mind fumbled through her plan. Should she agree? Should she say he was being transferred? Would that buy her more time? No that would never check out. She should stick to the plan.

Sara shook her head. "I'm just taking him for a neural scan."

"A neural scan? Who ordered it?" the brunette questioned further.

Sara was thankful for the paper face mask hiding the heat rising in her cheeks. She was a terrible liar, and she hoped it didn't show.

"Dr. Carver ordered it. It should be in the system." Sara prayed it was in the system. Maya had called in another favor to her baby's father with the promise that it would be the last one, that they wouldn't bother him anymore. Sara knew that if things went south, she would have made him an unwilling accessory to this crime, but she only felt a tiny twinge of guilt over that. He wasn't a good man. She was sure of that.

"Let me pull it up real quick," the redhead said, turning toward her computer station. She typed what seemed like an essay, and then gave a confused look to the computer monitor. Frowning, she said, "That's weird."

Sara's heart stopped. This was it. Dr. Carver hadn't followed through. She would be found out. She had failed. Her tongue was glued to the roof of her mouth. She couldn't breathe. She couldn't move.

The brunette asked, "What's weird?"

A million possibilities ran through Sara's head. The orders hadn't gone through in time. She had said the wrong type of scan. The doctor had ratted her out.

The redhead's reply was, "Carver ordered the scan, but he's not this guy's doctor. I don't know why he'd be ordering it."

Sara hadn't considered that. This wouldn't be the normal channel to get any type of tests performed. It would go through his normal doctor. But Sara didn't know his normal doctor. How was she going to get out of this?

"You know what?" the brunette volunteered. "I think Carver is taking an interest in his case. He came down here yesterday to check on him."

Sara suddenly remembered her phone call with Damian the day before. She had asked for Sam's room number, and the doctor knew it off the top of his head. He had said he went to see the patient. At the time, she had felt it was an invasion of Sam's privacy. She didn't like the thought of Dr. Carver standing by the Guardian's bedside. But now, she was thankful he had. She was also thankful that this nurse had apparently been on duty when Damian came by.

The redhead seemed to accept this explanation. "Okay, well if he wants a scan, give him a scan." She turned her attention back to the paperwork on her desk.

Sara stood there awkwardly. Was that it? Was she free to go? Did she have to ask to be dismissed? She decided to slowly turn back the way she had been heading and see if the nurses stopped her.

She took about two more steps before the brunette asked, "Are you new? I don't think I've seen you before."

Sara turned back to face her. "I'm fairly new," she said vaguely.

"What's your name?"

She couldn't give a real name. Was this woman going to check her badge? If so, she should say her name is Maya. But this badge was never going to check out anyway, and then, she would have implicated her sister. She had to think quickly. No one takes this long to think of their own name. She blurted out the first name that came to her mind.

"I'm Ananda." At least a dead girl couldn't be sent to prison.

The brunette replied, "I'm Sarah." *Of course you are*, thought Sara.

"Okay, we'll see you around, Ananda."

With that, she really was dismissed. She gave a small wave good-bye and pushed Sam about eight more feet to the end of the station, and then, turned the corner and disappeared.

Sara had no choice but to take the elevator now. She couldn't very well push the gurney down the stairwell. She would have to face the cameras. As she waited for the elevator to arrive, she double-checked that her face mask was in place and her badge was still backward. When the doors opened, she negotiated the gurney into the tight space and wriggled into the corner. She kept her head down and pushed the button for the ground floor, but the rear side of the elevator. There were doors on either end. The front side would open up to the lobby. The rear doors would take her where she needed to go.

The polished interior of the elevator showed Sara her own reflection. All she could see was her eyes over the paper mask. They looked accusing. Her own reflection was judging her for the actions she was taking.

She arrived at the ground floor, and the back doors slid open. Sara pushed the gurney and the Guardian out into another beige hallway. This one didn't have as many twists and turns, and the exits were clearly marked. She had to find the south side exit. That was where Maya would be stationed, and Tim would be waiting outside.

Noting the signs overhead, Sara found the last turn she would need to make before she was faced with the exit. She pulled the sheet up over Sam's face. It was better if he appeared to be dead for this next part. She noticed the sheet moved up and down ever so slightly with Sam's breathing. She hoped it was subtle enough that no one else would notice. If Maya did her job right, she would be outside in the night air in under a minute anyway.

Sara inhaled deeply and gripped the handles of the gurney tightly to steady her shaking hands. She squeezed her eyes shut as she turned the corner, afraid of what she might see.

When she opened her eyes again, she saw exactly what she was supposed to see, although it didn't stop her heart from skipping a beat. Ahead of her was the south side exit. Standing to the side of the door was a security guard who looked so young Sara had a hard time believing he wasn't still in high school. In front of him, partially obstructing his view, was Maya. She was talking to the young guard animatedly and, if Sara wasn't mistaken, a bit flirtatiously. She couldn't hear what they were talking about. Whether that was because she wasn't close enough or because all she could hear was her pulse pounding in her ears, she couldn't be sure. It didn't matter. All that mattered was he was smiling at Maya and paying no attention to Sam and Sara.

She pushed her way along the final hallway that would lead her out into the night. The sliding glass doors just past the guard's post reflected her own image back at her, getting larger with every step she took. Once again, she tried to control her pace.

Left foot. Right foot. Breathe in. Breathe out.

She was approaching the guard's station now. The young man in uniform was still listening raptly to Maya's story about something Sara couldn't quite follow. He maintained eye contact with her sister, but his body was turning toward Sara, preparing to ask her for her credentials. Sara's heart rate increased exponentially with each fractional movement of the guard's body. The blood was draining from her face. She must look ghostly. She felt dizzy and nauseous and electrified all at once.

As Maya continued her story, hardly pausing to take a breath, the guard raised a hand in Sara's direction, indicating she should stop. But he was too polite to interrupt Maya. He smiled and nodded and gazed into her eyes, all while trying to signal Sara that he needed to process her exit in the system.

Sara slowed, but didn't stop. If she raced past him, that would look highly suspicious, and he would surely follow her. She needed a better distraction. Maya could talk up a storm, but that wasn't going to cut it.

She was standing beside the guard now with the gurney still in front of her. Another inch or two, and it would trigger the automatic sliding doors. Sara could practically feel the cool night air filling her lungs. How was she going to get past this guy? How could she distract him from her presence?

Unexpectedly, Maya screamed midsentence. Sara and the guard both nearly jumped out of their skin. Sara's instinct was to run to her sister, to find out what was wrong. Thankfully, the guard beat her to it, giving Sara a moment to come to her senses.

"Are you okay?" he asked. "What's wrong?"

Maya doubled over, one arm wrapped around her bulging belly, the other pressed hard against the small of her back. Her face was twisted with pain. "I think my water just broke," she announced. She let out another scream and leaned heavily on the guard's station. "Can you call labor and delivery for me?" she begged of the guard.

He hastily fumbled with the phone and was now fully distracted. Sara still felt frozen. A tiny flick of Maya's fingers snapped her out of it. Her sister was telling her to go. This was her only chance.

Sara shoved the gurney forward. The sliding glass doors pulled apart, and she passed through them in slow motion. With her feet planted firmly on the concrete outside, she took a deep breath. Even through the paper mask she felt the foggy night air fill her lungs. She had done it. She had gotten Sam out of the hospital. But she couldn't stop now. There was no time to celebrate this small victory. Ahead of her, down a short ramp, waited Tim and his black station wagon, looking somehow more hearse-like than usual. She suspected she would never jokingly call it his hearse again.

She wheeled the gurney down the ramp, and Tim emerged from the driver's seat to help her. He opened the rear door as Sara pulled back Sam's bedsheet. Without discussing it, Tim positioned himself at the head of the gurney, sliding his hands beneath Sam's shoulders. Sara wrapped her arms around Sam's knees. Tim gave her a nod, and they both lifted. She was struck again by how light he was compared to how enormous he seemed in his ghost state. Maybe he wasn't really that big. Maybe his size was an illusion based on his enormous personality.

They negotiated his body so that he was lying down across the backseat. Sara shoved the gurney to the side of the ramp she had just walked down as Tim got in the driver's seat and started the engine. Sara raced to the passenger's seat and slid in beside him. Tim barely waited for her to buckle her seatbelt before he tore out of the parking lot.

Once they were out on the city streets, Sara felt safer. She wasn't alone anymore. She had half of her support team here with her. She didn't have to worry about running into any more nurses or doctors or guards. She certainly wasn't free and clear yet, but she felt like she could finally breathe normally. She pulled the paper mask off and buried her face in her palms.

"Are you okay?" Tim asked quietly.

Was she okay? She didn't really know how to answer that question. She had just abducted a comatose man from a hospital. Clearly, something about her was not okay.

"I'm fine. I'm just…" she trailed off as she turned to look at him, and he took his eyes off the road to meet hers. All his words came flooding back to her. Her best friend had confessed his love for her, had poured his heart out to her, and had made himself more vulnerable than she had ever seen him. She hadn't formulated a response yet. She still didn't know how to react. All her thoughts since she exited his car at the front doors of the hospital had been occupied with the Guardian and getting him out of his living prison. But now, she was faced with Tim again, and she owed him some sort of response.

"Tim, about what you said before," she began.

"Stop," he said abruptly. She was glad he had cut her off. She still had no idea what she would say if he allowed her to finish her thought. "Not now. Not here. I'm sorry I brought it up."

Sara swallowed hard and turned her eyes back toward the street ahead.

"That's not what I meant," he said, seemingly frustrated with himself. His hands tightened around the steering wheel. "I didn't mean I'm sorry I said it. I needed to say it. I just wish I hadn't said it now, tonight."

Sara didn't know what to say. She felt she should say something, but there were no words that would make this drive less awkward.

They weren't far from the subway station now. She would just have to live with the uncomfortable silence for a few more minutes.

Her phone buzzing in her pocket interrupted the silence. She pulled it out and saw a text from Maya. Her eyes widened, and she couldn't stop a faint, "Oh my god," from escaping her lips.

"What is it? What's wrong?" Tim was now even more on edge.

"It's Maya," Sara replied. "I thought she was just creating a diversion, but her water really broke. She's in labor!"

"Does this change our plan at all?" he asked urgently.

Sara looked over her shoulder at Sam sprawled across the backseat, his chest slowly rising and falling, but otherwise looking dead. "It can't. It can't change our plan, can it? I mean we've already got him here. We can't very well take him back to the hospital."

Tim stole a glance at the patient in his rearview mirror. "No, not really."

"We just have to be really fast." Sara began typing a reply to her sister. She told her they would be back as soon as they could and that she should call Aunt Joann. Sara couldn't remember what time their aunt's flight came in, but it was closing in on midnight. She should be back from her business trip by now.

Maya's reply came a few seconds later. All it said was, "HURRY!!!"

When Sara looked up from her phone again, Tim was bringing the car to a stop just around the corner from the Sixteenth Street subway station entrance. There was plenty of street parking at this time of night, thank goodness.

"Did you get a wheelchair?" Sara thought to ask as he put the car in park.

"Yeah, it's in the back. They had a bunch lined up at the entrance to the emergency department."

Tim retrieved the wheelchair as Sara stripped off the scrubs she was still wearing over her regular clothing. Then, together the two of them negotiated Sam's nearly lifeless body into it. They wheeled him toward the street-level elevator as quickly as they could. There was no longer any reason to try to control their pace or appear casual. They were just three people making their way to the train station, one of whom happened to be in a wheelchair. Much stranger sights had been seen in the middle of the night on the streets of San Francisco.

They wheeled Sam into the elevator and pushed the button for the fare gates level. As the door closed in front of them, Sara found herself faced with another awkward silence in another enclosed space. She was going to have to figure out what to say to Tim at some point. But until she did, she felt like she couldn't say anything. She tried to get a look at him out of the corner of her eye. He was staring at his shoes. The door opened, and they rushed through the fare gates and then over to the platform elevator.

It was out of service.

Sara and Tim looked at one another and then simultaneously looked toward the stairs at the end of the station. They had no other choice. They broke into a run toward the stairway. At the first step, Tim positioned himself in front of the Guardian and hoisted him up by the front of his chair. Sara stayed at the back, holding onto the handles of the chair and leaning back to keep gravity from taking control. They bumped gracelessly down the stairs. When they finally reached the platform, Tim and Sara were both sweating. Sara checked the overhead sign. The next train would be arriving in two minutes. She wheeled her patient into position.

Tim paced along the edge of the platform nervously, glancing into the tunnel where the train would emerge and then back down the platform to ensure no one was around. At the moment, it looked like they had the station all to themselves. There might be someone on the train when it arrived. They had no control over that. There was no point in worrying about the things they couldn't control.

Again, Sara felt like she should say something, anything to ease the tension between them. She knew Tim was right, that now was not the time. But it felt like an eternity had passed since he had made his confession in the car, and she couldn't believe he was okay with her just leaving it hanging like this. The train could not arrive soon enough.

It was approaching now. Sara could feel the air in the station beginning to stir. A plastic bag that had been dropped off the edge of the platform was lifted by the wind and floated on down the tracks.

The tiles beneath her feet began to rumble. The train could be heard at a distance. She couldn't allow herself to think about Tim anymore. She had to focus on the task at hand.

The wind grew stronger as the train pushed a column of air toward the Sixteenth Street subway station. The headlights began to illuminate concentric circles of light within the dark gaping mouth of the tunnel. Then, the lights reflected off the metal rails as the train approached the last curve of the tunnel, creating two parallel bright white beams shooting into the station. The sound grew deafening. Even if Sara could find the words now, Tim wouldn't be able to hear her. There was a spark from the electric third rail and then the train burst into the station.

That was her cue. Sara flipped the wheelchair with Sam still in it on its back. His head cracked hard against the unforgiving tile. Tim pulled the chair out from under the patient so he was lying flat on his back on the station floor. Sara kneeled down beside him. She placed her ear close to his lips. He was still breathing, slow labored breaths. She didn't know if this was working. She had to get through to him.

She put her face right up to his, so they were nose to nose. She yelled at him, "You have to let go, Sam. There's nothing for you here anymore. I'm sorry, but it's true. There is a chance for you to start over. I promise you that. But first, you have to let go." The train was beginning to slow down. Soon it would be stopped. She didn't know how much time she had. "Now, Sam! You have to let go now!"

Whether by coincidence or because she had actually gotten through to him, Sam's eyes suddenly flashed open, staring straight up. She saw their unique shade of pale blue surrounded by whites marred by a maze of red veins. He looked not at her, but through her. It only lasted for a second and then the lids went slack, and he let out a slow, laboring exhale. There was no inhale. He was gone. The last fraction of his soul had finally let go.

Sara felt a strange pull. Something, some unseen force, was pulling her down. Catharta was pulling her in. She succumbed. Throwing herself onto the platform right alongside Sam, she grasped the dead man's hand tightly and opened her eyes as wide as they would go. It felt different this time. She wasn't falling. She was being pulled in by a vacuum. She was pulled down into a black nothingness until everything was silent and the wind and the noise and everything associated with the living world was gone. She didn't move, didn't dare to breathe, until she felt a hand squeeze her own.

Sara turned her head to see Sam staring up at the ceiling, blinking, but otherwise motionless. They were in Catharta, but this was not the Guardian lying next to her. This was Sam. This last bit of his soul was no longer trapped in a body that refused to let go. It was in the ghost plane with her. She had brought him here.

She whispered, "Sam."

Slowly, he turned his head to look at her. His eyes had transformed from their already pale blue to a colorless clear glow. He was dead. There was no living body tethering him to her world anymore.

Sara felt safe here. She had escaped the hospital, had escaped the real world. She had momentarily escaped Tim and her tangle of feelings about his confession. Here among the dead, none of that could touch her.

Then the thought of Maya burst into her head. Sara's work was not yet done, and she had promised her sister that she would not let this baby come into the world without a soul. She propped herself up on her elbows and saw Ananda, waiting for her as promised, staring at Sam, wide-eyed and slack-jawed.

She had never seen him in this emaciated stated. He was all bone and skin and sinew, no muscle mass, no fat at all. People in Catharta didn't look like this. They didn't look like corpses because they looked the way they last remembered themselves. This last remaining piece of Sam may have been in a coma for three years, but he had some level of awareness. He knew that this husk of a person is what he had become.

Sara didn't have time for Ananda's shock. She asked, "Did you bring him?"

Snapping out of it, Ananda peeled her eyes off of Sam's supine form and looked at Sara. She nodded and then stepped aside, revealing the Guardian looking as enormous and intimidating as ever. His long hands were curled, not into fists, but into claws. His fingers looked more talon-like than ever. His broad shoulders heaved with each breath, looking like giant wings, tucked away but ready to take flight at any moment. His teeth were bared, and his eyes were narrowed as he stared down at the shriveled version of himself.

"What is this?" he hissed.

Sara couldn't tell if he was angry or scared or shocked. She had nothing to relate this experience to. How could she imagine what it would feel like to live a lifetime trapped in an afterlife from which there was no escape and then be suddenly confronted with herself, like some sort of twisted out-of-body experience?

She pulled herself up to a sitting position and then stood to confront the Guardian face to face.

"This is the rest of you," she said with as much confidence as she could muster. "This is what has kept you from being reborn. This is the part of you that has been clinging to life all this time."

Sam looked disgusted. "What life?" he spat. "You're a fool!" He didn't say it to Sara. He was yelling at himself. He took a few steps toward the crumpled soul on the floor. "All this time, what were you hoping for? What did you think was going to happen? Did you think you would wake up one day, and everything would be perfect? Did you think you'd get out of bed and someone would hand you your old job back and you'd be living in your old house, and your wife would love you again?" The Guardian fell to his knees, but still towered over the hospital gown-clad version of himself. "You're a fool!"

The withered, comatose Sam tried to scramble backward away from himself. He moved with strange jerking motions, as though he had forgotten how to work his limbs. This whole experience must be bewildering to him. He may have had some awareness, some sense of what was going on around him in the world of the living. But he knew nothing of the ghost plane or of his splintered soul. Nothing could have prepared him for the sight of his strong and healthy form bearing down upon him. And those eyes. He had never seen anything like those ghostly eyes in all his life.

Sara had to intervene. Placing a hand upon the Guardian's shoulder, she calmly and quietly said his name. "Sam." He didn't look at her, but he stopped advancing on the sickly version of himself. "It's not his fault. It's not your fault."

Finally, he looked at Sara. Still on his knees, he looked like he was begging her for something.

"All this time," he pleaded for her understanding. "He's been hanging onto hope for something that doesn't exist anymore. He's an idiot."

"Sam, he is you. You are him. You are two parts of the same soul." Sara had to get through to him. She had to complete what she came here to do. Maybe if she kept herself calm and spoke to him rationally she could make him see what she already knew to be true.

"He is not me!" Sam raged. He rose to his feet and came toward her, one talon pointed directly at her nose. "That is Sam Johnson, a pathetic excuse for a man. I am the Guardian."

His voice cracked when he said his self-assigned title. There was no confidence behind it anymore. He had been playing this role for so long, but now, he was breaking inside. The facade he had built was crumbling like some of the dilapidated buildings three stories above their heads. Even he couldn't believe in himself anymore. He was Sam Johnson. These two figures were one in the same.

The finger he still held in her direction went limp, and he looked back at the scared and trembling man on the floor. The Guardian asked his weaker form, "Why didn't you just let go?"

The zombie-like Sam replied with a dry and croaking voice, a voice that had not spoken in three years, "I wanted to, but I didn't know how."

These two very different parts of this man's soul were in agreement about one thing: they were both ready to move on.

"You can let go now," Sara encouraged as calmly as she could manage. "This is your chance. You can move on and have another life."

The Guardian's shoulders slumped. He stared at the missing piece of himself and asked Sara, "What if I've missed my chance? What if no one gets a second chance?"

She wasn't going to let him back out of this. She had to convince him. "If that's true, then you've cost a lot of people their only chance to get out of here. I have to believe that's not true. Please, just try. You owe it to every soul you've ever trapped here. You owe it to Ananda. You owe it to yourself."

She could see the struggle behind his eyes. He had convinced himself this was all there was. He had accepted his fate. He was meant to walk the barren landscape of Catharta for eternity. Now, she was offering him an alternative, and although he wanted to believe it could be true, it was frightening just for being different.

Finally, he asked, "What do I need to do?"

Sara didn't know, but she didn't want to sound unsure. He was placing his trust in her. She couldn't lose that. "You need to get back into one piece. You need to come together."

He nodded, and then, the towering figure of the Guardian extended a hand to the frail and withered Sam. Uncertain, the Sam Sara had brought here from the hospital looked at the outstretched hand and then looked at Sara.

"It's okay," she reassured him. "This is how you move on."

He reached out his own skeletal hand. It passed right through the palm of the Guardian, like there wasn't enough soul there for him to hold onto. Sara was confused. Sam had gripped her hand as they lay side by side on the platform. He was solid. Then, it occurred to her. They passed right through each other because they were each other. They were one soul. This is how she would put them back together.

Sara stepped forward and helped Sam off the platform floor. She propped his arm over her shoulders to help support his frail body. Then, she looked at the Guardian and instructed him. "I need you to hold very still."

He didn't reply. Sara took his lack of response as agreement. She addressed the Sam she was supporting. "Are you ready?"

He looked despondent. "I honestly have no idea."

That was close enough for Sara. She spun him around so that the Guardian was looking at the back of Sam's head. She could see both of their faces now. They looked so different. Side by side, they looked like two different people. But they had the same eyes. That much was unmistakable. She took a deep breath, and she pushed Sam gently backward. As his back met the Guardian's chest, they both inhaled sharply, experiencing some sensation Sara could only imagine. It looked painful. She hoped it would be over quickly. She kept pushing. The sickly Sam was disappearing into the Guardian. They were becoming one. Sara tried to ignore the anguished look on both their faces until there was only one face. There was only one man standing before her. Sam and the Guardian were one. They occupied one space. The two pieces of his soul had been reunited.

Sara studied his expression. He no longer appeared to be in pain, but he looked vacant. He stared blankly past her, through her, into nothingness. "Sam?" she asked cautiously. "Do you feel okay?"

"I feel…," he began, but then paused.

When he didn't finish his thought Sara coaxed him on. "You feel what, Sam?"

His expression relaxed and something as close to a smile as she had ever seen on his face appeared. "Whole," he finished his thought.

Ananda, who had be staring dumbfounded at the whole inter-action, finally snapped out of it and approached him. She studied his face closely, peering into his eyes, examining the set of his brows, his relaxed shoulders, his not-quite-there smile. Then, she said, "This is the Sam I used to know. This is the Sam that used to be my friend."

"Ananda," Sam said, his eyes finally coming into focus. A look of remorse washed over him. "I'm so sorry. I'm sorry for trapping you here."

Ananda shook her head. "When you stopped me from being reborn, that was a mistake. You didn't know what you were doing. You thought you were protecting me. You don't have to apologize for that."

His head hung low. "But everyone else. I've stopped so many people from moving on to the next life. What if there are no second chances? How can I ever atone for that?" It was as if the part of his soul that contained his conscience is what had been missing all these years. He finally regretted what he had done.

Ananda put a hand on his shoulder. "We can find out now. We can find out if there are second chances. But only if you're just Sam. You're not the Guardian anymore. No one here needs a guardian."

He nodded his head in agreement. Ananda wrapped her arms around his chest, and he hugged her close in return. They looked so strange together. Her tiny form made him look enormous.

Suddenly, the quiet moment was interrupted by an electric crackling sound. A white light began glowing within Sam's chest. Ananda pulled away from his embrace and stepped back, standing beside Sara. The glowing grew brighter and brighter until his whole body was lit up like a bright white beacon. Sara wanted to shade her eyes from the blinding light, but she forced herself to keep looking. Something inside of her told her it was important for her to bear witness to this.

Sam blinked, long and slow. Sara was worried he was going to deny what she believed was happening to him. She was afraid he was going to reject his rebirth. She approached him, but didn't touch him. She didn't want to do anything to disturb this process.

"Sam," she said, forcefully. "Look at me! Don't close your eyes. Just look at me. This is it. This is you starting over. Don't be afraid."

Sam stared at her, wide-eyed and unblinking. As he stared, his expression changed from fearful to desperate to hopeful in a matter of seconds. The light was overtaking him, and he was accepting it. Then, all at once, he was engulfed in a ball of bright white light. It was like staring into the sun. Sara finally had to look away.

When the light faded away and she could look again, Sam was gone. The process had completed. He had been reborn.

Exhaustion and relief hit Sara like a tidal wave. This was what she had been working toward. She had accomplished what she set out to do. She hadn't failed, and now, this journey could be over. She had no way of knowing if all the other souls in Catharta would get a second chance, but that wasn't up to her. That involved the rules of the ghost plane, which were something she couldn't understand let alone control.

Her body felt weightless, but her mind was heavy with fatigue. She nearly collapsed onto the platform. Ananda caught her and wrapped her in an unexpected embrace.

"You did it," she sobbed into Sara's shoulder. They were mostly happy tears. Sara was sure there was also some sadness at having just rediscovered the friend she thought she had lost to hatred and bitterness and then losing him again. But mostly, Ananda was happy for Sam and happy that the Guardian would no longer be able to terrorize the souls of Catharta.

She sniffled and pulled away, wiping her eyes with the back of her hand. "You really did it. You saved him. You should be proud."

Sara should have felt proud. She knew that, but she didn't. She felt a loss that she couldn't quite describe. It had only been a week since she stumbled into Catharta, but it had given her a purpose. It had made her feel like she was working toward something. Now, that was gone. She would have no choice but to find something else to work toward in her own life. She couldn't stay stagnant anymore. She had to do something with her life to make it worth living. She had to move toward something, but she didn't know what.

"What's wrong?" Ananda asked her. "Are you okay?" Concern creased her young face.

Sara thought of how to explain her feelings to this girl. How could she explain that her life didn't have enough purpose to someone who'd had her life ripped away so young. She couldn't. There were no words that she could say that would not sound petty and unimportant compared to what Ananda had been through.

She opened her mouth to try to explain that, but what came out was something different altogether. "My best friend just told me he's in love with me." Saying it out loud made it feel more real and more terrifying. This thought didn't encompass the bigger worry that was weighing on her, but it was definitely a big part of it. She hadn't had any time to process it yet, but she needed to very soon. "When I go back to my world, I have to say something to him, and I don't know what to do."

Ananda gave her a sympathetic look. "I'm not the best person to ask for love advice. I don't have much experience with that." Sara felt guilty for even having brought it up. This was just one more experience Ananda had been denied by having her life extinguished so early. "But I know someone who might have some advice for you."

Ananda made sure Sara was able to support her own weight and then led her further into the subway station. As they passed one of the brick support pillars in the middle of the platform, Sara caught sight of a figure seated on a concrete bench wearing a hospital gown. Her first thought was that it was Sam, that somehow the broken piece of his soul she had brought here had been left behind. But then he turned toward her, and she saw the familiar face that had brightened her childhood.

"Dad," she whispered.

He stood and walked toward her. "Hi, pumpkin," he said as he wrapped his arms around her.

She allowed herself to be enveloped by him. "I didn't think I'd ever see you again," she told him. "This is my last trip to Catharta, and I don't have time to go back to the hospital. I never dreamed you'd be here."

He hugged her a little tighter and then released her. "Your friend brought me here," he said, smiling in Ananda's direction. He looked his daughter up and down. "If this is your last trip, does that mean you accomplished what you set out to do? Did you stop him?"

Sara nodded. "He's gone now. He won't be able to trap another soul here ever again."

He looked at her a little smugly, but with a definite aura of pride. "I told you that you could do anything you set your mind to." The corners of his mouth turned down slightly. "You don't look happy."

In life, Sara never talked to her father much about her love life. It felt uncomfortable. But this wasn't life, and she would never have another chance to talk to her dad. There was no longer any point in holding anything back.

"Dad, Tim just told me he loves me."

Her dad gave her a knowing smile. "Well, it took him long enough."

Sara stared at him, nonplussed. "You knew? How could you have known?"

"Sara, honey, I've seen the way he looks at you. I'd have to be blind not to know."

She couldn't control her puzzlement. Had she been blind all this time? And for how long? "But you haven't seen him in over three years."

He gave her the warm, safe look that only a father can give. "I saw it from the first time you introduced me to him. He looks at you like you're the eighth wonder of the world or like you're from another planet. It's as if he's never seen anything like you, and he wants to stay close to you to make sure you don't get away from him."

This was unbelievable. How could Tim have had these feelings for so long and she never knew? "Why didn't you ever tell me?"

Her father shook his head. "That's not my job. It's his. Besides, would you have believed me anyway?"

Sara thought it over. "No, probably not." As shocking as this revelation was, she still had no idea what to tell Tim when she went back to the real world. "What do I do now? We've been friends for six years. This is going to change everything."

"Only you can decide what to do next. You need to think about how you really feel about him. And you're right—it is going to change everything. But you know, life can't stay the same forever. Change is inevitable. And even though it might seem scary sometimes, more often than not, it ends up being for the better. The outcome is almost always worth the risk."

Sara thought about that. She tried to see the way Tim looked at her, tried to see it through her father's eyes. It seemed impossible. Tim was just Tim. She didn't know how he looked at other people, so how could she know if he looked at her any differently?

She thought about how he had been there for her through this past week, even while he was dealing with a breakup. He had driven her all over town at all hours of the night. He had taken her to San Quentin without a moment's hesitation. He had helped her abduct a hospital patient without so much as a second thought. Surely, that went beyond the call of friendship, even for best friends. Maybe somewhere deep down inside, she had known he loved her. If she didn't, she probably should have.

She tried to think back on all the time they had spent together. She thought of the dozens of concerts they'd been to together, all the Sundays they'd spent watching football, the late night venting sessions about their boss, and all the times he'd brought her coffee without her asking. She thought about the microscopic changes to his facial expressions that sometimes drove her up the wall, but she still liked them because she felt like they allowed her to read his soul. She thought about their verbal sparring that made her feel so comfortable around him. She thought about the ache she had felt in the pit of her stomach when he had introduced Melissa as his girlfriend. She thought about the way his face looked while he slept on Aunt Joann's couch. She thought about his hazel eyes and the curve of his jawline. She thought about the shape of his lips and the way she felt when he said her name. It gave her goose bumps all over her body.

She did love him. She wasn't sure for how long, but suddenly, she knew it. She was in love with her best friend, and she had never allowed herself to acknowledge it because that would have meant taking a chance, reaching for something she wanted, risking failure. Those were things she just didn't do. So she had buried her feelings so deep that even she didn't know where to find them. But now, they were at the surface, and she couldn't deny what she felt. She felt love. And she owed it to Tim to tell him so.

Looking into her father's eyes, she knew he could read her expression. He had known exactly what to say to help her figure this out on her own. How could she go back to a world without him in it?

"I miss you so much, Dad."

"I know," he told her. He wrapped his arms around her again. "I miss you too. I miss you and your sister all the time." Maya!

"Oh my god, Dad!" Sara exclaimed. "Maya's in labor. She's going to have the baby. Maybe tonight."

He released her. "You should go be with her."

"But if I go, that's it. I'll never see you again."

"I know. But you can't stay here. You have to go live your life." His warm expression suddenly collapsed into a frown. "Your eyes."

Sara felt a panic rise in her chest. She looked around for somewhere she might see her own reflection. Nearby, there was a fire extinguisher set into a pillar with clear glass covering it. She stepped toward it and peered at the faint reflection of her own face. She saw her dark brown eyes looking back at her. Then, she noticed a prickling of glowing light, beginning in the whites of her eyes and burning toward the center like a sparkler burning down its fuse. The glow swallowed the pigment of her irises, and for a second, her eyes looked clear like Ananda's or her father's or any other soul in Catharta. Then, they flickered back to their usual state. She turned to face her dad and Ananda.

"But I haven't been here that long yet. I should have more time." She was desperate for as many minutes she could possibly get with her father.

"But Sam is gone," Ananda reminded her. "His gateway isn't needed anymore. It's closing."

"You need to go," her father ordered. "Now."

She hugged him again hastily. "I love you, Dad."

He squeezed her in return. "I love you too, Sara."

She turned toward Ananda. After a moment's hesitation, they embraced as well.

"Thank you for all you've done for us," Ananda said into Sara's shoulder. "Thank you for not giving up."

Sara pulled away and looked her friend in the eyes. "Thank you for believing in me."

Ananda smiled at her and then said urgently, "Okay, you need to go."

The three of them rushed back to the spot on the platform where Sara had appeared earlier. She lay down on her back and looked up at her dad and Ananda standing over her. She felt like there was so much she wanted to say to both of them, but she couldn't find the words, and it wouldn't matter if she did because there was no time to speak them.

Instead, she gave them both one last smile and then turned her gaze toward the concrete ceiling. It was time to go home. She closed her eyes and cleared her mind and tried to leave thoughts of Sam and her father and Ananda behind her. Instead, she thought of Maya in labor at the hospital. She thought of her little niece or nephew whom she would soon get to meet. She thought of Aunt Joann and the home she had provided for their little family. She thought of her job and her city and the life she had built for herself. Finally, she allowed herself to think of Tim, her best friend, the man who loved her. She thought of every time he had ever looked at her, every time their skin had made contact, and every minute they had spent together. Then, she opened her eyes and felt the familiar rush.

She was rocketing upward even though it appeared she was lying perfectly still. The edges of her vision blurred, and the pressure in her head increased. Nausea rose from her stomach, up through her chest, and into her throat. The moment that she felt she couldn't take it anymore, it all stopped. The invisible elevator arrived at its destination. She was staring at the same concrete ceiling. Fluorescent lights flickered in her periphery. But she was no longer in Catharta. The air moved ever so slightly. Sounds of the life in the world above crept into the subway station to let her know she had returned. She was in the world of the living. She was home.

She shifted her jaw to release the pressure on her ears and wiggled her fingers and toes to bring some life back into her body. Tilting her head to her right, she came face to face with Sam. Seeing his lifeless eyes set into his skeletal face sent a little chill through her. He was no longer Sam, not even a piece of him. This was just a body, a used up vessel. Beyond him was an empty platform. The train had already departed.

She turned her head the other way. There was Tim. He was sitting on the platform next to her, watching over her body while she abandoned it. He gave her a small smile. Only one corner of his mouth turned up. He looked tired.

"You're back," he said.

She knew what she wanted to convey to him. She wanted him to know how she felt, what she had allowed herself to realize in the few short minutes she had been away. But looking at his face, his soft eyes, she found she still didn't have the words. She didn't know how to explain what she felt or why it had taken her so long to let herself acknowledge her feelings. The way she felt about Tim could not be contained by words.

So instead of speaking, she acted. Sara pushed herself up with one arm and wrapped the other around Tim's neck, pulling him close to her. She didn't stop to think. She didn't want to give herself a chance to back out of it. In half a breath, she closed her eyes, cleared her mind, and she kissed him. At first, he was almost resistant. His whole body was rigid, and he was frozen on the spot. But she denied her urge to pull away, to believe it was rejection. She wrapped her other arm around him and wound her fingers through his hair. Finally, he softened, and he kissed her back, urgently, almost force-fully; his lips pressed hard against hers. She felt like electricity was running through her. Her whole body was awake. His hands found their way to her ribs and then around her back, and he pulled her close. His lips felt like they were meant to fit with hers, like perfect puzzle pieces that had found their way to one another. She felt lost. She was lost in his lips, in his embrace, in the warmth of him.

Finally, he pulled away, if only by a fraction of an inch. Breathing hard, he pressed his forehead to hers. His eyes were closed, but hers were wide open as she whispered, "I love you too."

He squeezed his eyes a little tighter, like her words came from a dream from which he didn't want to wake. Then, slowly, he opened them, and his eyes met hers. She didn't blink. She had to face this head on. She could not allow herself to be afraid of taking chances anymore. She had just jumped off a cliff, and now, she needed to trust the parachute of Tim to save her.

"I've spent years thinking I would never hear you say those words. I thought I was a fool for believing you might feel that way about me. I tried to move on. I tried to just be friends, but honestly, I think it was killing me inside." His eyes looked glassy. "But now I'm afraid I forced you into this. I didn't mean to spring my feelings on you like this. I wanted to tell you I love you, but I didn't want you to feel like you had to say it back. And now I said it while you're under stress and not thinking straight and I'm just afraid...," he trailed off.

Sara shook her head, which was still pressed firmly against his. "I'm the one who was afraid. I was so afraid of taking a chance that I hid my feelings, even from myself. I don't know if there was a right time or a wrong time for you to tell me how you felt. But I can tell you that I wasn't ready to say it until just this moment. And it's not because I didn't feel it. I felt it, but I was too afraid to let it be true.

But I'm learning that a life without risk isn't really worth living." He shook his head and sighed, like he couldn't allow himself to believe her. "I do love you, Tim. I think I have for a very long time. And I think now I'm brave enough to believe it. I hope you're brave enough to believe it too."

With that, he kissed her again, a slow and thoughtful kiss, like something he had spent years imagining and planning in his head. She felt herself melting into him, allowing her fear to melt away. They might have stayed locked together like that forever, but the overhead speaker announced that an eastbound train would be arriving in one minute. That was their reminder that time had not, in fact, stopped. There were other people in the world besides the two of them. Some of those other people might be on that approaching train, and they needed to be gone by the time it arrived.

Tim pulled away from her and took both her hands in his. He looked deep into her eyes, like he was searching for something. Suddenly, he looked satisfied, like he had found what he was looking for. His eyes softened. His mouth flattened out into a shadow of a smile. His eyebrows went up about one millimeter. He had allowed himself to believe her. He had put his heart on the line, and she had met him there.

He stood first and helped her to her feet. "What do we do about him?" Tim asked, gesturing toward Sam's body on the platform.

"We leave him here where he'll be found." Sara had gone over this part of the plan in her head many times. It was one of the things she had the most doubt about. She had to weigh what she thought was the right thing against what she thought was the smart thing. "A part of me wanted to take him back to the hospital and make it look like he had just finally given up. But it's a miracle I got him out of there at all. I can't try to sneak him back in. At least here, he'll be found quickly. Besides"—she said, looking back at the lifeless form of the man she had risked so much to save—"this body isn't who he is. His soul is who he is, and that's gone now. This is just a shell."

Tim nodded, and together, they made their way to the stairs. They heard the sounds of the eastbound train approaching as they left Sam's body and the wheelchair behind. Climbing the stairs hand in hand, Sara knew they were moving quickly, but she felt like they were in slow motion. She listened to her own breathing. It was slow and measured without any effort on her part. She was calm. She had let her heart take the lead, and it was the most cathartic feeling she had ever known.

They reached Tim's car and headed back to the hospital. Sara had about five text messages from Maya telling her to hurry. The whole way back Tim kept stealing glances at her, as if he wanted to make sure she was still there, she was real. She reached over and took his hand to let him know it was all real, everything this night had brought had really happened.

Tim pulled up to the front doors of the hospital and let Sara out with the promise that he would park the car and then come meet her at labor and delivery. Sara felt a strange feeling as she walked through the front doors. It was like a ghost of the panic she had felt when she walked in with the intention of abducting Sam. She pushed it down, reminding herself that she was done with that. She had helped Sam. He had been reborn, and now, she was relieved of that duty. She could move on with her life.

She found her way to labor and delivery and signed in as Maya's visitor. It felt strange stopping at the nurses' station, looking them right in the eyes and giving them her real name. She had to keep reminding herself that she was here for legitimate purposes this time. The nurse directed Sara toward her sister's room, and she pushed the door open. She was unprepared for what she saw.

As she stepped into the room, she saw first a couple of nurses, then the doctor, and then Aunt Joann smiling, standing by the foot of Maya's bed. As she stepped closer, she finally saw Maya, sitting up in the hospital bed with a tiny little baby clutched tightly against her chest. A pang of guilt shot through Sara. She had missed it. She hadn't made it back in time to be there for Maya's baby's entry into the world. She had let her sister down. But the look on Maya's face told her it didn't matter. None of it mattered because she had this brand new life in her arms. She looked tired and sweaty, and her hair was a mess, but she looked peaceful. This baby had brought her peace.

Maya peeled her eyes away from her newborn long enough to notice Sara had entered the room. She smiled serenely. "You're here."

Sara approached her bedside and kissed her sister on the forehead. "I'm here." She looked down at the little ball of life in her sister's arms. "Well, is it a boy or a girl?"

Maya smiled down at her little bundle and said, "It's a boy. I named him Sam."

Sara felt like she'd been struck by lightning. Sam. After months of brainstorming and debating and second guessing, Maya had named the baby Sam. Sara thought back over the last week. She tried to think of any time she had said Sam's name in front of Maya. She couldn't come up with a single moment. To Maya, he was the Guardian and nothing more. Tears welled up in Sara's eyes, and she let them fall. She didn't even try to wipe them off her cheeks. "That's a beautiful name," she whispered over the lump in her throat.

"Do you want to hold him," Maya asked.

Sara just nodded because she couldn't manage any other words. She scooped her nephew up in her arms and held him close, breathing in the smell of him. It was like nothing she had ever smelled in her entire life. It was heavenly.

"Look at his eyes," Sara faintly heard Maya say. "They're the lightest shade of blue I've ever seen. They almost look clear."

Sara tried to blink the tears out of her own eyes well enough to see clearly, and she smiled. Maya was right—they were a very unique shade of blue. As she stared into the little boy's eyes, she felt sure she had seen that precise shade of blue once before, but she decided to keep that to herself. This baby boy had the whole world before him. This was a soul with a fresh chance at life.

CHAPTER 20

Body Found in Subway Identified as Coma Patient
by Sara Jenkins

The body of a man found dead last week in the Sixteenth Street subway station has been identified by the San Francisco County Coroner's Office. The deceased was discovered by a janitorial worker in the early hours of Thursday, September 28th with no identification on his person. He has now been identified as 41-year-old Sam Johnson of San Francisco.

Johnson had been in a coma at Saint Gertrude Memorial Hospital for three years after being struck by an oncoming train, also at the Sixteenth Street subway station, on September 27, 2014. Following the incident, he was legally dead for several minutes. Paramedics who arrived at the scene were able to revive him, but he never regained consciousness. He had remained in Saint Gertrude since that time.

Johnson's body was discovered last week still wearing a hospital gown and a bag of intravenous fluids was still connected to his arm. A wheelchair, found nearby, has been identified as property of Saint Gertrude. The transit system janitorial worker who found the body reported that initially he thought the victim was sleeping. "He looked like he just lay down on the floor and went to sleep. There was no blood or anything. He looked peaceful. I tried to wake him up, to tell him he shouldn't be there. When he didn't respond, that's when I reported it."

Police suspect Johnson awakened from his comatose state and made his way to the station under his own power. Representatives of the hospital, however, are baffled as to how the patient was able to exit the hospital without detection. Mary Rowell, Public Relations Director of Saint Gertrude, released a public statement. "We are currently reviewing the situation to determine when and how Mr. Johnson left the premises. While that investigation is underway, we are increasing security measures to ensure patient safety." Rowell was not available for further comment.

Dr. Damian Carver, a surgeon with Saint Gertrude familiar with Johnson's condition, said it is not unusual for coma patients, upon awakening, to attempt to return to their last known whereabouts. "They wake up confused and in shock. They're disoriented, and they don't understand where they are. Sometimes they just try to go back to the last thing they remember. They may not even realize any time has passed." The doctor did find it strange, however, that the patient awakened at all. Carver commented, "I didn't expect he would ever wake up. Someone who suffers that kind of brain trauma and who has been comatose for that long usually doesn't make any sort of recovery at all. But I guess stranger things have happened."

Johnson was a software developer who had worked at several different startup companies in the Bay Area over the past two decades. In more recent years, he had been doing in-house technical support for a national car rental chain located in San Francisco. He is survived by his wife, Marie Johnson. The couple had no children. Attempts to reach Marie Johnson for comment were unsuccessful.

An autopsy of Johnson's body is scheduled to be performed next week. It is unlikely that it will reveal how or why the victim awakened from his comatose state. That and the fact that he seemed to have awakened on the three-year anniversary of the accident that put him in the hospital in the first place are mysteries that are likely to remain unsolved.

EPILOGUE

here was no real warmth or cold in Catharta. Those were sensa-
tions that went away with death. Ananda knew that well enough
from all the time she had spent there, but she felt cold nonetheless.
It was a memory of a sensation, tied purely to an emotion having
nothing to do with the temperature. She hugged herself and shivered
a little standing in the middle of Mission Street.

Standing beside her was Sara's father. He was the last piece of
her friend. Ananda would never see Sara again. She had come to save
the lost souls of Catharta, and she had done that. The gateway was
now closed. Within a matter of minutes, she had lost both the people who had meant the most to her in this wasteland of wandering
ghosts.

Sara had brought her hope. She made Ananda hopeful that she
might not wage this war all on her own. She had been fighting on her
own since she was alive. She had spent her teenage years fighting for
her life with little support from her mother and her sisters, and she
had failed. She had spent another lifetime fighting for the trapped
souls of the ghost plane, and she had felt hopeless. If she were being
honest with herself, she had been on the verge of giving up. But then
Sara showed up, and she was alive, and she wanted to do something
about the Guardian and suddenly Ananda wasn't alone anymore. But
now Sara was gone.

After spending a lifetime hating the Guardian and what he had
become, she finally got her friend Sam back. He had been a beautiful
soul once, someone who truly cared. She got to look into his eyes

one last time and feel like she had a friend again. A moment later, he was gone.

It was for the best, she knew. She should be happy for him. She looked for some warmth deep inside herself, some sense of joy that he was now free. Instead, she felt trepidation. She was alone again. She didn't know what would happen to the souls Sam had trapped there. She didn't know if they would be given a second chance. Somehow, she felt responsible for them, like she was their keeper. She needed to let go of that idea. She had never been able to keep them safe. Why should it be any different now that Sam had been reborn? The cold feeling sunk deeper into her bones.

At her side, Sara's father touched Ananda's shoulder with one hand and pointed up at a window in a nearby building with the other. "Look," he whispered.

Ananda followed the line of his finger and looked up at a second-story window. The shades were drawn, but they were sheer, allowing her to see just a hint of what went on inside the small apartment. What she saw was light. It was a soft glow, but it grew brighter every second. The brightness increased until she could make out the fully illuminated form of a human. Then there was a bright flash and the light faded. Someone else had been reborn. Ananda felt a little bit of the chill fall away from her.

Without thinking, Ananda broke into a run. Sara's dad followed just a few steps behind. Before she knew what she was doing, she found herself yelling at the empty streets, her own voice bouncing back at her off the buildings on either side.

"It's safe now! You don't have to hide anymore! The Guardian is gone!"

All around her, a slow stirring began. Blinds and draperies were cracked open. Some street-level doors opened just enough for the occupants to peek out. The residents of Catharta heard her call, and they wanted to believe her. What looked like a deserted city was actually a very crowded place crawling with souls who spent the afterlife hidden, cowering in fear? They were coming out of their caves now, rallying around the hope she was trying to give them.

Down the street a ways, just around the corner of an alley another light began to glow. Ananda spun around in a circle, trying to take in the entire city from where she stood. Here and there, she saw dots of light appearing, growing brighter.

"Open your eyes!" she exclaimed. "Don't be afraid!"

One by one, the lights around her grew into brilliant flashes and then slowly faded away, taking their souls with them, sending them off to start another life.

She locked eyes with Sara's dad, a man she hardly knew, yet now felt eternally bonded to because of what he represented: Sara, friendship, salvation. A soft glow began in his chest as she looked at him. A faint electric crackling could be heard. He looked down and touched the light, cautiously as if it might burn him. Then he looked at Ananda and smiled. It was a small smile, soft and grateful. The glowing increased and engulfed him, and although it made her eyes sting to look at him, she did not look away. She held his gaze until he was fully obstructed by the brilliant light and when it faded he was gone too.

She was happy for him, but it did not melt the chill she felt through her whole body.

But then she felt a spark of warmth. It felt like more than a memory of a sensation. It felt like true heat, something she had not felt in the lifetime she had spent in Catharta. It was in her heart, like a tiny ember smoldering there. She pulled in a deep breath, and it fueled the flame. She turned to face the building next to her. She could see her reflection in the glass windows of the store front. She could see the soft glow of her crystal clear eyes and an equally soft glow in the middle of her chest.

She touched her fingertips to the spot, and it grew, like a flower blooming. The light covered her torso and then her arms and legs, her whole body. She was a beacon. She was a woman made of fire. She looked up at the slate gray sky, and tears streamed down her cheeks. She didn't blink them away. She kept her eyes open wide. She was going to begin again.

ABOUT THE AUTHOR

*L*auren Weston was born and raised in Martinez, California, where she currently lives with her husband and two beautiful children. She began writing in her spare time while working as an accountant in San Francisco. After receiving tremendous support and encouragement for her fan-fiction novel, The Walking Dead Files, she began writing her own original stories. Now, she is a full-time writer. Catharta is her first published novel. You can connect with Lauren on Twitter using the handle @LKWestonFiction.